I0668123

AH MEN

A man's gotta do and a woman does too!

Letitia Richard

www.LetitiaRichard.com

Ah Men, published by Letitia Richard Copyright ©2010 All rights reserved.

No part of this book may be reproduced, stored in or introduced into a retrieval system, or transmitted, in any form, or by any means (electronic, mechanical, photocopying, recording, or otherwise) without prior written consent from the publisher, except brief quotes used in reviews.

First printing September 2010
ISBN 13: 978-0-9830179-1-2
ISBN 10: 0-98301-791-3
Printed in the United States of America by Instantpublisher.com

This is a work of fiction. It is not meant to depict, portray or represent any particular real persons. All of the characters, incidents and dialogues are the products of the author's imagination and are not to be construed as real. Any references or similarities to actual events, entities, real people, living or dead, or to real locales are intended to give the novel a sense of reality. Any similarity in other names, characters, entities, places and incidents is entirely coincidental.

For information, please contact Letitia Richard at P.O. Box 7815, Torrance, CA 90504 or email to: CONTACT@LETITIARICHARD.COM

Editors: Letitia Richard
Paula R. Thomas
Connie Love

Dedications

This novel is dedicated
to the loving memories of
my dearly missed Brother, my 2 Big Mama's
and to so many more who have passed on
yet remain near and dear in our hearts.

You will never be forgotten!

Willie "Joe" Richard, Sr.
7/7/49 – 8/31/10**

Aaron David Pennix

Eloise Holmes Williams

Beulah Simmons Richard

Acknowledgements

First and foremost, I give praise and honor to GOD for everything I am and for everything HE allows me to be! For without HIM, I am nothing and I know it!

(Mom) Creasie Pennix, you have been my biggest cheerleader since birth. Your love and generosity cannot be measured. I hope that I am able to repay you for everything you've done for me. I love you!

(Pop) Lonnie Richard, you are my hero! God knows your hard work gave your family the security they would have never had without you. I wish you much, I love you much and I will always have your back!

Connie Love, World of Publishing - Girl, your friendship is irreplaceable. Thank you so much for all of your support and encouragement through the years!

Samuel Dickson - Dude, you mean more to me than words can say. You've been there for me since I was a kid and I will never forget that! Thank you for everything for all of these years!

Paula R. Thomas - I so appreciate everything you've done to assist me with my endeavors. You are truly a Godsend and may your blessings abound!

And to everyone who gave their time, kindness and support, I thank you with all of my heart!

Kalika Robinson, Bonnie Pennix
Renee Mendscole, Zahra's Book Store
Walter and Amber Mitchell
Stephanie Matthews

AH MEN

Prologue

"I think I'm falling in love with you," I said breathlessly to him trying my best to sound as sexy as hell. I was panting hot and heavy; hardly able to catch my breath as I rolled off of him. We were drenched in each other's sweat after just satiating ourselves in a triple-header session of pure, raw, sex!

And yes, I said it partially because I thought that it could be a little true, but I also said it as sort of a test for Vincent. I knew he would be shaking in his boots after hearing me say something like that, so I had to do it.

I thought I knew him well enough to know that I didn't want to be just another woman in his harem of women. Plus, he's always so damned self-assured and arrogant, as if he didn't have a care in the world, or as if he didn't care for anyone in the world but himself. I wanted to put a little of his fire out and let him know that he was dealing with a different breed of woman; a trick I peeped from my mother.

Even though I knew what type of man Vincent was before I got involved with him, I just had to make sure that the emotional table was equally balanced; by getting him to fall for me harder than I'm sure he would want himself to.

"Oh," is all he could get himself to say as if I really fucking meant it!

His male ego makes me sick, yet I can't help but respect him for it at the same time. Stupid! I know his super inflated ego would terrify most women, because they already know he's gonna be an ass.

When accepting the differences between men and women, you often find that women care a whole lot more than men usually do. Not me. Not only do I know the difference, I count on those differences to play on for an upper hand, and I am counting on those differences to help me now…'cause just for him, I'm going to act out the worst kind of ego on his ass; his own! I venture a guess that Vincent ain't never met a chick like me before.

So anyway, his single word response to my declaration of love didn't upset me or surprise me, it just merely set the stage for my mission at hand which is to make Mr. Vincent Cruthers truly fall for a woman…Me!

I guess he started to feel a little guilty since he just sexed me, (though it was really me clearly having just sexed him), and here I was declaring my undying love to him. So he started making those sexy, throaty, noises. "Mmm," said he, as I kissed him and he kissed me…all over…as if to smooth-over his non-response.

"Ha!" I laughed to myself. I had to catch myself so I wouldn't laugh out loud. "Piece of cake," I thought, knowing damn well this was going to take every inch of my femaleness to pull this shit off successfully. I would let him think that I was just another vulnerable woman totally blinded by the animalistic charisma we shared in the bedroom. I'm sure his ego will let him think nothing more of it than that. And because of this, Vincent Cruthers is in for the ride of his promiscuous life.

In the meantime I eagerly responded to his purr, and was once again dripping wet in anticipation of the climactic chain of events which were sure to come. So I climbed on top and stuck one of my breasts into his mouth. His juicy lips took it eagerly, sucking on it so hard I could hardly contain myself. One thing is for sure, I have never experienced sex as good as I experience it with Vincent!

***

"What does she want me to say?" Vincent thought to himself while he sucked on one of the firmest tits he ever had the pleasure of knowing. Women were always declaring their undying love to him. He knew the main reason for that was probably his big dick, which was currently, steadily growing in-between Jax's lean thighs.

"Women are interested simply in having sex with me," he thought. So as long as he was a good provider, then he would continue to be the recipient of the nicer things in life that he had become accustomed to. He simply did not feel it a wise investment to reciprocate the love of a woman...of any woman.

He preferred his lifestyle of, "love 'em and leave 'em" dangling at an arms-length. At least that way he would always have a woman hanging around. This was his line of thinking, and for all intents and purposes it had served him well for thirty-something years.

He had acquired lots of material objects from these women whom he'd loved at an arms-length. Things like, airline tickets to anywhere in the world, Hugo Boss suits, Vermeil watches and let's not forget the rent payments. Vincent had it made. Now why did Jax want to go and fuck up everything by falling in love with him?

When he'd met her at that library, he'd been studying her for almost an hour before he decided to approach her. Not that he was lacking self-confidence, but it was just a matter of timing. Everything was a matter of timing for Vincent. He knew how to pace himself and he knew that patience was one of his best attributes.

Luckily for him, the moment he began to approach her she was mumbling something about massaging her shoulders. Well, opportunity presented itself and Vincent jumped on it, like he did most opportunities and most women.

Jax was refreshing to him because she was so much younger than him, hella fine and confident beyond her years. For some reason he felt the impulse to want to take care of her, which made the situation even more difficult. She was the kindest, but most outspoken woman he thought he had ever known. She had an ego like a man, but never got upset when other women acknowledged him in public.

She exhibited extreme patience when his answering machine would begin to record in-coming calls from other women, of whom she had heard plenty say, "...Vincent, if you're listening, pick up the phone." And for some of those voices, yes, he did pick up!

As attractive as she is, Jax always gave her full attention to him, never acknowledging other men in his presence. And she clearly didn't feel threatened by other women, which struck Vincent as being quite odd and definitely not the trait of any woman he had known before. But he really likes her a lot, still not being able to figure out the reason, except for the obvious. It couldn't be the "gifts" she gave him because she didn't give him anything but her time.

"Well," he thought, "perhaps it's simply the way she climbs on top of me and insists on doing most of the work and doesn't stop until the job is done." He wasn't sure, but as she again lowered herself onto his hard dick, he discontinued the thought and concentrated on her grind.

He began to move with her and grabbed on to her small waist. He looked into her luscious brown eyes and provocatively licked his lips at her. "Yeah, Miss Jacqueline has got it goin' on, but she will not be allowed to disrupt my lifestyle and that's final! She had better fall in line with all the others, or fall out of bed!" Vincent said this to himself with both of his heads.

He was soooo wrong!

(1) – Jax – The Learning Curve

I first met Vincent in 1993 when I was a senior in college, researching for my thesis. Immediately he blew me away with his style, because he was so different from all of the other guys I knew. Not that I was interested in my nerdy lab partners, rowdy frat guys, or the boy's in my hood, but I had never been interested in smooth operator's either. And oh, was Vincent a smooth operator. We met at a library in Hollywood…that should have been my first clue my ass was headed for drama!

This Hollywood library was referred to me due to its historic location and its specialized content on early Los Angeles, the topic of my thesis. It had books galore on my research material but I had not imagined in my wildest dreams, a library so old, so historical-looking, so, interesting. The library's gray granite walls, cedar beams lining the high ceiling, and vast collection of books was so plentiful, I guessed that it must have been here for centuries.

It is, supposedly, located near where a small township of black settlers, around 1887, had made a successful peaceful coexistence with the Mexicans and whites. Their diverse journeys had led freed men, women and children to the "California Mountains" to start new lives for themselves.

The promise of freedom, equality, and the likelihood of jobs stemming from the gold rush to the railroads kept them coming. Eventually however, their lives would be shredded to hell by ignorant whites who couldn't stand to let things be.

No one really knows what happened to the township and the black people in it, but suffice it to say that every trace of evidence of their upward mobility and progress was burned down to the ground, more than once. But the church always seemed to survive.

Very few clues remain as to who or what sparked the beginning of the end for those brotha's and sista's, but folk-lore and innuendo has surrounded Freedman Hollyhill Library for generations.

I thought writing my thesis on the early days of Los Angeles would be romantic. Imagining what California might have looked like in those days: Men, sporting those gaudy thick mustaches and wearing poncho pants, with women wearing those dainty ankle length dresses with corsets.

Having been born and raised in L.A., it never occurred to me that blacks even lived here way back in the day, or that they would be just as disadvantaged in every way. This was not an era in which to fantasize about. Instead it was just another lesson learned about the history of our savage country taking form.

These poor people probably all wore Levi's for digging in all of that dirt while looking for gold. They probably strived to work hard and keep their mouths shut for fear of any trouble. And their peaceful existence was no doubt short lived, in spite of the fact that they broke their backs to bring life to their town.

No, my thesis would not be a romantic telling of the days of old. It would certainly be another recount of the struggle of the black man. This library was probably built with the wealth of gold that was found in those days, by those people, who would never to be able to receive any of the benefits of their hard labor. So with briefcase in one hand and my backpack in the other I walked around this huge place and took in all of my surroundings.

"Now how in the world am I supposed to get any work done in a place like this?" I thought, as I toured Freedman Hollyhill Library from aisle to aisle.

The majority of people here are older and the place smelled like a combination of Ben Gay and rotten wood. The smell wasn't the problem; I was more concerned with a fragile book falling apart in my hands, and then being charged a king's ransom for its destruction. My girlfriend Sabastian would get a kick out of this place though. I've got to call her and tell her to check it out.

Sabastian is one of those free spirited, guru type people. She wears the oddest collection of clothes made in America or abroad, and is as skinny as a rod. She lives for places like this, with historical relevance and creepy. I'll tell her about it just as soon as I finish my assignment, because if I tell her before I'm done, she'd sneak up on me during my studying and say something like, "Girl, we should hold a séance for you in aisle 4 section 12, so you can seek the special advice of the spirit dwellers." I swear that girl is weird. Professor Cunningham told me about this place. I swear that lady is weird too.

Well, I finally settled down, found myself a work station, and was already wishing that I was kickin' it at the beach instead. In my back pack I unload a jug of hot cocoa, a box of Graham Crackers, a pack of Double Mint Gum and a worn out letter from Frances.

I met Frances in Bermuda last summer and we have written each other only once since I returned home. I keep his letter with me to remind me that I am still a woman, since I haven't been getting out of the house lately.

The letter is so full of "...darling, you are so beautiful," and "...any man could fall hopelessly in love with you," that I have a tendency to fantasize about him, a lot! This is normal, isn't it?

Well, after searching for and pulling at least eight books off the shelf I began my long and tedious search for the information which would see me finally graduate from college. I began to apply every technique I learned for writing term papers in putting this project together. I munched occasionally on my crackers and sipped on my cocoa, and more than that, I wrote down quote after quote after quote from those dirty, dusty boring ass books.

By the time I was halfway done I had probably read an excerpt from every book there. I was so tired that my eyes were beginning to blur, my mind started playing tricks on me and all of that damned reading was starting to tense up in my shoulders.

So, I thought, clearly the best thing for me is to get out of here and go stretch my legs or something, or at least get a change of scenery from all of this historic-ness. But I didn't budge because I had entirely too much work to do. I was not about to blow it off and take the chance on not receiving my bachelor's degree on time.

I must admit I've never been very disciplined in much of anything, including studying, but the anticipation of walking across that stage at CSULB was my driving force.

I haven't even been on a date for more than two months due to my eagerness to get it over with already! I don't need a man hanging around all the time, but considering it's so close to my last official Spring-Break, I'm starting to stress that I'm not going get a date before Summer's all over. I'd stuck to my word to finishing my assignment on time before I start having some fun.

I've been turning down several eligible dates lately, and my mother is already worrying about me a little. She says things like, "Jax, you sure better be careful by turning down these men honey, 'cause one of 'em could easily be your ticket out the ghetto."

And I say back to her, "Mom, we don't live in the ghetto, we live in Hawthorne. Besides, I have Frances."

Yes, I do live at home with my mother. For one thing I'm a total mama's girl, and for another, it would be totally stupid to live elsewhere when I have total seclusion in my own half of the house that my mother and I share. I could have easily lived on campus at LBSU, but I just didn't see the need for it.

My mother and I have lived together my whole life so why should I leave her now just because I was going to college? Anyway, my mom is always looking out for me. She does the weirdest things to try and hook me up with men, to marry!

Once, I was dating this guy for only about three months when she decided that he was the one for me. She took it upon herself to make out an entire wedding guest list and left it on my bed. When I saw her hint, I laughed so hard I started to cry. I didn't know if my mom thought I was that serious about, what's his name, or if she was just giving me a not so subtle hint to get out of her house. However, I wasn't about to go out like that. Mom would simply have to be more direct than that if she wants me to go.

A lot of my friends think my living at home with my mother is not very healthy at my age. In fact, most of them think it is downright pitiful. Unfortunately for them, I don't care. I've never spent a dime on rent either. I couldn't imagine throwing money away on rent like they do. I would rather buy a house, which is exactly why I've been saving my little trust fund all this time.

As it turns out, mom really doesn't mind me staying in the house with her. I'm her only child and she just wants me to be happy. She simply loves my companionship, as long as I stay the hell away from her men and she stays the hell away from mine! Sabastian says I'm experiencing Infantile Syndrome. I say, again, she's just weird!

My mother, Christine Winters-Perdue, has been married three times and each of her husbands, including my father, have all lived in this house with us.

My father died when I was two years old so I never got the opportunity to know him very well, therefore, Harry became the only father that I ever really knew. He and mom got married when I was six and stayed together for 15 years. And it's just a matter of time before they end up back together.

Harry is only about 5 foot 7, 175 pounds and nobody you want to mess with. He and mom made a cute couple, for a while, until their arguments started interfering with my ability to sleep at night. I never did find out what they were arguing about. Mom just always told me," Mind your business child."

Harry and I, however, still maintain a great father-daughter relationship. Soon after I graduate I'm going to work with him at his independent research firm. It's something like investigative work, but it involves a lot of government and large corporations. My dad has my back.

Mom's third husband, Jules, was the step-father from hell. I think she married him to prove that she was still a desirable woman. He's eight years her junior which isn't a big deal these days, but Jules was and is a jerk.

He wears too much cologne, drives an ugly '69 Corvette, and is sneaky as hell. Mom and I both knew he was no good, and a year after she married him, he knew it too. She can do much better than that. Mom kept my dad's name and hyphenates her current, latest ex-husband's.

After all of the drama, mom and I still have each other. As far as I'm concerned I have it made, and once I complete this final assignment I can concentrate on my professional future and on the rest of my life. My living arrangements should be the farthest thing from my mind right now, but I swear my mind wanders like a child. Like I said before, I am not a very disciplined person.

I knew I had done as much studying as I could do for one day when I started thinking about Jules. So, I thought I would re-read the last paragraph of the book in my hand, when I became curiously fixated on this one phrase; "...and with the gifts of the Gods I was the recipient of..." and the first thing to enter my mind, of all things was a shoulder massage.

Now I knew damn well that it really said, "Gold" but I happened to say, "Shoulder massage" out loud because I was hallucinating or something.

Anyway, no sooner than I said, out loud, that I wanted a shoulder massage did this handsome stranger appear from nowhere and start giving me a shoulder massage! I couldn't move. In fact, I wasn't entirely sure that someone was actually touching my tense shoulders. So like a fool I sat there for a moment, with my eyes closed, moaning in satisfaction and fantasizing about Frances and the crystal clear waters of the Caribbean.

I accepted those strong warm hands without hesitation. I suppose I would have eventually dosed off to sleep had I let him continue. But then suddenly, I realized that I was letting a stranger in Hollywood touch me and I jumped a clear 10 feet out of my chair!

He looked at me with this amused look on his face and said, "You said you wanted a massage. I always try to give the ladies what they want."

Oh God what a line! I hadn't heard anything like that since I was in high school. But for some strange reason I wanted to believe him. He was a really good looking man, so I was trying to convince myself that he was being sincere.

While observing him closely I noticed that he wasn't wearing a wedding ring, which really doesn't mean a damn thing for men these days. He had on an expensive looking pale green suit, a nice pair of shoes, a handsome face and a firm tight ass. I said in response to him, "Does that include touching women you don't even know?"

"Not unless they look as good as you," he said with a grin on his face.

"Don't you think your lines are becoming a little typical?" I said while sitting back down, thinking this is a waste of my time.

He said, "I am not in the habit of exchanging such lines with women that I don't know. I know too many women to waste my time doing that. However, I am a gentleman and because I overheard you talking to yourself, wishing for a massage and because anyone can plainly see that you have been hard at work doing something, I thought I would take time out of my own studies and make this beautiful woman's fantasy come true, if only for a moment."

Needless to say, not only was he reading my mind, again, but that was entirely too much bullshit from so fine a man for me to just let pass by, so I kept him.

He introduced himself to me and asked if he could sit down. My curiosity got the best of me and so I said, "Yes."

"My name is Vincent Cruthers, what's yours?" he said as he extended a well-manicured hand to me.

I accepted his hand in mine then began to blush as I was taken away with the heat illuminating from his hand onto mine. "Jax. How do you do?"

I could tell that he was watching me intensely as if trying to figure out some mysterious puzzle. I felt so insecure as he watched every move that I made-from the licking of my lips, to make sure that my lipstick was still on, to the nervous finger rub under my eyes to make sure that my eye liner had not caked up in the corners and made eye jam.

And though I am as direct as a person could possibly be I could not find one thing to say to this gorgeous man who had just planted himself in front of me. Self-consciously I looked down at my clothes and wanted to hit myself for leaving the house looking so tacky; worn out black stirrups, an un-tucked denim shirt and brown military style ankle boots. My hair was in a ponytail tied with a shoe lace and I had on a dangling silver crucifix earring in one ear and a small diamond stud in the other. I was a mess!

He obviously saw the despair in my eyes, being that I was not able to make any reasonable conversation, and so he decided to rescue the moment. "I've never seen you in here before."

I thought to myself, "You're right about that, and had I known what I'd find in here, I would have dressed for the occasion." "No, this is my first time...visiting this library I mean." I was starting to feel like a school girl flirting with my 9th grade band teacher.

"And what do you think?" he asked.

"Oh, I think you're a very nice man."

"Pardon me," he asked with this sexy ass smirk on his face.

Oh my God, oh my God, oh my God! What did he ask me and what did I just say? I was trippin', and he knew it. I was bothered because I've never been one to let a man get to me like this. I thought, "Jax, you better get yourself together girl if want to get to know this man and not just let him get to know you." So I got my thoughts together as best I could and summoned up every drama class I ever took.

"I'm sorry. My brain has been on over-drive for the past hour. To answer your question I think this library is quite interesting. And from what I can tell, you do appear to be a nice man." There, I got it all out without sounding like a complete idiot.

"I didn't mean to startle you by touching you like that. You were just so irresistible, the way you were mumbling to yourself that is, I found it simply impossible to pass you by and not respond to your unintentional request. I really didn't mean to offend you."

He sounded so sincere and so non-conceded. But something inside me knew better than to take his words verbatim. I don't know why, maybe it's the stereo-typical label that is often placed on smooth-looking, smooth-talking men; that say they are not to be trusted. "Don't worry about it," I said as cheerfully as I could. "What are you doing here?"

"Well, believe it or not, I often come here just for the mere opportunity to pick up unsuspecting women such as you." He smiled this most perfect smile, and then said, "No, actually I'm here just expanding my mind."

Hmm. A man who likes to expand his mind for no particular reason. Very interesting. "And do you come to this library often, Vincent?"

"Yes."

He was looking at me as though he could see straight through me...looking like a young ass Billy Dee Williams with a fade. I decided to challenge him. "I realize that my clothing is not matching today Vincent, but it really is rather rude for you to stare at me like that." There, I said it. Maybe I came on a little strong, but I needed him to know that I am a woman in control. I needed to make a stand with him, or so I convinced myself.

"I like it when you say my name."

I thought I would melt. Oh well, enough of being in control. "So, Vincent, what do you find interesting about this place?" I asked with enough charm to hypnotize a cobra.

"I find that it's a very calming place. It's far away enough from where I live for me to get away and see another side of the city."

"And where do you live?"

"I live in Los Angeles," he said.

"That's pretty vague," I said. "That can literally mean anywhere in the county."

"Well, you're not thinking about visiting me are you?" He shifted in his seat and placed his hand underneath his chin as though he were thinking.

"That's not my point, at the moment Vincent," I said, feeling a little nosy about my question all of a sudden.

"If you want specifics Jax, then you'll have to take down my address and my phone number."

That did it. This guy was too smooth for me. At that point I wanted to get up from my seat and excuse myself from him. It was obvious to both of us that he was playing some sort of game with me and I had not the time, nor the want to play. Who was I fooling? I did want to play, and I wanted to play to the very bitter end. So I thought I would play for a couple of more points and if he didn't let me win, then I would be on my way.

"Vincent, is it? I'm a little hard at work here in case you hadn't noticed, so you can either continue massaging my shoulders while I read this last paragraph, or I'll have to take my chances and look forward to seeing you again on some other occasion."

He looked at me like I had just stepped into a pile of dog shit. I thought to myself, "Now you've gone and done it. You wanted to play with this guy and you've just gone and practically given him an ultimatum that I know he'll reject." I waited until what seemed like an eternity before he spoke again.

"Would it be all right if I were to call you sometime soon?" he asked, as charming as he had spoken before.

I answered, "Yes, Vincent" like some damn fool in a trance. I tore out a blank piece of paper from my tablet and began to write down my phone number but he stopped me before I had a chance to finish.

"Don't write it down."

"If I don't write it down then how will you be able to call me?"

"I'll keep it up here," he said, pointing to his head.

"Oh, you expect me to believe that you're going to memorize my phone number now, and call me at some other time in the future?"

"Yes." Silence.

Well I'll be damned. This guy is either crazy or too caught up in himself to know what he really sounds like right now. Fine. If he wants to continue on like this then I have to let my ego know right now that it was never meant to be. It's not my fault that he's not going to call. This situation is totally out of my hands and I'm not going to give in and let him assume that I am an easy target. And yes, he is a very nice looking man, but there are several of them walking around out there, right? I tried to convince myself.

One thing bothered me, though. Vincent had this look of sophistication and arrogance all rolled up in one nice clean cut package. Why in the world is he interested in me, looking as I do, today of all days? That doesn't sit well with me at all. For all he knows I can be a bag lady sitting in the library trying to keep warm. Or I could be a prostitute who lurks in places like this, looking for easy targets. No rational thought came to mind why he was pursuing me. Oh hell, it must be my perky personality and my fascinating charm, right?

I recited my phone number for him and I guess he memorized it. Together we sat and talked a little while longer while he gave me a brief history about the library - some things that I had never heard before. All along I kept wondering if he still had retained my phone number after all of this idle chit-chat.

I finally decided to leave, but still was not able to tear myself away from him so I offered to buy him coffee across the street. He declined and said that he himself was not yet ready to leave; that he had some more research that he wanted to do.

After I stood, he stood also and I noticed for the first time that he was wearing very familiar cologne. I couldn't remember right away, but when I finally did I realized that it was the same cologne that my ex-boyfriend Tucker used to wear - Hugo Boss. Yummy! If he smells this good and looks this good, I wonder if he...

"Well it was very nice meeting you Jax," he was saying.

"Same here Vincent. Maybe I'll see you here again, if you don't call."

"Oh, I'll definitely call. When do you think you'll be here again?"

"Probably tomorrow," I said. "I'll keep coming back until my work is done."

"And what exactly is your work, if you don't mind my asking?" he asked curiously.

"I'm working on my thesis for graduation," I said, trying not to sound too school girlish.

"Oh, a college girl," he said slightly teasing.

"No, a college woman," I said correcting him.

He smiled. I reciprocated.

Vincent called me later that evening and somehow I was not surprised. Shortly after our initial meeting, we met several times in that old library in Hollywood. I, of course, had to complete my thesis by the semesters end, and he wanted to find more books on, shorthand?

I told him that I would not have a lot of leisure time until after I graduated. He acknowledged that and was very supportive for those final weeks. But when I finally did graduate from college, it seemed as though all of my time now belonged to him.

We went to dinner, ate picnic lunches in the park and walked hand down my favorite beaches. He'd put the top down on his convertible and laugh out loud as my hair twisted and turned and knotted in the smoggy wind. We were having a wonderful time together while getting to know each other. It was the perfect time for romance. I was out of school and I wasn't to start my new job with my step-father for a while. It was the perfect summer so far.

Later I learned that Vincent was a total gentleman in some areas. I couldn't stand it because he wouldn't touch me...there was no immediate romance. Yes well, we held hands and hugged and kissed and he was good at all three of those things, but I wanted more. I knew that there was a lot more to him than he was letting on.

Sometimes when I would visit his apartment, we would be all into each other and then the phone would ring. You can always tell by the way someone is talking to the person on the other end of the line whether it's a male or a female. And from what I could tell Vincent only received phone calls from women and he wasn't afraid to let me know.

Once we were at his place getting hot and bothered on his sofa when the phone rang. Well, he continued to sit with me, nibbling on my neck and told that someone on the other end of the phone that he would see them later that night and not to bother him again until then. I swear I didn't know what to make of it.

I knew Vincent and I were not exclusive, but damn, how in the world is a girl supposed to take this shit, especially since it was obvious to me, by all of the phone calls, that somebody was getting some from him. Well hell, I wanted some too and I was starting to think that he didn't find me desirable in that way.

Sometimes when we returned to his apartment late at night after being out on the town, he was still a gentleman even then. We would kiss and pet and sometimes get over-heated by the moment, but then that would be it! I was totally convinced during our first months of knowing each other that he was gay.

"What a fucking waste," is all I could say to myself each and every time he dropped me off at home from a date without trying to lay me. I could not stand the thought of having a brother/sister relationship with someone as fine as Vincent Cruthers. I would rather indulge in incest. As it turned out, he was just testing the waters before the big plunge!

The night he decided to stop being a gentleman, we were lazily lounging around his apartment watching television, drinking wine and sharing a Big Daddy caramel sucker. He was kissing me with such precision and expertise I started feeling a little dizzy.

His kisses are good; I hope he likes mine too. And though, we were always touching and panting and exploring each other's body, this night felt different to me somehow. I don't know exactly why, I just had a feeling that it would turn out different from all the other nights before.

"Here you go Jax," he said as he mischievously handed me yet another glass of wine, snapping me out of my own thoughts.

I took the glass from him and asked, "What are you up to?"

"Nothing. You told me you like this stuff."

Yeah, I do. How many bottles did you buy anyway?" As if I didn't know. "Three," he said while trying to hold back a sly smile.

"Uh huh," I said in such in a way that let him know that I knew he was trying to get me drunk. He started to settle back down on the sofa with me when the phone rang. I said "I'll get it," jokingly. He faced me suddenly, and the look on his face told me that he didn't like my joke.

He took the phone call in the bedroom and when he returned he said, "We have to talk."

"About what?"

"About us."

"What about us?"

"Jax, I like you, I really do. But I think I should lay some things down on the table for you, right now."

He was looking so serious now, as though he were going to tell me that he had a lot of women in his life and wanted to keep it that way, as if that wasn't obvious enough. "Go ahead Vincent," I said with an innocent voice. But, I was thinking to myself, "I like you too, but I'm not head over heels in love with you asshole. You're simply a guy that I am savoring for the moment."

Some things you do for the simple thrill of the moment and that's what Vincent is…a moment to savor for the time being. I didn't expect to be his only woman, nor did I want to be. I just graduated from college and I start my new career soon. He was simply my vacation.

His lifestyle didn't bother me…I wasn't stupid enough to let it. Oh he thinks that he owes it to me to tell me these things because our time together is "our quality time," and no one else's.

Vincent is an experienced man when it comes to handling women, but he didn't have to take the teacher role with me. I guess I made it too easy for him to see me as a vulnerable little woman. I certainly did not reveal all of my true self to him, as I suspected he did not reveal all of his true self to me.

"You're too easy to play with," I thought.

He had a lot to tell me, so I let him. In fact, he told me everything a woman needs to know about a man and some things a woman shouldn't know about a man. As he spoke, I couldn't help but think that he was a little feminine. But not a girlish feminine, more like a masculine version of the singer Prince type feminine. I say that because, I think he's just feminine enough to know what a woman thinks and feels, and masculine enough to give her what she needs...the perfect combination.

I think Prince is the ultimate and the most perfect combination of both femininity and masculinity, though some muscle and some height would help. He probably has most, if not all, of the ingredients some women like to see in a man, like; sensitivity, compassion, understanding, patience, honesty, and a freak of the week! I think I see those qualities in Prince; I know I see them in Vincent, even though he tries his damnedest to keep me at an arm's length.

"...so don't take what I'm telling you as negative" is what he was saying by the time I realized I wasn't listening to him. "I'm not drunk," I finally blurted out while trying to conceal the fact that I was a little tipsy.

"I didn't say you were. Hey, have you been listening to me?"

"Yes." I lied.

"As I was saying Jacqueline..."

"Jacqueline?" I said to myself. He's using my full name. He never uses my full name. Something must be up. I turned to him to listen for the first time that night.

"...and I do consider myself a thorough man...a well-rounded man, which is why I would even dare to divulge certain information about the male species..."

I couldn't help but think this man certainly loves to hear himself talk.

"...and particularly tonight, before we decide to get any closer than we already have, Jax."

"Go on Vincent."

"A man is a complicated tool. He runs on empty, he runs on full, and he simply runs, because he's expected to be a fine-tuned engine; which is to say that because a man is expected to do these things, he indulges himself with rewards. So never underestimate a man...any man, not even me. Now I'll tell you the truth, a man can easily love a woman...one woman even, with all of his heart and his mind and soul, but because a man happens to have a third leg...and if that third leg gets an itch, that third leg will seek a scratch."

He was watching me now, looking for any response from me. He was getting none. I was too horny to care. "Scratch me, scratch me," is all I could think about.

He was saying, "...that third leg is so powerful, that it deceives wives and lovers every day. It has deceived you before too Jax, and no doubt, will deceive you many more times in your life. Now some women like to call us dogs and sluts and whores, but all of that doesn't say what we really are. The plain and simple truth is we're just men."

What was he saying about sluts and whores? All I know is that I've got to tinkle, again, so I stood up and excused myself during his speech and said "I'll be rack bite baby," as I stumbled to the rest room. When I returned, Vincent was waiting patiently and as I approached the sofa he took my hand to help me sit down.

I thought we were going to get back to the kissin' and huggin', but Vincent said, "As I was saying Jax, we are just men. And Lord knows that I tend to look over you like my kid sister, but I want much, much more than that."

"Oh goody," I thought, "he wants more, he wants more!" I looked at him as though I had been paying close attention all along.

"The only way I can give you more is to first be completely honest with you so that you know exactly what you're getting, OK?"

"Yes Vincent," is all I could say.

"OK. Now, I know that you were only joking when you said that you would answer my phone when it rang, but all joking a side, don't ever answer my phone."

I had an angry defensive tone now. "I wouldn't want to answer your phone anyway!"

"Good, because you might not like what you hear on the other end of the line. Now Jax, I'm not telling you all of this to make you upset or angry, I'm telling you all of this because you need to know. Every woman is not prepared to hear what I'm saying but I think that you are, and I want to be the one to prepare you for what's to come.

To be quite honest with you, I'd sort of like to keep you tucked away for myself, because you have a rare quality about yourself that I haven't seen in a woman in a very long time. Any experienced Man like me couldn't help but be attracted to a woman like you, and so I want you to be prepared for the worst, even the worst in me."

What in the hell is he yapping about? And why has he chosen tonight of all nights to lay this heavy crap on me...and why are my clothes still on? Vincent is such a character. I already know he's a gigolo, what else is there for me to know? But he went on relentlessly, telling me things about men that I already knew, things I thought I knew, and things I had no idea of.

He told me not to trust a man as far as I could throw him. He told me that a man would screw your mother if he could get away with it. He told me that even though he cared for me so much, if he could get away with screwing my best friend, he would. He told me that a man will say or do anything to get in the panties. "You should know that a man tries his best; he's only flesh just like a woman, but a man is supposed to be a rock, with something more to prove."

It suddenly then became very clear to me as I sat there with my mouth hanging wide open. And as he went on, it became easier for me to listen to the things that Vincent had to say. So when I looked at him, I knew for sure that Vincent was a dog, a man-whore even! He had admitted that he was some kind of womanizer. He claimed that if every man in world had the opportunity to do so, they would be too! Yet, given this, I now knew exactly where I stood with him from that forward. And as stupid as it may sound, it was a wonderful feeling.

I would much rather want to know where I stand with my enemy rather than have my friend stab me in the back. I wanted to know where I stood, he told me, and I appreciated it. I came to see him as my "mentor" so-to-speak. I think he likes teaching me these things because I'm a fresh, 25-year-old, who he was grooming for his stables...some sort of prize to have. In any case I thanked him for all of the knowledge that he shared with me that night, and then I asked him if I could lick his Big Daddy again.

"Have you been listening to anything I've said?" he asked almost exasperated.

"Yes Vincent," I said with a sigh. "I heard every word. And I want to thank you for being so honest with me by letting me know that you don't give a damn about me or any other woman, and that you'd gladly take any woman for granted if given the opportunity. But don't get me wrong, I for one can appreciate your honesty. And just by looking at you, I've pretty much already labeled you as a 'ladies' man'. I figured that out the day we met and you've confirmed it every day since." I stood up and started to pace the room.

The conversation was getting a little old, and I was pissed that he was throwing this shit in my face like I was stupid. So I went off on him...a little. "As a matter of fact, the fact that you have thrown this shit in my face tonight is reason enough for me to leave!" I dramatically reached for my purse, but he snatched it up before I could get to it.

"Look Jax," he stood up facing me and reached for my hand. "You've gotten to me like no other woman has; in fact, I'm quite taken with you. I'm not telling you any of these things to piss you off, or to insinuate that you're stupid. I'm telling you these things so you don't ever have to do any guess work about me." He looked so good standing there it was hard pretending that I was upset with him. The fact of the matter was I was upset because my buzz was fading.

"Look," I finally said while taking my purse from his hand and setting it on the end of the sofa, "we were having such a nice evening, why spoil it with all this talk about who's a hoe? I'll take you any way I can get you...for now." I took his Big Daddy from his other hand and began to lick it.

He smiled. I reciprocated.

"Can I get you some more wine?" he asked, picking up my empty glass.

"How many bottles do you have left anyway?"

"Oh, enough to get you where you want to go," he said smiling again.

"I'm already there, or I will be in a second," I said as I handed him back his candy and started for the bathroom again. When I returned, he handed me another glass of wine and everything returned back to normal. Soon, we were kissing and exploring each other again.

It was getting close to one o'clock in the morning and I knew that I should stop drinking to make sure that I was going to be sober enough to drive myself home. Vincent was resting his head against my chest, fondling the back of my neck with gentle finger strokes. And as I sat there with him, I started to rehearse this seduction scene in my mind: When I return from the bathroom, I'm going to stand right in front of him, in the glow of the television light and drop my summer dress off of my shoulders, wiggle out of my panties and then throw myself on top of him.

I'm sure he'd take me then wouldn't he? Who am I kidding? First of all, I had been planning to seduce him like that all night, each and every time I returned from the bathroom, but I never did it. And I had been at his place drinking wine since about eight o'clock that evening, but something kept holding me back, as I kept telling myself, "I don't want to throw myself at him. If he doesn't want me, he doesn't want me. But oh, how I want this man."

Vincent is a caramel covered 6 foot 1, 185 pounds of solid muscle. No excess body fat at all, with a firm butt and a rippled stomach from nipple to navel...Drop dead gorgeous is how I see him, even if I've only seen him with his clothes on.

I could tell by the way he looked at me...by the way he surveyed my body from top to bottom that he really wanted me too. And I could sense that he knew that I wanted him just as badly as I sensed that he wanted me.

Perhaps he also sensed that I was hesitant in going through with my seduction scene, because of all of that talk about "why I shouldn't trust a man." Anyway, I think Vincent was starting to dose off on that damn sofa, so I figured that it was time for me to go home disappointed, once again.

I excused myself from his grasp and headed for the bathroom. The thought of seduction was now farthest from my mind. I was prepared to bask in the thought of my seduction of him in my own bed at home.

I came out of the bathroom for what seemed like the hundredth time that night, relieving myself of all of the wine I had somehow managed to consume. But this time, as I exited the bathroom and turned off the light, I was engulfed into a house of darkness.

There was no longer the television light that had been guiding me back into the living room where Vincent and I had been groping each other on the sofa. There was nothing. For a moment, I figured there had been a power outage or a black out. But then I saw a bright light to my left and I decided to follow it.

As I entered the doorway of which I had never been through before, I saw that the bright light was several lit candles, and the door through which I had just entered, was Vincent's bedroom.

There in contrast to the bright light, Vincent stood naked in front of his king sized water bed. I was saddened briefly that my plan to seduce him failed. He had taken the reigns of seduction and flipped it on me, as only a knowledgeable man of women could do...a womanizer in all his glory.

As delightfully dumbfounded and equally pleased as I was, I was finally going to get my wish from him. There I stood, taking him in all of his naked splendor, from head to toe. He was as gorgeous as I had anticipated he would be and I could plainly see that he was already ready for me.

Then for some reason, I was overtaken with shyness and was unable to speak. There was no need for further words, because he could plainly see in my eyes that I was ready for him too. Why he had waited this long, I'll never know.

He quietly took two steps toward me, took each of the shoulder straps on my dress, tilted them to the side, and allowed them to fall freely from my body onto the floor. I stepped out of my shoes as he swept me up into his arms and laid me on top of the bed.

He hovered over me and eased my panties off of me with expertise...too slow to bear as it seemed an eternity before they finally dwindled off the tips of my toes. And from the tips of my toes, he began to kiss me slowly and reassuringly.

All I could do was lay there and think, "Oh this is going to be heaven. I've waited so long and I hope I'm not too tipsy to enjoy it."

Interrupting my thoughts, I heard Vincent say to me, "I've been counting the days too, Jax."

Afterwards, I stared at the ceiling and wondered what type of transformation my body had just undergone. It was a miraculous feeling...hardly contemplative for one person to be able to comprehend. It was a feat that I had never experienced in my life. It was heaven.

We both laid there in silence for what seemed like hours. Vincent then quietly rolled out of bed and walked towards the bathroom. I could see his naked body silhouetted in the candle light. It was a sight to remember.

He returned carrying a ceramic basin filled with water and a sponge. He approached me with the sponge in hand, dipped it into the basin full of water and began to sponge down my body. He took extra care with my breasts - he seemed to know they were sensitive and swollen due to all the sucking they'd received all night long. Then he washed the sweat from my neck, my chest, my stomach, my thighs and every other part of my body that made contact with his.

When he finished he got back in the bed with me, laid on his side with his elbow on the bed and his head resting in his hand and asked, "So, is that what you wanted Jax?"

I could have died right then and there with embarrassment. He had been reading me all along. The truth of the matter is, *that was* what I wanted, and I told him so. In the morning we showered together, and I knew that I had found a very special friend in Vincent. Yes, I knew that he could never be all mine, but with a condom and the skills he had, I was willing to share!

The first thing I did when I left his apartment was drive straight over to Sabastian's house since it was on my way home. Luckily, she was standing outside with her nephew, kissing him goodbye from a night of baby-sitting. She turned as I drove up and walked over to greet me at my car.

I got out and started walking towards her, when she asked, "Girl, what's wrong with your legs? Why are you walking like that?"

I couldn't hide the expression on my face. I laughed out loud and said, "Remember when I told you that Vincent must be gay?"

"Yeah, I remember." She placed both hands on her skinny hips striking a pose and already smiling from cheek to cheek.

I said smiling also, "Well, he's not. He's definitely not!"

(2) – Joseph – Ships a Hoe

The familiar sights and sounds that seemed to wake him up at exactly the same time every morning was always a relief to Joseph. It meant that he was still on board the S.S. Cruxia, and as detached from reality in the States as he could be.

His only reminder that he was missing something at home was his ever present early morning erection that poked through the sheets while he lay on his back. He hadn't been with a woman in a very long time…for him.

As he lay there, he hesitated before getting out of his bunk because of the cold nip in the air. Joseph preferred to be the first one on deck, even before the wakeup call sounded. He didn't do it to impress anyone for status; he did it simply for his love of the ocean. He loved the way the ocean breeze shot through the very soul of his manhood and he appreciated the aquatic life that lived in the ocean beneath him.

He needed this alone time on deck. He looked forward to it every day, early in the morning before the sun rose. He appreciated it even more so than any of the other sailors on board. And he needed this time to escape alone because he knew that upon his return to the States he would finally have to make those wedding plans with Veronica, like he promised.

How could he think of marriage? How could he have been so foolish? Yes, he loved her, she was his childhood sweetheart, but why do people make the assumption that they have to follow through with childhood feelings? He's a grown man and she's a grown woman and they shouldn't have to do this. But there is the small matter of the child.

Joseph knew that he had to do the right thing by marrying her. Oh hell, he didn't want to go out on deck thinking about deep subjects like marrying Veronica. There was plenty of time for that. He would prefer, rather, to think ahead to the island of Fiji that they would be embarking upon soon. And he knew without a doubt he would not be able to resist the beautiful women that lived there.

It had been way too long for him, and though he tried to contain himself, he *is* only a man. If he was lucky, he thought, and were to find the right woman, any woman, he would fuck her. Hell, he needed to think about something else besides his problems waiting for him at home.

He was already making a mental note of how much extra cash he would need in order to be with that special someone to last him the few weeks the S.S. Cruxia would be in Fiji. Joseph laughed and thought, "I wonder if they'll be waiting for us at the docks?" He hoped so. But he knew for sure that he had two more days on board the ship before they would reach land. And he would have to make due with 425 or so, men for a short time longer.

So far he had avoided contact with the ships known homosexuals. He'd always heard the rumors. As for the others, he didn't ask and they didn't tell. He found it natural and had grown accustomed to living with large groups of men throughout most of his adult life. However, the latest headlines about gays in the military did pose as an interesting question regarding all of the friends he had made and whether or not they themselves were gay.

He didn't worry about it much because standing at 6'3, 210 pounds, looking like Denzel he'd fuck a faggot up. It was the farthest thing from his mind, but secretly he did wonder about the sexuality of those less masculine looking fellows that ran amuck aboard the ship...not too much thought though.

Before getting out of his bunk, he was always very careful not to wake the others. He did not want anyone to learn of his desire to start the day this early. This was his special time and no one else's. So he quietly put on his civilian clothes as he always did and ascended to the deck from the back staircase as not to alarm any of the crew men on duty.

When he found a quiet spot under the moonlight, he relaxed and took a deep breath. He looked overboard and looked down at the white water crashing against the side of the ship and wondered how many knots they were traveling at.

Just then he heard a faint sound to the right, and as he turned and looked he saw a huge rat tugging away at a supply bag obviously left on deck by one of the crew men on duty. He instinctively reached inside his pocket for his sketch pad and pencil and began to capture the little rodent at work. He etched away at his drawing trying his best to capture the rat in earnest.

Suddenly the rat took notice that it was being watched and turned to investigate. When it was sure that it was not in danger it returned to its mission at hand, which was to tear the bag in shreds and to consume as much of the contents as it could. Joseph was amused that this little creature was so openly bold and determined, though grateful at the same time, that the rodent had not taken flight before he finished his drawing.

When finally he was done, it had taken all of four minutes to capture each detail of the rat at work. And as quickly as he had turned his attentions to the rat, he just as quickly lost interest and returned his gaze to the open sea. He found it more rewarding to sketch in the early morning with only the humming of the S.S. Cruxia's engine to remind him that he was not entirely alone.

He sketched not only of the things that he could see such as the moon, stars and oh yes, the rat. But he also drew things created by his vivid imagination such as, prehistoric women with big tits, Angels with magic wands, sports cars and mammoth sized beer cans.

Joseph had such a creative imagination he could draw nearly anything and make it comical and believable at the same time. He and his pencil could do no wrong. He was pretty good too. He had often wondered had he gone to college for his drawing skills if he would have amounted to much.

He hadn't thought about going to college in a very long time, ever since he opted to join the Navy - the same United States Navy that both his father and grandfather proudly served. If ever there were a true sense of a man, Joseph always though that he was it. He was very proud of this feeling, for he felt that he got it from his father, who also had a love for the sea as he did.

During times like these, when he sat alone on the deck of the Cruxia, he often pondered about the times he spent with his father as a young boy. They would drive down the coast, rent a fishing boat and sit on the water for hours eating spam sandwiches and having those precious father-to-son talks.

His father told him great tales of his days as a sailor and of all of the exciting and different ports that he visited. Joseph looked forward to these times more often than any other, because of the precious time that he got to spend with his father, of whom he was so much alike. He also loved to hear those wonderful tales that he just knew one day he would emulate.

Most of the time, they would ignore the catfish tugging on the ends of their fishing lines, and just bask in the each other's company; father and son. He wished that he had been able to spend more time like that with his father, but his father had long since passed away leaving his mother a widow and himself a fatherless only child.

So very saddened by his passing, when he became of age, he too joined the Navy, to honor his father. Perhaps he did it just to get back those lost feelings of closeness, but probably more so to test his own manhood as compared to his father. He himself wanted to experience all of the wonderful things that his father had experienced in order to become the man that his father would want him to be, but would never know.

And as he finished a series of drawings that he'd just completed, he noticed the rainbow colored hue of the sunlight appearing from the east as the start of a new day was beginning. He was transfixed while looking at the beautiful colors the clouds made in contrast against the sun. And as always, he was soothed by remembering the things that he had done with his father as a young child, and in his pursuit of happiness in trying to be all of the things that his father would want him to be.

The beauty of the ocean had never ceased to amaze him. And out of the purple ocean he saw what he thought was a dream, a nightmare perhaps of one of his drawings coming to life. The ocean opened up with a thunderous splash and a force so volatile that he was suddenly afraid. And then he saw that it was actually a pod of whales leaping through the waves with what appeared to be a great urgency. Perhaps they were headed to the warmer waters of Fiji to commence in age long rituals unknown to man.

These were the wondrous things of the ocean that Joseph enjoyed most, and he was the only one in the world witnessing this spectacular show of nature at work, early morning, in the raw. Joseph took this wonderful sight to heart, and when it was over he tried to return to his sketches and just enjoy being a man at sea, but this morning his mind was troubled and he just couldn't shake the feeling that he was making a mistake by marrying Veronica.

Was he ready? He wasn't sure, though he did love her, which is why it was so hard for him to understand why he was having these doubtful feelings. Oh, but then he thought, "It must be pre-wedding jitters. Every man must get them I suppose. I am at the marrying age, I do have a child with this woman, and we could make beautiful love together for the rest of our lives. But shouldn't I wish more for my daughter, than my father wished for me?"

And so he thought of Veronica, and he remembered when he first met her. They both shared the same sixth grade class with Mr. Peterson. Joseph liked girls then, but Veronica didn't stand out very much. She was sort of shy and didn't seem to get along with the other girls very much. But because she didn't stand out, she wasn't one of the many girls that he and his buddies would chase toward the bungalows of their school and try to sneak peeks under their dresses.

No, he preferred Valerie, Allison and Belinda for that. They were considered "hot to trot" even for eleven years old. They would expertly lure him into the bungalows and allow him to steal feels and kisses. They would pretend to be upset to have been cornered by him, as he moved in for the kill, but he knew better.

Joseph figured if he got an erection by being so near to a girl, then they must cream their panties by being near to boy. Touching and grabbing at them was one of the highlights of each school day. He knew at that tender age that he was a lover of women and that he would have to conquer as many as he possibly could before he got married. Damn, back in those days girls were a lot simpler.

By the time he graduated from grade school and entered Jr. High, he noticed that Veronica had started to blossom. He took notice of her more than he ordinarily would have because they lived in the same neighborhood and were often thrown together by fate on their walks home from school.

They were very cordial to one another and spoke, as did their parents, who were all very active within the PTA. But he was always a little hesitant in trying to get to know her because she often times seemed so shy and he was uncomfortable with that because he himself was so outgoing. He wanted the world to be his friend and he wanted the world to know that he wasn't afraid to be its friend. Veronica didn't fit well within that picture, not at first.

In any case, he took notice of her and as she blossomed she took notice of him. By the time they had reached Sr. High School it was she who asked him out for their first date. He was totally blown away. As a matter of fact, he stuttered his reply to her because she had taken him by such a surprise.

She picked him up on their date in her father's, 4X4 pickup. Oh he knew that she could handle it pretty well, because he had seen her, the summer before, receiving driving lessons from her father. She was after all, daddy's little girl. Besides they were only going for pizza and a movie at the local mall right around the corner. So he supposed that her father trusted her to drive at least that far with a neighborhood boy, who had lived in the neighborhood just as long as they had.

He remembered their first kiss, which was so tender and innocent that he couldn't resist going back for more. He remembered their first sexual encounter, suspecting that he was the one who took her virginity, though she never admitted it and he liked her even more because of that. He thought it was impressive of her trying to demonstrate to him that she was more of a woman than anyone would ever believe. And he remembered every first thing they ever did together.

She was his childhood sweetheart, and even though through the years they managed to break up several times, she was always very cordial when it came to seeing him with other women, though he couldn't admit the same whenever he noticed that she was seeing other men.

She would nod hello when he and his dates passed by in the car. She would even initiate conversations with the other women whenever they happened to see one another in the mall or the movie theater. But they always ended back where they started, together in each other's arms, falling in love.

Veronica fell in love with Joseph, Joseph fell in like with Veronica and then he fell in love with the sea, and she just couldn't compete. But then she got pregnant and so she didn't have to.

After he showered, he put his uniform on and checked the roster to see what his duties would be for the morning. Unfortunately, he received the kitchen for the day, which meant that he had to report down to the kitchen immediately and help prepare and serve breakfast for several hundred fellow crew men. "Damn!" He thought, "Why did I have to get stuck in the kitchen on such a good day like today?" He had no time to waste before having to report, but he decided to do 50 quick pushups anyway just to get the adrenaline pumping.

Everyone considered kitchen duty the worst duty that you could receive in the Navy. It was three levels down under, it was stuffy, had no windows, and always smelled like ammonia. It was also the place the men teased each other about getting their "salads tossed." Perhaps his subconscious instructs him to do pushups, while crew members are around, in an effort to appear more macho before entering the kitchen.

After going down into the kitchen discovering that the crew the night before had not scrubbed it down as it should be, he instinctively took the initiative and began spot cleaning everything, making it shine. Coincidentally, the Captain had decided to do a spot check that morning and was very pleased with his findings.

Joseph was observed by the Captain as being "prepared as usual." Some of the other men on board didn't like the fact that he was always getting pats on the back by his commanding officers. A lot of them knew that he always got out of his bunk early in the mornings, but they never knew that he was out on the deck sketching or meditating. They just assumed that he was trying to impress his officers by being the first one up.

The men assigned with kitchen duty finally served everyone their breakfast and were waiting for them all to finish up so they could clean up. They would all take this opportunity to either go out on deck to relax for a while, or to simply sit down somewhere in the mess hall and wait for the last sailor to leave.

During this time, Joseph took a seat on one of the stools next to the sink and closed his eyes in meditation. He was completely lost in his own thoughts when something zoomed inches past his head, hit the wall behind him, and scattered scalding hot liquid all over him.

Alarmed, he opened his eyes, jumped up and saw that he was drenched with coffee. He was furious and about to kick somebody's ass when he noticed that there was a riot in the mess hall. He didn't have the slightest clue as to what triggered the fight.

Punches were coming from across the table, eggs were flying everywhere, and biscuits were being thrown all over the place. Heads were being bashed in with chairs, people were being kicked in the groin and they were all shouting bloody murder to one another.

The bull horn sounded but they ignored it and continued to fight. It was a pitiful sight as some of the men had bloody noses and knuckles, and others ran out looking for their superior officers to break up the fight. Joseph, without even thinking, being the kind of man he was decided to try and help.

He jumped straight over the counter into the mess hall and jumped into the middle of the frenzied activity and started throwing men off of men. "Stop this shit! What the hell is going on?" Joseph tried to scream over all of the yelling, but no one bothered to pay him any attention. "We're all gonna get in trouble for this shit," he was saying!

"Fuck you Man!" somebody said as Joseph was hit in the back of the head and the men continued to fight.

When Joseph turned around to fight the person who had hit him in the head, he received another punch in the nose. This time he grabbed his nose in pain because he thought it had been broken. He was definitely ready to fight now and started hitting whoever was close enough to him. Suddenly he was on the ground with several others, and before he could get up, somebody jumped on his hand and Joseph yelled out in pain.

The fighting continued on all around him as he yelled out, "My hand, my hand!" He grabbed his hand with his other to protect it from being stepped on again. But because he was still on the floor, he was hit and kicked along with the others. And finally, he blacked out.

When he woke up he was in the infirmary. He was still high and groggy from the pain medication. With his good hand he instinctively grabbed his injured hand and saw that it was set in a cast. His hand was broken, which meant he couldn't sketch...which meant that his time on the ship would seem to go on endlessly with no passing of time, with no relief, and he was miserable with the thought.

He vaguely remembered the fight, but he didn't remember what had happened after the fight and he didn't remember why the fight broke out in the first place. He felt his nose and to his surprise there was no cast on it.

He turned toward the bunk on his left and then on his right, but there was no one else in the infirmary. He was alone. He thought that it was stupid he had been brought here in the first place. Just because he had been kicked in the head and had a slight concussion was no reason to be carried off into the infirmary like a little bitch. But there he was, tucked in all nice and neat in his little bunk all by himself.

He figured that someone would come in and explain what had happened to him soon. And because he didn't want to make a big fuss over nothing, he waited and waited and he waited, but nobody came.

Finally, sometime during the course of the afternoon he fell asleep because when he woke up his lunch was sitting beside his bunk. "This is strange," he thought as he poked at his sandwich, "that someone would bring me food and not wake me up to eat it." He figured that everybody was being reprimanded for the fight that morning and they were all trying to keep their distance from the only one who had sustained an injury.

He decided not to worry about it and he ate his sandwich. Afterwards, he stared at his hand in disbelief and wished that he could sketch, which is what he would have been doing at this very moment.

Shortly after he ate, a crew member returned for his lunch tray and Joseph asked, "Hey, what happened in the mess hall?"

The younger man replied, "We're under orders not to discuss it." And that was that. No sooner than he had entered he was gone.

Joseph being a dedicated sailor decided that these are the rules and he wouldn't press it. But he was so bored laying there he thought he would go out of his mind. He wished one of his buddies would sneak in to check up on him, but nobody did.

And although he knew that he was fine, he figured that they just wanted to keep him near the medical supplies in case he lost consciousness again. Besides, he felt that everybody had been acting weird anyway, especially in the infirmary. And though he had never had cause to visit this place before, he got the strangest vibes from it. This was a strange and cold place as compared to the barracks where the sailors slept.

As the afternoon turned to night, he began to feel the effects of the drugs he had been given, and so he drifted off to sleep only to be awakened sometime during the night by the sounds of passion, or what he thought were the sounds of passion?

He told himself "Nah, I'm just horny again – just dreaming." So he tried to go back to sleep to get some rest before they docked in Fiji the next day. But he couldn't shake a weird feeling he had, so he opened his eyes.

He was trying to distinguish his dream filled state apart from his awakened state of reality, and to realize that he was not sleeping anymore. But, yet, he still heard these sounds of passion, and they were definitely coming from one of the bunks right next to him.

He couldn't believe his ears! He was actually hearing the grunts, moans, groans, and the squeaking mattress, that go along with sex! "Where the hell did she come from," he thought?

But suddenly, he was revolted as he realized there was no woman, this is some homosexual ass shit going on! Obviously, two sailors, two men were fucking in the dark, in the infirmary, a squirt away from a threesome with him!

Joseph couldn't move, and he didn't want to give away his presence by making any noise. And so he said nothing, but he was disgusted by the whole thing. He began to feel nauseated at the very thought of what was going on. And then he thought again, "Maybe, somehow, some way, a woman *did* stole away on the ship, 'cause that sure sounds like some squishy, wet, pussy fucking."

So he tried to make himself believe he was hearing sex between a man and a woman. For a moment, he felt a sense of relief that this *was* the case, and he smiled at the very idea that a woman *had* been on board the Cruxia all along and had gotten away with it!

But, just when he had convinced himself that it was normal fucking, he was about to allow himself to yank out his own penis and get off, when he heard a man's voice ask, "Am I hurting you?"

Joseph expected to hear a woman's voice reply. "No. Just keep on doing what you're doing" It was another man's baritone voice.

Joseph couldn't hold back his silence any longer. He sat up in his bed and demanded, "What in the fuck is this sick shit?!"

The two men were obviously startled as they both jumped up and one of them said, "Oh my God, there's someone in here! You said no one was in here!"

The other voice said, "Hurry up, take it out, take it out!"

Joseph thought he recognized one of the voices, and leaned from his bed to reach for the lamp. As he finally found it in the dark, he accidentally knocked it over because he couldn't turn it on with his hand in the cast. So he jumped out of bed to run towards the light switch on the wall. He felt his way through the dark looking for it.

When he finally found it and was able to turn it on, he saw two white asses scrambling out of the door with their pants around their ankles. A second later, then they were gone!

He stood there feeling disgusted and ashamed of having been in a room with two faggots. "So it is true," he thought, "they do toss salad on the Cruxia. Ugh!"

He looked back at the bunk that they had been on, just feet away from him, and noticed how the bed covers were crinkled up. He threw the remains of the broken lamp in the trash, sat down on his bed and put his good hand to his head.

He wondered if they would have tried to do anything to him had they known he was in the next bed. He regretted the thought as soon as he had it, and shuddered at the thought. Then he considered sounding the bull horn and having those two faggots busted with their dicks out and their pants down, but decided against it because some fool was bound to confuse the situation and a rumor would spread that he was gay too. So he wasn't going to mention it...for now. Instead, he would do a little investigating on his own and find out whose voice it was that he recognized, and then settle the score.

Looking at his hand he laughed to himself, thinking if he was able to sketch right now he would be drawing two men doing it doggy style. Joseph lay on the bed, leaving the light on and said out loud, "This has been one fucked up day!"

He was paranoid and didn't sleep for the rest of the night, thinking that someone was going to come in and try to suck on his dick, or something. He didn't exactly know what the homosexual rituals were, but he wasn't about to take any chances.

In the morning the medic came to check up on him. He took a look at his right hand and asked Joseph a couple of routine questions about how he was feeling. Joseph told him that he felt fine and then thought about telling him about what had happened the night before, but something inside told him to keep his mouth shut. Besides, he didn't want to get involved and he did not want his name associated, in any way! So, he said nothing.

The medic told him that he had a slight concussion and a broken hand, and that he could return to his assigned sleeping station that night. As the medic was leaving, one of Joseph's buddies was coming in to visit him.

George was the craziest sailor on board the S.S. Cruxia. He was a short, chubby, dark skinned, hard-core looking brotha who got much respect on the open seas. He used to get into all kinds of trouble when he was younger.

He used to steal, sell and use drugs and create total mayhem wherever he went. Fortunately, he saw the error of his ways after being arrested and faced with the possibility of going to prison. Sometime after this, he decided to join the Navy and has since turned his life completely around...well almost.

"Hey, what's up Man?" George asked. "I'm sorry to hear what happened to you over in the cantina. How's your hand doing?"

"Thanks for asking Man, but I'm alright. My hand is fucked up though!"

"I can see that. Is it broken?"

"Yep. Any word on who's the fool with the appointed ass kicking for doing this to me?"

"No. From what I hear, it was too much of a mess going on down there for anybody to be singled out. But the word is, everybody down there was acting up and are all in big trouble."

"What did Captain Grey say?"

"He is royally pissed. He has some of them confined to the barracks, some are on toilet scrubbing duty and some of them lost their rank."

"So I was the only one hurt?"

"Yep, you were the only fool hurt. Ain't that something? That's what you get for trying to mix it up with those idiots."

"Hey, what's up with Carrera and Green?"

"From what I hear, Green got out before all of the action got too bad because he didn't want to be nowhere near them fools when they started to throw some serious blows. But Carrera stayed in the mix and got busted, the dumb bastard. You know he already got written up once before for smoking weed out on the deck one night when he thought everybody was sleeping."

"Yeah Man, I remember that because I was on deck that night too. I remember thinking to myself, why do I smell weed If we're in the middle of the ocean? But I didn't say anything though. You know me, I mind my own business."

"Yes, we know Joe. Well at least we used to know before yesterday, that is."

"Yeah well, I'll never do that shit again."

George stood up and walked toward the door. He turned and said, "By the way, the ship is docking in Fiji tonight and the boys and I are all going to hit the streets as soon as they let us. You want us to swing by and pick you up?"

"My hand is in a cast, but my dick ain't," Joseph said with a grin.

"That's my Man. Try as you might, but you're still a dog." Joseph gave an innocent look to George and said, "I'm gonna be good this time."

George mocked him, counting out on his fingers, "That's what you said in the Philippines before you met Fawn. That's what you said in Taiwan before you met Song. There was some girl in Germany; Eliza or something. Shall I go on?"

Joseph was suddenly embarrassed. He knew, all too well, that he had a habit of tasting the waters of his travels, and after each affair he promised never to do it again. But it wasn't his fault, it was his dicks. Besides, he was marrying Veronica soon and planned on being faithful to her when that happened.

He remembered all the great stories his father had told him about his adventures in the Navy, so he always assumed that this is what his father and his grandfather did. He had tried to get the other girls out of his mind, but he did wonder if they were still writing him at home, trying every trick in the book to get him to marry *them*, so they could come and live in the States. Joseph said to George, "No, don't remind me. Just swing by and pick me up on your way out."

George laughed and said, "Yeah alright Romeo," and opened the door.

"By the way," Joseph was saying, "I've got to tell you something. I know I probably shouldn't tell anybody this, but you might be able to help me figure out what's going on."

"What is it?" George asked curiously.

"Last night when I was heavily under the drugs the doctor gave me, I was kicked back, falling asleep and I started to dream that somebody was fucking in here and I was watching them."

"Damn Man, you're a peeping tom, you weird motha fucka." George laughed as he returned to Joseph's bedside, waiting to hear more. "That's funny Man, was she fine?"

"That's the whole thing man. Number one, it wasn't a dream, and number two, it was two faggots!" Joseph squirmed uncomfortably in his bed, looking for a reaction from George. He didn't want him to think that he had dreamt the whole thing, or that he was crazy.

George's eyes grew real big and he said, "Say what?!"

"I said it wasn't a dream. It was two faggots in this infirmary last night, doing what faggots do right there in that bed over there!" Joseph said pointing to the empty bed which was still in disarray.

"Ugh, that's nasty Man! For all you know, while you were sleeping they could have tried to bust you wide open."

"Fuck that George. Nobody is gettin' to this booty," he said defensively. "All I know is that two fools must have snuck out during the night, not thinking anyone was in the infirmary, came in here, to their little rendezvous spot and got busy. Thank God they didn't pick my bunk. They probably picked their usual bunk."

"Did you get a look at who it was?"

"No. I reached for the lamp and knocked it over because of this stupid cast. But when I jumped up and said, 'What the fuck is going on here?' I was running for the light and by the time I finally turned it on, I saw two booties with their pants hanging around their ankles." Joseph told this to George with the same look of disgust on his face as he had had last night.

"Damn, that shit is nasty. We've got this kind of stuff going on not only on the Cruxia but every other ship out there." George was looking as disgusted as Joseph. "I thought the president signed in a policy that says, 'Don't ask, don't tell', or whatever?"

"Yeah well, they didn't tell," Joseph said.

"That's too close for comfort."

"I know that's right, especially for my comfort."

Trying to lift Joseph's spirits George said, "Well hey, you'll be back in your own bed tonight, so you'll be all right."

"I know I'll be alright. Those mutha fucka's better not come near me."

"Come near you?" George slapped Joseph on the back.

"Fuck you Man, you know what I mean." Joseph playfully punched him in the stomach.

"Well, you might as well go ahead and get some more rest before we dock, because if you come out now they'll put your ass to work, cast or not." He was walking back towards the door.

"Yeah I know, but it's boring as hell in here. I can't sketch or anything with this cast on my hand."

"Sketch with your left hand," George said as he disappeared behind the closing door.

"Sketch with my left hand?" Joseph repeated while wondering if he could in fact draw as skillfully with his left hand as he could with his right hand. He had never even given it any thought because he was right handed. But George had given him a bright idea that he would have never thought of on his own, since he had been pre-occupied with the sex scene from hell the night before.

He reached for a pad and pencil sitting on the night stand next to him and clumsily, at first, began to draw simple objects with his left hand. And as he continued to draw, the objects became more definite to him. At first the chair he drew didn't look like a chair, but more like chimney. And the telephone he drew looked like the head of a dog, but the drawings were coming together rather well, he thought.

He continued practicing his sketches with his left hand for the next several hours, completely lost in his own world. He hadn't even noticed the bull horn which signaled their arrival into Fiji.

At 18:30 hours George and the crew swung by to pick Joseph up from the infirmary. They had finally docked in Fiji and were ready to hit the town. As they all jumped off of the ships ramp and on to the dock, George was the first one to look around and ask, "Where are the women? I know they're close 'cause I can smell 'em."

After spotting a group of women walking past the docks, the guys all looked at each other and ceremoniously said, "Whoop, there it is!"

Hundreds of men were coming off the Cruxia in drones by 18:42 on a Saturday night. They were all planning something big...something special.

Most of them had on full Navy attire, but others were less obvious. The women of Fiji must have known what they were in for, because they were all dressed to kill. They were wearing their most tight fitting and shortest skirts and dresses, walking around the docks as though they were really waiting for someone in particular. Everybody knew that they had been waiting for...the Cruxia to pull in.

When several of the women walked toward the guys, George took the initiative and said, "Excuse me young ladies, but could you please point us out to the nearest strip bar?"

One of the women looked at him confused, as though she did not understand what he had just asked. But the girl standing to her left said with a thick accent, "Strip bar is on Winola Lane, the Tiki Room. Take route 3, turn left on Winola. We see you there maybe?" the girl was saying with a determined and experienced look on her face.

George just ignored her. He turned to Joseph and said, "Hail a cab. If a cab driver can spot anybody, he can spot that big ass cast on your hand." They all laughed, including Joseph, because he knew that George was probably right.

Joseph, George, Green and Paul walked to the end of the pier to find the cab driver who would first, try to rip them off with the fare, and then take them to the Tiki Room. Unfortunately, Carrera couldn't come along with them because he was given clean up duty for the weekend after the kitchen fight. But both Green and Paul had avoided detention by getting out of the way.

Carrera was a young, but out spoken Cuban who was sort of adopted by the guys. When he first came aboard the Cruxia, Joseph took it upon himself to try and calm down the youngster so he wouldn't get into any unnecessary trouble, which was always the case. After that he couldn't shake Carrera lose, because it gave him too much status with the other sailors to hang around the guys, so they just let him tag along.

Paul Green and Paul Tippit; brown, long and lanky, had served in the Marines together. And though they weren't brothers or best friends or anything, they usually ended up together, even in the Navy, because of this association and their similarity in looks.

Most of the sailors didn't like Paul Tippit, however, because of his blatant attitude. But everyone figured that they would tolerate him because of his association with the more likable Paul Green. And so the five of them were their own crew and took watch over each other on the Cruxia and abroad.

When the guys arrived at the Tiki Room they were all in full anticipation of what the evening would bring them. George was immediately interested in the half naked woman on stage in a cage, grinding against the cold metal bars, motioning for him with her tongue. So he went to her.

Paul and Green found a booth big enough to seat all four of them and motioned for a waitress to bring them each a beer. But Joseph had decided to get a better look at this place they were in and walked over to the bar in order to see a wider view of everything that was going on around him. He has seen many strip joints like this in his adventures as a sailor. He wondered if he would be able to control his sexual emotions this time.

Joseph was ordering his second beer, watching the men of the Cruxia go stir crazy over a blond haired woman juggling her breasts with the palms of her hands. He thought it strange that this woman of Fiji would dye her hair blond when the other women looked more attractive and exotic with their natural black hair. He looked up and saw George and the other guys touching and grabbing women as they passed by the booth.

They were all laughing and drinking and Joseph decided to join them until he heard a woman's voice say, "I'll have mineral water with lime," to the bar tender. When he looked up to see what woman was ordering a soft drink in this place of drugs, alcohol and sex, he knew that his attempt to "be good" was lost.

She was beautiful in the most simplest of ways to Joseph. Her hair was black but it wasn't straight like most of the other women. It had a waviness about it that made her look almost American. It was cut in layers from short to long around her face. She wore tight fitting jeans, a Marlboro T-shirt, a pair of flat, black loafers and a distinctive gold locket around her neck.

When she took a bill from her pocket to pay for her drink, Joseph immediately motioned to the bar tender that he would pay for it. She looked at Joseph with sharp eyes and said, "I can pay for my own drink sailor."

Joseph was taken back a little, as he had expected this woman to be an easy target as were the rest of the women in the Tiki Room. Then he thought she was playing hard to get and so he decided that he didn't want to play the game with her. He looked at her and shrugged his shoulders as a sign of compliance to her comment and turned his back on her once again.

When he thought she was gone, he turned around and saw that she was still there sipping on her drink watching the other women do their strip routines. Joseph concluded that she was a lesbian and so he picked up his beer and walked over to the booth with the other guys.

"Why did you leave that fine woman sitting all alone over there? Was she too expensive?" George said as he patted the ass of a woman as she walked by.
"She wasn't for sale," is all Joseph said.

"That's bull. All of these whores are for sale. You must not have the knack boy. Let me show you how it's done." George got up from his seat and walked toward the woman at the bar. It was obvious that he was drunk, as he was not able to walk a straight line in her direction.

Green got up from his seat too and started towards George to stop him from making a fool of his self. But Joseph grabbed hold of his arm and said, "Let him go. I want to see this shit."

The guys at the booth started taking money out of their wallets and placing bets on whether George would succeed at picking up this woman. Joseph's money went against it because he thought the woman was gay. But Paul and Green were confident that George would eventually find the right words, through his slurred speech, to convince this woman that she should fuck him tonight.

After a few minutes George returned to the booth and said without hesitation, "That bitch is gay!"

The guys laughed so hard that two of the beers fell off of the table and broke on the floor. Joseph, still laughing said to the others, "Alright, pay up."

It was close to one in the morning and most of the men in the bar were starting to head back to the Cruxia. Joseph, George, Green and Paul were among the last few to leave. They were still laughing at George having made a complete fool of his self with that woman at the bar. They had been making jokes about it all night and were completely unaware that the woman had moved over to the booth next to theirs hours ago.

When Joseph stood up to go to the bathroom he noticed her at the booth sitting with one of the strippers. He thought this must be her lover and she was probably there to keep a close watch over her, with all of the American men in the bar. When he came out of the men's room, he saw the two of them standing in the doorway of the ladies room.

The woman at the bar was saying, "Papa's going to whip you if he ever finds out what you do here." She had tears in her eyes and was holding her sister.

The younger stripper was crying also and said, "We need the money Lea. Papa would be too proud to take it if he really knew what I did at night."

"I don't like the way they touch you, like you are an animal, Cela. Don't you have any pride?"

"No! Why should I have pride when these men come here and pay me for having such a beautiful body?" the younger stripper said while pulling away from her older sister, drying her eyes.

"They call you a whore and spit on your body if you let them, especially the Americans who are so arrogant. They think I am a woman lover because I come here to watch over my little sister," Lea said drying her eyes also.

"Then don't come anymore, Lea. I could make more money if you let me have a few minutes with one of these Americans." She said the word "Americans" as if it were a filthy word.

"It's not the American's fault that you make yourself available to them. Some of them are nice men, even if they are misinformed."

"You met someone you are interested in, maybe?" Cela asked curiously.

"Of course not!" Lea said defiantly. "I could never..."

Joseph stepped out into the hall way taking both of the women by surprise. He looked straight into Lea's eyes and saw a glimmer of interest. She blushed and immediately turned away from him. "I hope I'm not interrupting anything ladies?" staring down Lea.

Cela noticed that her sister had turned away from the sailor, so she, being obviously more open to men asked him, "You like my sister?"

Lea's eyes grew wide and she shook her finger at her little sister and said, "Cela! You are impossible! How can you embarrass me like this when I only try to protect you?" She was covering the sides of her face now with her hands as if to hide her reddened cheeks.

"Oh Lea, this a nice man. He paid just to look, not to touch. Look at him? He's a pretty man. What's your name sailor?"

"Joseph. Joseph Pride." He extended his left hand towards Cela and she took hold of it and shook it.

"Big strong hands sailor. What's with the cast, you break your hand in a fight? You know my sister Lea?" Cela took his hand and placed it in Lea's hand. Silence fell between the two of them as they starred into each other's eyes. Cela was getting a big kick out of watching her sister's unusual reaction to a man, but she said nothing.

Joseph finally broke the silence and said, "We've met."

In an attempt to give the two a little privacy, Cela said, "I go and get my stuff from the back room. I come back soon." Before Lea could protest, Cela briskly walked away leaving the two of them standing alone in the dimly lit hallway.

"I really must go look after my sister. She gets into trouble easily." Lea was pulling her hand out of Joseph's.

Joseph tightened his grip in an attempt to hold on to her. "Don't go. Please don't go, Lea. Tell me what to say to make you stay?" He regretted it as soon as he said it, but he had already begun to dig himself into an emotional hole that he wasn't quite sure he wanted.

He was absorbing everything about her. The fresh scent of flowers that lingered off of her hand and her hair, in spite of the smoke filled building, was intoxicating. He saw traces of gold in her big brown eyes and longed to kiss her natural tanned lips. All he wanted to do was to feel this way forever, and he knew she felt the same way.

How did he always get himself in these predicaments he wondered? No answers came to mind, as he was too occupied, too overwhelmed by Lea's natural and innocent beauty to consider that question any further.

Lea finally said, "It could never be anything but sex. You know it and I know it."

"Oh it could be much more than that if you let it," he said with hope in his voice.

"My sister was right about one thing, you are a very pretty man."

The next morning on the Cruxia, George approached Joseph while he was struggling to make up his bed with one hand. "Man, what happened to you last night?" George asked with curiosity.

"Nothing, I just got a little tied up that's all," Joseph said while trying not to look George in the eyes.

"Yeah right tied up, my ass. You met with someone, didn't you?" George triumphantly asked.

"What makes you think that?"

"Because we waited for you outside and you never came out. We figured you had a hot date and we left it at that."

"Well I am a big boy I can take care of myself, not like your drunken ass."

"Hey, I wasn't drunk, I was fucked up. Now stop trying to avoid my question. Who is she?"

Joseph could no longer resist throwing Lea back in his face. Besides, he was a little upset with George, having been called a boy by him last night, even though he knew George always acted like an ass hole when he was drinking. "Her name is Lea. You remember, the girl at the bar that you tried to pick up but couldn't?" Joseph said it with a smile on his face.

"You mean that lesbian?" George asked puzzled.

"No. I mean the one we *thought* was a lesbian."

"How do you know she's not AC/DC?"

"Because, she told me, besides, she wasn't there waiting for her woman, she was there waiting for her little sister, you know, the one who did that little trick with her tongue?"

"Oh yeah? Say, you think you can hook me up with her sister?" George joked.

"No. And five bucks says that you can't hook up with her on you own either." They laughed out loud and talked about how much fun they had had last night, and about how fun their stay in Fiji was going to be for the next several weeks. And later that night, Joseph met with Lea again, as he did every night for the duration of his stay in Fiji.

He didn't even think about sketching the whole time he was there. He was having the time of his life, and Lea was too. They spent every available free moment they had together, making love in hotels, in cars, on beaches, in trees, on toilet seats, in alleys, on counter tops and any and everywhere they could get away with it. They made love with such fury and passion as if each passing day were a testament to the brief lifetime that they would share together.

And with each new position that they explored, Joseph was testing his ability to work with just one working hand. He was very successful. When they spoke about his inevitable departure, they were optimistic with one another in saying that one day they would always be together. Little did Lea know that Joseph had made these promises before, although he always meant it at the time, he always knew deep down, it wasn't true.

Finally the day that the S.S. Cruxia was to depart from Fiji arrived, and the men would finally be returning to their homes in the States. Hundreds of men stood on the pier with the women with whom they had become involved with over the course of three weeks.

Joseph stood there with Lea and tried to comfort her with the promise that he would send for her one day. And although Lea loved hearing him say these things to her, she knew that it probably wasn't true. But she preferred to be treated this way than to be treated like a whore. And so she listened to him say goodbye and took in all of his beauty for the very last time.

She wondered how many other women throughout his travels had fallen under his flirtatious spell...how many other women had he sketched over and over again. She hoped she was the only one. At least, she knew she would always have something of his that no one could ever take away. And she knew that through his emotional eyes, Joseph hadn't even noticed that expectant, special glow about her face.

(3) - Gregory - Our Father

Gregory stood over his dying father, watching him lay there with sullen eyes. He knew that there wasn't much time before his father would eventually pass away into another life.

When he sat down on the bed next to him and reached for his hand, he noticed that it was missing the strength and the warmth that it used to. Instead it was cold and frail, and this saddened Gregory even more because the inevitable was written all over his father's sunken body. The doctor had briefly explained to him that the pneumonia had run its course and that there was nothing more that they could do to save him.

Though his father had been a shrewd business man over the last 30 years, he had never been shrewd enough to learn that three packs of cigarettes a day will surely kill you eventually in some form or fashion. Gregory never could stand the stench of cigarette smoke, or any other kind of smoke for that matter. He thought it deplorable that anyone would put something so vile into their mouths.

The lawyers had explained to him that he would need to take control of his father's corporation immediately in order to avoid any complicated take-over attempts by certain chair members of Thomas Childs Incorporated. He wasn't even sure as to the enormity of his father's holdings. They hadn't been on speaking terms for many years, but when his father fell into this fatal state of health, Louise, his father's longtime companion, called him and said that he should come to his father's ailing side before it was too late.

Louise was always like a mother to Gregory. His mother, Sara, wasn't dead, she had simply ceased to be a mother, not just to himself but to his brother and sisters; Lisa, Theresa and Jeremy. He guessed she simply got tired of being a stay at home mom. Thomas would never let her be anything more than that, except to rear the four children.

She should've been content in allowing him to make all of the decisions. So one day when Thomas was at work, Sara packed her bags, and left a note for Gregory to give to his father. Unmoved and emotionless, she walked out of the house leaving behind her husband and their four children.

Growing up all of them had easily adapted to their mothers absence, except for Gregory, which was unusual because he was the oldest. He missed his mother the most perhaps because he was at that age when he needed approval from both of his parents. And, like his mother, he was more fragile than any of the other children and his father seemed to always resent him for it.

But he did have strong ties with his father. They loved each other very much even though they didn't express it as much as they should have. And so, early on, Gregory took on the role of surrogate mother while Pops worked through the day. He took care of his younger siblings, and because of that they all had a very tight bond, loving and caring for one other.

However, Gregory did have very deep under-lying emotional problems that he did not want to admit. The fact is he was insecure with his feelings and himself. He wasn't sure if he was ever going to be able to trust a woman again since his mother had abandoned them. His father didn't seem to have any problems with it however. He bounced back a couple of years later with his girlfriend Louise, though he never married her. Sara therefore became a long term companion who never had kids of her own. He and the others liked Louise, but under no circumstances were they ever going to call her "Mother."

Gregory was grateful that Louise had notified him in New York when it became apparent that his father was deathly ill. He had to admit to himself that he was a little surprised that Louise had not taken advantage of the situation in trying to take control of his father's assets.

Thomas Childs is a very wealthy man and he assumed that given the opportunity, any long term companion such as Louise, would try and get her "just rewards" for having spent so many years with someone and to never have been rewarded with a commitment in marriage. But that obviously was not the case with her. In fact, she had turned out to be more of a mother than his own had ever been to him and the others.

And as he sat there holding his father's frail hand, he thought about calling Sara, though just for an instant, but decided against it as his mother had already caused his father enough grief in one lifetime. And there was no need to send him into another life with the same grief. As far as he knew his mother was still living in Europe somewhere. He had lost track.

They had spoken to his mother on only the most, rarest of occasions throughout the years, and he had long ago begun to think of her as more of a distant relative rather than his biological mother. The others stopped expressing their feelings for her in his presence long ago, because they knew he did not share the same feelings about her as they did.

He wished that he had returned back to California on a more positive note. It had been far too long since he had seen his father, though he had kept in close contact with his brother and sisters. They had visited him in New York quite often and he was very happy to know that they were all prospering in their endeavors.

His sister Lisa was a house wife, obviously following in the direction of Sara. She married right out of college, and though she had received her teaching credentials she was never able to put them to use because she kept popping out babies year after year. Last count she was working on number five.

Jeremy had long ago begun working with his father at one of his real estate offices. He had been promoted to operations manager and was also a top notch salesman who was accredited with having sold several of the estates in Beverly Hills, to movie stars and major corporate executives.

Theresa was still in college working on her degree, though he wasn't sure what that was this year, because she changed her major often. She was a sweet kid and Pops encouraged her to stay in school and get a degree in anything she wanted, as long as she did it successfully.

He thought about his life in New York and what he had left behind. He was a successful stock broker there and had done very well for himself, without his father's money, though he had access to it when things got a little tight. He wondered if he would be returning back to home now, if not for his pending death. Though he was not necessarily in love with New York, it had been his home for the last six years, though he'd never quite gotten used to the bitter cold winters there.

Gregory was interrupted from his thoughts as his father stirred. He looked down at the sick man and prayed that he would open his eyes and look upon him. He wanted Pops to realize that he was there with him, finally. But Thomas didn't open his eyes. He seemed to be fighting the inevitable in his nightmares, looking for the light...the direction that would finally take him home to peace eternal.

Gregory also prayed that his father would not pass-on without knowing that he cared for him a great deal. And as he continued to sleep, he placed his father's hand back under the covers, stood and walked toward the window.

He hated hospitals. He always did, because the sterilized stench made him nauseous. And as he looked out of the window and saw how beautiful it was outside, he cringed at the comparison, of how dreary it was inside. When he looked up from the window he saw Louise walk into the room.

She quietly motioned to him with her hand. When he walked towards her she spoke sadly and said, "Come on baby, the doctor has something he wants to tell the family." He slowly nodded his head and took hold of her out stretched hand as they left the room together.

His whole family was gathered outside of the hospital room and Theresa, the youngest, ran into his arms as tears streaked her face. Gregory held her close as they looked at the doctor and waited for him to speak.

Dr. Nichols finally said, "I'm sorry, but the prognosis for your father is bleak at best. He has developed double pneumonia as a result of several respiratory failures, including emphysema, which has worsened over the years, probably due to excessive cigarette smoking. He's not expected to live for very much longer. I suggest you make sure his will is in order and that you contact a clergy man as soon as possible."

There. It had finally been said, at least in a professional capacity. They had all heard from Dr. Nichols' mouth what they had been dreading to hear; the confirmation of Thomas Childs' immanent death. Though they all knew it to be true, they still wished for a miracle, but a miracle was not going to take place in room 4-16.

They were all too overcome with grief to speak, and so as usual, Louise took the reins and said, "Doctor, do you think it will be alright for us to take him home so that he is surrounded with things familiar to him before...?" She was unable to finish her question due to a sudden lump in her throat.

The Doctor noticed her emotional state and said, "If that's what you want. But I'm afraid that he probably will not come out of his state of unconsciousness and, therefore, will not be aware of his surroundings."

Theresa began to cry again at this news, as Gregory continued to hold on to her while stroking her hair. He realized that she was probably closest to Pops than any of them. Because she was the baby he loved lavishing things upon her; as though trying to make up for all of the mistakes he had made with his other older, and with Sara.

Lisa quietly said, "We're glad you're here Gregory. Pops would be glad you're here too."

"Your father *is* glad he's here, Lisa" Louise interjected.

"Well, that's what I meant," Lisa explained.

Louise continued talking to her, "Don't talk about him in past-tense baby. He's still with us, and let's try to keep him that way for as long as we can."

Jeremy stepped in between Louise and Lisa and said, "I can't take being in this hospital any longer. Let's go back to the house and think about making final preparations for Pops. If we start now we can be thorough, and you know how Pops like thoroughness." Louise looked at him coldly, but the others nodded favorably. And so one by one, they all walked back into Thomas' room to say good night.

Each of them whispered their own special something into Thomas' ear before kissing him on the cheek and hurrying out of the room. When Gregory approached him and once again looked down at his sunken body, he promised himself that if it was the last thing he did, he would maintain his father's assets, and carry on the tradition of the Childs family.

When they arrived back at the house, Lisa's husband, Michael, was waiting there with three of their four children. It had been quite a while since Gregory had seen his nieces and nephews.

They were growing up so fast that he was a little upset with himself for not being around to watch it more closely, as he had intended. But now he intended to keep this family together, and that meant he was going to bond with his sisters children, no matter what. So he greeted each one of them with a warm kiss, a big hug and an enthusiastic hello. Little Alex, the twins Robin & Raven and Jonathan were Pops' pride and joy, as well Lisa and Michael's.

He greeted Michael with a hand shake and asked where Jonathan was. Michael said that his mother had volunteered to keep the four month old infant, who was a crier, and would surely get on everyone's nerves within the hour.

As they walked into the house, slowly and uncertain, everyone fell into a weird silence that can only be described as eerie. And as they entered the main entryway, the reality of what had brought them together on this day, hit home. Without warning they all embraced one another and began to cry, as a family.

Louise finally composed herself and asked if anyone was hungry. They all said "no" except for Lisa, who said, "Well, I could go for a little something." Everyone looked at her with a question in their eyes, but before anyone could verbalize what they were thinking she replied, "No I'm not pregnant."

"Don't worry about it baby, I'll fix a little something for everybody," Louise was saying as she exited the marble floored hallway and headed towards the kitchen with Alex, Robin & Raven on the heels of her feet. "Gregory?" she called back. "Why don't you go into your father's office and call his attorney and invite him over here too."

Gregory had already spoken with Timothy Callahan earlier in the day upon his arrival into Los Angeles. Timothy was a good friend of his father's and had represented him financially for nearly thirty years. And so the news of Thomas' decline of health was very upsetting to him.

When he walked into his father's office he was overwhelmed with the way it looked; it had remained the same for far too many years while the rest of the estate was beautifully modernized.

The wood paneled walls, shaggy burgundy carpet, the huge oak desk and fading brown leather chair were all still there. The pictures on the rear wall were of all of his children, grandchildren, and of course Louise. And some of his finer pieces of art that he had collected throughout his travels in the Orient, Africa and the Middle East hung on every wall.

Gregory somberly walked towards his father's desk and hesitated from sitting in the big and familiar leather chair. But he shook the feeling and sat down, grabbed hold onto the arm rests and closed his eyes.

He reminisced about his younger days when had often been summoned into the office. But back then, he would be standing on the opposite side of the desk, while his father would sit in his chair. And Thomas, with a stern look on his face and a stern voice would ask him "Gregory, what do you plan on doing with your life son?"

And Gregory being only a young boy would say, "I don't know Pop, what do you think I should do?"

This infuriated Thomas. He hadn't raised any of his children to be indecisive, especially his sons, the ones who should automatically want to follow in his own footsteps in the world of real estate where big dollars could be made. He had begun to acquire his fortune at a young age, and had built up a substantial empire, able to support generations of his family for years to come.

Thomas had an illustrious career that had given him recognition throughout the state, country and in some cases throughout the world, as a formidable entrepreneur, with meager beginnings, who eventually rose to lead a fortune 500 company.

Gregory was always slightly intimidated by his father, though he was never afraid of him. He was persistent in his plight to be his own man. Though he wanted to please his father, he wanted to do it on his own terms, not at the beck and call of his father. I guess he had something to prove to himself...something to prove to his Pops, and something to prove to his mother; that with or without their support, he could succeed.

He *had* succeeded, and though he was always too passive in his attempts to find that special woman to share his accomplishments with in New York, he felt that fate would eventually lead her to him. He wished that she could be with him now, whoever she was, to give him the strength to go on. As the head of the family, he would need to take charge and secure the financial future of the family, as his father would expect him to; as his siblings would expect him to; as Louise would expect him to; and as he himself expected to do.

He picked up his father's old worn and familiar rolodex and began looking for Timothy's office phone number. When he found it and started to dial, it was as if he were in a trance. He snapped out of it only when the secretary had put Tim on the line and he was saying, "Hello...Greg? Are you there?"

Slowly and painfully Gregory began to tell Tim of his father's final prognosis. A silence fell between both of them when he was done. When Tim finally spoke, he said, "Well, then son, it's totally up to you now."

Gregory knew exactly what he meant and responded by saying with a new vigor, "Tim we need you to come by the house as soon as possible. We don't have much time. I'll need all records of my father's financials, including Stocks & Bonds, T-Bills, Escrow Accounts, holdings and anything else I'll will need to make a smooth transition as the new President and CEO of Thomas Childs, Inc.

Now, I know he had a lot of property business transactions pending in the Caribbean, so I'll need to see the proposals from the Time Share packages, as well. Are we going to have a difficult time in getting the other board members at TCI to cooperate with the change over?"

"No, I don't think so. Thomas has always been a good judge of character. The people at TCI wouldn't want to make trouble for you or for your family during this rough period. Besides, that traitor Stanley Bunch sold his stock two months ago to invest somewhere else, and he was really the only one that made trouble around here."

"Good. Tim, I want you to know, from my father's mouth to your ears, that you are truly more than a friend to this family. You are family and I intend for it to stay that way.

Even though I am going to be the new head of TCI, nothing will change your status with the company or with this family. To be quite honest with you, if you were not a part of this team, then I'm sure that I wouldn't be able to do it."

"Nonsense, Gregory. Not only are you a bright and successful young man, but you are and will always be the one whom your father intended to run this company after him. Regardless of any differences you may have had over the years, he made sure that a vote by the board would not be necessary for this. He has a lot of faith in you. I know you won't let him down, as I won't let you down. But as far as the will is concerned, well, you'll just have to wait to see what's in that."

With that exchange, Tim said he would be by the house within the hour bringing with him all of the necessary paperwork to ensure the safe and quick change over from one CEO to the next.

Gregory sat back feeling relieved. He took notice that he had just begun to take the reins of his father's company and would very shortly be the head of a mega-conglomerate. And as he opened each desk drawer, one by one and studied the contents, the pieces began to fall into place. He quickly determined that he would need to hire a data research firm to acquire files and data to help him in his new capacity.

So he sat there contemplating the future and thinking of his father, and occasionally his mother. He suddenly felt overwhelmed as though he was going to drown. From this moment on, TCI would be dependent upon someone who had never even had an initial interest to participate in it, let alone run it.

As he looked up from being lost in his thoughts, Jeremy was standing in the door way holding a silver tray holding sandwiches and a glass of orange juice. "Hey Man, how you holding up?"

"I've been higher," Gregory said with a weak grin.

"You know, Pops really would be real happy to see you sitting there."

"Pops *will* be happy to see me sitting here, 'cause he's coming home."

"When are you going to arrange that?"

"Actually I was going to ask Louise if she would arrange it."

"Louise really loves Pops. But I know she must feel a little left out, seeing that he never married her." He walked over to Gregory and offered him a sandwich.

"No thanks." Gregory declined the offer of food. "I think Louise is feeling everything we are feeling right now. Even though Pops never married her, she's always seemed content. For all we know, she could have turned Pops down. Besides, I bet the old man makes up for it in his will."

Gregory stood up and walked over to his younger brother, taking the tray from his hands and setting it on the desk. He inspected him from head to toe, admiring that he had turned out to be a handsome young man in spite of the big nose that everyone used to tease him about as a child.

Jeremy is a thin man weighing around 165 pounds standing at 5'9. He took after his father and chose to wear custom made suits with suspenders, brown patent leather shoes and oval rimmed glasses. If anyone didn't know him any better, they would swear that he was a nerd. But that wasn't the case. The fact was Jeremy was a bit of a ladies man, dating three to four women at a time.

Gregory put his hand to Jeremy's shoulder and squeezed. "You're going to have a lot more responsibility now Jer. Can you handle it?" Gregory asked his younger brother.

"I wish that I didn't have to handle it. I wish that Mother never left us and that Pops never started smoking after she left. I'm really hating that bitch right now!" he said as he walked around to his father's desk and opened the lower left drawer, pulling out a family portrait of their family, taken more than 20 years earlier. "You didn't know that he kept a picture of her in his desk, did you?"

Gregory was surprised to see that he had missed the picture when he was roaming through his father's desk. He reached for it out of Jeremy's grip. He examined it carefully and lovingly as though it were made of precious stones. He looked into his mother's eyes and saw an unhappy woman. She was holding Theresa, who couldn't have been more than two years old at the time. "Why's this picture in here like this?" he asked puzzled.

"Your guess is as good as mine. Maybe it was wishful thinking" Jeremy said.

"You think after all this time Pops was wishing for her to come back home?"

"Once you get through his tough exterior he's really soft at heart. I think that his love of family might have convinced him that she might come home."

"How'd you get so smart?" Gregory asked smiling.

"Pops invested in me a long time ago." He smiled back.

Together they looked at the old and new photo albums that Thomas Childs had lying around in his office. The picture hidden in the desk was the only one with Sara Childs in it.

"Do you think Louise has seen this picture?" Gregory asked his wise little brother.

"I don't think anything gets past Louise" he said as they both began to laugh. They were laughing so hard that they didn't even see Louise when she and Timothy Callahan entered the office. When the brothers looked up, they were suddenly embarrassed for having found a moment of comic relief.

Gregory motioned for Tim to come closer and said, "Don't get the wrong idea about our laughter Tim. Both of us needed to get some frustration out of our systems," he said as he looked at his younger brother, who nodded in agreement.

Timothy nodded his head in understanding, sat down in one of the empty chairs and placed his briefcase in his lap. Louise asked him if he cared for a sandwich, orange juice or coffee. Tim declined.

She walked back to the door, turned towards the three men and said, "I'll be making the arrangements to bring your father home. You three take your time and discuss whatever needs to be taken care of. However, I'm sure the girls would like to join in on this conversation once you've handled the business."

They all agreed and Gregory stood to close the door behind Louise. When he turned around he faced Jeremy and Timothy, stuck his hands in his pants pockets and said, "Let's take care of this as soon as possible. The faster we can settle all this business, the more time we'll have to spend with Pops...before it's too late."

They only took an hour or so, before they had laid out all of the topics for discussion to have with the rest of the family. Gregory led the way as they all exited the office and entered the family room. Lisa, Theresa and Michael were all sitting around waiting for them. Louise, having made all of the arrangements to bring her lover home, had her hands full in the kitchen with the grandchildren.

Theresa rose and said, "I'll go get Louise."

But her older sister Lisa interjected by holding out one hand and said, "Wait, Theresa. I really don't think Louise needs to be here right now. Yeah, she has the right to know what we're going to go over, but Louise has had just as hard, if not harder a time of this than any of us. I say we do the main planning and fill her in later." Lisa then looked around the room for approval. Theresa quietly sat back down and crossed her arms in defeat, as a spoiled child would.

"With that taken care of" Tim said, "Let's get down to business."

As soon as the meeting was over, Tim stood to leave and asked, "When will your father be coming home?"

Lisa said, "Louise has been arranging that. Knowing her, she'll have him here by tonight."

Tim acknowledged this and began walking toward the door. "In that case, I'll be back a little later. Please inform Thomas that I'll be back, would you?" He seemed to ask the entire room.

At around a quarter to six in the evening, a silent ambulance pulled into the Childs estate driveway. Louise was already waiting outside to assist the drivers with Thomas. She had his room all prepared for him. Though she had no intention of leaving his side for a minute, she had thought about hiring a nurse for him, but Dr. Nichols didn't think it was necessary, as there was nothing a nurse could do to help Thomas.

After Thomas was settled into his room, Louise sat with him, stroking his hand and talking to him as though she were sure he could hear every word that she was saying. Gregory hung just outside of the door eavesdropping and standing there as though he were summoning up enough courage to enter the bedroom of his father. When Louise eventually took notice of him, she motioned for him to join her at the bed side.

As Gregory struggled to move his legs toward their direction, he was afraid. He was afraid of seeing his father laying there motionless. He was afraid that his father would never look upon him again. And he was afraid of the responsibility that he was about to take on. He was afraid that nothing would ever be the same again.

Theresa, though 23, was clingy, needy and awfully immature for her age. She was indeed daddy's little girl, and the baby of the family. Since his return, she constantly sought out physical contact from Gregory as though needing to replace Thomas' affection for her.

Gregory found it flattering, yet, at the same time he was unsure because he didn't know the first thing about nurturing a young lady into the world of womanhood. He was sure that this responsibility should fall into the hands of their sister Lisa. Lisa, however, had her hands full with a husband and four of her own children. Aside from that, it was obvious to Gregory that his sisters didn't have a strong bond as sisters should. He speculated that it probably had something to do with all the attention Pops gave to his youngest child.

Knowing his father, Gregory figured that Pops had already given Lisa her special treatment when she was the baby of the family and his only daughter. He hoped that the entire family would rally together in making this rough situation as smooth as possible. Just because he was the oldest of the Childs children, he wasn't sure that he wanted to be responsible for absolutely everything. And as he stood next to Louise looking down at his father, he knew that he too would need a shoulder to lean on.

All through the night the family kept close watch on Thomas. Each of them sat with him, spoke with him, read to him or just caressed him, in the hopes that the closeness of the family unit would bring him around somehow. And as Gregory sat with his Thomas, while nodding off in the chair beside his bed, he sensed something which caused him to open his eyes.

He had expected someone else to be in the room, but when he looked around, he saw no one. He slapped his face to wake himself up completely, thinking that he must be paranoid. And as he turned back around he looked at his father once more and saw that this time he was looking back at him, with ghostly eyes.

Shocked, his first instinct was to stand up and yell at the top of his lungs so the family would join him at his father's bedside. But when he saw the clock on the wall which read 2:03 am, he decided against it. His little nieces and nephews were sleeping in the purple room, and Louise, with loads of nervous energy, was probably checking in on them. Realizing that he was the only one present to witness the awakening of his father, he began to cry.

He reached quickly for his father's hand, as if he knew that this was his last chance and said, "Pops, I'm here. I'm here."

With all of his remaining strength, Thomas squeezed his son's hand and tried to speak, but could not. Very calmly as though speaking to a child, Gregory said to his father, "Don't try to talk Pops. Just know, that I'm here...the family is all here." He paused while holding back his cracking voice. "Tim was here to see you too, Pops. He's a good man. He loves you, you know. Now, don't you worry about a thing, 'cause I'm gonna take care of everything for you...for the family you hear me? You hear me Pops?" Tears streamed his face as he squeezed Thomas' hand. "What I really wanna say is...is that I love you...and I wanna thank you, for my life."

No sooner than Gregory was able to say all of these things did he hear a ghostly swishing noise that sounded to him like air being squeezed out of a beach ball. Within that instant his father closed his eyes, released his grip from Gregory's hand, and was dead.

Thomas Childs was a big and strong man in life, but in the end he was mere skeleton of himself. Long ago he had been an attractive business man that caught the attention of many women. Gregory and his siblings resembled their father's good looks in life, and now they would only be able to look in the mirror to remember what he looked like alive.

Gregory's tears streaked his cheeks, his neck and shirt collar. He began to shake uncontrollably because he had just witnessed something that would haunt him for the rest of his life. He slowly released his father's hand and stood to his feet. He walked to the door, holding his stomach with one hand and his mouth with the other. As he paused before opening the door, he looked back, fell to his knees and yelled out in the quiet house, "Noooooooooo!" Thomas Childs was dead. Gregory Childs had just inherited more than he would ever be able to handle.

The funeral was grand in the way movie stars are laid to rest. He obviously had lots of friends, acquaintances and business associates that held a great amount of respect for him and chose to show it by attending his burial services. There were rows of Lincoln Townhouse Limousines transporting his immediate family, as well as his step-brothers and sisters, in-laws, cousins, and his good friend and attorney Timothy Callahan.

"It's a beautiful day for a burial, if that's appropriate to think," thought Gregory. And as he rode in the back of one of the limos with his siblings and Louise, they were silent. He was quiet for entirely different reasons than was everyone else. Looking for an escape from all of his newly acquired responsibility, Gregory had let one of his old college buddies talk him into popping pills to calm his nerves.

The first pill didn't affect him immediately so he had taken another one. Soon after, his head began to spin and when he tried to talk he realized that he wasn't making much sense. So he decided to keep his mouth shut until the effects of the drugs wore off. And though he figured he wasn't the kind of guy to get mixed up into drugs, had been searching for a vice that would give him some comfort.

Soon, the procession ended at Rose Hills Cemetery and everyone got out of their cars and followed the casket to the grave site. Lisa held the twins' hands, while Michael carried their two toddlers. Theresa held onto Louise and Gregory and Jeremy walked side by side to the front row of awaiting chairs.

When everyone was seated or standing still on either side, the minister began to speak. As he spoke, Gregory was feeling good or better, yet, feeling high. He felt like doing summer saults all of a sudden. "Damn," he thought, "I thought those pills were going to make me cruise, not crank." But he sat there determined not to give away his secret.

He looked around the crowd trying to distinguish all of the saddened faces dressed mostly in black. He saw many people whom he recognized, who smiled and blinked one eye at him as if saying, "Keep your chin up." He smiled back and continued scanning the crowd in order to keep himself busy.

As his gaze penetrated through a massive mound of flowers dedicated to his father, he saw the profile of a woman that he thought he recognized. So, he shifted in his seat to get a better view, but there was nothing but flowers to see in place of her face. So he shifted again to get back his first view of this her, but she was gone. Occupied as he was, de didn't hear the minister say, "And this concludes our internment for the beloved, Thomas Childs, may he rest in peace forever. Amen."

The family remained seated as the attendees walked past each of them, ceremoniously shaking their hands and kissing them on the cheek out of respect for their loss. Gregory anxiously greeted each guest in the hopes of seeing that familiar profile...that woman of whom he thought he recognized.

As the crowd began to diminish and started to return to their cars, his high was beginning to diminish and he began to believe that he had been hallucinating. When he saw that the others were all standing, looking at him as if asking, "Why are you still sitting there?" he immediately stood up.

He looked once more at the casket containing the remains of his father and followed suit as everyone placed a single red rose upon it. They each said their final good-bye to Thomas Childs and then headed towards their limo which would take them home to greet the anticipated hundreds of guests who would be arriving soon.

After he assisted everyone into the limo he got in as well. But before closing the door he noticed that someone was still standing next to his father's grave. He watched the woman, only able to see her from behind, as she knelt beside the grave and laid something on the casket. He could see that it was not flowers as the other mourners had placed upon it, but something much smaller.

When finally his curiosity got the better of him he decided to get out of the limo and approach this woman at his father's gravesite. When she turned away from the grave, Gregory could see that she was the woman who he had seen earlier...the woman who's vision had been concealed by the flowers during the ceremony. He could see that this woman was his mother, Sara Childs.

Before anyone knew what was happening he was charging at her yelling, "What in the hell..."

As Gregory made a mad dash back to his father's gravesite, Louise was shocked when she recognized Sara standing there. She told the others what was happening and they all looked up to see what was going on. Theresa screamed with nervousness when she saw her mother. Lisa and Jeremy were concerned about what would happen next, but by the time they got out of the limo to stop the confrontation between Gregory and their mother Sara, it was too late.

He had stopped just short of his mother and before she could speak, he slapped her in the face. Theresa leapt from the limo trying to run towards them but Louise grabbed her by the arm and said, "Give him a minute baby. He has a lot of anger for that woman. Just give him a minute."

Theresa hysterically screamed, "But she's my mother too! I need to go to her!" But Louise kept a firm hold on her arm. Michael stayed with the kids as Lisa and Jeremy ran towards the gravesite, trying to get there before things got uglier.

Jeremy got there first just in time before Gregory was able to slap his mother again. He jumped in front of his mother and yelled at his brother, "What in God's name are you doing?" But before he let Gregory answer him, he turned around to face his mother and said to her, "And what in God's name are you doing here?" Both of them stood there unable to answer Jeremy. Sara was holding the side of her face that had been slapped, with tears running down her face, carrying her makeup along with it.

Lisa arrived huffing and puffing. "Sara, are you alright?" Sara nodded yes to her daughter. "What are you doing here? You shouldn't have come, you know that."

Sara said through broken words, "I only came to pay my respects to your father."

"You should have paid your respects to our father when he was alive!" Gregory snapped.

"Alright, that's enough!" Jeremy finally said. Gregory you have been acting weird ever since this morning. And this...this tantrum you're having with Sara is not like you, so get it together Mr. CEO!"

With that bit of news, Sara's eyes lit up. She said to Gregory, "So he did leave it to you. I knew he would. He was always a man of his word."

Gregory said mockingly, "Yeah, like when he said 'til death do us part.'"

In addition to the slap to the face, Sara was hurt by this as well. When she turned away to hide her shame, she saw the youngest of her children running towards them at full speed. Theresa approached them, crying as usual, and ran straight into her mother's arms. Sara held her tightly and comforted her daughter with the love that only a mother can give her child. The others looked on as if sickened by this show of emotion between the two of them. Louise remained standing by the limo, looking alone and vulnerable, with Michael standing next to her watching the commotion.

Gregory strayed from the group in search of the item that Sara had placed in his father's grave. After finding what he was looking for, he returned holding the object in his hand. "Look at what our loving mother left behind in our father's grave. Was this supposed to send him off to heaven feeling better, Sara?" He said this with contempt in his voice, all the while holding out the diamond engagement ring that Sara Childs wore as Thomas' wife. Everyone looked at the ring in Gregory's hand and then they all looked at their mother with questions in their eyes.

Theresa was the first to speak. "Leave her alone! What's wrong with her giving Pops back the ring anyway?"

"Nothing's wrong with it, Resa, it's just not the adult way to go about doing things," Lisa said pulling her little sister out of her mother's arms. "How did you find out, Sara?" she asked while helping Theresa wipe away her tears.

"I read it in the newspaper," Sara said wiping away her own tears.

"You get the Los Angeles Times in Europe?" Jeremy asked Sara.

"No. Actually I've been in the States for quite a while now."

Frustrated, Gregory asked, "And you didn't even bother to let any of us know, did you?" He turned to his siblings. "You see, this woman has never faced up to her responsibilities. She left a child to do most of it for her."

"That's not fair Greg. You don't know what I went through with your father," she said pleading.

"First of all my name is Gregory. Second, Pops gave you everything a woman could ask for. How dare you talk about him now when he's not here to defend himself? But then, self-convenience has always been your way out, hasn't it?"

Sara Childs had finally taken enough from her oldest son. She knew that he had been the most bitter out of all her children, due to her departure from the household years ago. But she was still his mother.

"Listen here, *Gregory*, I don't have to defend myself to my own son, but, if it will make you feel any better by telling you...by telling all of you that I'm sorry I left you, then I'll tell you. And regardless of how many years have gone by, I was once married to your father, had a relationship with your father, had four children with your father and I too am also mourning the death of your father.

Yes, I left you Gregory. No, I couldn't handle the responsibilities of being a wife and mother all those years ago. And oh, yes, I have regretted and will regret until my dying day that I was not mature enough to maintain a mothering relationship with you. But one thing has remained the same...I love you all. I always have and I always will!"

This outburst of Sara's took them all by surprise. They had never heard her speak so outwardly before. It took a great deal of courage for her to come here today. Gregory suspected that she had planned all along to conveniently be seen by them at the gravesite.

They all looked at one another unable to speak. Sara was about to spill more of her feeling out in the open when they were all distracted by a series of slow, methodical hand claps. "Clap...clap...clap...clap. Very well spoken, Sara." Louise was standing behind them now. She had had enough of watching them from a distance, being unable to hear what they were saying.

She walked closer to them and continued to speak. "These children have had a rough day, don't you think? And don't you think you could have waited until all of the cars pulled off before showing up as the lone woman at the grave site. I'm surprised you're not wearing a black veil."

The children were stunned. They couldn't believe what nice, quiet Louise was saying to their mother. They all looked at each other again for confirmation as though they suspected that an old fashioned cemetery-style cat fight was about to take place.

Sara just stood there calmly taking the abuse from her ex-husband's longtime lover, for what seemed like an eternity to her. She knew of Louise, but had never met her before and she had often wondered why Thomas had never married her. So now she looked Louise up and down taking in her appearance and everything else she could about this woman who had just as well become her children's mother.

Louise continued. "Thomas told me you might try something like this." Sara raised an eyebrow. "Yes, Sara, Thomas and I have spoken of you many times over the years. And yes, he spoke to me about the fact that he would die soon. That's what people do when they are in love…talk. But then, you wouldn't know that, or at least could never show it.

Now I'm not out here trying to get in the way of you and your babies; they're all grown and can take care of themselves now, but I do have a problem with you staging your little performance over my man's grave.

See those cars over there?" Louise pointed to the slow moving line of cars exiting the funeral, but had been able to witness everything going on. "A little more timing on your part could have saved this family a lot of embarrassment. Now if you don't mind, these children need to get home to greet their father's friends and be present for the reading of his will."

Having said that, Louise turned and walked away, not giving Sara a chance to reply. She stopped after a few steps and looked at the children. "Invite your mother over to the house if that's what you want, or if you think that's what your father would want. She *is* your mother and I'll support you all in your decisions because I couldn't love you any more if you were my own. The choice is yours." She returned to the limo and Michael was standing there to help her inside.

No one knew exactly what to say, not even Gregory. By now his high was completely gone and he was pissed. So he, his brother, sisters and their mother stood around feeling very awkward.

Sara had received more than she bargained for in coming to the funeral; she knew that now. Not only had she been physically attacked by her own son, she had been beaten down with words by her ex-husbands lover.

Though Gregory wanted very much to tell his mother that he never wanted to see her again, he knew that he couldn't. As much as he tried not to, deep down inside he did love her. But, he was not going to allow her to come back into the picture now and tear the family away from Louise. If he did that, he would be falling right into her hands. So with the ring in his hand he looked at his brother and sisters and said, "You can see her anytime you want, but not at the house...not today."

With that, he put the ring in his pocket, turned his back on them, and returned to the limo. He was sure he'd be seeing his mother again really soon...they all would. "Maybe I should score some more pills, or something stronger," he thought, as he strolled back to the limo.

(4) - Jax - Make That a Double

It was three o'clock in when I crept in the house on a Thursday morning. Well, I wouldn't exactly call it creeping since I come and go as I please, but out of respect for my mother, I didn't want to wake her up.

I was halfway up the stairs when I heard my mother say, "Jax, is that you?"

Now why did my mother always ask me the same thing each and every time I walked into the house when she knew it was me? I was the only one who came in from the side door, which is triple-bolted by the way, and I was the only one to use the rear staircase which is hidden in a closet in the kitchen. Only Harry would think of putting a hidden staircase in the kitchen for added security. I'm grateful, 'cause you can never be too careful. "Yes mom, It's me. What are you doing up this early?"

"I was waiting for you," she said.

"Why are you waiting up for me?"

My mom took an early retirement from teaching at St. Mary's Academy High School, thanks to all of her husbands. She has entirely too much time on her hands, for my nerves. I am the spitting image of her in every way; just add twenty-four years and subtract three husbands. Everything I am is her gene pool's fault.

"Well, I just want to talk to you."

I was curious to hear what this is all about. "What's up?"

"Harry called."

"He did? What did he want?" I asked anxiously. My step-father usually doesn't call on her phone, he calls on mine.

And I just know she wasn't in my room snooping around again for God knows what.

"He wanted you to call him when you got in last night. But I guess it's a little late for that, isn't it?"

Oh hell. Why of all nights, or mornings, is she giving me attitude about coming home at this time. I swear that woman needs a man in her life. I just hope she doesn't marry him before I move out of here. "What did he say Mom?" I asked as I dragged myself up the last remaining stairs. I walked down the hallway to her bedroom where I could see her peeking through the door.

"You're supposed to go over to the business today. Didn't he tell you?" she asked, ready to get an attitude with him if this was my first time hearing about it. She would always find any and every excuse to get in an argument with that man. I think she's a little jealous of our relationship, but what does she expect me to do, just stop being the man's daughter just because she divorced him? Shit she divorced him, I didn't.

"Yeah, he told me," I lied. Damn! I was forgetting everything lately since I started spending every free minute with Vincent.

I haven't let my mom meet him yet because she'll probably try and get with him her damn self. Plus she'd probably freak out a little because of his age. His salt and pepper hair, though only at the temples, might make her wonder about it.

I was tired of talking to her and all I wanted to do was go and soak in a long hot bath tub. I guess I wasn't going to get any more sleep this morning, especially if I had to be at the office by 7:00. "Mom, I'm really tired. I'm going to my room, is there anything else that you wanted?" I asked her, praying that she would answer, no.

"No child," is all she said before slamming her door.

"She must be going through the change," I mumbled, as I walked down the hallway to my own room. I undressed, ran

myself a bath with Neutrogena Bath Salts, and got in. It stung
a little when I settled down into the hot water.

Vincent and I had another wild time last night and my
"poony" was really feeling it now. It was still throbbing as
though it had a heart of its own. I wonder why he thinks he
needs to go at it like that, with me. Could it be that he goes at
it like that with every woman he sleeps with? Shit, I could
drive myself crazy trying to figure out what he does with
other women.

As I started to relax in the tub, I began to let myself drift
off to another place...another time. I started to fantasize
about meeting a handsome stranger who'd sweep me off my
feet and carry me off into the sunset. I imagined him to be
about 6'5, weighing about 220 pounds, with delicious caramel
skin and intoxicating hazel eyes. He'd be younger that
Vincent, about 31, have big feet and bow legs. You know
what they say about big feet and bow legs? Anyway, we
would meet in a small restaurant or a coffee house:

*I would be sitting alone sipping on a cappuccino and eating a piece
of cheese cake with my fingers. He would walk in through the
door...standing there looking around the room as if he were looking for
someone, and then he would see me. I would see him at the exact same
time that I was sucking cake off my finger. Our eyes meet, and we both
freeze. When the host walks up to him to escort him to a seat, the
stranger whispers something in his ear and makes a gesture in my
direction. The host looks up at me and smiles then whispers something
back in the stranger's ear, probably his approval of me. Together they
walk towards me, looking straight though me the entire time, but they
stop just short of my table. The host pulls out the chair for the stranger
and leaves him alone, sitting at the table across from mine, facing my
direction. And as our eyes lock on to one another, I am suddenly shy and
turn away. All this time I hadn't even noticed the cream which was
sticking to the side of my mouth. So I go on as though nothing were
unusual about this sudden attraction to this handsome stranger. And I
continue to eat my cheese cake with my fingers and sip on my cappuccino
and I can feel the stranger looking at me, so I return his stares. He*

makes a gesture with his hand to the side of his mouth, telling me that I was wearing cake on my lips. With that, I flick my finger from the side of my mouth and then put my finger in my mouth, sucking the cream from my finger. I can see that the stranger is watching me more intensely now, and so I continue to suck as I continue to stare at him. Finally, the stranger can take no more, and he rises from his chair and kicks it aside. A young waitress is passing by us with a cart of deserts and he takes the cart from her and pushes it in my direction. As he reaches my table, my breath is taken away as he lifts me from my chair and holds me in the air with firm hands and a tight grip. He asks me my name and I say with breathless words, "Miss Desire, and yours?" and he responds, "Mr. Destiny." After that he lays me down on the tray of creamy desserts and rips off my clothes. And all gazes are upon us as he begins to rub creamy pies all over my body. I moan in response to his touch and I begin to help him dress me in layers upon layers of whipped creams. He then lowers himself over me and begins to lick the sweetness off of my body. His tongue is so warm and soft that I start to shiver. He takes off my shoes and dips my feet in chocolate syrup. And he is ferocious as he is careful, as he sucks up this special treat from my feet. I wiggle and squirm as to escape the torment of this pleasure that he is giving me, but he is relentless as he works his way up to my thighs. After spreading whipped cream on them, as one would butter to bread, I part them allowing him access to every part of my flesh. He is sure to keep a firm grip on me as he works his way up on the inside of my thighs, but I am no match for this stranger, and so I submit to him. When he is done there, he moves even higher to my belly button of which a warm marshmallow sauce has been awaiting his arrival. He laps at it as though it were water quenching his terrible thirst. And when he looks at me with desire in his eyes, I take his mouth into mine and suck at his lips which are full of this rich delicacy. It's as if I were sucking the nectar of the gods. I wanted him. I wanted him then and there! Our tongues clashed and melted as one, until the need to breathe brought us apart. Then he nibbled my neck in places that I thought had no feeling. And as he lay on top of me, I felt his desire searching for a way into the warmth that would surely accommodate him well. At the very moment of entry I heard a familiar voice. I didn't want to acknowledge it because it was very faint at first, but then it became clearer and clearer. It sounded like...

"Jax! Jax you better get out of there girl, you're gonna be late!"

Damn! It was my mother! Why can't I ever get through one fantasy in this house? "What!?" I yelled at her, suddenly realizing that I had fallen asleep in the bathtub, thankfully without drowning myself. I jumped out of the water and beheld my wrinkly, pruned body. Mom had managed to save my life...again.

"Child, what are you doing in that room? You still in the tub, 'cause I never heard the water run out and you know that water makes a lot of noise running out," she said talking through my bathroom door.

I just ignored her because she was really beginning to get on my nerves. I let the water out of the tub, stood up and began to dry off. When I got to my thighs, I started cracking up to myself. I turned on the radio and the DJ said that it was a quarter to six. Oh shit, I'm going to be late if I run into L.A.'s famous early morning traffic.

I pulled my hair into a ponytail, rubbed myself down with moisturizer and made a mad dash to my closet, deciding on my pale grey skirt, conservative silk tank top and black blazer. The last thing I want to do is to have some fool flirt with me at the office for looking like I'm going to the club.

I sure hope Harry wasn't expecting me to make a full day of this today. I'm still on my last school break and I intend enjoy every minute of it before I start my permanent position with Research Limited. My step-dad is cool but I've got a social life to maintain. Ever since Mom divorced him he hasn't had one at all.

So now here I am running late on my first training day with him, all because I've been up all night long doing the wild thang with Vincent, and fantasizing for hours about some stranger with a kinky thing for desserts. I'm trippin'!

I arrived at the office ten minutes late, with bags under my eyes, a throbbing poony and an attitude because I didn't get a chance to finish my fantasy about pie boy. I didn't know that much about Research Limited, except that it had something to do with research, which is obvious. I was bored already. This day was getting off to a lousy start.

"Hey honey." Harry was waving to me from across the lobby.

I walked over to greet him with a hug and a kiss on the cheek. "Hey dad. Sorry I'm late, but I had a rough night," I said grinning.

"Well that's OK honey, as long as your mother gave you the message. How is she these days?" he asked as usual.

"She's OK. Nosy as ever," I said with a slight smile, not willing to get into my mother's business with him. When it comes to men, Mom and I have an understanding about that kind of thing. Seeing that I wasn't going to tell him that she really was miserable without him and he needed to rush home and sweep her off into the bedroom, he changed the subject.

"I won't keep you all day, but you need to know what's going on around here as my new office manager," he said as he led me down a long corridor.

I followed alongside him taking in all of the faces staring at me as people sat behind desks lined on either side of the corridor. I sure hoped that they didn't think I was his woman or something. To make sure I loudly say, "Dad, what are they doing?" I pointed to the two rows of employees on either side.

"They're doing their jobs, I hope," he said with a smile as he eyed everyone closely. All eyes returned back to their computers. "The ones on computers over there," he pointed to the employees seated on the left, "are hooked up to every kind of information networks you can think of. And most of the ones over there," he pointed to the right, "are my field reps. They sometimes go out and dig up whatever kind of information they need. It depends on which contract they're assigned to and that's where you'll come in."

We finally reached his office at the end of the long corridor, entered and sat down on the sofa. It reminded me of a newspaper editor's office because it had glass walls, so he could keep a close watch on everyone in the office. I'd never been to this building before. His business had recently relocated and this was my first visit. I could see that he was doing very well for himself. "Dad, this is great."

"Thank you Jax. We're all very proud of the work we do here." He rose, walked over to his desk and pressed his intercom. "Pearl, hold all my calls." He sat on the end of his desk and faced me.

"I started this company some 22 years ago after working in the aerospace industry for many years. My job was to contact government agencies in order to verify certain specs. I was promoted rapidly and eventually made manager over my department. As manager, I was able to oversee what everyone else did and to improve upon how they did it. Soon after that, I had a brainstorm. Why work for someone else when I can work for myself? So, here I am today, owner of Research Limited.

I sat there facing him with my briefcase sitting on my lap and a pad and pen in my hand waiting to write down something useful. Nothing he said was useful. I had heard this story too many times to count. "How do your acquire contracts?"

"I've been using old contacts for years. I made several friends while working in the aerospace industry and I've been able to expand on that, making new contacts with government and independent companies."

"As office manager, what will be my job, making sure office supplies are ordered and stocked?" I asked teasingly.

"Girl," he said, sounding just like my mother, "you're gonna learn this business upside down. I want you to become friends with everyone in this building and to become familiar with every contract we have." He rose from his desk and gestured for me to follow him. We walked into the corridor again and headed for a woman sitting at one of the desks.

"Joanne, this is my daughter, Jax. She's going to sit with you for a while and I want you to share what it is you do all day around here."

Joanne and I shook hands. "It's very nice to meet you Jax. We've been hearing a lot about you lately."

I looked at Harry and grinned. "I hope he hasn't been boring you with little girl stories about me."

"No Jax. Actually he's speaks very highly of you like any proud father would. By the way, congratulations on your college graduation," she said with a smile.

"Well thank you very much."

Harry said, "Well, now that you two have become acquainted, I'll leave you to get to work. Jax, I'll be out of the office for a while so this is the perfect time for you to take charge and get to know everybody." He turned and walked away.

So here I am the new girl on the block and daddy's little girl. He never had any kids of his own so I'm it. How will these people respond to me I wondered.

Joanne was a sweet lady and I could tell that she was in her early 60's. She was short and a little plump, with her hair in a bun-looking thing sitting on top of her head. She was wearing an outdated tweed skirt suit, with coffee colored stockings, a beige ruffled blouse with black patent leather shoes. She definitely was not making a fashion statement and I wouldn't have to worry about her as the competition if a cutie pie ever visited the office.

I sat with her at her desk allowing her to do her work without asking too many questions. She entered data on her computer and made notations on the note pad which read TCI, at the top. A file on her desk also had the same company initials on it. I noticed that there were several letters and business forms that she was referencing.

She explained, "Whenever we get a contract from someone, we make up a folder like this." She held up the file. "These forms tell us what kinds of research they would like for us to do for them. Sometimes they write and sometimes they call to request what they want. As the requests get more complicated the forms and letters all get added to their file.

This company is huge and we had done business with them for years but all of a sudden, new research requests have been coming in. This letter on top is their latest request for us. They want us to do some research on an investment group which supports timeshare properties in the Caribbean."

"Does that mean someone will be going to the Caribbean?" I asked sounding like a fool, thinking about island-hopping over to visit Frances, in Bermuda.

"No," she answered patiently. "That means that we dig up everything we can on this investment group, including everything they've been involved in for the past five, ten or twenty years."

She continued her endless task on her computer and sometimes stopped to make notes on her note pad. I got bored and picked up the file she had shown me earlier. It made for boring reading. Some CEO died and his preppy son inherited his position. The new CEO was making inquiries into the personal life of some of his employees, especially someone named Stanley Bunch.

Apparently Stanley sold his stock in the company but was rumored as trying to buy back stock illegally after the original CEO died, so the newest CEO, Gregory Childs, wasn't taking any chances with any trouble-makers. He also wanted details on certain investment groups, timeshare properties and the going rates for several properties around the country.

Though it was as boring as hell, I knew that I couldn't let on to anyone that I was not having a good time. Who the hell did I think I was anyway? No one is supposed to have a good time at work, are they? Well, I didn't know for sure, because all of my jobs have been minor ones to help me pay for my school expenses. I always knew that I would have a job waiting here for me when I graduated, so I never bothered to look for another job.

As time went on, I was beginning to get the hang of what was going around this place. I took the initiative and began wondering around the corridor's introducing myself to different employees. Some of them looked at me like I was crazy but most of them seemed to be nice people.

I could sense a few of the women looking me up and down as though I were dressed inappropriately or something. But most of the men couldn't take their eyes off of my chest, even though I had purposely worn a high cut blouse to completely cover my boobs.

I was somewhat timid in my approach because I didn't want to come on as a tyrant, right away. There had never been an office manager in this company before. I was the first. They had always worked directly through Harry but now they would start working through me. I knew that the transition would take some getting used to for everyone.

When I felt my stomach rumble I looked at the clock on the wall and saw that it was already passed noon. "Time sure fly's when you're having fun," I said to myself while walking into Harry's office to use the phone.

I called Sabastian at work. "What's up girl?"

"Jax, is that you?" she asked with her most impressive business voice.

"Yes dear, so drop the accent," I said joking.

"Where are you? I called you at home and at Vincent's but you didn't pick up at either place."

"Did Vincent pick up?"

"Nope."

"Hmm, he's probably in bed with some slut right now," I said to myself. "Anyway, I'm at Harry's office," I said to her.

"Are you starting today?" she asked confused.

"No. I'm here getting myself familiar with what I'm going to be doing when I do start. He doesn't want me coming in here as an untrained stranger."

"Oh, OK. Well, are we still on for later?" she asked.

"Of course, I'm looking forward to it, especially since Vincent isn't picking up his damn telephone when my friends call."

"What's the big deal with that? He never picks up the phone when I call."

"Yeah well, at least now he lets me give out his phone number to my good friends and he lets me answer it when I hear that it's one of you guys. The least he can do is pick up the phone when he hears that it's you or someone else calling for me," I said letting myself get worked up over a hopeless cause.

"Girl, you know that man is not going to change his spots, so why do you insist on acting like he is doing something that you don't know about?"

"I don't know girl, pride maybe? Anyway, so be it. One day Vincent Cruthers will realize that I'm the only woman he needs," I triumphantly said.

"Yeah right," Sabastian said, bursting my bubble. "So where do you want to meet after work?"

"Same place as usual, I guess."

"Alright, I'll meet you at our lookout spot at 5:30. I hope some men are going to be in there tonight, since tomorrow is a holiday."

I agreed and hung up the phone with her. I was still a little upset thinking about Vincent, so I decided that I was going to make him jealous someday if it was the last thing I did. I had once thought about sleeping with his friend Tony, but I figured that wouldn't make him jealous it would just make him hate me. So I'd just have to think of something else.

First, I'd start seeing other men and if I become interested in one of them, I'm sure he'd take notice that. Part two of my plan was still a work in progress. So with that pleasant thought, I decided not to go all the way home and then drive back this way to meet Sabastian. Instead I would stay here and eat lunch in the buildings cafeteria. If I'm lucky, I'll be able to sit with some of the employees and try to make some friends. If that fails, I'll simply fire them all!

I was at our favorite booth waiting for Sabastian when she switched her tiny ass into the bar. She was right, there were a good number of attractive looking men coming into Newton's this evening. I guess everybody was thinking the same thing about getting the party started a little early this weekend.

She dramatically waved at me from across the room, probably to get some attention, and sexily walked over to me. That girl is a trip. She'd use every trick in the hand-female book to get a man. But then again so would I. No wonder we're such good friends.

"Hi honey," she said as she approached the booth and gave me a mock kiss on both cheeks.

"Hey honey."

"You been here long?" she asked sitting down.

"I've been here for about an hour," I said sipping on my glass of red wine. "I had to get out of that place. It's going to take a lot of getting used to; going to work instead of school every day. I guess I'm spoiled or something, living with Mom and having Harry pay for almost everything for me my entire life."

"Well, at least we had the good sense to stick it out and finish college, not like a lot of people. You've had your free ride, so now you're going to have to pay back into the system."

"Yeah well, had I started right out of high school like you and not waited, I might not be feeling so old right now."

"Old? You're only 25. What's so old about that? Shit I'm 28. If anybody's old it's me." She laughed out loud, just enough to get the attention of two men in business suits taking seats across the booth from us. "Check it out, girl," she whispered.

I turned my head around in time to see the two men taking seats across from ours. One of the men was really cute, but the other one looked like death. Sabastian must not have seen *him*. I wonder why it is that nice looking men let ugly men hang around with them. Is it so that they can pick up the leftover's the cute one's not trying to get with?

They saw us looking at them and nodded their heads hello. We did the same and immediately turned away from them. One thing is certain about Sabastian and I, if both of the men don't look good, then we don't bother, because neither one of us is going to chance being picked up by the ugly one.

"There you go Sabastian," I said pointing to the ugly one.

"I don't think so," she said smiling. "I'd rather be celibate."

"You are celibate."

"Yeah, and now you know why."

We both laughed so hard and so loud that everyone in the club looked up at us. The other women rolled their eyes as if thinking we were purposely trying to get the attention of every man in the place. But Sabastian and I ignored the stares and continued to have a good time. We were always making jokes about her being celibate, which isn't very far from the truth. The truth of the matter is she gets some...sometimes.

Sabastian ordered a drink from the waitress and I ordered another and as we talked about the events of the day the men kept rolling into Newton's. "Why aren't you at Vincent's?" she asked me.

Because I'm with you, silly woman," I said teasing her.

"Girl, you know what I mean. Now why didn't you go over to his place tonight like you do every other night?"

"Because he expects me to," I replied.

"Oh, I see, playing hard to get are we?"

"No. More like hard to find." I really wasn't in the mood to discuss my relationship with Vincent, so I changed the subject. I knew if I gave her a dare, where a man was concerned, she'd more than likely take me up on it. So I dared her to walk past a group of men sitting on the far side of Newton's and innocently drop a handkerchief.

I know it sounds a little childish, but you don't know Sabastian. She is such an unusual person that I think she finds these challenges as being spiritual or something. I can pretty much ask her to do anything, but unless it's in the form of a challenge she usually won't do it. When I question her rationale for doing some of the things I ask her to do, she simply says, "That question has fire...I'll do it."

Sabastian gulped down the rest of my wine, winked at me and said, "I'll be over there choosing the man I'm gonna marry someday." With that, she scooted out of the booth and walked towards a group of men with a paper napkin in her hand. I watched her switch her skinny self towards them.

The outfit she wore was cute, but she would say that she was "spiritually attired." That simply meant that everything she was wearing was all matching. She had on a print dress which dropped to her ankles and had loose strings all over it. It was fitted in the waist but hung loosely everywhere else. Her pumps, handbag and earrings were made of the same fabric, probably taken from a scarf that came with the outfit. I'd say that she was definitely "spiritually attired" tonight.

As she made her way over to the men, she stopped. She turned around and looked at me, just as she dropped her make-shift handkerchief, then she started eye balling each and every man within her view, but no one offered to pick it up for her. I started to feel a little uncomfortable for her after about a minute or so, until this short scrawny little fellow leaned over to pick it up for her.

He barely had to bend his knees in order to get it and hand it to her. I wanted to laugh out loud, but I held it in as to not break her concentration. I thought she would run back to me laughing about the whole situation but then I saw that she was actually enjoying her conversation with this little bitty man.

She stood about one foot over him and I thought that she was just passing away the time with him until someone else tried to talk to her. That never happened. In fact, they found an empty table and sat down together, ordering drinks and everything. So I sat there observing the whole thing by myself.

The waitress came by and said that the men sitting in the next booth would like to buy me a drink. I looked up at them and saw that they were both watching me very closely. I told the waitress no thank you. I knew better than to accept a drink from two men especially when one of them was butt-ugly. My luck, it would be the ugly one actually offering to buy me the drink. And the next thing you know he would plop his ugly ass in my booth and try to pick me up. That was the last thing I needed right now. No, if I'm going to be picked up by anyone it's going to be someone who I can at least take out in the daylight.

I bought my own drink and watched Sabastian and her tiny man from across the room. I tried to remember the wonderful fantasy that I was having this morning in my bathtub, but all I could remember was my mother yelling to me at the top of her lungs.

As time lingered on, I noticed a variety of men and women coming into Newton's. Some of them came as couples, but most of them were alone. I found it interesting that the majority of women coming in were dressed in skimpy dresses and skin tight pants. But then again, it was the Thursday before Independence Day. Hell, it might as well be Friday.

Soon the band came in and started warming up. I didn't mind that Sabastian hadn't come back because this band was pretty hot. They were called Justus, and consisted of five good looking men.

The lead singer and I had made eye contact on several occasions, but nothing more. Maybe tonight he would ask for my phone number, although I don't usually give out my phone number casually. I guess in that respect I'm like Sabastian; it has to be sort of cosmic or at least there has to be several sparks. No, I'd just watch them from afar and enjoy their funky music like I have on many nights.

Soon the band was in full swing. Newton's was really jumping and people were mingling and dancing all over the place. I noticed that Sabastian and the little man were busy on the dance floor quite a bit. Shortly after the first set, the lead singer introduced a guest singer. When she walked on to the stage, the men howled and hooted at her.

She was a big woman, though an attractive one, with long black hair, a huge ass and big thighs. You could easily see her thighs rubbing together in the skin tight mini-skirt that she wore. I wondered how she even got her big ass in that skirt. "She probably lied on the floor and wiggled her ass in it like the rest of us do," I thought.

When she started to sing "International Lover" by Prince, I immediately began to think of my overseas friend Frances, whose letter I hadn't even read lately. Sorry Frances. The tranquil water of the Caribbean had been replaced by the Vincent's tranquil water bed.

The dance floor began to fill up with couples holding each other close while slow dancing. The ugly man sitting in the booth next to mine asked me if I wanted to dance and I immediately said, "No."

This woman was bad. I had never heard anyone else sing one of Prince's songs, or whatever his name is these days, as infectiously as she did. When she finished she introduced herself to the audience. She said her name was Unique. I thought to myself, "That's unique."

As she continued to talk to the audience, I thought I recognized her voice. It was somewhat husky with a kind of twang to it. I just knew I had heard that voice before, and so

I assumed that it had been in another night club somewhere. Before long I was convinced that I had heard her voice on Vincent's answering machine saying, "Pick up the phone if you're home Vincent." That was it! That was where I had heard her fat ass voice before, on my man's answering machine! But he wasn't my man, was he?

"Jack...Jax...Jacqueline...Hello, is anyone there?"

I was staring that fat bitch down. "Hey Sabastian, are you and the little man having fun?" I asked, embarrassed that I had been busted staring down a woman.

"His name is Bart, short for Bartholomew," she said in the defensive.

"Short is right," I said teasing her. "No, I'm just kidding. Are you having fun?"

"Yes girl," she said enthusiastically. "I think I've met my soul mate."

"Oh yeah," I said half interested.

"...because his zodiac is...Jax?"

"What?"

"What are you looking at?" she said, irritated because I hadn't been really listening to her.

"I'm looking at Unique."

"Why?"

"Because I'm almost positive she's fucking Vincent."

"How do you know that?"

"Because I recognize hearing her voice over his answering machine," I said in disgust.

"Now how can you be sure that it's her voice? You've heard several voices on his answering machine haven't you?" she asked trying to reassure me.

"Yeah, but I know that voice," I said determined.

"Well, what if it is her? What are you going to do about it?"

"What am I going to do about it?" I thought. What *am* I going to do about it? What can I do about it? Absolutely nothing! I'm not his woman I'm just one of many. And the reality of that hit home like it has no other time since I've known him. The fact of the matter was that I couldn't do a damn thing about it!

Sabastian sat there staring back and forth between me and Unique, not knowing exactly what to say. I could tell that she wanted to discuss the new love of her life, Bart, but I couldn't tear my stare away from that fat lady on the stage.

What did she and I have in common anyway, besides Vincent? She's fat and I'm thin. She's tall and I'm short. She's old and I'm young. I couldn't figure out any resembling factors besides the fact that she has a poony, and so do I. Fucking men! What they all wouldn't do for something to poke on?

"Jax, are you alright?" Sabastian was asking me, tearing me away from my thoughts.

"Yeah, I'm alright girl." I was lying. "So, tell me about Bart."

"Well, he's a 36 year old accountant who's never been married, doesn't have any kids and owns a home in Rancho Cucamonga. I'm in love," she said elated.

"It doesn't bother you that he can't kiss you unless he stands on a chair?" I asked smiling.

"Height is irrelevant in the bedroom, Jax," she responded slightly annoyed.

I guess she *was* in love. "I'm sorry honey. Where is he? Why is he still sitting over there all alone?" I asked her.

"I'll talk to him tomorrow," she said. "We both thought it rude to leave you by yourself."

"Well, well, well, I guess my little dare made your evening, didn't it?"

"Yes it did," she said. "Jacqueline, will you be my Maid of Honor?" she said with a sinister smile.

"Girl, you're trippin'. You think this is the man you're going to marry?"

"If the stars say so," she said.

Just then, Unique began to sing another song, "Truly" by Lionel Richie. What was it with these slow songs and this woman? People started piling up on the dance floor again and that ugly guy asked me to dance again. Again, I said, "No." Why don't you dance with him so you can get a closer look at Unique?" Sabastian asked.

"I'm sure I'll be seeing her close up soon enough," I told my friend.

So for the duration of the evening, Sabastian and I listened to Justus play and Unique sing. I found myself analyzing everything about her out of curiosity. I watched the way she wiggled her hips, and the way she pouted her lips. I watched the way she touched herself when she sang sexy lines from a song, and the way she closed her eyes during each climactic ending. In turn, I labeled her a slut. But, Unique was a beautiful woman, and even I couldn't take that away from her, unless I were to hit her in the face with a baseball bat.

Sooner than later the evening ended, with me not engaging in one single solitary dance. Something or someone had taken me out of the mood. So instead I spent my time at Newton's watching other people dance and flirt.

By the time I realized it, I had consumed almost four glasses of wine and I didn't even have a buzz. Maybe I should start drinking something stronger...nah, that's the last thing I need. Being a drunk didn't fit very well with my agenda.

Anyway, Sabastian and I were headed out of the club about to go to our separate cars. She had said good night to Bart a few hours earlier and so we had to watch out for each other while walking out into the night.

Just then I heard someone say, "Can I escort you ladies to your car?" When I looked up I saw that it was the lead singer from the band. He sure was looking good standing there with traces of sweat still trickling down from his temples.

Sabastian was saying, "No," before I could poke her in the side with my elbow. I guess she didn't know that I had secretly been admiring this man from afar, for a while now.

He ignored Sabastian's premature answer and looked at me.

"My name is Jerome."

"Hello Jerome, my name is Jax and this is Sabastian," I said her name with a sarcastic tone as to tell him to excuse her rudeness.

He continued to look at me. "I've seen you in here before Jax, but this is the first time you never danced. I hope that you enjoyed yourself tonight." He was flashing his pearly whites now, looking like a wolf out on the prowl.

I decided to bait him. "The music was superb as usual Jerome, but tonight I was in the mood to do the looking, not to be looked at." Sabastian looked at me like I was crazy. I could tell that she was not in the mood to stick around and watch me carry on with this guy.

I said to Jerome, "I was about to walk my friend to her car. You're welcome to walk along, if you like."

"I'd like that as long as you let me walk you to yours afterwards."

I agreed, and the three of us walked over to Sabastian's blue Ford Taurus. After she and I hugged, she got in and whispered to me, "Are you going to be alright Jax?"

I tapped my purse jokingly as if I had a weapon inside it and whispered back to her with a smile, "Oh, we'll be just fine honey." Sabastian said that she would talk to me tomorrow, started her car and was gone.

Jerome and I stood there in the parking lot checking each other out as people walked to their cars in every direction. "Where are you parked?" he asked.

I pointed to my little bucket and said, "See that silver Volkswagen Fox over there?"

"Yeah," he answered.

"Well, it used to be black," I said with a chuckle.

He laughed at my joke, took hold of my arm and started walking me in its direction. But I wasn't ready to leave him just then because I had a plan.

I was hoping that he and I could get to know each other better so that my name would become common in his conversations with his band, and eventually maybe Unique would hear it. Maybe then she would somehow hear my name again from Vincent and then I could confirm my suspicions that the two of them are fucking. At the same time, Vincent could learn that I was seeing someone else too. My plan was perfect, but I didn't have the nerve to suggest that he and I get to know each other better in order to put my plan in motion. Wimp.

"When will I see you again?" he asked.

"Perfect," I thought. Now I can put the motion to the lotion. "When would you like to see me again?" I said as demur as I know how.

"How about in fifteen minutes," he said flashing those damn teeth again.

Does he think that I'm that damn easy. Fifteen minutes, what in the hell was that supposed to mean, anyway. "What's happening fifteen minutes from now?" I asked cautiously, all the while clutching my purse ready to throw down on his ass if necessary.

"I need to go help the rest of the band secure the equipment for the night," he said. "It should only take about fifteen minutes and then I'd like to take you out for a cup of coffee."

"And what shall I do in the meantime?" hoping all along that he would invite me back inside so I could get a closer look at that Unique heffa.

"Please come back inside with me and we can take it from there."

Needless to say, this opportunity was perfect. My curiosity with that woman had held most of my attention for the entire night. I needed to know if it was just my paranoia that made me think it was her voice on Vincent's answering machine, or if it was my insecurity in the relationship that I had with him.

"Sure. You can follow me in your car to this all night coffee house I know of." There. That was a safe, mature response to his implying question, I thought.

"Cool," he said somewhat disappointed, I think.

Together we walked back into the club, which was nearly empty by that time. Chairs were being placed on top of tables and the lights were turned up sky bright. I casually looked around for Unique, but I didn't see her anywhere. I hoped that she hadn't left yet. If she had, I would wait for another time to get to know Jerome. Fortunately for me I saw her coming out of the ladies room, tugging on that ever rising mini-skirt of hers.

I was standing next to Jerome as he was unplugging some cords. I wanted to make sure that she'd see me, and she did. She immediately turned her nose up at me as though I was trespassing on her turf, or something. I had the inclination to stab her with some tweezers, but I needed the bitch alive.

"Jerome? Why don't you introduce me to the band members, if you don't mind," I said standing closer to him as Unique approached the stage.

"I'd love to introduce you," he said. One by one he introduced me to the other members of Justus. I told each of them how much I enjoyed their music and how I was looking forward to hearing them again. They were all very pleasant but were obviously eager to wrap up for the night. I acknowledged this and told them not to let me tie them up. When Unique started collecting her jacket and purse from behind the keyboards, I wondered why Jerome didn't introduce me.

"Maybe, they have a thing going on," I thought to myself. The hell with them if they did, I wanted to meet her. "Jerome? Tonight is the first time I've seen her," I said pointing to Unique. "Is she a new member of your group?"

"No," he said. "She's on again off again. She popped in tonight at the last minute wanting to sit in on this gig, so we let her."

He seemed to speak of her with a disinterest, but he still made no attempt to introduce me to her. Finally I decided to take matters into my own hands. "Unique, is it?" I said walking in her direction holding out my hand to her. "You have a very lovely voice. It was a pleasure listening to you tonight," I said with my most sincere voice.

She looked up somewhat surprised, but took my hand and shook it as she spoke. "Thank you very much. Are you a friend of Jerome's?" she asked with a curious look.

"As of tonight, yes," I said ready to grab my tweezers out of my purse. "My name is Jacqueline. Jacqueline Winters, but my friends call me Jax. It's very nice to meet you." As soon as I said my name twice, I thought I saw a hint of recognition in her eyes, but she didn't let on if she did recognize it.

"Nice meeting you too," she said vaguely. With that, she picked up her belongings and walked out of the club without saying anything more to me, or anything at all to the guys in the band.

Jerome had been watching our exchange and was looking a little worried, but he said nothing.
"What's with her?" I asked him when I saw him looking at me.

"She's a little fickle, especially when there's a beautiful woman around," he said.

"Why? Are the two of you involved?" I asked bluntly.

"Not anymore," he answered honestly. "As a matter of fact, she's not involved with any of us anymore," he said as he pointed to each member of the band.

Ugh, that's nasty. "You mean all of you have had a relationship with her?"

"I'd call it more of a re-*lay*-tionship." He had this triumphant look on his face.

Well, that did it for me. I accomplished my mission by throwing my name out at her, and now I wanted to get the hell away from this pervert. But I had to think of something fast, so being one a little on the dramatic side, I faked menstrual cramps. I told Jerome that my period had just started and that I had to get home in a hurry. Men. He bought it hook, line and sinker. I guess he figured that I couldn't give him any tonight, since I was bleeding and all. I should have known better than to try and talk to a musician anyway.

He walked me to my car without trying anything, thank God, and I got home before I knew it. I walked up the back staircase and headed down the hallway to my room. I knew my mother wouldn't be bothering me tonight because I could hear her tiny little snores coming from underneath her door. I undressed and climbed into my bed, exhausted.

My answering machine was blinking off and on, but I didn't make a move to check it. It's probably Vincent, wondering where I was tonight. I was pretty pleased with all of the things I had accomplished today; my first training day at work, meeting Jerome to get to Unique and making Vincent wonder where I was tonight. No wonder I was so tired. I wasn't about to let that man get to me without getting to his ass first.

After I said my prayers, I started to let my mind drift off into space. But tonight, Vincent was not going to be the last thought I had before falling asleep. No, it was time I put him on a shelf. Tonight, I had a date with a tall and handsome stranger who had a kinky *"thing"* for desserts.

(5) – Vincent – We Make Our Own Beds

"…Ninety eight…ninety nine…one hundred." Vincent finished counting having completed his daily pushups, stomach crunches and weight lifting. He was pumped up and ready to start his day.

He grabbed the towel from off the floor and began to wipe the sweat from his forehead. As he patted himself down, he smelled a woman's fragrance coming from the towel. He smiled to himself wondering whose it could be. It was impossible for him to try and guess exactly which one of his many lady friends the scent belonged to, so he just savored the thought.

Good thing for him that Jax decided not to come around last night like she usually does. That girl was getting too attached to him anyway. But he couldn't help but wonder where she was and who she was with, though he'd never admit it out loud. Shit, she was his and his alone, or so he would like to think. It wasn't a good idea for her to be out there fooling around with other guys who would eventually hurt her. "She should just stick with what we have," he said to himself. Deep down, he couldn't stand the thought of her being with someone else, but that would be calling the kettle black, wouldn't it?

Without a further thought Vincent jumped into the shower and began bathing with his Fahrenheit soap-on-a-rope that a *friend* gave to him last Christmas. After bathing, he stepped in front of the bathroom mirror and looked at his face. He didn't have any stubble but he decided to shave anyway.

He pulled out his shaving kit from the medicine cabinet and looked long and hard at the leather casing. It was one of the many gifts that he had received from women, though he couldn't remember which one had given this one to him. He had been trying to remember for a long time now, but the memory of who had given this gift to him had long since faded from his memory.

He made himself return his concentration to shaving and took the gold handled brush out of the kit and lathered it with shaving cream, brushing it on and around his smooth face. And oh, what a face it was, clear of blemishes or defects of any kind. And knowing this, he was always very careful when he shaved. He couldn't afford to nick himself, especially not today.

After shaving he put on one of his more expensive designer suits, he left his apartment, jumped into his black Mercedes 560SL and drove off. He had a lot of things to do, so he was in a hurry to get his day started. The first stop was Western Union. He hoped that he wouldn't have to wait for the money he was to receive from Cynthia. He needed the six thousand dollars to help pay his rent for the month and to pay on his suits he was having made-to-order.

When inside Western Union, he filled out the process card and slid it underneath the glass to the elderly woman sitting behind the bullet proof window. She took the card and looked at Vincent. "You a regular here, huh?" She smiled flirtatiously at him with a nearly toothless mouth.

He smiled back at her and winked his eye and said, "Yes. And I hope I continue to be." With that, the woman counted out the six thousand dollars and handed it to him. Vincent took the money and put it in his Mario Valentino wallet, and then placed it in the breast pocket of his suit jacket. He turned back and smiled at the woman before leaving through the door. "I might as well flirt with the old bag. She might be able to do me a favor someday," he thought.

Now it was time to return to Larry's On Sunset, the shop that customized and tailor-made his suits. He had an appointment to receive the final fitting on two suits he ordered almost a month earlier. He knew Larry would be a little upset with him for having kept Pablo, the tailor, waiting for so long. But he was a regular and knew that he could sweet talk even a straight man out of being angry with him.

He planned to receive the final fittings and pay for the suits out-right, to make up for any inconvenience he had caused Larry. Good thing for him Cynthia had come through with the money, again. He had to make it up to her somehow, and he knew just the thing. He figured, what the hell...if her husband can't give it to her right, he would.

When Vincent pulled in front of Larry's, the man himself was standing outside smoking on that old pipe of his. He smiled as Vincent pulled his Mercedes next to the curb, in front of his Corvette. As Vincent approached him, Larry extended his hand. "Where in the hell you been you cock-sucking son of a bitch?" Old Larry was a foul talking, chubby, suspender wearing, pipe smoking, cane walking, four-eyed, filthy rich ass old man.

Vincent admired the hell out of him. He wanted to be just like him, though not chubby, pipe smoking, cane walking or four-eyed. "Hey old man, what's shakin'?" Vincent greeted him with the same enthusiasm.

"The money in my pockets son," Larry said as he shook Vincent's hand. "We been a little worried about you."

"Oh. And why is that?" Vincent asked.

"Well, you ain't been comin' around here on schedule lately. What's wrong, some lady done gone and thrown the perfect pussy to ya, huh?" he said with a crooked smile.

"Now Larry, you know me better than that," Vincent cringed at the thought.

"No, can't say that I do. But one thing I do know is that you got two thousand dollars' worth of imported silk and linen in there that ain't worth a damn 'til we can get yo narrow ass fitted right."

"Well," Vincent said, "that's why I'm here, old man. I've been a little busy lately with certain things going on in my life." He was starting to get annoyed. "Hey man, I'm sorry I had to keep rescheduling the fitting. Damn. Now can we get on with it?"

"Well, you're here now. So go on in there and kiss Pablo's ass. He'll like that." Larry grinned at him. Vincent knew that Larry wasn't kidding about that. Pablo would surely give him a hard time for having been stood up so many times. He also knew that if he didn't kiss his ass *well*, that he'd be wearing two tacky fitting suits.

He left Larry standing on the sidewalk in front of his building. He walked through the waiting room where several "high-end" clients were reading either, Fortune, Forbes, Gentleman's Quarterly or the Wall Street Journal. It's true. Impressive clientele did keep Larry's pockets full of money.

Pablo was in the main dressing room, prancing around with a tape measure draped around his neck and stick pins clinched between his lips. He was skillfully marking chalk on, what looked like, a shirtless mannequin, in a pair of slacks in the making. The song "YMCA" by the Village People was softly playing on the sound system.

"Don't swallow those pins. I wouldn't want you to die on me without finishing my suits," Vincent said with a smile as Pablo turned around and looked him up and down.

"Mmm...mmm...mmm," Pablo was saying without realizing he still held the pins between his lips. He spat them out into the trash can beside him and said to Vincent, "Well, well, well, If it isn't the little drummer boy. You sure have a lot of nerve, honey," Pablo said with a girlish, arrogant tone.

"Why, whatever could you mean?" Vincent said as charming as he knew how.

"Don't you dare try to play me. You and I both know that you've been a bad boy lately. I just hope she's worth it."

"Now why do both you and Larry think that a woman has something to do with my not being able to make my last few appointments?"

"Vincent," Pablo said with a laugh, "everything you do or don't do has something to do with a woman. Now, who is she, and does she have a brother?" Pablo stared intently into Vincent's eyes, as if to pull some juicy gossip out of him.

"Am I fucking glowing? Is it that obvious to everyone that this new woman in my life is getting me?" Vincent thought to himself, "If that's the case, I've got to distance myself from Jax even more." Yes, she did make him feel young and more alive than he had felt in a long time. Yes, she did have an arrogant way about her which turned him on. And oh yes, she was an excellent student in Love Making 101. But from now on, she would have to be treated like just another skirt.

His way of life had been determined a long time ago...way before she entered the picture. Things were about to come to a grinding halt right now! "No she doesn't have a brother Pablo. Don't you have a man?" Vincent finally said after snapping out of it.

"Honey, the world is full of men that should be mine. Now take your butt over there in the waiting room with the rest of the pant legs. I'm sure you all have something in common." Pablo turned back around and continued chalking and pinning the pants on the mannequin man.

Vincent was relieved that he had not given him more of a hard time about his missed appointments. So he walked back to the waiting room, as instructed, and took a seat on the black leather sofa. He crossed his legs, exposing the French silk socks that he wore, and put his hand to his chin.

Lost in thought, again, he didn't see the many faces of men coming and going from the waiting room. One man politely asked him if he wished to see the Gentleman's Quarterly, after he had finished with it himself. But Vincent was too lost in thought to even hear the man. He was too busy trying to convince himself that it was best to stop treating Jax like she was different from the others...like she was special. He needed to think about something besides her. He needed to think about...about...Tracey!

That's right! He had made a lunch appointment with Tracey and unless Pablo called him next, he was going to be late. Just then, Pablo signaled for Vincent to come back into the main dressing room.

When he stepped out of Larry's into the sunshine, he felt a sense of relief. He had paid the balance on his suits, decided to put Jax on the back burner and had a pretty woman waiting for him to take to lunch.

Larry was still standing outside and noticed the smile on Vincent's face. "What's the matter with you, boy? Why you smiling like that?"

"Larry, did I ever tell you that you are nosey as hell?"

"You didn't have to tell me that, boy. My wife tells me that all the time; besides, how you expect me to know somethin' if I don't ask nothin'?"

"Well, I guess you got me on that one. Say Larry, when did you know that you wanted to marry your wife? I mean, when did you know for sure that she was the one for you?" he asked curiously.

Larry took one long and hard look at Vincent and puffed twice on his pipe. Finally he walked over to his shiny red Corvette, with the help of his cane and opened the door. He pulled a framed picture out of his car and then walked back over to Vincent. "See this here picture? This is my wife."

Vincent took one look at the beautiful woman staring back at him from the picture and was mesmerized. He couldn't take his eyes off of her. Finally, he realized that Larry must be watching his reaction and so he looked up from the picture. Vincent didn't want to insult the old man by being attracted to his wife, and so he was very deliberate about what he said next. "She is....she's a nice lady I bet, huh?" That was all he could get himself to say. The fact of the matter was he was surprised as hell, that a fat, old man could snatch a young beauty like the woman in the picture. She looked young enough to be his granddaughter. "My hero," he thought.

Larry laughed a little and said, "Nice my ass. When you have a woman who looks like this, and does everything as good as she looks, I say you marry her."

Vincent looked the old man square in the eyes and knew for the first time that wisdom was certainly acquired from age. They said goodbye and Vincent promised him that he wouldn't be a stranger. He looked at his watch, jumped into his convertible and pulled away from the curb en route to have "lunch" with a woman named Tracey.

He arrived at exactly noon to what appeared to be an empty building, except for the one Nissan Sentra that sat in the parking lot. "Hmm, a Sentra." Vincent hadn't counted on a grown woman with a prospering career having a car like this. "Well, maybe she's just practical," he thought.

Tracey had already explained to Vincent that she would be the only one working at the law firm on this 4th of July holiday. She wanted to impress her bosses by working extra hard and doing the menial tasks that the prior Legal Secretary refused to do. Vincent was impressed with her for that, as he always was with well-spoken and well paid women.

He met her in a supermarket in Beverly Hills one day last week. She was standing over the avocados, testing them for freshness by squeezing them. He was browsing through section by section, not actually looking for anything in particular. When he browsed into the produce section, he saw her standing there squeezing the avocados, looking... edible herself.

She was one of those redbone sista's with freckles; high yellow, petite with pretty brown hair and eyes. Vincent figured that she was a 40 something professional who worked or lived in the area. He also noticed that her grocery cart only contained enough food items to serve one person for dinner:

1 Cornish hen, 1 sweet potato, 1 head of lettuce, and 1 tomato.

She picked up the avocado and sighed. That's when Vincent decided that she was probably done shopping and about to leave. He wasn't about to let her get away without first checking to see if she had a wedding ring on her finger. If she did, he would question her to find out just how devoted a wife she is. Quietly he rolled his cart next to hers and asked, "Pardon me. May I get close enough to squeeze the avocados?"

She looked up with apparent disgust written all over her face. "Excuse me," she said as she quickly began to push her cart away.

"Don't let me run you off. By all means, if you weren't finished here I can wait aside." He changed his expression into a look of concern.

"Oh, no," she said embarrassed. "I'm all done here. You can go ahead."

"Does squeezing the fruits and vegetables really tell you if they're ripe for the picking?" he asked.

"Well, I assume so. I've been doing it for years, so it's just a matter of habit for me now. Why? Didn't your mother or your wife ever teach you how to inspect your food?"

"Hmm, she's asking about family already. She definitely needs a friend," he thought. He said, "No. I roam the supermarkets for friendly women, such as yourself who are kind enough to give me on the spot, crash course training." This got her to smile so he continued. "Do you live around here?"

"No. I work around the corner. I'm on lunch break and thought that I would pick up my dinner now, so I wouldn't have to stop at the market later on. Why, do you?"

"No. But I take care of certain business in this area and I'm often in this market. And since I've never seen you in here before, I was simply going to welcome you to the neighborhood," he said grinning.

"Well, thank you anyway." She very slowly started to push her cart away. "Listen, if you're sometimes in this area, and I work in this area, maybe I'll see you in here again and I can instruct you on the fine details of choosing the right melon." She grinned back.

Vincent decided to go for the glory. "Why don't I just take you out to lunch or dinner and we can have someone else chore over the minor details for us?"

"That would be very nice." She reached inside of her purse and pulled out her business card and handed it to him: McKenzie and Swine Law Offices: Tracey Jones, Legal Secretary.

"Your friends wouldn't, by any chance, call you T.J. would they?" he asked after reading her card.

"Why as a matter of fact they do. How did you know that?"

She was looking more and more interesting and interested every second. "I just have a knack for nick-names, that's all."

"Well, you can call me T.J. if you like." She was definitely flirting.

"I'll call you tomorrow, if you like."

"I like. By the way, what's your name?"

"Vincent."

"Well, Vincent it was very nice chatting with you. I hope to hear from you soon."

"Oh you will," he said, as he watched her roll her cart into an aisle, pay for her items and leave the store. He called her the next day and arranged to meet with her for lunch. They had spoken only one other time to confirm this lunch date. He was impressed, so far, with everything about her. He was looking forward to getting to know her much better.

He rang the security buzzer and waited for a reply from her on the intercom. When he didn't receive a response within a few seconds he rang it again. "She probably had to go to a certain location in order to answer it," he thought, and so he waited.

Tracey either trying to surprise him, or she just wanted to see him right away because she flung the door wide open, nearly hitting him in the head. It surprised Vincent and he jumped back thinking that he would rip his suit if he had to kick somebody's ass. But then he saw her and was relieved that he would not have to fight off anyone.

She was wearing black high heels, Bermuda shorts, and a deep-cut body suite. Vincent's first thought was that she looked totally different from the way she looked in the grocery store, with her nice dress and a jacket. But she looked good just the same.

"I hope I didn't startle you. Come on in," she said as she held the door open for him.

Vincent took a look over his shoulder to take in a photographic memory of his surroundings. His car seemed to be in a secure space and there were plenty of exits posted on the building. He knew from past experience that a man should always know his options when going anywhere, especially for the first time.

"I was expecting you to buzz me from inside the building" Vincent said.

"Well I was going to, but I was close enough to the entrance when you rang to run over and let you in," she said as she closed the door behind him and proceeded down the hall. "Well, this is where I work. And no, I don't usually dress like this, but I figured since I was going to be the only one working today I might as well be comfortable. By the way, you look very handsome. You've just come from another one of your business meetings?"

"No. Actually I've just come from a fitting for a couple of suits I'm having made." She grabbed Vincent's hand and guided him down the hall, towards her office. He instantly liked the way her hand felt in his. It was moist and soft and small, just the way a woman's hand should be. "You're the only one in the building, huh?"

"Yes I am," she said as they finally reached her office and she released his hand.

"Aren't you afraid being here all alone?" he asked as he took a seat in the chair facing her desk.

"No. No one can get in here unless I let them in. So if my judgment in character is bad enough for me to let the wrong person in here, then he deserves what he gets." She sat behind her desk and leaned in towards him.

He smiled. "You know, a person could take what you just said in a whole lotta ways."

"I know." She smiled back. "I also know that we were supposed to go out to lunch, but as you can see I am hardly dressed for that, especially since you've managed to out dress me. Why don't we have lunch here? Would that be alright with you?"

"Sure. What you got?"

"What do you want?"

Vincent was getting the impression that this woman had more that food on her mind. "We could order pizza."

"Yeah, we could do that." She reached across the desk for his hand again.

"Or we could order Chinese."

"Yeah, we could do that too." She started making little circles in the palm of his hand.

"Is there anything in particular that you would like me to eat?" Vincent asked her, now realizing that this woman was hoping he'd fuck her. "Or do you want to read my palm?"

She looked up almost startled by his questions. "I'm sorry, am I making you uncomfortable?"

"It would take a lot more to make me uncomfortable Tracey. Is that what you want to do....make me uncomfortable?" he asked her while leaning forward in his chair and placing his free hand underneath his chin.

"Would making you uncomfortable, make you comfortable, Vincent?" She put one of his fingers in her mouth and began to gently bite on it.

Vincent wasn't impressed, yet. He wanted to see just how far this woman was going to go before he let himself get too excited. "Do you have a finger nail file?"

"Is that what you want, a manicure?" she said with his finger still between her teeth.

"And a pedicure while you're at it," he said in a smug voice.

"In which manner will you be satisfying this bill, Sir?"

"I'm sure you'll think of something."

Tracey stood up still holding his finger in her mouth and walked around her desk to where Vincent sat. "Do you have any plastic?" she asked while kneeling down in front of him, releasing his finger.

"I never leave home without it. But, I'll need to know if you have your references in order. These are tricky times we live in my dear."

"Oh yes. I've had my references verified at least twice this year, and you?" She began taking off his shoes and socks.

"My references have all checked out too." Vincent was beginning to let himself enjoy what was apparently about to happen. "I guess avocados are an aphrodisiac, huh?" he asked, looking for an answer from her as to why she was coming on to him like this.

"Either that or they just make you see things more clearly."

"So we clearly understand each other?" She didn't answer him except for a brief nod. She took both of her hands and held his fingers in place as she sucked on them, one by one.

Vincent felt himself stir within and tried to contain himself, but he knew that he was about to have the ride of his week.

He gently took his hands from her and stood, removing his jacket and hung over the back of his chair. Then he removed his wallet from the breast pocket, retrieved several condoms from it and returned the wallet to his breast pocket.

He placed the plastic on the desk in front of Tracey, unzipped his pants and returned to the seat in front of her.

She looked at him and then at the opening in his pants. Vincent sat there with his legs parted and his hands resting on his thighs. He told himself that she would have to make the first move. Apparently she read his mind, because she reached inside his pants and began to massage his penis. She felt it pulsating through his briefs, trying to escape from its confinement. So she freed it and let it bobble in the air.

On her knees she crawled closer to Vincent and began, again, to massage his massive rock. She looked at him with intensity, as if to stir any emotion out of him. Vincent motioned for her to continue, by sliding forward in his chair, bringing his penis directly in front of her face. She took it in her mouth.

She began to suck and massage and lick on it with such a passion that finally she did get a response out of Vincent. He encouraged her to continue by holding onto her head and by stroking her hair. He could feel his penis going further and further down her throat, putting a nice kind of pressure just in the right spots. So he began to wiggle his body in rhythm with hers to let her know that she was doing a good job. She was slurping and rubbing him everywhere, as though she'd done this sort of thing before.

Vincent started to rub her too. First he rubbed her breasts until she started to moan. Then he stuck his hand inside the front of her body suit and found a nipple. She responded very well. Finally, he started to peel down the body suit from her shoulders until it was resting at her waist. She didn't stop working on him. Vincent was massaging both of her breasts in his hands and tugging at her pants with his feet. He had done this sort of thing before and so he was successful at freeing her shorts from her hips.

When finally she looked up at him, he began to slide out of his pants. She helped him out of his pants, shirt, tie and briefs and dropped them to the floor. Neither of them said a word as Vincent motioned Tracey to stand up and he pulled her clothing from her body and onto the floor. He took her arm and guided her to her desk and she sat on top of it.

He took a condom from the desk and put it on himself. Then he rose and lay Tracey onto the desk. She herself knocked everything off of it onto the floor. Vincent climbed on top of her and slowly eased his penis into her. She moaned at the moment of entry and began a rhythmic dance with him.

They danced forever, with Tracey content to let Vincent move her around like a piece of furniture from one position to another. He knew that if she had gone through all of this to get it, then he was going to give it to her, thoroughly. All the while Vincent had been wondering to himself if there was a security camera in this place. That would be all he needed. When they were done they both put their clothes back on and sat back in their chairs as though nothing had just happened.

"Was that form of payment satisfactory?" Vincent finally said.

"Oh yes. As a matter of fact, we encourage using that kind of plastic."

"Well, I do believe you still owe me change back," Vincent said with a smile.

"I don't have any right now, but I'm sure I will this weekend."

"Then I'll call you to collect it."

"Do that."

Vincent leaned over the desk and kissed her on the cheek. He hadn't even thought of kissing her on the mouth the entire time he was screwing her brains out. And giving her oral was definitely out of the question...for now. He opened the door, looked back at her sitting at her desk and said, "I'll talk to you soon."

"I hope so," she said.

He walked out of the office and out of the building. He saw his car in the same place, and the coast was clear. His day was turning out better than he thought it would.

But as he began driving down the street, his car began to make a clicking noise. He didn't panic because he had heard this noise before. His car had occasionally been making this noise for a couple of months now. But now he felt concerned about what could materialize into a major problem, if it hadn't already happened.

He had at least $4000 in his pocket, but $1500 of that had to go towards his rent. So, that would leave him with about $2500 dollars to get his car serviced and to have some extra spending money. So after dropping off his rent money at his land lord's office, Vincent called the Mercedes dealer to tell them he was bringing in his car.

Although he knew several men who called themselves mechanics, he had never once even thought of leaving the care of his car to either of them. He preferred to take his car to the one place he knew would take care of it as well as he did, even if they did charge up to 300% more for the repairs.

He decided to have lunch in the Sizzler across the street from the dealers shop to wait for his car. Besides, he hadn't eaten a thing today and he needed to strengthen himself due to his earlier activities with Tracey.

As he sat there picking over his Lemon Herb Chicken, he wondered why women like Tracey give themselves so freely. Didn't they know that he, and men like him, would take and take and take, without giving anything back in return? Except maybe a good stiff one from time to time.

And yes, Vincent thought about AIDS all the time. He remembered the days when, fucking was the most natural thing anyone could do, until weird shit started happening. People started dropping off the face of the earth with this disease that no one could explain. He had put a halt on his dick, for a little while anyway. And up until then, he had never once used a condom. But now he kept a steady supply of condoms by ordering them factory direct, which saved him a ton of money.

And he was cautious enough to know when to stop fucking and change his condom on the spot. Women hate that shit…when you stop the rhythm like that; their juices seem to stop flowing. But he usually makes up for it.

A hostess walked up to him and asked if everything was OK. He said yes, and as she walked away he found himself visualizing her naked. Sex was always on his mind. No, it wasn't a hang up, it was a man thing. He's a man who loves to use his thing!

After eating, he picked up his car, spending almost $500 on the repairs and headed for home. Right before he got there he changed his mind. He didn't want to be there when and if Jax decided to stop by. "Avoid her," is what he found himself saying out loud. If he avoided her, then he wouldn't have to look into her pretty eyes. And if he didn't look into her eyes, he wouldn't have the need to touch her, to undress her, to make love to her. And although Jax was the one woman he needed to be with, his nature could never let her be the only one. So until she learned that lesson, he would simply avoid her.

When he got home later that night, after the neighborhood kids finished with their fireworks, he figured enough time had passed for Jax to have called or stopped by. He assumed that on a Friday night, she and her weird friend Sabastian were probably getting dressed to go out to watch some fireworks display or go to some night club somewhere.

One of the things he didn't have in common with Jax, was that she loved to party. He knew all too well, the life of partying. He had had enough of that earlier in his life. Besides, every time he did go to a club, he ran into women that he knew, women who he had been with, and the friends of women who he had been with. Hell! It was just too damned complicated going to a public meat market and then running into several women who he had fucked before.

Sometimes he wondered how soon it would be before Jax had one of those famous conversations in the ladies room of a club, and discover that they both knew and had been fucked by him.

Vincent checked his answering machine and discovered that Jax had not called him. Blair, Joyce, Miranda and Sherry did call wanting to know what he was doing tonight. He didn't bother to call any of them back, because he was a little disappointed that Jax hadn't called, though he'd never admit that either. He didn't bother to turn off the machine, but instead went into the kitchen and started looking for something to cook himself for dinner.

He found a steak, some frozen vegetables and a can of biscuits. Vincent was well adapted to cooking his own dinner. As a matter of fact, he often made dinner for his female friends. Afterwards there would be dessert and steamy sex, all mixed together. However, tonight was different. He wasn't in the mood for anyone touching his stomach and chest, or sucking on his dick to get him in the mood. No, tonight he just wanted to eat dinner by himself and catch up on his sleep...something he hadn't been able to do in a very long time.

After broiling his steak, boiling his vegetables and baking his biscuits, all in ten minutes, he ate it in five, and was in bed in two. His water bed swished as he tossed and turned while trying to get comfortable. He couldn't even remember the last time he had been in his bed alone.

About three o'clock in the morning his phone rang waking him up from a sound sleep. Because he had left his answering machine on, he didn't make a move to answer it. Instead he just lay there listening to his own voice, and then the voice of a woman saying, "Vincent, if you're there, pick up the phone." He didn't seem to recognize the voice on the other end so he waited until the voice said something else. Maybe then he would be able to distinguish this woman's voice from the other women who were constantly calling him. He almost fell off of his bed with what he heard her say next.

"I hope you're happy now, you self-centered son of a bitch!" The voice was slurred, the woman was drunk. "From fucking around with your whorish ass, I got infected with the HIV virus! Did you hear me?   Did you hear me mother fucker? I'm going to die with AIDS...and so are you!"

Vincent's heart stopped beating...his blood ran cold...his mouth died out to the bone and he broke out in a cold sweat! Had he just heard that woman correctly? Did she say that he had given her AIDS?! No! That couldn't be, because he wore a condom, sometimes two. This must be some kind of April fool's joke...but it's July, not April!

"I must be dreaming," he thought, but the voice rang out again. "I don't give a fuck whether or not you get your ass tested, but you better not let me ever see your ass with another girl, else I'm gonna..." The machine beeped and cut her off.

"No! Not yet!" He hadn't worked up enough courage to pick up the phone before she was disconnected. Panic struck him like a nuclear bomb! Shaking uncontrollably, he reached for the machine to rewind it and listen to that disturbing message again. But who was she? For the life of him he could not recognize that voice. When his hand reached the machine he didn't have the nerve to listen to the message again. He was well aware of what he had just heard; he was going to die of AIDS!!!

Vincent crawled out of his bed and onto his knees, and began to pray for the first time in years. He prayed for things he didn't even know he cared about, like; feeding all the children of the world, stopping all of the violence of the world and for the restoration of faith in God for everyone.

He was as selfless in his prayers as he had ever been before in his life. And though he trembled through clasped hands, and his naked body was drenched in his own sweat, he prayed. The prayers of a dead man were sure to reach the ears of God sooner than that of the prayers of a live one. And according to the words spoken on his machine, he was dead!

He didn't have the heart to even think of how many women he had probably infected with the deadly disease; he hadn't reached that far in thought, yet.

Vincent Cruthers at 37 years old had just listened to "death" on the other end of his telephone. He would never have any children, (if he didn't already have any), and he would never get married, (not that he ever thought he would), and he would not live to a ripe old age and die of natural causes. The fact of the matter was he wanted to die right then and there, so he prayed for death to swallow him up whole, and suck him into the mighty earth. But he wanted to die now, not years down the line when his condition would be obvious to everyone and he would suffer a slow and painful death.

He didn't want his family to visit a living corpse in the hospital, and to be fed through sterile tubes. Nor could he stomach the thought of taking tons of medication that would eventually betray him. But most of all, the thing that instilled more hurt in him than anything else, is that he would never have the opportunity to fuck a woman again!

As day broke through the shades of his bedroom window, Vincent still knelt at the edge of his bed. He hadn't moved for over four hours and he barely noticed the cramps shooting through his body. Also, he ignored the phone as it rang off its cradle, time and time again. Vincent didn't even have the presence-of-mind to hear the many voices of women, as they asked him to pick up the receiver if he was at home. Instead, he continued to kneel as though his life depended on it.

With his eyes tightly shut and his fingers woven into one another, he knelt...he prayed. The silence that swept over his world was more than he could bear. He could hardly relive those terrible words which had just torn his life apart. But there they were, eating at his flesh and his very soul. There they were!

When he thought he could take no more of the thoughts dredging around in his head, he regained enough strength to stand. And although it was as if his soul had leapt from his body, leaving it to fend for itself, he began to move about his room. He moved from corner to corner, in a drugged state of mind, without any control or reason.

When he found himself in front of his full length mirror, he stopped. Slowly he began to inspect every inch of his naked body from head-to-toe, searching for signs or signals that he over-looked while not knowing of his illness. His eyes inched upward and downward with the attention to detail of a bald eagle. He noticed moles he had never once seen before and imperfections in the color of his skin. He took everything he saw as a flaw, as though this were the proof he needed to confirm his deadly dilemma.

Without realizing, he grabbed his sagging piece of flesh that had served him in many sexual exploits; more than he could take note of, and began to tug at it. This time though, not to hasten his hard-on for a woman sitting in the next room, but as though to pull it out from its foundation. He had always admired this flesh, this piece of masculinity for which women had always begged for, lied for, and sometimes cried for.

Vincent could feel no pain as he tugged and yanked on his penis. There was no hope, no sunshine, no way out of his death sentence. The fact of the matter is, he had already submitted to the fact that he was infected with the HIV virus; he didn't need a doctor to confirm his situation...that would be too embarrassing. No, he would live out the rest of his days alone and out of the public eye. In his eyes, that would be the most selfless act of all. But the temptation to be with women would always be there, he knew that. He was a man born to satisfy the women of the earth.

And so, as he stood in front of his bedroom full length mirror, while tugging at his penis, he prayed this time for strength. It was bad enough that a strange woman's voice had told him of his destiny, but the voices of strange women had been his destiny for years.

Vincent had given up trying to figure out the voice of the woman who had delivered his death sentence. He took her word as gospel because of the lifestyle that he had led for a very long time. He did not think that anyone could ever be so cruel as to fabricate something of this nature. And although he did not recognize her voice, was of no consequence, for Vincent had slept with a variety of women without even knowing their names. Therefore, he knew that the probability of this allegation had to be true.

He had always tried to convince himself that he would not become a statistic who would contract the AIDS virus, but deep down inside himself, he knew that the opposite was true. He was a "ladies man" so try as he might, he knew he'd find great, if not impossible difficulty in giving up the pussy.

Visions of his penis drying up and falling off made him abruptly drop it in disgust; it didn't look like a trophy anymore. He looked at his reflection in the mirror and saw a defeated man. He no longer saw a confident charmer who used his guile's to seduce women, nor did he see a handsome face that had been one of his best assets.

"Oh God! Is this my punishment? Is the rest of my life to be lived as a nightmare? Am I deserving of a punishment this horrible?" He asked himself these questions as tears began to streak his face. Suddenly, he was aware that he looked his age. Never once had he thought that he looked his age, which was why he could snag chicks, young and old. But now, his face seemed to sag under the pressure with the news that he had received from the woman unknown.

In a panic, Vincent ran into the bathroom, turning on the hot water in the shower. Steam rose from the shower head and consumed the entire room with a foggy haze. He found serenity in the setting as he slowly allowed himself to succumb to the scalding water. He didn't even seem to mind that his skin was beginning to slowly scald.

He reached for the soap and a towel and began to scrub his skin with a great urgency and with such fervor, that the skin on this chest began to blister. His penis, however, was receiving the most damage from this self-affliction. It turned a bright burgundy in color and started to pulsate with each splash of hot water that it came into contact with. He would have ignored the pain, had it not been for his natural instinct to kick-in and protect what had always brought him so much pleasure.

Finally, Vincent turned his back on the scalding hot water in an effort to finally protect his swollen penis. He dropped to his knees and fell to the bottom of the shower, crying out in great, great pain! The pain was either from the scalding hot water or from the pain that now consumed his every thought. He didn't know which, but he unleashed a loud and gruesome shriek that consumed his apartment throughout.

A defeated man, Vincent lay in the shower unable to move. He wasn't aware of his ringing phone, he wasn't aware of his ringing doorbell and he wasn't aware that Jax was scampering to turn off the hot water, throwing her arms around his naked body.

As Jax cried, screamed and pleaded with Vincent to respond to her...to explain what was wrong, he couldn't. As far as he was concerned, he was already dead!

(6) – Joseph – A Man's Gotta Do

In the early morning, it was more of a pleasure than a burden for Joseph to respond to Sayla's hungry cry. So he eagerly got out of bed, hour after hour, heating up her bottles and feeding her until she would fall back to sleep in his arms.

Given this last opportunity, he decided to do his morning exercises and shower before she awakened again. Afterwards, he lay next to her on his bed and watched her sleep, sucking on her little fingers as though some delicious liquid was being extracted from them.

So precious is his baby girl that looks so much like him. He was pleased that she had been born with distinctive features that would label her a Pride for the rest of her life. Pride is what he felt for his daughter, as his father had felt for him and as his father's father before that.

Sayla Pride would carry on the tradition of sailors in his family, with her name, if not with anything else. Her name was no coincidence, either. When Veronica asked him to name their daughter, he immediately blurted out, "Sailor!" But Veronica wouldn't go for that, so she shortened it to Sayla.

When the phone rang, he caught it before the second ring, so not to wake up his sleeping daughter. He figured that it might be Veronica, since she was so reluctant to let him keep Sayla overnight, without her. "Yeah?"

The voice on the other side of the phone asked, "Is that how you answer the phone when your fiancé, calls?"

"Had you let me know it was you, I would have answered differently," he said with a sarcastic tone.

"How is my baby?" She ignored his attitude.

"My baby is fine. How are you Ronnie?"

"You know how I am Joseph. But I'd be a lot better if we could continue the discussion on the wedding."

"Damn, here we go," he thought.

Ever since he returned from overseas, Veronica was raring to get moving with the inevitable wedding plans that plagued his every thought with fear. He promised her that it would take place, and soon. She had already taken it upon herself to put together a guest list and a tentative dinner menu. The when and where were the only other details to complete. She had even received permission to wear his mother's wedding dress and had begun the alterations on it herself. Damn! Out of the ocean and into the fish tank.

"Joseph, are you there?" Veronica sounded annoyed now.

"Yeah I'm here, but I've gotta go. Sayla's waking up. We'll call you later, OK?" He hung up the phone before she could answer him.

Sayla was still sleeping in a fetal position, sucking away at her little fingers, looking like a little Angel without a care in the world.

But Joseph was suffering from pre-marriage jitters, probably more than any other person in the history of the world. He wasn't sure if he could go through with it. It's not that he didn't love Veronica either. The fact of the matter is he does love her, enough to have a relationship with her, enough to have a baby with her and enough to marry her. "But now...so young, so soon?" That was the question ringing in his ears every time the subject came up.

Whenever he tried to look back on all of his overseas lovers, no names came to mind, only the faces of beautiful women with beautiful bodies who had taken away the loneliness. So he couldn't blame his hesitance on any of them, because he knew that they were merely distractions.

His father had taught him to think of them that way, as did he, when he was traveling from seaport to seaport. But still, there was this fear that he could not ignore, and he didn't know how much longer he could keep Veronica at bay.

He stroked his daughter's head and kissed her cheek very gently as to not wake her up. He reached for his pad and pencil and began to sketch her, laying there in his bed. Without thinking about it, he drew with his left hand, though his right hand had mended weeks ago. I guess he liked change, as well as chance. When he was done sketching his daughter, he checked her to make sure she was still breathing, as he always did when she slept late.

After making himself a cup of coffee, he walked out onto the balcony and stared out in the direction of the swimming pool with a dead gaze in his eyes. He had to think long and hard about a major decision in his life.

Turning his head to check on Sayla, he saw that she didn't even stir. She was the one constant in his life that he would make good on. His daughter was worth all of his effort to make his relationship with Veronica work, as was the thing that the Prides had always done. And so, his decision was made. He would marry Veronica.

"Hello."

"Hi baby. Miss me?" Joseph asked Veronica.

"Of course I miss you, I miss both my babies. How is she?"

"She's fine. You know, you don't always have to ask about her like that, as though I'm going to do something wrong, Ronnie."

"I know Joseph, but she is only a baby, and mothers are more adept at taking care of them, you know."

"No. I don't know!" Now he remembered one thing he absolutely hated about her, she was a little miss know it all! He gritted his teeth. "By the way, you wanna get married next month?" Silence.

"You mean it Joseph?" she asked almost astonished.

"Of course I mean it, girl." He had a frog in his throat when he said it. "So set it up for next month, and let me know what time to show up, OK?"

"I'll get right on it, baby."

"By the way, I'll bring Sayla back to you soon. I have a few things I need to do today." He hung up the phone and gathered Sayla in his arms. She was opening her little eyes and smiled at her daddy. He kissed her and said, "Daddy's going to take care of you forever, Boo. I'd do anything for you."

And with that he bathed and dressed her in the cutest little pink sailor suit. He tried to give her some juice, but she wouldn't take it, so he drank it himself. For some reason he liked Gerber's Apple Juice better than any other brand.

He carried Sayla out of his apartment to his car, securing her in the baby seat before climbing into the driver's side. After dropping off little Sayla with Veronica, he would start his mission to find George and ask him if he would be his Best Man, even if it killed him.

Sayla was fussing with her pacifier the entire ride to her mothers, but Joseph had to keep his eyes on the road. He didn't believe in spoiling her...too much. She would cry and whine for her daddy's attention, but he wasn't paying her any attention, and that seemed to piss her off. Sayla was definitely her mother's daughter, requiring his attention every possible second.

When he pulled into the visitor parking lot he was able to return his attention to her, who was fussing profusely by now, so he began to sing her the song he had made up in honor of his only child:

"My little Sayla,
so soft, so plump,
wrapped her fingers 'round my heart,
for her I'm just a punk."

Joseph sang the lines over and over again while pushing his nose in her face, until finally she stopped kicking and shifting in her baby seat and starting smiling and drooling all over his face. He kissed her drool, picked her up and took her inside to Veronica, who was waiting at the front door dressed in a skimpy silk robe.

"How's Mommy's Little Angel?" She held her arms open to receive the baby from Joseph. Sayla was smothered with tiny baby kisses from her mother. "You got here quick, is there something wrong?" she asked him after putting the baby down in the swing.

Joseph closed the front door behind him. "No, nothing. I just didn't want you to worry about her for one second longer than necessary," he said.

"I'm not worried about her when she's with you, baby. I'm just a new mother who is always missing her baby. I miss you too, baby. And I've got something for you."

"Oh yeah, and what is that?" he asked curiously.

She untied and dropped her robe to the floor and said, "This!"

Joseph let his eyes take in her body from head to toe, and back again. He took in the fullness of her breasts, slightly sagging from the added weight of mother's milk and her stomach was not as flat as it used to be, but not too disgusting.

She walked toward him and extended an invitation to him that he couldn't resist, so he took her right there on the living room floor in front of Sayla, who must of liked what she was seeing because she appeared to be clapping and cheering them on.

As he lay on top of Veronica, he was disappointed in the lack of tightness of her pussy. Even though he knew recently giving birth would cause her body to change, he was still disappointed. But he made love to Veronica, all the while knowing that he better get used to it fast.

She seemed to sense his disappointment and attempted to experiment with him to keep his attention. She rolled on top, underneath and even side-ways to satisfy him, and when she had exhausted herself, she was pleased to let him finish up the job.

Veronica knew that things had not been the same between them since he returned from overseas, but she was damn sure going to do whatever it took to keep him and have the family she always wanted. So, after Joseph was finished with her, she sent him on his way because she had some sit-ups to do.

"I'll call you later," he said on his way out the door.

"You better," she said as she kissed him good-bye and brushed up against him before closing the door behind him.

"Well, I've gotta hand it to her," he said to himself as he walked to his car, "she sure is trying hard." He smiled while getting into his car. "Now it's time to find old George."

George wasn't home, as usual. Ever since they returned from overseas, George had been scarce. Joseph figured that he was trying to make up for lost time by catching up with as many women as he could lie to. But just as Joseph was about to pull off, George pulled up in his car. "Hey man. What's up?"

"Where have you been? I haven't seen you around lately," Joseph said.

"Oh just trying to get back into the groove of things, man. How's the hand?"

"It's OK."

George got out of the car and opened the front door to his small house. "Come in at your own risk. I haven't cleaned up for days." Joseph followed him into the house.

"You can say that again. What the hell you been doing in this here?"

"Absolutely nothing!" George replied.

"Well, I can see that. Hey, you got something to drink up in here?" Joseph asked.

George looked up surprised. "It's eleven o'clock in the morning. What the hell you wanna drink for?"

Joseph was walking around in the living room looking at old pictures that hung on the walls. He had seen all of them before, but he didn't seem to recognize any of them. George was playing back his answering machine listening to his messages. The voices of at least two women were leaving their phone numbers and asking him to call them back at his earliest convenience. The third voice sounded like a much older woman. Joseph caught the last sentence. "...so come by before then, to mow the lawn."

"Damn man, your women get older and older," Joseph said laughing.

"Shut up. That was my mama."

"I'm just playing. How is your mother doing, anyway?"

"She's fine. Just as bossy as ever," George replied.

"You gotta go by the old house and do the lawn for her?"

"Yeah, but not until later on this afternoon. She probably figures that she has to call and remind me about the shit, not realizing that she's more senile than me," he grunted and walked over to his mini-bar. "I've got some Gin, Tonic Water, E&J, Tequila, some Boone's Strawberry Wine and a case of hot beer on the back porch. What's your pleasure sailor?"

"Give me a shot of Tequila," Joseph said, wiping his forehead and then sticking both hands in his jean pockets.

"Alright," George said. "It's your hangover." He reached for a shot glass, poured it full of Tequila and handed it to Joseph, who downed it with a gulp.

He sat down on the sofa, slammed the empty glass down on the table and said, "Give me another."

George said, "Damn man, I ain't ever seen you drink except for when we're overseas somewhere." He handed the bottle to him and sat down in his lounging chair and stared at Joseph. "Female problems, huh?"

"Yep, you know it. But this is more than a problem," he said while settling into the sofa after pouring himself another drink.

"Ah shit! She done backed you into a corner, huh? What, is she pregnant again?" George asked with a smirk.

Joseph's eyes bucked open. "Don't be jinxing me like that! Shit, you know a woman is more fertile after she has a baby then at any other time! And I knocked those boots this morning!"

"Well then what's the problem? You sitting over there downing Tequila like your name is Juan Gonzales."

"I want to ask you a favor," Joseph said after downing his second shot of Tequila.

"A favor? Ah shit, last time somebody asked me for a favor I was done out of $500 and can't find the fool to this day. So you see, favors ain't somethin' I'm big on," George said with an exclamation point.

"No, it's not that kind of favor."

"Then what is it?" But before Joseph could answer him, there was a knock at the front door. "Hold on, man." George got up to answer the front door. "Green, come on in, right on time. What is this? Are we having a S.S. Cruxia reunion or something?"

Green walked through the front door. "Hey Joe, what's up? How you doing man?"

"Hey, Green. What's up?" They shook hands and Green took a seat next to Joseph on the sofa.

George returned to his lounge chair. "Why is everybody meeting at my house on this lovely morning?"

"Cause you're the only one that lives on the out skirts of town. And whether we're coming in or leaving out, we always think of you," Green said to George and then turned to wink at Joseph.

George asked Green, "Would you like some coffee, tea or perhaps a shot of Tequila?"

"Tequila?" Green said surprised. "You're acting like we're back in some third world country across the ocean somewhere. We can't drink like that this early in the morning, can we?"

"Yeah well, old Joe here seems to need one for some reason," George told Green.

"Why is that Joe? What's up?"

"Well, I was just about to ask George..."

Just then, George interrupted him and stood up. "Hold on, hold on. Let me go throw the beer in the freezer. We might as well get it cold now."

Green said, "Forget all that, man. Get me a glass with some ice. It is sort of hot outside; I'll knock a few back."

"Alright. Joe, you want one too?" George yelled from the kitchen.

"Yeah, why not," Joseph replied.

George said, "Alright, three hot beers coming up."

"So what's been up with you Joe? How's your hand?" Green asked Joseph.

"The hand is fine."

"Have you talked to that girl from Fiji lately? You know the fine one you hung with over there?"

"Nah. Matter of fact, I can't even remember her name," Joseph said annoyed.

Green reminded him. "Lea, Cela or something like that."

"Oh, great, thanks for reminding me man. I've trained myself not to even think twice about that overseas shit, let alone remember their names, and your little pip squeak ass comes along and fucks up all of that," he said even more annoyed.

"Whoa! Hold up, hold up. Sorry man." Green threw up both of his hands.

"Ah, no big deal Green."

"So you don't talk to her huh?"

"Nope. I probably gave her a wrong phone number and address, I don't remember."

"Well you still receive packages and letters from those other chicks," Green said. "You should be getting one from her, too."

"I don't know Green. Now that I think about it, she was different," he said. "I mean, she was like all the others, but, just different."

"I hear you, man. I'm the same way, though not as much of a playa as you are," Green said with a chuckle.

Joseph was laughing too. "Hey I'm not a playa I'm just an old seaman like my father and his father before him."

"Yeah, yeah, yeah, we know, we know. The famous Prides. We all know all about you Pride men."

"That's right! And don't you ever forget it." They gave each other a high-five.

George returned with three glasses of ice and a six pack of hot beer under his arm. "Here you go boys." He handed each of them a glass and set down the beer on the table. "Cheers! The Cruxia men are back in force in the big city once again!"

They all cracked open a can of beer and tilted their glasses to the side while pouring the hot liquid over the ice. The thick foam exploded over the sides of each of their glasses and spilled all over the coffee table. They each downed the glass of beer at the same time. Then they all sort of agreed, "What the fuck?" as they began to take shots of Tequila one after the other.

They began to reminisce about life on the Cruxia and when they would all be reporting back to duty for another mission. Not excluded from the conversation was; women, sex, politics, sex, sports and sex, but mostly they talked about much of nothing in particular.

The three of them drank on a Saturday morning as though none of them had a care in the world. Everything around them became obsolete as they gossiped like farm hens.

No one heard the Jehovah's Witnesses knocking at the front door, or even the crashing sound of a car accident outside. Joseph, George and Green were friends, sailors and rapidly getting drunker by the minute. With each drink they became more determined to outdo each other so they started playing a game called, Sailors Bluff.

The object of the game is to fool each opponent into thinking that you are going to throw back your drink first, when actually you are not drinking at all, so that the other opponent gets drunk and you don't. But, the problem was, nobody ever played the game fairly. Everybody always drank, nobody ever even attempted to fool each anybody else, and always did exactly what the intention of the game is...get drunk.

By the time they looked up at the clock it was mid-afternoon, which meant that they had been drinking half the day with no food in their stomachs. George took it upon himself to call Pizza House for a home delivery of two extra-large pizzas with everything. He slammed down the phone after ordering and said, "An hurry da fuck up!" with a slurred tongue. They all laughed.

Green said to George, "Sit yo drunk ass don!"

George replied, "Kiss ma duck!" Again, they all fell out laughing. Still laughing George said, "Hey Joe, member on da Cruxia you say two men was in da firmary doin' the nasty next to you, an you thunk they was comin' to git yo booty next?"

"Hey, waita damminute. I forgot 'bout dat shit til yo ass just brought it up just now. Still can't put my finger on who dem fools was," Joseph was trying to explain.

"What'n da hell you say?" Green blurted out, wanting to know what they were talking about.

Joseph went into the sorted story, as best he could, about his weird night from hell on the Cruxia. He explained to Green, as he already had to George, what happened when he was sleeping in the infirmary after the brawl in the kitchen. He ended the story about two "mystery" men who were engaging in homosexual intercourse on the bunk directly across from his.

He couldn't be sure who the two men were, but he was positive that he recognized at least one of their voices. When he startled the two men and reached for the light, they both scampered out of the infirmary with their pants wrapped around their ankles and their lily white asses pulsating in the after-glow.

He had also found it hard to believe that everybody on the ship didn't know that he, or someone, was actually in the infirmary that night. Everybody on the ship knew that there had been a brawl in the kitchen that morning. How could anyone not know the infirmary wasn't empty? But the first question was still, who were those two faggots?

Joseph slurred out his ordeal to the half sleeping men in the living room. He was mostly talking to himself, but that was OK, as he hadn't really given it the kind of thought that he had planned to. However drunk he was, he was always careful to speak "hard-core". So he added, "I'll kick any mutha fucka who come near me ass."

George laughed so hard his elbow lost its grip from his lounge chair. "Hey Joe, it's yo turn to da porch to get mo beer."

"I thought you said it was all n'da feeza?" Joseph asked.

"I lied," George said and laughed to himself as though he had just said something funny.

They played a few more rounds of Sailors Bluff, and no sooner than the pizza arrived did they gobble it down as though it were their last meal on earth. Before they knew it they had nearly drank the entire contents of George's make-shift mini bar.

They were a horrific sight, lying around in the middle of the living room with beer cans, booze bottles and shot glasses all tilted over on their sides. Good friends hanging around not causing a bit of harm to anyone, except maybe their livers, was a deserved treat for them all. Joseph hadn't even remembered why he had even gone over to George's house in the first place. But it didn't matter now, his mind was clear. As a matter of fact his mind was so clear, he passed out.

When he woke up he was so disoriented, he didn't know if he had been asleep for a few minutes or a few hours. He found himself in an empty living room even dirtier than it was when he arrived. There was no sign of either George or Green. He grabbed his head and moaned, while looking around the room for any other signs of life. He found none. Even George's plants had managed to pass out due to lack of sunlight.

Joseph finally stood up dragging himself into the bathroom to splash cold water on his face. When he looked at the image staring back at him in the mirror, he saw a good-looking man, a drunk man, a single man, a seaman, with blood-shot eyes, walking down the aisle in less than a month. Fuck!

Looking around the bathroom, he saw several pairs of George's underwear scattered about the floor. Shaving cream, a razor blade, a tube of toothpaste, a box of Black Belt condoms and a near empty bottle of cologne was lying atop the counter.

Even though he had been in the bathroom several times during the course of the afternoon, he was too disoriented before now to notice the mess. Joseph looked around in disgust. "Damn he's a slob!" he said out loud. But never the less, he splashed some of the cologne on his face and squeezed a finger full of toothpaste in his mouth to try and get rid of the lingering taste of liquor, peppers and anchovies.

He took a quick glance in the direction of the window and noticed that it was later than he had realized. The sun would be setting soon and so he decided that he should probably go home. In the living room he stopped to use the phone to check his messages at home. He wondered if Veronica had called to check up on him or left him any messages. He hoped not.

Right before picking up the phone, he noticed a torn piece of paper with his name on it. It was a note which read, "Joe, sleep it off and lock up when you leave. Had to mow ma's lawn. George."

"Perfect," he thought. He had just found another excuse to not go home or to his future wife. It was like he was running from a losing battle. He was not going to let a decision such of this be made until first trying to exhaust every recourse in talking himself out of it. He locked up the house and jumped in his car, headed for George's mother's house. As he was drove he noticed Sayla's car seat and couldn't help but think of her. He knew that he should do the right thing by her by marrying her mother. What else could he do?

He thought of doing the right thing for his mother, and how she was never one to give him advice on matters as personal as this. The name Pride suited her well, as she was a proud woman.

He recalled the memories of his mother telling him of how Alexander and she met, when she was 16 years old. Alexander Pride took her on a whirl wind romance. When Georgia first looked at Alex, she somehow knew that he was the man she would spend the rest of her life with.

Alex was already a seasoned sailor, having just recently returning from overseas exploits. When they were married and had their only child Joseph, their love had only blossomed into more. When he died, leaving her a widow and Joseph without a father, she never once spoke ill of his exploits that he had had overseas. And though she was a wise woman and knew well of them, she would only say, "That Alex sure was a rascal."

Georgia Pride was blessed with knowing true love when she saw it, and though she never saw it in her sons eyes, she would never tell him that. She loved her granddaughter with all of her heart, yet, she knew that this decision was totally on Joseph and she offered no advice to him on the matter. As for herself, she had never even considered the possibility of marrying again. Instead she honored Alex's memory and the life that they shared together.

Joseph took these things into consideration; that his mother and father had a love strong enough to surpass the grave. He found it difficult to go against the grain, by not doing what his father had done in marrying one woman; the mother of his child.

He returned his thoughts back to the road as he drew nearer to his destination. Out of the corner of his eye he saw a jewelry shop which had a sign that read, "SALE" in big red letters. He took this to mean a sign from God that he should go into that shop and purchase a set of wedding rings for himself and Veronica. But no sooner than he gave the idea another thought, he remembered he didn't have any credit cards on him, so this became his next excuse.

Joseph turned the corner as fast as he could, trying to get away from the jewelry shop. Sweat was dripping down from his forehead and his hands were so clammy he thought he might lose his grip on the steering wheel.

Realizing that he was on the street that he had been looking for, he was lucky enough to see George's car which snapped him out of it. As he recalled, George's mother lived on the second house from the corner.

He was amazed to find so many cars parked on the street. He first thought that there might be a block party going on. But when he saw that the street hadn't been blocked off, he shrugged off that thought, even though he was finding it very difficult to find a parking space. Fortunately for him, George who had been working behind some shrubs, looked up and saw him slowly driving down the street.

He motioned for him to pull up into the driveway. When Joseph got out of the car George looked at him and said, "Are you following me man, or what?"

Joseph approached him and said, "Looks that way, doesn't it." George was steadily working on his mother's lawn. He was stooping beside the lawn mower refueling it. When Joseph asked, "Why did you leave me passed out like that?"

George just smiled and said, "Well, you were out of it, and I had to go. What did you expect me to do?"

Joseph smiled too, looked around at the scattered leaves in one corner of the lawn and asked, "Do you need any help?"

"I was wondering when you were going to ask."

They worked side by side; George mowing the lawn, while Joseph raked up leaves and stray fragments of grass that had eluded the mower basket. He was somewhat relieved that his mind was being occupied elsewhere other than Veronica and the liquor that he had consumed earlier in the day. When George turned off the lawn mower and finally asked Joseph, "I take it you been wanting to talk to me. You want to get it off your chest?"

Joseph shrugged while holding the rake handle underneath his chin and said, "Yeah, as a matter of fact I do." But before he could get into it, two women were approaching up the driveway. Joseph had been cut off once again. The women were looking in their direction and smiling. Joseph and George smiled, nodded and studied the women up and down with great care.

After the women entered the house, George turned to Joseph and said, "I forgot to tell you that my mother is having a crystal party. And all kinds of chicks… young and old have been coming house in groups of two, three and more. Let's finish up this mess and head into the backyard where we can talk." Joseph agreed and helped George move all of the equipment into the garage.

After they were done, George sprinkled grass seed onto the bald spots on the lawn and turned the sprinkler on low. He joined Joseph in the back yard, having a seat next to him on the back porch. When George spoke to Joseph, saying "Well man, spit it out."

Joseph had found himself suddenly speechless. He didn't know where to begin. This had been the opportunity he had been waiting for all day; to shed his feelings on Veronica, and to seek the advice of his good friend, and perhaps to even ask him if he would do the honors of being his Best Man. So with a deep breath, he spilled his guts. He told George of his conflicts with the situation and of his desire to do the right thing. George listened intently.

When Joseph had said all that had to say on the matter, he turned to George and said, "What do you think?"

"What do you mean, what do I think?" asked George.

Joseph was obviously annoyed. "Man, you've been giving me advice for years on things that I've never even asked you about. And here it is that I am finally asking you and you have absolutely nothing to say? What's up with that?"

George stood up and opened the back door. He turned on the back yard light and then returned to his seat on the porch. For the first time since their discussion began, Joseph could see the expression on George's face, since the sun had set several minutes before. George had a large smile on his face, and that pissed Joseph off even more. Joseph anxiously said, "What in the hell is so funny?"

George looked his friend square in the eyes and said, "Nothing's funning Joe. As a matter of fact I think the situation is pretty damn sad; sad because Veronica has you just where she wants you. I'm not saying that she's trying to force you to do anything that you don't want to do. And I'm not saying that she got pregnant on purpose or anything like that. But what I am saying is that, she knows the Pride's better than almost anybody else, and she knows that the Pride's always try to do the sensible thing."

Joseph interrupted him. "Sensible? What in the hell does that mean, sensible? Does that mean the right thing?" Joseph was looking at George for an explanation.

All George could say was, "To me Joe, sensible means whatever is sensible in the eyes of your family." He searched for more words. "I guess what I'm trying to say is, it's the way you were brought up. Everybody's got choices to make and most people make those choices based on how they were raised."

"Well, does that mean I should marry her, or not?"

George looked at his friend and said with compassion, "All I can say, my man, is do what you gonna do. No matter what you decide, I'll stand up for you either in the church, or in the dog house." George patted his friend on the back and excused himself to go into his old bedroom to find something decent to put on with all of the ladies present.

He asked Joseph if he was coming in the house or if he was going to hang out on the porch. Joseph hung back; he wanted to try and make sense of the advice he had just been given, besides, he didn't want to be seen looking like he was, with all of the pretty ladies inside.

Left alone with his thoughts, again, he sat there figuring that the reason that he was so hesitant about marrying Veronica was partially due to what his mother had told him; "True love only comes along once in a life time." And although he wasn't sure if Veronica was his true love, he was sure that the reason he had told her to rush the wedding was so that he wouldn't have the opportunity to find out.

George returned to find his friend still pondering his thoughts on the porch. He slapped Joseph on the back and said, "Man, you would not believe all the chicken heads in that house. Ma really out did herself this time."

Joseph looked up and said, "What are they doing in there?"

"Looking at brochures, crystal, plastic containers, make-up and shit like that. But they're mostly eating her macaroni and cheese pie."

Joseph looked up at George. "What's macaroni and cheese pie?"

"It's macaroni and cheese filled with meat. It's pretty damn good too. You want some?"

Joseph could go for something else to eat. His stomach did need some more food to dry up the last bit of alcohol in his system. "Yeah," he finally said. "I could go for some of your ma's macaroni and cheese pie."

George opened the door and said, "Go on. It's right through there."

"I'm not going in there looking like this, man. At least you had the opportunity to clean up first. Look at me, I look like a bum," he said.

"You don't look like a bum, you look like a drunk. Besides, the food is in the kitchen, not in the living room. You won't run into anybody."

Joseph looked at George, and then stood up to go for the food. Before entering the house he extended his hand to George and said, "By the way, I'm looking forward to you standing up for me at my wedding next month."

George's mouth flew open while grasping onto his hand. "So…you decided to go through with it, huh?"

"What more can I do? I do love her. Besides, there's no guarantee that she's not the love of my life, right? She's the mother of my child and a good person. I would probably be a fool not to nab a woman like that." He tried to convince himself as he entered the house.

Joseph found the plastic plates right next to the macaroni and cheese pie. He could hear the voices of women echoing from the other side of the wall so he was quick to dip up his food before being seen by anyone. After taking a large portion of the pie, he grabbed a fork and rushed back outside. The pie was good! It was so good that when George told him that there was another pie in the oven, he went back for seconds, and then thirds.

He and George sat there eating and discussing his wedding plans. Joseph decided that he should call Veronica and give her the good news, but then remembered that he already did. It was he who had been struggling with the idea all day, not her.

George heard his mother's voice ring out and he went into the house. He was gone before Joseph could ask him for something to drink. If you eat enough macaroni, it'll dry up your mouth, and that's exactly what it had done to his. When George didn't return right away, he decided that it would be alright for him to get something to drink out of the refrigerator.

When he opened the refrigerator, he saw all kinds of food in there; good stuff too; puddings, pies, cakes, soda's, even beer. "Damn," he thought. "George's mom sure eats a lot."

He had his head completely inside the refrigerator looking for something else to consume, when he sensed someone standing behind him. He smiled to himself, thinking he would see ugly George's face when he looked up, so he took his time on purpose. When Joseph finally did turn around, he noticed a pair of legs that George couldn't fit into, if his life depended on it.

His gaze continued upward to curvaceous thighs, hips, waist and breasts. Finally when he saw the face that went along with the body, he was speechless. It was obvious that she was speechless too.

When George entered the kitchen and happened to walk in on them, they both reacted as though they had just been caught fucking on the kitchen table.

(7) – Gregory – Outta Control

"Give me another!" Gregory snapped to the bartender as he slouched in his bar stool. He was quickly becoming a regular at this little dive located around the corner from Thomas Child Incorporated, in Downtown Los Angeles and it was obvious that he was already worn out from his new responsibilities as CEO at TCI.

The bartender, conveniently named Sam, eyed him suspiciously then poured him another glass of brandy. Feeling a little awkward, he was quick to walk over to the other end of the bar and tend to the unruly bunch of men gathered there. Hard hats and after five shadows were the prerequisites for entry into this dive, not Armani suits, which is why Gregory stood out like a sore thumb.

Gregory just sat there staring at his reflection in the mirror behind the bar, looking into lifeless eyes and trying his best not to think about his chaotic existence. He did not go to the bar every day after work to get drunk, he used it as an excuse not to go home, where he would also have to fill his father's shoes. That is exactly how he felt he was expected to behave, like his father.

Everyone at TCI expected him to behave as his father did, and expectations were put on him when he returned home in the evening, as well. So he developed a routine, whereas he would put on a disguise at work, but by the time he reached home he would be a totally changed man...buzzed! Though things had begun to return to normal after the death of his father, he still felt the pressures being placed on him as the new head of the family.

After the reading of the will, everyone involved became familiar with the enormity of Thomas' holdings for the first time. No one ever anticipated the compensation that they would receive from his death. Gregory, himself, was still in shock over the news of the large trust funds that were left to him and his brother and sisters.

Thomas Childs was obviously a very successful man, more so than anyone imagined, except for Timothy Callahan. Perhaps Sara had an idea of the enormity of his holdings, Gregory suspected, because she had been hanging around quite often, since the death of her ex-husband.

Theresa, on the other hand, was delighted that their mother was becoming a constant in their lives. Gregory had allowed Sara to visit the house on a few occasions to see Theresa and Jeremy. He would always conveniently excuse himself from the premises whenever she made her famous appearances. Louise on the other hand, kept a close eye on the comings and goings of Sara Childs. She had her own reasons for not trusting this woman.

Soon after the funeral, she overheard Sara asking Theresa why it was that Louise continued to live in the Childs family house when she was not a Childs herself. Theresa, not being too wise on interrogations, said innocently, "I don't know. But now that I think of it, all of her mail has said Louise Childs for as long as I can remember."

Louise couldn't help but smile when she overheard this sweet child tell her own mother, in so many words, that she was indeed a Childs...she *was* family. No one had ever mentioned the possibility of a common-law marriage between Thomas and Louise; quite frankly the subject never came up. But that *was* the case.

She had been using her lover's name for more than a decade, which is why she and Thomas didn't find it necessary to get married. And she had been living with them for so long that the thought of her leaving after Thomas' death never crossed anyone's mind, except for Sara's. Louise took great pleasure in seeing the expression on Sara's face when she realized that a common-law marriage had been in effect for years.

Gregory didn't want any part in the potential for a cat fight in their home, which is why he found it easier and easier to hang out in a bar after work. He hadn't forgiven Sara for her lack of being a mother to him and the others, and he sure in the hell wasn't about to make any exceptions for her, especially not right now.

He looked down into his empty glass, then back at his reflection in the mirror. All he could see was his father...taking one last gulp of air before dying. Damn! The significance of seeing someone die, especially a parent, is a trip! Gregory should have been seeing a therapist the day after...didn't anyone notice?

He took his family and the family business very serious, but hell, he was still a young man who was entitled to have some fun. Nobody seemed to want to let him have any these days. Everybody was always asking him, how is the business is going? How is the transition with the knowledge of the business going? How is the knowledge with the business records going?...and this, that, and the other; blah blah blah? Nobody ever asked him about him.

This bar, this dive, this hole in the wall, was the only place for him to go to forget about everything and be himself. His social life, since returning to L.A., had ceased to exist and he was trying desperately to create one.

As he sat at the bar listening to the scratched record in the background, he wondered about the woman that he should be sharing his life with...someone that could put some meaning back into it. He thought about a puppy too, but soon thought that people would think it strange if they saw him cuddling with a puppy. What the world didn't realize is that he was desperate to have the kind of love that perhaps only a puppy could deliver.

The desire to find the meaning of life was at the forefront of his mind and he believed that a woman, to go along with his status and his growing addictions, was the key. However, underneath it all was quite disturbing; the idea of suppressing his very "bad thoughts" with the help of something, or someone…perhaps the ideal woman would solve all of his problems.

There were always a few women at TCI giving him the eye, but he decided it best not to pursue women working at his company. And though Gregory isn't a shy man, he isn't very forward when it comes to women either. Considered a catch, the only thing he knew how to do was to wait for a woman to give him a clear signal that she wanted him to approach her.

Having lived in New York for the last six years, he was quite used to having women, pretty much demand something of him, if that's what they wanted. Upon returning to California, he wondered if the women would be just as aggressive. He thought, perhaps his New York demeanor was written all over him and no California women would be attracted to it.

Every now and again a female customer at the bar would approach him, but he figured them to be prostitutes, since that was the type of neighborhood he was frequenting. Who did he think he was fooling? He was sitting in the middle of skid-row; and he just knew there were hookers looking to give him HIV. His paranoia sank in and he cringed at the thought!

Wearing an Armani suit and driving a convertible Jaguar was normal for executives who worked in the high rises a few blocks away, but they were not common-place here, in the area that he was frequenting so often, but he didn't care. Perhaps deep down inside he wanted someone to mug him or steal his car to give him a reality check. Let's face it, he found it difficult confronting this new role of his.

He didn't ask to be the CEO of a mega-corporation; he didn't ask to be rich; he didn't ask for any of it and would rather have it all taken away than to have all of this responsibility fall on his troubled shoulders.

His thoughts were floating all over the place as the sun set behind the concrete skyline and the bar filled-up with more weirdoes by the minute. Most of their attentions were focused on him and his fancy suit as he sat at the bar alone. They didn't know what to make of him. Some of them thought that he had amnesia and didn't know who or where he was. Others speculated amongst themselves that he was an undercover cop waiting for his informant. But most of them figured that he was down-and-out and on the verge of committing suicide.

But, because no one in the dive could figure him out, he was safe from them, for now. Sam kept the gossip going. He over-exaggerated every word Gregory spoke, every move Gregory made, and because most of the people there had no real lives of their own they all listened.

After a while, people in the bar started speaking to him and treating him like he was an alright guy. Gregory was getting a kick out of his little secret life. He thought about everyone that knew him. "If they all could see me in here, they'd shit themselves!" This new found alter ego was responsible for leading him to some pretty hot night clubs in the city too.

He began going out on the town all of the time, and his nights after work became longer and longer. His family was not very vocal about the transformation that was coming over him. He surmised that they knew the transition in all of their lives would bring about changes in their routines. And for the most part, they were grateful that Gregory had not exploded with the amount of stress in his life.

However, they were not aware that Gregory was not handling it very well. He was taking pills, drinking entirely too much and had begun a very reckless spending habit. He also began frequenting ritzy night clubs. The more he went to them, the more women he began to meet. But, he wasn't stupid enough not to know that he was meeting so many women because he looked like big money. But, again, he didn't care.

The nightmare of seeing his father die had done so much to him. He was haunted with eerie visions and ghostly sounds that haunted his dreams. The pills were a way to medicate his thoughts, and the alcohol was a way for him to forget and get some sleep. The women were a way to stroke his ego and to reaffirm that he was not just a CEO, but that he was a man.

He was careful not to let his job be effected by his personal life, so he was always on time to work and was always prepared for his meetings. But the whole CEO thing was more time consuming than he had expected, so he relied heavily on information acquired from the independent research company he contracted.

He had nearly become completely dependent on their analysis of the goings on of TCI around the world. And because Gregory was dedicated in preserving the memory of his father, he had to know what he was doing at all times. This was a crucial point in his life and he needed to do everything within his power to do the job that Thomas Childs would still be doing today, if he were alive.

In fact, he was doing such a good job that, Jeremy, in an entirely different office location was often compared to his brother and the amazing job that he was doing. Jeremy could have easily taken this and become jealous and resentful, but he didn't because he knew that his father had made a wise choice in choosing Gregory as the next head of the company.

Although he hated to admit it to himself, even he knew that he was not up to the challenge of running a mega-corporation. So he was content in his managerial position in one of the off-site real-estate companies and learned to take pride in the fact that his brother was controlling all of it.

On occasion, Jeremy and Gregory would double date. Gregory was amused at all of the women that he saw his brother begin to manipulate. At the same time, he was impressionable enough to take on some of the same traits as far as flashing their money.

They were two rich brothers on a mission, trying to conquer as many women as they could, as fast as they could. They ran through women like women run through panty hose, by being young and impetuous. At the same time they were having fun knowing that sooner or later they would probably crash and burn.

Louise sat back watching, the whole time shaking her head in utter disgust at the shenanigans of the Childs brothers. She busied herself by being that missing link to Theresa and the grandchildren and by being strong for the family.

The nights that Gregory went out alone, he would sometimes go to that dive bar on skid-row and have a couple of shots of brandy, while rubbing elbows with some of the fellow "skid-rowdians." Then he would intentionally put the top down on his Jag and head out for some of the finer clubs in L.A. This was becoming an all too familiar routine for him, yet, he was quite enthralled with it all.

One woman he met, Venus, instantly became a fascination with him. She was beautiful. She had the body of a Goddess, the hair of an Angel, the face of a Saint and the eyes of a Queen. Gregory romanced Venus like he had romanced no other woman he had ever known.

He didn't even take the time to notice that she was demanding more of him than any other woman had ever demanded of him. Had he looked closely, he would have known that it was all about his financial status that was dictating the relationship. Before he had acquired all of this money, he was pretty much an average Joe. And even though he always lavished nice things on his women, he had never been able to do it in such a grand fashion before.

But Gregory was not his self these days. He wanted everyone to think that he was in total control of his life, which is what everyone expected of him and that's what he tried to portray.

In this portrayal, he let things get by him that he would not have ordinarily. One of those things was Venus, so skillfully pulling blinders over his eyes. The family watched in disbelief as Venus wrapped him around her pinkie finger and was able to get a car out of him, a new wardrobe out of him, several trips out of the country out of him, jewelry out of him, and anything else out of him that she could form her luscious lips to ask for.

Not convinced that she was in love with him but that the opposite was true, his family said nothing except, for Jeremy of course, who noticed that she was doing to him what he had been doing to women recently. Gregory warded his brother off by telling him that he knew what he was doing. Besides she hadn't even put a dent in his pockets yet.

Little did anyone suspect, Gregory was not as foolish as he appeared. Somehow he knew, sadly, that the only reason for Venus' attention was the fact that he was rich. But again, he didn't care. At this point in time he couldn't distinguish between those who cared for him, or for the money. He included Sara Childs in this group, and attributed Venus to being just like his mother. And so, he reeled her in just as fast as she reeled in him.

Though he looked the part of the fool, he had every intention of dumping her when he was no longer interested in playing the game; just like his mother had done to his father.

In the beginning of the relationship he had no idea that he could be this way. He wasn't himself; he was in another state of mind all together. And thanks to Venus, he had begun to pop pills to keep himself going and to wake himself up in the morning. She demanded so much of him...this Venus, the woman with the angelic name, who was actually a devil in disguise.

Gregory thought he really deserved to be tormented now. He thought he was haunted by the memory of his father since he was feeling the weight of the world falling on his shoulders. "Why me?" is what he asked himself time and time again. He thought he was getting everything he deserved; payback for staying away from home for so many years. So he stayed with Venus and they continued to torture each other.

Sometimes when they went out on the town, he made sure that they were seen by everyone. She, of course, would be wearing something he purchased for her because their "friends" were always watching them. Gregory took these occasions to make the most out of his use for Venus.

Once in one of their favorite restaurants, The Ivy, he invited her to take his penis into her mouth underneath the table. He told her that this would keep the excitement in their relationship, and because she wanted to keep him around, she did it.

Luckily, they were sitting in a booth and she was able to give him head but play it off…somewhat. Gregory, however, always made sure to give away the goings-on underneath the table with his facial expressions. And sure enough, whispers and rumors circulated like wildfire around the restaurant.

Because they were using each other, Gregory always presented every idea to her as her choice; there was no forced entry going on. He knew that she would always agree to do what he suggested because he knew that she was a user, through and through.

By the time he finished with her, he was going to make sure that her reputation was that of a cheap whore. His anger was fueled by the similarities he saw in her and in his mother. Because he felt a sense of hate for his mother and wanted to hurt her, he decided that hurting Venus was the next best thing. So occurrences, such as the one in the restaurant, took place all of the time…all over town.

Sometimes she would take her panties off in the car, before stepping out with him. He liked it when she wore little skimpy dresses so he could actually visualize that she was "commando" underneath. Somehow he was always able to make sure that her body was exposed by as many people as possible during these times. Also, during these times, he suggested intercourse between the two of them in obvious situations such as park benches, the laundry house and even elevators.

On a park bench, in an upscale setting in Century City, he asked her to sit on top of his lap facing him. Because she had no underwear on, he was able to easily unzip his pants and slide his penis into her ever waiting pussy. He wondered if she also knew that everyone around them knew that they were fucking.

In the laundry house, he would sit her on a high counter and stand in between her legs, also unzipping his pants and moving his penis in her. But the elevator was always more of a challenge to Gregory. They would find an elevator to ride up and down until it was the most crowded. He'd back himself into the corner, with her standing in front of him and raise only the back of her dress, exposing her ass to him for penetration. Gregory dogged her in every way he could think of and he paid for it with his wallet.

He was fighting the world, and fighting Venus because of what she represented to him. It was sort of a self-afflicted torture that he was unable to tear himself away from. And he would rather deal with her than deal with his mother, who was coming around the house more and more. The more he tried to avoid her, the more he saw her. In his eyes, she was pathetic; moving in on poor little vulnerable Theresa.

Thank goodness for Louise, who busied herself in the garden and taking care of Thomas' grand-children. She stayed out of their way, for the most part, but was the eyes and ears of that household. Gregory admired her and was pretty perceptive when it came to her. He admired her more than he had ever admired his own mother.

He knew that even though he had avoided Sara, trying to stay far away from her grip, Louise was just around the corner, eyeing the entire situation and knowing everything before it happened, especially when Sara was involved.

His intentions, however, continued with Venus. Jeremy nick-named her, "Venus Fly Trap" and Gregory agreed. Yes, she was a beautiful caramel complexioned woman, but Gregory was tired of playing with her, looks aside. He was suddenly an important man about town, and she was not necessary anymore.

Her Black Barbie boobs and weave eventually played out, so he dumped her. It worked out fine, because as it turned out they were both using each other anyway. She was using him for material gain, and he was using her for orgasms.

He didn't like the person that he was becoming; vain and arrogant, not at all like the thrifty and sincere person he used to be. For the life of him he could not figure out what to do to become a normal, happy person.

He had inherited so much...it was almost inconceivable for him to believe, not just the money, but the power and the status and everything else that went along with being the first born of Thomas Childs. The more he thought about it, the more depressed he got, the more he drank, and the more he did these reckless things. After all the glitter faded, it seemed to throw him into a pit of further depression.

Jeremy, on the other hand, was lucky. He didn't have the enormous responsibility that Gregory had and he played only a minor role in the family business. Yet, he was more comfortable with the family life, because he had remained at home all of his life, while Gregory had fled to New York to escape it.

In a perfect world, Jeremy should have been the first born. He was mentally stronger and more like Thomas Childs than Gregory. But, the fact of the matter is that Thomas left the company in Gregory's hands; family reputation, legacy and all.

"One day, I might need to procreate," Gregory thought. So then, he began to stress about producing an heir. Not immediately, and definitely not with Venus. It could be a difficult thing, trying to find the right woman in this town; one who is kind and sincere...who is not too overbearing, but has a mind and a career of her own. "That would be perfect."

Venus was more of a snake; cold blooded and spineless like no other woman he had ever met before. That was too bad, because he really had had high expectations for her. But she burst his bubble and that made him hard-nosed, and a little bitter...and it probably made him drink even more.

In the meantime, he couldn't help but watch his sister, Lisa with her husband Michael. They were more in love than ever, raising their four children. He wondered if he would ever be so lucky.

He watched Jeremy juggle women around with none of the problems he had experienced. And he watched Theresa; young, innocent and beautiful, getting much action from every young man in the neighborhood. He seemed to be the only one not able to handle being young, black and rich. The walls were closing in on him and it was just a matter of time before things were going to seriously get outta control.

One day at work, he received a surprise visit from his mother, Sara. His secretary was announcing her just as she made her way into his office. He couldn't believe the gall of this woman. He had intentionally avoided her at the house because of his disgust for her, and now here she was forcing her way into his office as though she had some kind of got-damn right! He was furious! "What in the hell is your problem, woman?!" he said spinning around in his chair.

"I want to talk to you right now, young man," she said with authority as she closed the door behind her and headed toward him.

"Young man? Are you losing your mind? I haven't been a young man since you walked out on me 20 years ago."

"You can be angry with me all you want," she said standing across from him "but I'm not going to ignore what I've been seeing and hearing lately."

"What gives you the right to question me about anything, Sara?" He said her name with contempt.

She ignored his attempts to make her feel bad. "Whether you acknowledge it or not Gregory, I am your mother, and I will not stand by and watch you throw your life away. I've seen you around with that whore, and the things I've heard about the two of you is...is disgusting."

Gregory cut her off before she could continue. "Wait...wait...wait! Do you mean to tell me that you've been following me and Venus?

"Of course not, Gregory! There's been no need to follow you two anywhere because you've left behind a trail of sex and drugs and God knows what else. Now, son, I know you hate me but I don't care because I love you and no matter what, I'm going to look out for you now that your father is gone."

"How dare you mention my father to me you bitch!" He lunged forward, looking like a demon about to leap on an innocent lamb. His head and his chest were pounding entirely too fast. He probably should not have taken that second pill this morning.

Sara was startled with fear. She was afraid of her own son; thinking for sure he would leap across the desk and hit her, like he did the day of the funeral. She backed up from the desk. "Gregory, you need help," she whispered. "I know you're on something that's making you act this way. You're angry with me yes, but I can't help that right now. I love you, and I need to help you realize what you're doing to yourself. The drinking...the drugs...and what else baby boy? What else is eating away at you?"

She was speaking in a calm and soothing voice. He just stared at her with confusion in his eyes. "You've turned out to be a fine young man, Gregory. You have always been smart and sensitive…loving and caring. Don't fall down now that you're at the top. Nothing is worth you making those kinds of mistakes; not Venus, not me and not the terrible death of your father."

Suddenly, as though her words had snapped him out of a trance, he stood and began walking towards her. She froze and looked him square in the eyes. He stopped just inches away from her. "What do you know about my problems or what's eating away at me?" He said this in an almost eerie tone.

"I've been there too," she said.

"How can you know what or how I feel, Sara? How can you know how any of your children feel?"

"I know what I know, Gregory. And what I know is that you, in particular, are having a tough time of everything, lately."

"And what else do you know?"

"I know that when the pressures mount, you want to turn and run for cover. I know that you think you have to live up to the reputation of your father, and take care of the family. I know that you are lonely and scared and confused and have been looking for a crutch to help you through, 'cause you're too proud to up and leave…like I did."

He was beginning to understand what Sara was saying to him. "Like you did?"

"Yes, like I did. Living down the reputation of your father is not easy. But living up to the expectations of being a Childs is even harder."

"How can you compare what you went through, with what I'm going through? You were a housewife with the simple job of raising four children. I've been made CEO and the new head of a closely scrutinized family. I don't see the pressures as being the same, Sara."

"Trust me Gregory, they are the same. The fact that what I went through was more than 20 years ago attributes to it. The rolls of men and women were completely different than they are today. And when you're not as strong as the person you are supposed to live up to, it's even harder. I admit, I was not a very strong person in those days, but I did the very best I could under the circumstances."

"What circumstances, Sara?" Gregory watched her with watery eyes. He wanted a real explanation as to the reasons she left her children behind.

She seemed to sense that he was pleading to save his own life. And as she looked back into his desperate eyes, she knew that now was the time to save his life by doing or saying whatever it was that he wanted…needed to hear.

Sara slowly walked over to the sofa and sat down, then extended her hand to her son. Gregory looked at her for a moment before walking in her direction. And though he did not take her hand as she had hoped, he did sit down next to her and faced her, once again.

Sara began by telling Gregory how much she loved Thomas - how when they first met it was love at first sight. In the beginning, it was hard to make ends meet, but Thomas was totally against her taking a job. Instead, it was her job to always look the part of a respected and loyal wife. Sara didn't mind pleasing her husband in this way, but she found herself bored each and every day.

After making Thomas breakfast in the morning before he left for work every day, it took her a maximum of at least one hour to clean the house from top to bottom. For the rest of the day she would try to find other things to do to help pass the time away, but usually ended up twiddling her fingers.

Once she found out she was pregnant, her life lit up like a light bulb. She busied herself with sewing and knitting for the baby. Thomas was pleased as well, but was busy building an empire for his wife and future child. Sara had to work very hard to keep his attention because he worked such late hours. Once Gregory was born, Thomas was the proudest father on earth. He paraded around the hospital, handing cigars to everyone he saw. That's when he first started smoking.

During the day, Sara and Gregory were left at home to bond, while Thomas was off purchasing property and making mergers with other companies. Life was fine, but Sara was not the object of her husband's attention. She suspected that he was having an affair, but she didn't have the nerve to ask him.

By nature, Thomas was a harsh spoken man, though he was gentle. And Sara did not want him to think ill of her because of her own insecurities. So she said nothing. Instead, she doted over Gregory by being the best mother that she could be. But it wasn't enough for her. She was still a very young and attractive woman and felt that she was deserving of some attention from her husband. But in those days, women were supposed to stand by their husbands and wait for them to make the first move.

Sara was filled with desires that Thomas either would not, or could not satisfy. This hurt her very much. Because she was so in love with him, she wanted to believe it was because he respected her as the mother of his child, and didn't want to jump at her flesh at every given moment. But the fact of the matter was he simply took her for granted by believing that she would always be there for him. He believed that she would be content while he was off securing a future for the family, no matter how long it would take or the pain it would cause.

Psychologically, Sara could not handle the rejection. She began to have sleepless nights and a loss of appetite. She began to grow thin and pale and started to neglect Gregory. When she finally went to the doctor, he prescribed some medication to help her sleep and to calm her nerves. That was a big mistake. Sara took to those pills like a fish takes to water.

Thomas never knew the extent of Sara's problems, so he ignored her for the most part, though unintentional. Sara knew that Thomas loved her and so she took her pills so that she could cope…so she could take care of her husband and her baby.

Eventually, the pills lost their effectiveness, so she had the doctor double the dosage. By this time, she was hooked. She believed that she had to take the pills. She used the pills as a crutch, just as Thomas used his smoking as a crutch. But he was getting richer by the day and thought that the money was going to make up for everything in their lives.

Soon Lisa was on her way to being born and Sara had a rough time getting off of the pills during her pregnancy. She complained to her doctor, begging him if there was something else she could take that would not affect the baby. The doctor advised her not to take anything during this time, so she had to quit cold turkey for the sake of her child.

The withdrawals added to the misery she was already feeling these days. All the while, she was hiding all of it from Thomas, which was easier than she expected, since she rarely saw him anyway. To top it all off, he purchased a new estate for them in Pacific Palisades, which meant Sara had to pack and leave the neighborhood that was so familiar to her, again.

The current house was perfect for their growing family; one of the only things in her life that was familiar and good. But Thomas wanted to move into a more upscale neighborhood with more upscale homes, so this meant up-rooting the family, again. Movin' on up!

Originally from Cleveland, Ohio, Sara Jackson's people had for years passed for "white," if they chose to. Many of her relatives were able to take advantage and enjoy their lives with less stress, which was what she was missing right now.

After marrying Thomas there was no reason to stay there anymore; his skin color wasn't nearly as light as hers. After being seen around town with him, everyone would certainly know for sure that Sara Jackson was "black."

Gregory was about to turn three years old, and the baby in her womb, (Lisa), was two weeks past her due date. Sara had managed to stay off of the pills during her pregnancy, but the tension was written all over her face.

The doctors finally had to take the baby from her, but Lisa had to stay in the hospital for complications for a month before she was able to come home. Thomas hired a house keeper to help Sara take care of things, but he himself continued to stay away. She was convinced that her husband was having an affair, but she did nothing to stir up trouble in her "fantasy world" of a life. She was used it by now.

The next baby, Jeremy, popped out almost immediately, which was a blessing in disguise, because it kept Sara busy and away from the pills. But she was very fond of Gregory and had a tendency to show him extra love and attention.

Guilt was a factor in this because of the lack of attention she had shown him when he was a small child. But now she showered him with love as if her life depended on it.

They were very close as mother and child and it seemed possible that if anyone could pull her out of a life of depression, it would be him. Lisa and Jeremy were less clingy, and they did not seem to need her as much as Gregory did. However, her relationship with all of her children blossomed.

Prior to their move into their latest and largest Childs family home, Sara found herself pregnant once more. Unfortunately, the pressures of her marriage and her life had caught up with her once again, and she found herself on pills. She was not able to kick the habit, and for the duration of her pregnancy with Theresa she took them.

Thomas was alerted to the situation one morning when she thought he was still asleep. She was taking a pill when he snapped at her, "What are you doing, Sara?"

She was startled and replied, "An aspirin, it's just an aspirin." He immediately snatched the bottle from her hand and read the prescription. He had never heard of the drug before, but knew right away that it was not aspirin, but an amphetamine.

He ranted and raved at her abusively, telling her of the dangers of taking this kind of medication while pregnant. He told her how everything he had done in his adult life was all for her and that she was turning out to not even be worth it. He had said, "Thank God for my children who will inherit my fortune and my good sense, not like their mother!"

This broke her heart. She was not strong enough to hear him talk to her this way. It should have been obvious that she was not strong enough for much of anything he did to her. He forbade her to take anymore pills and told her that he would deal with her further, after the birth of their child.

When they had moved into the grandest home that any of them had ever seen, Thomas immediately moved into a separate bedroom. Sara had finally lost her husband in the way that she needed the most.

Deep down inside, she could still feel the love between herself and Thomas, but it was so hard for him to show his emotions. She dealt with it as best she could and tended to her four children like a prominent housewife should. Sara didn't dare take pills anymore, she was too afraid of the consequences. Instead she retreated into herself, relying more and more on her one true comfort...Gregory.

Though she knew she was exposing her son to emotional stress, she couldn't help herself. He was the only one that she could really talk to, though he was just a child. But he loved her unconditionally and that tugged at her heart like nothing else.

He was a fine young boy, who, like all of her children, had received traits from both herself and Thomas. They were not light enough to look "mulatto" but inherited that beautiful light brown sheen of their father. "That, along with their black "good hair" was a relief for Sara.

Eventually Thomas moved back into their bedroom and things finally started to look up for the family. Thomas' company had grown and expanded considerably and was soon incorporated, and Sara, for the first time in her marriage was totally fulfilled. She had a large spacious home to tend to during the day and four restless children who kept her busy during the afternoon. She was in mother heaven.

Theresa was blessed with good fortune, as the drugs Sara took while pregnant with her had no real effects on her. Yes, she was timid and soft spoken, but so was Gregory and Sara took no drugs while pregnant with him.

Because Sara was so blissful in her current life, she began to plead with Thomas to quit smoking. She herself hated the smoke and the smell, and was convinced that eventually something bad would happen to him. But Thomas being a smart ass told her to keep her pretty head out of his business. She dropped the subject and never brought it up again.

When things were at their most perfect, Thomas dropped a bomb on Sara. He told her that he would be expanding Thomas Childs Inc., worldwide and that he needed to leave the country for an unspecified length of time. Sara was too through!

For the first time, she spoke up to her husband, telling him that she forbade it! She went on to tell him that she had been the perfect, doting wife and mother for years, and had been treated like shit as a result of it! Never before had she told him that she suspected him of having affairs over the years until now. And she even brought up her years of drug dependency, and blamed it on his lack of attentiveness toward her and the children. When she was done venting all of the complaints she had about him, he excused himself and left the house. She was certain that she had lost him forever.

When Thomas didn't return home for three days, Sara thought she would lose her mind. She had no idea how she was going to take care of four children with no job skills. Thomas could be a very cruel man when he wanted to be and she thought he might make her situation destitute. The love between the two of them seemed damaged beyond repair, so Sara made a decision that was meant to secure the future of her children. When, through a friend, she discovered that

Thomas was coming home, she packed her bags, wrote that damn letter, and left!

To her, this was the only way Thomas would be forced to be a father to his children. She knew if she were gone, he would not be able to leave the country for business and the children's futures would be secured. If she stayed, she was sure he would someday leave her and the children penniless. Either way, a life of faking it, undiagnosed depression, and addiction to prescription medication was no way to live. At least she thought so at the time.

Sara really thought that she was doing the right thing by leaving behind her life, so that her children could have one. But she wasn't thinking of the hundreds of other consequences that would arise...how could she? Sara had always exhibited questionable behavior.

When Sara finished the story of her years as Thomas Childs' wife, Gregory sat there in utter disbelief. He had never heard, "back in the day" stories about his parents before. When his mother ended her explanation of events she looked him square in the faces to see if she could find any compassion in her son's eyes.

Gregory didn't know how to respond to what his mother had just told him. He didn't know if he should embrace it as truth or to throw it out as mere fiction. He stood and paced across his lengthy office. Now and again he would look in her direction and then turn away.

Sara was still a very beautiful woman. He tried to imagine her living as a stay-at-home mom raising four small kids. Even though he knew that his father was a hard man, he wasn't sure he could just take her word for anything since Thomas wasn't there to defend himself.

Sara could no longer bare the silence. "Gregory, do you understand where I'm coming from, baby...or at least where I've been? I left your father because of deep problems I had with myself. I didn't handle those problems very well and I made a lot of mistakes along the way. But you know how he could be sometimes. He could make you feel worthless in trying to live up to him.

I could have killed Theresa because I was hooked on pills while pregnant with her, all because I couldn't cope with your father. Now, I'm not blaming him; I blame no one but myself for not being a stronger person. I wish I were a stronger person so that I could have stood up to your father and kept our family together."

Gregory stared out of his window and without looking at her asked, "You and I were close?"

She smiled. "Yes. We were very close."

"How did you stay off of the pills?" he asked.

"Well," she said with a sigh, "I gave up my children to give them a better life, but I didn't want to die in the process. So I guess you could say I quit for my kids. But believe me, the moment I drove away seeing your little face in the window, I knew I was making a mistake that had to be made.

I could have easily used my situation as an excuse to fall deeper into the pit; I came close many times, too. That's why I left the country. It was too easy for me to be tempted to do drugs in this country as opposed to other countries. I didn't leave because I didn't love you...I left so that I could stay alive to keep an eye on you."

"Why couldn't you and our father work out custody arrangements, or something? Kids do need both parents, ya know?"

"Gregory, by the time I was sure that your father was going to take care of you kids the right way, I was just on my way to recovery. A couple of years went by and the next thing I knew Louise was in your lives. He wouldn't let me come around much anymore after that. I watched you all from a distance...not saying much of anything over the years. I knew that I had given you up and that I had to pay the price for it."

"Why are you telling me all of this now, Sara? Are you afraid that I'm going to marry a whore, like Venus and get strung up on pills, and lose control of my life?"

"Yes, something like that. Gregory, first of all you must understand that you and I are more alike than you know. I think we both have dependency tendencies, and so we have to be careful. I've been watching you very closely and you have not been handling the loss of your father very well at all."

He turned to face her for the first time. "What in the hell do you expect? My father was a great man."

Sara stood and approached her son. "Yes, he was. Are you up to the challenge of living his reputation down? That's what it all boils down to, Gregory. Let me help you. If anybody knows what you're going through, it's me."

"What makes you think I need your help?"

"You don't need my help, but you need somebody's. I can see that you're speeding right now. I know how pills can make you feel. I know that you drink entirely too much at night. I know Gregory. Why not let someone who knows, help you? Why not me?"

He stood there, speeding just like she had suggested, unable to think clearly, but somehow knowing that she was speaking the truth. "How did you know?"

Sara took one step closer to her son and took his hand in hers, knowing that she was taking a terrible chance of being rejected or worse, being hit. "Easy baby."

She inched even closer and slowly reached up to place her arms around his neck. "I got you son. I'm not letting you go this time!"

(8) – Jax – Tired Of The Pain

I've got to get a new alarm clock. Here it is, Monday, and I'm running late for work again. To top it all off, I woke up with my period and now I'm sick as hell. Karma!

Every month I receive each and every symptom that a woman can have with her period; the bloating, the cramps, the nausea, the headaches, the irritability, the muscle aches, and the list goes on and on. To add to the list, I can't find a damn thing to wear because none of my skirts fit around my bloated waist today. All of my blouses are hugging too tight around my swollen breasts, and it's too hot to wear slacks.

So I go through my closet throwing everything off their hangers in search of an outfit that I can wear on a scorching hot day, while running extremely late for work, while on my period, worried to death about how weird Vincent's been acting lately, and trippin' off that fine ass man I just met the other day. This day has barely begun and already it's fucked up!

Finally, I find my blue polka dot dress…I know, but it was a Christmas gift from my mother. It makes me look like I'm wearing a circus tent, but I don't care. I complete my outfit with some comfortable shoes and run out to my car only to drive myself smack in the middle of a traffic jam. What else is new? I wish they made cell phones that everybody could afford. At least then I could call Harry and tell him, "I'm stuck in traffic but I'm on my way."

Everybody in that office must think I'm crazy. They all think I have Harry wrapped around my little finger, which I do, but I don't exploit it. I mean, what do they expect? I am his daughter, but I'm not taking advantage of the situation, I'm just not a morning person, that's all.

Besides, this "work" thing is new to me and I'm doing the best I can. Actually, I've been working really hard so that no one will think that I'm taking advantage of the situation. If they looked at my work, then they'd know that I'm not squelching, but rather good at my job.

I've been working over-time at every turn and God knows I'm not getting paid for it since I'm salaried. One account in particular, called TCI, has been taking up a whole lot of my time. They must be really lazy over there because they want us to do damn near everything for them.

Investigate this, investigate that...I have the mind to walk over to that office and ask, "What in the hell do you want from us? You use up so much of our time; I should increase your rates and make you our only customer." Yeah, right. I guess I'll just take it all in stride and do the job that I'm paid to do. I don't have a problem with it I'm just being bitchy. Cramps! Hell, in 72 hours when I'm feeling better, I won't even remember today.

While I was sitting there stuck in traffic I couldn't help but think about the weird event that took place with Vincent last week. Ok, ok, we've both been playing games trying to give each other that extra space, so it won't seem like I'm rushing him and he won't feel like he's rushing me. That's fine and dandy, but when you get right down to it, he's my friend first because I really do care about him. That alone is enough for me to be worried about him.

When I stopped by his place last week and I heard him screaming, I knew something was wrong. At his front door, I hesitated going in because I first thought the noises were from him fucking some woman's brains out. But I know his screams of passion and it didn't sound right to me, which is why I used the hidden key over the door frame to go in.

I found him crouched in the shower with scalding hot water running all over his body. Poor baby. He looked so helpless lying there. He must really have received some tragic news, or something. But for the life of me I couldn't make him open up and talk to me.

That pisses me off too; the fact I care enough about him to check up on him and he won't even open up to me and let me know what the hell is going on in his life. Maybe I should just butt out of it all together. I'm kind of tired of the games anyway. I guess that's easier said than done, I don't know. But that guy I met Saturday was gorgeous...just gorgeous enough to make me forget all about Mr. Vincent Cruthers.

That was weird too - the fact that I couldn't even get my mouth to say anything intelligent when we met. I mean, me, Ms. Jacqueline tongue-tied when it comes to a man? I don't think so! But he caught me off-guard, just like one certain other guy I met a while ago.

I was expecting to see some ordinary Joe scavenging for food out of Mrs. Clark's refrigerator but that's not who I saw. Instead, I saw the finest, handsomest, most gorgeous man I had ever seen; well, next to Vincent that is. But they're both handsome, in different ways. This guy had a more rugged exterior about him. More manly, I think.

I'll never forget the way he looked at me. I'll never forget the way I felt, when he looked at me. Oh, God, I'll never forget how embarrassed I felt when his friend walked up on us and saw us looking at each other. I thought I would die!

Good old mom. Thank goodness she met some lady on one of her turn-around trips to Vegas, who happened to invite everybody on the bus to her crystal party. And it's a miracle that I even tagged along with her to the party. But as it were, things turned out just fine. Now If only I could figure out a way to find him so I can see him again. I know that he was there with Mrs. Clark's son, which makes my mission a little tricky.

Thirty minutes later pulling into the office parking lot and feeling sick as a dog, I finally realize that I don't have any Advil. Oh my God, I'm gonna die! There is no way I can get through the day, let alone the first day of my period without any Advil. So I had to turn back around and head for the nearest drug store.

This is an emergency! Midol and Pamprin is mere dog food compared to the painful cramps that I get. This calls for the fillet mignon of pain pills, and fast.

When I got to the drug store, I felt that everybody was looking at me like I was crazy. I thought, "What? Do I have mud on my face?"

Oh my God, I panicked thinking that I must have blood spotting through my dress. So I ran down an empty aisle and turned my dress around and saw that there was nothing there. That's odd. People were probably looking at me funny because I'm green in the face. I feel awful. The best thing for me to do is to grab the pills and a 7-Up while I'm thinking about it, and get the hell out of here.

While standing in line, I'm so overcome with cramps that I buckled over. The cashier asked, "Are you OK?"

"No I'm not. I'm going to have to take these pills right now."

"You can't open those until you pay for them," she said like she owned the damn store.

"Look lady! I'm paying for them now, but I'm also going to take them now. Do you have a problem with that?" I said with an attitude.

She rolled her eyes at me in disgust. That bitch! How dare she give me lip at a time like this. If I had enough strength, I'd ask to see the manager, but I don't have enough strength and I'm late for work. Boy, am I late.

Even after popping the pills with my soda, I knew that I had taken them too late. The cramps had already set in so bad, that by the time the medicine starts to work won't do much good for the first few hours anyway. When I got back into the car I was so uncomfortable that I could barely shift gears. Damn, I knew I should've got an automatic.

Though I can only imagine what labor and childbirth feels like, I bet my cramps come pretty close to both of them. My friends keep telling me, "Once you have a baby you won't have cramps anymore." Screw that!

By the time I made it to the office and got to my desk, I broke out it a cold sweat. Harry wasn't around to interrogate me about being late, so I took this time to try and gain my composure. I really didn't feel well, but I couldn't keep using my cramps as an excuse not to show up for work, even though it was a real problem. I had been to the doctor about my problem and he told me that there was nothing wrong with me.

All of my pap-smear results have come back as normal, so I guess I'll just have to suffer through my child-bearing years. My doctor had even told me about the, "once you have kids theory…" but I most certainly am not going to have a kid just to possibly get rid of some annoying cramps.

I was pissed off that the pain hadn't stopped and was just reaching for those stupid pills again when my phone rang. "Research, Jacqueline speaking."

"Hey, girl It's me."

"Hey hey Sabastian. What's going on?"

"Nothing girl. I was calling to see if you want to do lunch today."

"No, I don't think I can. I've got tons of work to do, plus, I just walked in the office a few minutes ago."

"Oh, so you have it like that, huh?" she said jokingly. "You can stroll into the office anytime you feel the urge."

She was beginning to annoy me, but I kept my cool because I knew it was the cramps. "No Sabastian, I don't have it like that, I really woke up late. I think the problem is my alarm clock is not going off. I need to buy another one pronto, but not today 'cause I'm sick as a dog."

"What's wrong?"

"Cramps."

"Wow, you really suffer bad with them, don't you?"

"Yes, I really do," I said to her in the most pathetic voice I could muster up.

"Well, I'm one of the lucky ones. I don't have any pain or bloating, what so ever. As a matter of fact, I carry a supply of tampons with me everywhere I go because I never have the slightest warning of when my period is going to come. I guess some of us are just lucky, huh?"

"I guess so." I got off the phone with her as politely as I could. She can be infuriating sometimes, but that's just Sabastian. I swear that girl is weird.

After my conversation with Sabastian I picked up the closest file on my desk, opened it and got to work. I could barely concentrate on the work in front of me, let alone think about the looks and snarls I was receiving from the people working around me.

Apparently, one girl in particular, Pam, was vocalizing her disapproval of my position. From the very beginning she never seemed to take a liking to me. She was one of the clerks in the department and had verbally expressed, to several other co-workers she thought it unfair that Harry had brought in his step-daughter to become office manager over everyone else who had all been working here longer than me.

I got wind of the office talk since the day I started, but I decided not to let that affect my work. I knew that I had worked hard in school and graduated with the intentions of coming to work with Harry. And as long as he was pleased with my performance and as long as I did not take advantage of the situation, I was not going to let any of the talk get me down. Aside from that, I had so many other things going on in my life, that this little girl Pam didn't even scratch the surface of my interest. However, on this particular day I was not going to let her get away with her obvious subordination.

I went down to personnel and grabbed her file. I never had the opportunity to get to know her, like some of my other co-workers, because she was always so distant with me.

So my reason for getting her file was to see her background within the company.

As I looked through her file I noticed that on a couple of occasions she had been previously written up for similar acts of insubordination. Nothing serious, but it was pretty obvious to me that she had a personality problem.

I buzzed Harry and asked him if I could come into his office and speak with him about her. He said, "Yes," and so I took the file and headed for his office. Everyone's eyes were affixed on me as I walked into his office. They knew that I had just left out of personnel and I had a file with me. I'm sure they were all wondering whose it was.

"Good morning, daddy," I said as I closed the door behind me.

He smiled as he swiveled around in his chair. His short, salt and pepper colored hair matched his grey pin-striped suit perfectly. My step-father was as cute as a button.

"Daddy huh? You wouldn't just be saying that because you were late, would you?"
Damn, he did notice. "I really am sorry about that. I take full responsibility and I'm going to buy myself a new alarm clock on my way home."

"Well, you're getting the job done honey, that's why you're the manger. So what's that in your hand honey? What's going on?"

"I've been holding something back for a few months, and I don't want things to get out of hand with any of the employees. Rumor has it that Pam Watson doesn't think it's fair that your step-daughter has become office manager."

"Pam Watson? Pam Watson?" he said as he drifted back in thought, recalling her work record. "Oh. What has she done now?"

"She hasn't done anything yet, I just want to keep it that way. She's openly rude to me and verbalizes to her co-workers that she doesn't like the fact that I came in out of the blue and got this position. She's seems to be highly resentful of that. Did you promise her this position before I came on board?"

"No, she doesn't qualify for your position. As a matter of fact, I took a special interest in hiring her in the first place because she had a baby at home and couldn't seem to find a job anywhere else."

"Well, I don't understand what the problem is. I get along with everyone else in here, and she's doing alright with her work habits but can you tell me why there are two letters in her file, in regards to subordination?" I asked as I handed her file to him.

"I don't recall any particular occurrences other than her having a smart mouth," he said as he took the file from me and glanced through it with disinterest. "She's probably a little envious of you too. Ms. Jones had to deal with her in the past, and so I pretty much let her reprimand anyone that needed it and I followed up on it later.

Ms. Jones was an older motherly type of woman, who posed no threat to anyone in here, but you are a different story, being so young I mean. But here, you are in charge, so you can come up with your own conclusions." He looked at me, and with a stern voice he said, "I've given you a big responsibility Jax, I want you to use professionalism in your judgment. And because I have a lot of faith in you, and I know you're a good kid…pardon me, a good young woman, I'm going to leave those details up to you. We'll go over any final decisions together, OK?"

"OK." With that done, I turned to leave and was overcome with another terrible cramp in my side. I grabbed my stomach and quietly moaned.

"Hey baby girl, what's wrong?" he asked with concern.

"It's a female thing. You wouldn't understand."

"Oh, you forget I lived in the same house with you. I do understand. Maybe you should go lay in the lounge, or go home if you're feeling too bad."

"Yeah, I might do that, but I really don't want to go home unless it's absolutely necessary. I have so much work to do, and I want to get caught up before I go home."

"Well, you do what you gotta do and I'll see you later. I'm going to be out of the office for most of the day. If you need me, call me on my cell phone."

Ok, thanks daddy. I'll take care of everything around here." I left out of his office and returned to my cubicle. I could see Pam staring at my every movement. I sat behind my desk and opened her file. I intended to read every scrap of paper regarding this girl, which was making for some interesting reading, even though I could barely keep my concentration due to the pain and discomfort I was encountering.

She had been reprimanded twice for inappropriate language to figures of authority. She had been told during one of her progress revues, not to stimulate rumors through the office. She had been denied a raise based on these things, and she was turned down for a promotion based on lack of skill which was her own fault, because she did not sign up for a work program last year, intended for those who eventually would be able to move up within the company. Oh, Pam. She had an attitude problem alright, and I'm just the one to put a stop to it.

"Be professional, be professional," I kept telling myself while I tried to gain enough courage to speak to her. I wasn't afraid, or anything, but this was going to be my first confrontation with an employee as an office manager.

I knew that I couldn't just go off on her, or talk trash. It was up to me to set an example of authority and professionalism. Shit! I should just fire the bitch and be done with it! But I put her file to the side, deciding that I would talk to her at the end of the day.

I got to work on my computer, updating files for TCI. For a while I forgot that I wasn't feeling well. I was able to complete the TCI file with the information that Harry investigated for them. He was working very hard on this account, which was taking up most of his time…actually it was taking up most of everybody's time. And just because I was able to do the updating today, by no means, means that there's not going to be more to update tomorrow.

We were finding out a lot about this company as the months went by. That Thomas Childs was a smart man…sneaky too. He had business ties all over the place that the new CEO was just now finding out about. I wouldn't be surprised if he was in with organized crime, or something. But that's probably just my over active imagination at work.

When I saw Pam walk by and roll her eyes at me, I knew that wasn't my imagination, so I got up and followed her. When I walked into the bathroom behind her, I was glad to find that we were alone. I decided to initiate a conversation with her.

"How are you this morning, Pam?" I asked with a half-ass smile on my face.

She turned from primping in the mirror to look at me. "Fine, but the morning is all but over." After she said that, she walked out of the bathroom before I had a chance to say anything. That girl really doesn't like me.

I thought about going after her, but realized that I had to throw-up instead. Running into one of the stalls, I fell to my knees hoping that I could throw-up quick and painless, but nothing happened. I stayed on my knees for what seemed like hours but still nothing happened.

My head was spinning in every direction like I was going to pass out. I was sweating and panting so hard that I was hardly able to keep my balance. My elbows kept slipping off of the toilet seat, too. I felt horrible. I wanted to die. Finally, I heard someone enter the bathroom. Hoping no one would see me in this pitiful position, I tried to close the stall door, but I didn't even have enough energy to do that.

I heard a voice say, "Jacqueline, are you alright?"

I could barely shake my head in response to Vivian's question. She approached me and started to rub my back. "If you're sick you should go home," she said in a motherly voice.

I was finally able to answer her. "I know, but I can't seem to be able to get to my feet."

With that, she helped me up and walked me over to the sink. "Here," she said turning on the water. "Splash some water on your face. That should help you to feel a little better."

I did what she told me to do. "The only thing that's going to make me feel better is if I do throw-up."

"What's wrong? Do you have the flu or something?"

"No," I said looking at her with a pitiful and dripping wet face. "I'm on my period."

"Oh my God! I thought my daughter was the only one who has a bad time with her period and cramps and all."

"No, apparently not," I said, trying my best to smile at her. I then asked Vivian if she would have the completed TCI file couriered to their office, because I was going home. After she agreed I went to my desk to get my purse.

On my way out of the office I saw Pam staring at me once again. She was standing at someone else's desk, whispering something to them as she looked at me. I hesitated, and as sick as I was, I walked over to her and said, "Pam, my office at 8:00 tomorrow morning for a meeting."

"In your cubicle you mean?" she said with an attitude. The girl she had been talking to turned her attentions to a file cabinet, avoiding my gaze.

"Yes," I said with a fake smile. "Don't be late," I said as I turned to walk away.

"I never am."

I ignored her and continued to walk out of the building. She's got a lot of balls. I wonder if the state has enough money for her in her unemployment insurance account.

While trying my best to contain my disgust for this girl, I got in my car and headed for home. Like a fool, I jumped back on the 405 freeway from hell. There I was, stuck in traffic, inching my way home between first gear and neutral and nauseas...again.

I began to pray to God that he would not let me throw up now. There was nowhere for me to do it. I certainly couldn't do it out of the window. Gross. How in the hell could I have left out of the office without a plastic bag, or something? That damn Pam had me all worked up, that's how.

At last, the traffic broke and I was able to drive at a pace of around 45 mph. I kept on praying that I would make it home in time. There was a man driving along side of my car, motioning to me, winking, blowing kissing and whistling at me. Usually, I would be flirting right back, to the cute one's that is, but I was not in the mood today.

I wanted to be with Vincent right now. He was the one who rubbed my back and re-filled my hot water bottle for me. I wish that he was here taking care of me, driving me home through this chaos, but he's not. He's been off trippin' somewhere, doing God knows what, to God knows who.

The closer I get to that man the more distance he puts between us. And the closer I got to my house, the sicker I felt. Finally, I couldn't keep swallowing down the urge to throw-up, so I did.

Driving down the freeway with both hands on the steering wheel, I had no choice but to throw-up in my lap. I couldn't turn my head to do it on the passenger seat, because I might have run into another car or worse yet, off of the road...the same with trying to do it out of the window. I had no choice but to do what I did. And it didn't stop there.

I regurgitated over and over and over again, up-chucking food from last week that had apparently been sticking to my ribs. I threw-up every ounce, every drop of fluid in my weak body. This was the most disgusting thing that had ever happened to me in my life.

After I was finished, I spat out the remaining bitter taste in my mouth. I looked around at the cars passing me by, and was surprised to see that no one had noticed. I was at least thankful for that.

When I looked down at my lap and saw that bubbling sea of brown, lumpy goop, I was relieved to see that it was all swimming in the middle of my ugly dress and none of it had dripped onto my car seat or the floor, yet. I drove as fast as I could to get home before the goop started to drip through my pantyhose and into my crotch.

I was lucky to make it home in one piece and to not have spilled one drop of vomit. After pulling into the driveway, I very slowly inched my way out of the car, so I wouldn't drop any vomit. I scooped up my blue polka dot dress in front of me.

This reminded me of how my Grandmother used to carry freshly picked string beans in the front of her apron to the kitchen sink. I walked over towards Mom's rose bushes, grabbed the water hose and watered myself down on the front lawn.

Old Mr. Johnson from across the street was watering his lawn. He looked over at me in dismay. Lucky for me he's very old with limited hearing and I'm sure his eyesight is no better. I didn't care though, because I wanted to rinse off my clothes of that disgusting stuff before I tracked it into the house. In doing so, I ruined my dress, my pantyhose and my shoes. That outfit was goofy anyway. It's probably the reason I got sick in the first place.

I dragged myself into the house, up the stairs, out of my clothes and into my bed. Each and every step was painful and exhausting, but I managed to drag my wastebasket next to my bed. Thank goodness it was already lined with plastic. I had a feeling I wasn't through with throwing-up.

I tried to dose off to sleep but my head was spinning, so I took three more Advil. The bottle specifically says, "Do not exceed eight pills in a 24 hour period." Fuck that! I needed quick relief and I wasn't getting it fast enough.

I thought about calling Vincent so he could come over and baby me like he usually did when I wasn't feeling well. I missed him. I hadn't seen him since I got him out of his shower and put him to bed. He didn't say two words to me, but at least he didn't reject me or push me away. I know he's feeling better now, I've talked to him since then but I haven't seen him. I want to see him now, so I picked up the phone and called him.

To my surprise a woman answered the phone. This threw me off because one of the rules in Vincent's house was that no woman was to ever answer his phone, not even "special" me. So I figured that it must be his mother or sister, or somebody. "May I speak to Vincent?" I asked in a sweat voice. In contrast, she had a bad attitude and answered me by saying, "Who is this?"

Just what I needed, more attitude from another bitch. "Tell him Jax is calling."

"Hold on."

I heard her throw down the phone and start to mumble something to him in a highly agitated voice, but I couldn't understand what she was saying, though I could imagine. Vincent picked up the phone. "Hi baby."

"Hi back. Who was that?"

"Nobody."

Damn. If I was her, I'd slap the shit out of him. I didn't hear a smack, so I guess she didn't.

"Vincent I don't feel well. Come take care of me," I said talking like a baby.

"If only you knew Jax. I don't feel well either," he said down and out.

"Well what's wrong? You won't talk to me. Let me help you. Let's take care of each other."

"I don't think anybody can help me with my problem," he said in his most depressing voice yet.

"I don't like the sound of that Vincent. Look, regardless of where our relationship is going, we're friends, and if you need me all you need to do is tell me and I'll be there for you. Will you be there for me?"

"I want to be."

"Vincent, dump the tramp and get your buns over here."

He chuckled and said, "I'm on my way."

I love testing his will for me over other women. And nine out of 10 times I was satisfied. He told me time and time again, that I was the one he cared for most. And if I needed him, he would drop any other woman like a hot potato.

Well, he hasn't declared his undying love for me, or anything like that, but he was my friend even though he was an ass hole most of the time. I wasn't about to let some cheap harlot make me more upset than I was already, due to today's earlier events. Besides, I knew Vincent better than almost anyone, and I knew how far I could push him. I didn't expect much, but I pushed a hell of a lot anyway.

When he got to my house, I was so happy to see him. It really made my day that he came over at my request. The fact that he had a woman over his house when he agreed to come over topped it off with a cherry. "Hi honey," I said as I opened the side door.

"Hi there yourself." He walked in and kissed me on the cheek. He looked me up and down, observing me in my robe. "Don't tell me, you're on your period, huh?"

"Oh, you've got my calendar all figured out, do you?"

"That's my job, isn't it?"

He grabbed hold of me and we walked upstairs into my room together. He pulled back the covers to my bed while I climbed in and he climbed next to me. He stroked my head and my cheek, as we laid there together, in silence just being close to each other. I knew he had a lot of things on his mind, but I didn't want to scare him off. So I said nothing. I just let him hold me as I drifted off to sleep.

When I opened my eyes, Vincent was sitting across the room observing me. When I asked how long he had been sitting there, he answered, "Not long. I just want to remember you this way - looking so sweet and innocent."

I thought what he had just said to me sounded more dramatic, because I was just waking up from a deep sleep. In any case, I shrugged it off and said, "I didn't mean to fall asleep on you and keep you here for nothing. I just wanted to see you. If you have things to do, you can go."

He stood and walked towards me and said, "I don't have anything more important to do, but I am going to let you get some rest. I know you have to go to work tomorrow and you'll want to feel better by then." He pointed to my barf basket and said, "I'm just glad I didn't have to witness anything fowl. I saw what happened to your outfit floating in your bathtub." We laughed.

I asked him if he wanted to go see a movie tomorrow night and he said, "Yes." So we agreed that he would pick me up at eight o'clock. He wanted to see the movie "Philadelphia." That's the movie where Tom Hanks portrays a man with AIDS. I thought it was sort of a sad choice, but Vincent wanted to see it.

In the morning, I had my mother wake me up at six o'clock. I wasn't about to be late for work and miss my eight o'clock meeting with Pam. I was looking forward to this meeting. Besides that, I was feeling much better, having consumed half the contents of my Advil bottle.

When I arrived at work, there was hardly anyone there. I noticed that Pam hadn't arrived yet, so I went to my desk. I found a letter from Vivian saying that she had completed the task that I had asked of her the day before, and that there were no problems in the office for the remainder of the day. I was grateful for Vivian, in having a mature woman in the office that was hard working and dedicated to my step-dad, just as much as I was.

When I was sorting out papers on my desk, I noticed that I hadn't put away Pam's personnel file. I felt stupid thinking anyone who walked in here could have easily seen that I was checking up on her.

That's where my lack of expertise comes in. It had only been a short while for me and I was learning the ropes the hard way. So I shrugged off the thought of anyone having seen the file on my desk, except maybe for Vivian. I was sure I could trust her as far as I can throw her.

At eight o'clock, Pam stomped into my cubicle and said, "You wanted to see me?"

I could hear the attitude already. "Yes Pam, have a seat." She did, at a snail's pace. "Pam," I said in an authoritative tone, "I'm going to talk to you as your manager, I'm going to talk to you as your co-worker, and I'm going to talk to you as a woman. I'm going to do all of the talking first, and I don't want to be interrupted. When I'm finished you can say anything that you want to say and we'll have an open discussion.

I've observed you on several occasions doing a lot of whispering whenever I happen to be walking by. I'm not paranoid, so I'm not going to justify any paranoia you might think I have in regards to whether or not I think you've been talking about me. That's not the point. The point is I know you've been talking about me, and if you're not, you want me to think that you are. Now whether you are or you aren't really is not the issue. The issue is that it is rude, it's unruly and it's unprofessional and it needs to stop, today.

There's no reason for you to be whispering anything in anybody's ear, or staring someone down when they're walking by. You obviously want them to think that you're talking about them, and you want to be noticed. Well, I've noticed you. I've been patient and I've been very quiet about the entire situation. But I'm going to let you know that I'm your manager and it is my job to make sure that this office functions in a professional and efficient manner, and Pam, I find that you are failing the company with your lack of professionalism.

Now, I'm not going to attempt to get into the reasons that you might have a dislike for me. Whether it's because, I'm new on board or because, I'm new on board and have the highest position in this company other than Harry, or because I'm new on board and have the second highest position in this company and I happen to be the bosses step-daughter.

Whatever the case may be, it's none of your business. The fact of the matter is, what Harry does with his company is Harry's business. And neither you nor I have any say so in that. But I will let you know that Harry has given me a say so as far as you and every other employee in this company is concerned. I have your personnel file here, and I've gone through it very carefully.

I've read that Ms. Jones also thought that you have a personality problem, as I do. She was very lenient with you, because she was a very nice woman, so I hear. But Ms. Jones is no longer here. In her place is me, and I am not going to tolerate it. As far as I am concerned your work record is not strong enough to warrant your personality within this company. So, consider this a verbal warning, that if your attitude does not improve, you should know that your work habits are not strong enough to override that and to keep you employed at Research Limited. Any questions?"

I couldn't believe it when the little bitch didn't have anything defensive to say. She shrugged her shoulders and said, "Is that all?"

I opened her file in front of her and began to write down my comments on a performance sheet. Without looking at her I said, "Yes, you can get to work now."

With that, she stomped out of my cubicle just as she had stomped in. I give up. I'm not going to worry about it anymore. I've done my job by letting her know that I'm the boss and she's a peon. So I returned to the files on my desk and got to work. Later, when I saw Harry, I told him about the talk I had with Pam and he was pleased to hear how I handled the situation.

For the rest of the day, I went on as though nothing had happened. I greeted everyone in the office like I usually did and stayed busy helping people do their jobs. I met with Sabastian for lunch and we had a big laugh about the whole thing.

"I would've fired the bitch!" she said.

"Oh, Sabastian, you can't just fire someone because they're ignorant. You have to give them the opportunity to hang themselves."

"Well, you know she's really talking about you now."

"I don't care. As long as I don't see it or hear about it, that's her prerogative. Besides, look at me, I'm talking about her right now."

"You're a bigger person than me, girl," she said stuffing a fork full of salad into her mouth.

"Everybody is bigger than you, skinny." I smiled at my friend.

I was thankful that my cramps were being controlled with my pills. I had taken so many during the night, I was sure that I wouldn't have any more pain probably for the rest of the week. But as I started getting dressed for Vincent to pick me up, I was sure to put the bottle of pills in my purse anyway.

At eight o'clock, there was no sign of him. Time passed slowly by as I looked out of the upstairs window and still there was no sign of him. I eventually called him at 8:45 thinking that something was wrong. But he answered the phone and said that he was just running late and he would be there soon. Sure enough 9:00 came and went and there was no sign of him.

I was trying to keep myself from getting upset because he said he was coming. If he was going to cancel on me, I'm sure he would have done it by now.

When I called him again at 9:05, his answering machine picked up. I talked into the phone asking him to pick up if he was there, but he didn't. This made me feel a little better by thinking that he was on his way. But when thirty minutes passed by, I was pissed again.

My phone rang shortly after I called him and he was on the other line saying that he had been on his way when he got a flat tire. "That's funny," I thought. "It doesn't sound like he's calling me from a phone booth and he doesn't have a cell phone." But once again, he soothed things over and said that Triple AAA was repairing the tire as we spoke, and that he would be there in 15 minutes.

By 9:45 I was through. I knew something wasn't right and that Vincent was lying to me, so I jumped into my car and headed to his apartment. I timed myself on purpose, and as usual, I got there in almost 10 minutes. I pulled in front of his building and saw his car sitting at the curb and his living room light was on. My adrenaline was pumping. I knew I was about to have a confrontation with him and another woman.

Vincent knew that he didn't have to lie to me about anyone in his life, so the fact that I was about to bust him didn't feel right.

I walked up to the front door and knocked. I heard nothing. I knocked again, and out of my peripheral vision I saw the kitchen window curtains being peeped out of. Seconds later Vincent slowly opened up the front door with a goofy grin on his face. I ignored him and swung open the screen door, walking past him. I swiftly walked into the living room and without having a full view of the room I spoke.

Hi. My name is Jacqueline, what's yours?" As I entered into the center of the living room, I could see that I had not been speaking to myself, as I had guessed I wouldn't be.

"Peaches," she answered with a southern drawl.

I sat down on the loveseat across from where she was sitting and looked at her and smiled. I noticed that the television, not the radio, was on. I also noticed that she was pregnant! "So, what are you two kids watching?" I asked nicely.

Before she could answer, Vincent interrupted. "Jax, can I see you in the kitchen for a minute?"

"Sure," I said with a fake smile, as I stood. "I'll only be a moment," I said to Peaches.

I walked passed Vincent into the kitchen and he closed the door behind him. "Jax, I can explain," he said in a panic.

I exploded! "Explain what!? The fact that you just got caught in a fucking lie, Vincent!? The fact that you're trying to make a fool of me with that tramp bitch sitting in there, probably pregnant with your fucking baby!?"

My voice was getting louder and louder. "I should have known...I should have known that a no good bastard such as yourself can't do right by nobody! Why did you lie Vincent!? Why!?"

He tried to answer me but I didn't give him a chance! "How dare you lie to me and tell me that you're on your way to pick me up and you were sitting in here with her all along! How could you do that!? I guess a better question is why did you do that!? You know that I know that you're a got damn whore! You don't have to lie to me about who, when, where, and what you fuck! And what were you doing with her anyway!? What kind of kinky shit were the two of you doing in here Vincent!?"

Vincent lowered his head and closed his eyes. He didn't want to answer me or either didn't know how. I waited. "Jax you're blowing everything out of proportion," he finally said. "Now calm down and let me explain."

"No! I don't want an explanation! Fuck you and fuck her!" I reached for the kitchen door that he had been leaning on. I pushed him out of my way and rushed passed him heading towards the living room. When I got there, I saw one of Vincent's good friends, Tony, standing there. I didn't know where in the hell he came from but I didn't give a shit either.

I picked up my purse from the sofa and looked at Peaches. Despite all of my choice words for her, I knew she wasn't the blame for Vincent's bullshit.

"It was very nice meeting you," I calmly said with a smile. She was so flushed; I thought she was going to have the baby right then and there. I walked passed Tony and said, "Hi Tony, bye Tony."

I swung the front door open with such force the doorknob connected with the wall and created a huge hole. I pushed open the screen door and nearly knocked it off of its hinges. Boy was I pissed. I was expecting Vincent to follow after me and make me listen to his explanation…he didn't.

When I got into my car, I looked up to see if anyone was watching me from Vincent's front door, but no one was there. I drove away crying my eyes out! The man I cared so much for had just treated me like a piece of shit! To top it all off, he didn't even run after me like they do in the movies. I was so mad I could have thrown-up all over again!

I started driving around the city with no destination in mind. I wasn't about to go home. Instead, I wanted Vincent to try calling me at home and get nothing but my answering machine. My eyes were filled with tears and my heart was pounding a mile a minute. I wanted to hurt him. I wanted to hurt him bad. All of a sudden I got an idea.

I found myself on Mrs. Clark's street in the middle of the night. She was my only link in finding the guy I saw in her refrigerator the other night. I parked across the street from her house and was sad to find that all of the lights were out. Feeling pitiful and rejected, I started to cry again. Hormones right?

Anyway, what the fuck did I think I was doing and how in the hell did I think I was going to ever be able to find him? He probably didn't see anything in me but another skirt anyway. Who was I fooling? I know I was trippin' but I couldn't help myself. My brain knew the deal with Vincent, but I cried anyway.

Much to my surprise, I saw a car pull up in Mrs. Clark's driveway. I watched as two men got out of the car. They both went into the backyard and moments later I saw the back porch light come on. I got butterflies in my stomach even though, I couldn't be sure if the guy I was looking for was one of the two. But I knew that one of them had to be Mrs. Clark's son...or bungling burglars.

I dried my tears and tried to work up enough nerve to walk over to them, but I just couldn't. What kind of excuse could I possibly give for being over here, especially in the middle of the night? I thought about saying that I was having car trouble, or that I left something over here the other day. I got out of the car not knowing exactly what I was going to do, but I was going to meet this guy one way or another. I headed across the street and straight into the backyard. I heard one of the men say, "Hey man, do you here that?"

I took that as my cue to say something before I got shot or beat up. "Excuse me," I said as I entered the backyard like I owned it. "I'm sorry to intrude, but I was just about to leave a note for Mrs. Clark when I saw the light and heard voices back here." As I turned my head towards the porch, I saw him. He was as gorgeous now as he had been the other day. His mouth dropped open when he saw me.

Mrs. Clark's son stood and approached me. "Hi, I'm George. We met the other day."

"Oh yes, I remember. How are you?" I ignored his friend...for now.

"I'm fine. What's this about a note for Ma?"

"Well, I was just leaving from a friend's house when I realized that your mother lives in the same neighborhood. I have to have her recipe for that macaroni pie. It was delicious." I lied. It tasted like shit, but... "So instead of disturbing her so late at night, I was just going to leave her a note."

"OK. I'll give it to her," George said.

"Can you go inside and get me some paper and a pen?"

"Sure, I'll be right back. Joseph, keep the lady company." George disappeared into the house.

Alone at last! "It's you?" I said with a surprised voice.

"What a coincidence," Joseph said to me with a smile on his face.

"Oh, I'm not a believer of coincidences. I believe everything happens for a reason." I could see that he liked me. It looked as though he was staring into my very soul. "So are you enjoying this lovely evening Joseph?" I asked.

"Yes." He had a question mark on his face.

"Jacqueline. My name is Jacqueline."

"Yes, Jacqueline. I'm enjoying it even more, now." Joseph smiled.

"Surely I couldn't be the reason for your new found enjoyment?" I flirted.

"Oh, but you could." He flirted.

"Well, in that case," I reached into my purse and handed him one of my business cards, "call me and we'll discuss it in greater length." He took my card, but not before holding on to my hand for what seemed like minutes, but was actually seconds.

George returned from inside of the house at the same moment Joseph was holding my hand.

Damn! We were busted again.

(9) – Vincent - The Truth-Seeker

Vincent stood silently in the kitchen, shaking his head in utter dismay. He could not believe the scene that had just taken place in his apartment with Jax.

He wanted to storm out after her and try to explain the situation as she had found it, but his head was already filled with too much other shit going on. Plus, he was embarrassed when his friend Tony looked at him with eyes appealing for an explanation. Vincent simply shrugged his shoulders as to say, "I don't know what to tell you, man."

Slowly, he made his way to the front door and observed the hole that Jax had just created in his living room wall. He noticed that the screen door had nearly fallen off of its hinges, as a result of her angry exit. And he could just barely see the rubber marks in the street, made by her speeding car. He had really hurt her this time and was sure he had finally blown his ideal relationship with her.

Late that night when he was finally alone with himself and his thoughts, he resisted the urge to call her. Somehow he knew that she wasn't home or at least she would not answer her phone. He knew how strong of a woman Jax was, or how strong she would like people to believe she was. But he wasn't in the mood to appease *her* ego tonight, he would much rather have his own soothed.

Vincent wanted a woman in his corner who would do for him what he hadn't even asked of her yet. He wanted a woman to know his hurt without him having to tell her. He wanted a woman to take away the pain that he was unable to take away himself. He wanted a woman to do all of these things for him and more. But Jax was not able to fulfill these things for him, nor could any other woman, with the exception of his mother.

Vincent rationalized to himself that he would still need to be in the womb in order to receive the kind of attention he craved. If only that could be achieved for a while…to be back in the womb, safe and warm, and not able to use the penis that had been used so many times before – "the penis that is causing me so much grief now," he thought.

Oh, how he wished "it" could still be one-inch-long and useless, instead of ten times that length and full of erotic experience. Try and try as he might to not think of his inevitable fate of a slow death, he did anyway. And because he hadn't obtained enough courage to visit his doctor to begin receiving the proper medication, he believed he could feel his insides dying.

Thoughts of Jax, however, seemed to sustain him somehow. But now he had even succeeded in alienating her, his only "medication." It's not like he planned to ever fuck a woman again, so he didn't understand how he could let himself be put in this situation in the first place.

Tony phoned him Tuesday night, shortly before he was to pick up Jax, and wanted Vincent to play host to him and a couple of his women friends. Tony said that he was trying to get with Peaches' friend, Rhonda. Well, Rhonda wouldn't go anywhere without her friend Peaches and because Tony lives with a woman, he asked Vincent if he could "hit-it" at his pad.

Vincent was the sucker who was stuck with the pregnant one, Peaches and tried to make small talk with her while his homeboy was in the back room fucking Rhonda.

In the meantime, Vincent was busy lying to Jax over the phone because he was trying to do his friend a favor. If he gave Tony just ten more minutes to score, he could go back home to his woman, and Vincent could go and pick up Jax for their date.

He was already late picking her up to go see a movie, plus she had begun to sound suspicious behind his excuses. It was just a matter of time before she would drive past his house and investigate what's going on for herself. When she arrived, unannounced, he knew he was fucked!

The next day, Vincent was still thinking about calling Jax to explain last night's situation to her. But the more he thought about calling her, the stronger his urge not to call her became. He knew that his explanation was going to sound like a lie in itself. Why did he allow himself to get placed in these situations? Because of Tony and his bullshit, he was in the hot seat with Jax.

He sat on his bed ignoring his ringing phone, and the voices of women saying, "...pick up the phone if you're there." His mind had just about checked-out, and all he could think about was his carefree, childhood days filled with love and security that only a mother can give.

His mother was a devout Christian woman who brought him up in the church and taught him the things it would take for him to be a good man. One who should, respect women, one who should not lie and one who should remain faithful unto the Lord. Vincent regretted that he had taken his mother's words and teachings in vain. He had done just the opposite of what he had been taught. He grew up disrespecting women and being less of a man than he wanted to be. Furthermore, he had become a liar and a cheat.

He was hard on himself these days blaming his lifestyle for the curse that had been placed on him. He wished he had the sense of mind to pack up his bags and flee to his mother for her comfort. But his shame was too great and he felt that he had to stick it out alone. Vincent was as stubborn a man as ever there was created, and so he wallowed alone in self-pity.

He settled in his bed and closed his eyes, in the hopes of trying to catch some sleep. He had been unsuccessful the night before, and the night before that, as well. Tonight, his hope was that his worries and fears would drift away in his dreams. But he tossed and turned on his waterbed, not soothed at all by the usual swaying. Instead, he sweated profusely, was overtaken with chills and was tormented by his own dreams. Vincent couldn't find peace while awake or asleep.

Sometime during the next day, he awakened rubbing his eyes, bringing himself out of a deep sleep. He realized that he must have slept the entire night. It was clearly morning, as he began to slowly remember, that he had originally laid down early yesterday afternoon.

He got up and went into the kitchen to make something to eat. As he reached for a skillet over the stove, he was again overwhelmed with the strong urge to see his mother. The more he moved about in the kitchen, gathering utensils to make bacon, eggs and toast, the more he thought about his mother.

His dear mother; maybe she was calling him to her. Maybe going home to her was the best thing for him right now. It had been years since he had seen his mother and even more years than that since he had last been to Baton Rouge. A visit home was beginning to sound like his salvation. So, just like that, he decided to go to Louisiana.

He knew he would not be able to fly on such short notice - not enough cash without hitting-up a lady friend, so instead he scraped together enough money he had hidden around his apartment for a rainy day...a train ticket. He packed up a few clothes, locked his car up in the garage, and got Tony to take him to the train station.

Within a few hours, he was on a train headed for Louisiana. He hadn't even bothered to phone his mother to let her know he was on his way. Nearly three days would pass before he was to reach his destination, and he wanted to use that time to think. The passing landscape would be the perfect sedative for the thinking he would do. He needed to think about himself, about his family, and as hard as he tried to deny it, about Jax.

On the Amtrak, Vincent was finally able to unwind a little. He gave way to his troubles and began to imagine various scenarios in which his life could play out favorably for himself. He starred out of the window for hours at a time, watching cities come and go, hillsides come and go, and finally familiar looking southern towns.

Neither food nor sleep was on his list of priorities, so he hardly did either. He was slow to communicate with the others on the train for fear that they might be able to look into his very soul and discover what is troubling him. His only need was to be home with his mother, so that he could finally appease this overwhelming urge to be comforted by her. She was sure to make everything all ok.

He arrived in Baton Rouge in the early evening. The sweet, moist air was the first thing he recognized as he stepped off of the train. Being in the train station brought back memories of the last time he visited this place years ago.

People milled about, with a familiar, southern looking distinction. And, as he hauled his expensive luggage out of the terminal and onto the busy street, he smiled with a look of recollection as kids played stickball in the abandoned train graveyard across the street. So, with a glad heart, Vincent wiped his brow with his Versace silk handkerchief, loosened his Armani tie, and headed for his family home across the tracks.

It was such lovely evening that he decided to walk the few blocks. He headed west on Main Street facing the sun head on, as it slowly made its way down behind a row of quaint little houses, thick with green moss and vines. When he got to Le Grande he headed south and then east on Loop de Pierre. He took a deep breath, taking in the wonderful aroma of this quiet neighborhood. "At last, peace" he thought.

He approached upon a park and saw some children playing on the swings and some others playing an intense game of soccer. Before heading to his mother's house, he decided to sit on a park bench and watch the children play. It was a warm summer evening, and so he kicked off his shoes and rested his head back on the bench. He relished in watching the tree tops sway with the force of the warm breeze. It was beginning to feel as though all was well in his world…finally a place where he could find some peace.

"Ya mind ifa sit here?" he heard a thick Southern accent ask.

As he slowly lowered his head from gazing at the sky, he saw a tall, thin, dark skinned woman standing directly in front of him. The glare from the fading sunlight made her appear as though she were glowing. She was carrying a bag of groceries in one arm and what looked like a ripped alligator purse in the other. "No. Not at all." He moved his garment bag to the side and made room for this strange woman.

Her hair was disheveled with a green scarf tied around it. She was wearing a long flesh colored see-through dress, which hung at her calves. Shoes were not among her attire, and Vincent thought this was strange. Also, Vincent noticed that she wasn't wearing any underwear! Not even the fading sunlight was enough to keep him from noticing that she was completely naked underneath her dress.

He first thought that she might have been a homeless woman or maybe just a mental case, but then he had to remind himself that he was not in Los Angeles anymore. He was in another place where customs and attitudes about life were completely different. So he figured that this free display of her "ham and eggs" was acceptable here.

"Ya come a long way," she said.

Vincent looked around as though expecting to find someone else she might have been talking to. When he saw that there was no one else there, he said, "Are you talking to me?"

"Yeah, boy. Who else woul'da be talkin' to?" She kept on speaking. "Ya from da big city. I can tella mile away dat ya from da big city."

"What's da big city?" Vincent asked amused.

"Any place dat's not 'round here. But ya been here befo, ain't ya? Ya know dis place. Ya tink dis place find ya some comfort. Ya can't find no comfort by runnin' way, ya gotta find it in yo self boy, didn't ya know dat? Ain't no use in tryin' to get dat girl out yo system. She ain't goin' nowhere. Ya might be goin' somewhere dough...well, at least ya tink ya might be goin' somewhere. Ya otta not wor so much, tings ain't all dat bad."

Vincent was looking and listening to this crazy ass woman with disbelief. "Who are you and what do you want?"

"I ain't hurtin' nobody. I felt ya, so I came on over. Ya knew I'd come to ya once ya made da cision to try an straighten yo mind out."

"Come to you? What in the hell are you talking about? You're crazy. Get the hell away from me lady! You some type of witch doctor or something?" And though he was trying to talk hardcore, like a mother-fucking man, he was actually a little creeped out by this psycho bitch!

"I ain't no witch!" she rebutted. "Don't call me no witch. My mama wer no witch, ner was my granny. I jus be a Truth-Seeker, and dat's what dey calls me, da Truth-Seeker."

Vincent couldn't believe he was sitting in a park, in his hometown, in a very expensive suit, having a conversation with a deranged woman who is sort of kind of talking about his life. He couldn't believe how his long, overdue trip home had led him to this stranger than fuck situation. And he couldn't believe that his old neighborhood in Baton Rouge was just as country as it had always been.

"Well go and find your truth somewhere else, 'cause I'm not looking for your advice, sista," he finally thought to say as he inched himself further away from her.

She responded with a wicked laugh. "I ain't yo sista, we ain't kin. Ida known if ol' lady Cruthers was my mama."

Vincent slowly turned to her with his mouth hanging open, prepared to run for the hills. At first he was just entertaining her bizarre behavior but the things she was saying was too much for him to ignore. He got a strange feeling about this woman and gave her a cold look. "How did you know Mrs. Cruthers is my mother?"

"How'd ya tink I know?" she said with a snicker. "Ya tink it's 'cause I can read ya mind, since I be da Truth-Seeker?" She laughed that wicked laugh. "You look jus like ya mama…I'd know any of her youngins anywhere. Ya cuda called befo ya came to see her, though. She won't like ya surprise 'cause ya might give her a heart attack."

Vincent finally stood up, not able to take any more of this woman's non-sense and calmly said, "Look lady, I don't know who you've been talking to about me, or how you knew I was coming, but I'm not in the mood for this shit. So why don't you just go home, put some clothes on and leave me alone before you get hurt."

"Oh so now ya gon' hurt me?" she asked with amusement.

"No! I'm not going to hurt you," he snapped. "But if somebody sees you naked like you are, they might hurt you." He stepped into his shoes, grabbed his garment bag and started walking down the road. He could hear the Truth-Seeker laughing in the background.

"Boy, don't ya know ain't nobody gon touch me!" She was yelling to him. "Dey all know who I am. Ya gonna learn too - ya don know it yet, but ya will. I be seein' ya again, Vincent."

Upon hearing his name come out of her mouth, his reality fell from the sky. He froze in his tracks, dropped his bags and prepared for the gates of hell to open up and swallow him hole.

All the while he had been trying his best to ignore this woman, but she had gotten under his skin from the moment she approached him. Racking his brain, he couldn't figure out how this woman knew so much about him. And now, she just went and called out his name. What the fuck!

He slowly turned around to get another look at this *Truth-Seeker*, and when he did, she was gone. He blinked his eyes in confusion and looked in every direction, but she was nowhere to be seen.

Through the last flicker of sunlight, he could see the children still playing in the park, but he couldn't see her anywhere. Slow to regroup himself, he hazily turned around to continue his short walk to his mother's house. "I must be going crazy," he said to himself. He figured she had vanished on a bus that was passing by, or that she had simply blended into the darkness. Hell, he had left his troubles back in Los Angeles, only coming here to put his affairs in order. He didn't need this shit right now!

As he approached the old house, he could see that all of the lights were on. The front porch swing was slightly swaying in the evening breeze, with three cats atop, enjoying their evening siesta. He opened the screen door to the enclosed porch and walked up the squeaky, wooden steps.

Before knocking, he closed his eyes and listened closely to see if he could hear his mother humming. He could have sworn that he heard her humming in the kitchen, as she usually did when she was cooking - though he couldn't be sure if he just wanted it to be so. But he did smell something delicious coming out of the house. It smelled so familiar, so good, like the home cooked meal that he had been waiting for his entire life.

Suddenly he stopped, drawn back to his encounter with that weird woman. He couldn't help but take heed to the Truth-Seekers words: "Don gives yo mama no heart-attack." So Vincent carefully knocked at the front door, at the same time he called out to her. "Mama, you'll never guess who."

When the front door swung open and he saw that lovely old woman standing in front of him, he was so overjoyed. She cried out loud, "My boy, my boy," as she rushed into his arms and held onto him, as if for dear life. Vincent hugged her back with just as much urgency. He swept her into his arms, pulling her onto the porch, twirling her around in the air, startling the cats out of their sleep and sending them scurrying off the porch.

"Surprise mama! Surprise," Vincent said while still holding his mother for dear life.

"My boy! My boy!" she said over and over again. "What are you doing here? Oh Lord I must look a mess. Why didn't you call? Is everything alright? Are you sick? Let me look at you. Put me down." She was smiling and crying and so happy to see her son.

He could hardly get in a single word, because his mother was so excited to see him. "I wanted to surprise you mama," he said as he gently placed her back on her feet.

"Well, surprise me you did. You nearly gave me a heart-attack." As soon as she said those words, Vincent froze, remembering what that crazy Truth-Seeker had just said. "Boy what's wrong with you? You done seen a ghost?"

Oh no mama," Vincent said, trying to cover up this *coincidence?* "I'm just tired, that's all." He lied.

"Well, come on inside and let me make up my baby's room and get you something to eat. You ain't nothin' but skin and bones." She went on and on and on, fussing over him as she used to do when he was a young boy.

As they walked into the well-lit house, and left the darkness outside, Vincent felt a sense of relief. He was home. Walking up the familiar staircase was just as relieving. They went into his old room and sat down on his old bed. They caught up on everything; subjects big and small, but mostly, Vincent was overjoyed to be with his mother.

Iris Cruthers was such an adorable woman. She was short, and stout, and cute as a button, wearing a conservatively fitted flowered dress. She was a beautiful, old Creole sole who didn't look aged enough to be a grandmother to Vincent's nieces and nephews. But she let her hair cover with gray, and she wore it in a bun, all nice and neat on top of her head so it would not flow down her shoulders and get in the way. Vincent didn't look much like his mother, but he loved her with all of his heart.

That was another curious thing about what the Truth-Seeker said; "You look just like ya mama," which wasn't true. Vincent looked almost entirely like his father: tall dark and handsome, having received none of his mother's traits except for her long crooked baby toe. He wouldn't find out until later that he looked like his mother from within.

He sat with there with her on that old rickety bed in his up-stairs bedroom, the same room that he used to share with his brothers. He sat there holding his mother's hand, rubbing it against his un-shaven face while gazing into her beautiful hazel eyes. "I missed you mama."

"I missed you too Son. Somehow I had a feeling I'd be hearing from you," she said lovingly to her son.

"What do you mean?" Vincent asked. "Have you been talking to that crazy Truth-Seeker?"

Iris raised her hand over her mouth and gasped. "What do you know about that crazy binny!?" she demanded.

"I don't know anything about her. She came up to me right after I got off of the train and started talking to me like she knew me."

"Lord, I'll tell you, that Truth-Seeker might be crazy as a loon, but she sure got some un-told stories about her."

"What do you mean?" Vincent asked, trying to get a grasp on the strange woman.

"Well, I say it's better left unsaid. Nobody really knows what her story is for sure anyway, so let's just keep it at that," Iris said. "Now, is my baby hungry? I got a whole ham, collard greens, potato salad and some peach soda pop, waiting to be served up just for you. What you say?" she cleverly changed the subject with her enticing food.

"I say, it sounds like the best meal that I could ever ask for in my entire life."

Vincent and his mother sat down to eat at the kitchen table. He couldn't help but stare into her lovely, caring eyes the entire time he gobbled down everything she put down onto his plate. She was relentless in giving him seconds and thirds. And although he hadn't felt like eating for a very long time, he ate everything that she served to him.

Afterwards, they retired to the porch swing and watched the stars in the sky. He was reluctant to talk about the problem that actually haunted him, but he knew just by looking into his mother's eyes, and hearing her voice, that she somehow knew of the drama he was living through. Yet, being as kind and loving a woman as she was, she never asked. "So, how's the old man doing?" he finally asked of his father.

"Well, he's receiving better care in that hospital than I could give him here. Besides, he started moaning and groaning about having to climb the stairs every day and said he was gonna set fire to them. After that, I knew something had to be done."

"Mama, you didn't really take him seriously, did you?"

"Oh, you don't know your father. If he says he's tired of climbing the stairs, and he was gonna set fire to 'em, you darn tootin' I was gonna take him serious."

As Vincent sat there with his mother, he felt a sense of guilt for a lot of reasons. It had been so long since he had visited her and still he was reluctant to visit his father in the convalescent hospital.

He was afraid to look into his once strong eyes, and not be remembered by the old man. But he was willing to put all of that aside now and make peace with the people that he loved, in the hopes that they would rally around him when his time of need came. So, he promised his mother that in the morning they would visit his father and spend the day with him, hopefully bringing about a glimmer of recollection in his father's eyes.

That was his hope as he sat there on the front porch swing, holding onto his mother with the kind of love that only a son has for his mother. He didn't remember how long they sat there before they retired for the night but he couldn't help feeling that it wasn't long enough.

Later that night while resting in his old room, he lay there staring at the ceiling, drifting in and out of consciousness. He finally fell into a lovely dream:

Visions of a playground came to him with children playing, flowers blooming, and birds flying over-head in the beautiful blue sky. He saw his mother in the kitchen, stacking mounds and mounds of food on her old kitchen table. He saw himself as a child playing with his fire truck in the backyard, with the neighbor's dog chasing cats and squirrels, totally ignoring him as if he wasn't there.

His sleeping imagination was taking him back to a time and place, where he had no worries; just that of being a carefree child, in a loving home, with his mother's reliable apron to tug on. He was home and these dreams were a welcomed comfort. He was at peace with himself for the first time in a very long time. Even in his sleep, he was glad that he had made the decision to come home. He wished he had made it a long time ago.

In the waking hours of the morning, Vincent opened his eyes to the familiar sights and sounds of his parents' home. He clutched onto his pillow and smiled to himself, as though he held the keys to the secrets of life. Then it hit him: "How long will I be alive?" The disease, which was working overtime in his body, would soon take it over. He was suddenly filled with that stinging insecurity that had made him flee the big city in the first place.

"The big city? That's what the Truth-Seeker said to me in the park," he spoke to himself. And just then he saw her!

Although he thought he was hallucinating, there she was, a vision in his room…glowing it seemed; looking at him with that weird, almost haunting look on her face, wearing that see-through dress and as naked underneath it as a pig waiting for the slaughter house.

She stood near the bedroom window, looking as disheveled as he had first seen her. And then she spoke to him. "It ain't so, boy. It ain't so."

Starting to sweat profusely, Vincent was unable to move an inch; to either run from or towards her. He was only able to form his lips to say, "What's not so?" He spoke with only a faint whisper, but she seemed to hear him.

She answered him. "Come see me on dat old Genevieve La Rue Plantation and I show ya dat it ain't so."

As soon as he was able to move, he sat straight up in the bed. With a loud choking sound, he tried to catch his breath. In a panic, he looked all around the room, rubbing his eyes with urgency. When he opened them again, he saw that he was alone. The sun was creeping in through the window as he noticed that it was closed and the drapes were drawn.

"Was it possible that I was dreaming, or did that crazy woman get into this house?" Had that woman gotten into his dreams, or was she really there? He wasn't coherent enough to know the difference.

Like a child, he slowly leaned over to look under the bed. After seeing nothing, he got up to look into the closet, and still he saw nothing. He was convinced that he was losing his mind. He stood there thinking, "Is this what it's going to be like...dying?"

The very smell of his mother's cooking was enough to snap him out of the spell and encourage him to get dressed. Downstairs, he kissed his mother on the cheek and sat down to eat breakfast with her. They discussed the day's activities that they would share together. The first would be their visit to his father at the hospital and afterwards, Iris was very anxious to take Vincent around the town to visit old neighbors and friends, who hadn't seen him in many years.

They didn't have major plans for the day; they just wanted to spend their time together as mother and son. Iris wasn't sure how long her son would be staying in town, but she knew that she better make the most out of his unexpected visit.

"Mama, where's that old Genevieve La Rue Plantation?" Vincent asked, carefully avoiding his mother's eyes, while looking into his plate of ham, grits, eggs and biscuits.

"Now what made you ask me a ridiculous question like that?" she asked eyeing him carefully.

"Oh," Vincent decided to lie, "I heard some kids talking about it when I was at the park yesterday."

"Well, if you in the mood for some old fashioned hocus pocus, I suggest you trot up on over there, but I wouldn't advise it. You see, the stories about the Genevieve La Rue Plantation go back for many generations. It's been said that, the original La Rues that brought slaves there, had some weird goings-on. Some of those goings-on had to do with what some folks called witchcraft.

Now, it could have been that the white folk were just plain stupid when it came to the ways of old African folk, but when they got wind that some witchcraft was going on at their plantation, they became afraid of their slaves.

Of course, the plantation has long since been run into the ground. But back in the late 1800's, pieces of the property was sold to the ancestors of the slaves, for sharecropping. Some of their kin-folk still live there today"

Vincent's mother continued. "When I was a young girl, there was a woman named, Hattie Mae. Now, Hattie Mae was a direct descendent of the slaves that came on a ship and landed on the Genevieve La Rue Plantation. Hattie Mae was a beautiful woman. She had beautiful skin as black as tar, a tall shapely frame and pearly white teeth. I think, built like a brick house, is the term men would use today when talking about her figure. But, people also used to say that Hattie Mae was a witch.

Now, no one knows for sure whether she was or she wasn't, but because three of her four husbands all died in fires and the fourth one simply disappeared never to be seen again, the rumor persisted. And the children she had with these men all grew up and had children of their own, and all of them are said to be witches too.

Now, I'm not sayin' they evil, I'm just sayin' they different. And if you have any sense about you, you'll stay away from that old plantation just like I kept you and your brothers away from it while you all were growing up. But, now, it's totally up to you, if you wanna find out what all the talk is about."

When she finished, she threw her hands up in defeat as though telling Vincent, he should do whatever he wanted with the information she had just given him. Iris had said all that she wanted to say on the topic and then went dead silent, giving Vincent a chance to take in all that she had said.

His curiosity peaked even greater over the possibility that some *witch* had made contact with him. He found it interesting that he, for some reason, had been targeted by this Truth-Seeker. And although he did not want to upset his mother, he had already made the decision to find out what was going on for himself.

They finished their breakfast in silence. Vincent decided not to mention the Truth-Seeker or the Genevieve La Rue Plantation to his mother again. She was obviously unsettled by this talk, so he figured that he would have to sneak around town in order to answer all of the burning questions in his mind.

So instead they visited his father in the hospital and he saw an older, broken down image of himself. It nearly brought him to tears; like looking in a near distant mirror.

Afterwards, he and his mother went into the local cafe for lunch. But Vincent was in no mood to eat, as the sight of seeing his father in that place had made him want to vomit. Even though he knew that his mother had probably done the right thing by putting him there, he still could not swallow the lump in his throat and the guilt in his heart. "Mama, is he getting the best of care?" Vincent sadly asked.

"Baby, I know it's hard seeing a strong man like your father in a place like that, but there was nothing any of us could do. We not poor, but nobody is rich enough to supply for all of his needs at home either. And when he served in that World War, they promised to take care of him for the rest of his life so I let 'em do their job. And don't you worry; I'm on top of them people all the time, every day. There ain't nothin' they gonna do to your daddy that I don't approve of first."

With having said that, she smiled at her son, and reached for his hand across the table. He grabbed it, and brushed it against the side of his face. She smelled like wild flowers, just like she did when he was a kid.

"You think he recognized me?" he asked.

"I'm sure of it!" She smiled.

"Have Anthony and Stanley been up here to see him?"

"No. And I ain't blamin' them for not coming right away, just like I didn't blame you. Your brothers have busy lives and they'll make it up here sooner or later."

Neither of them ate at all. They just sipped on iced tea and made small talk. Their only reason for going into the restaurant was because it was just across the street from the hospital and Iris needed to talk to her son about what he had just seen. Had Vincent not seen it with his own eyes he would have never guessed that the big and bad Warren Cruthers, was now a confused, old man.

Born and raised in Baton Rouge, Warren Cruthers was a southern catch back in the day. Dark skinned, curly haired, conservative hard-working Christian, attracted every woman, single and married, while growing up in a small county.

Having worked the railroads, like his father and his father before him, he made an honorable living. He met his future wife, Iris, the day she arrived in town to join the rest of her family who had recently moved there. Warren laid eyes on her and volunteered to transport the young beauty's luggage to the station house; the rest they say is history, followed by a wife, a family, a life…and now this.

He felt bad for his father. He wished that he had become successful enough and financially stable enough to be able to take care of his father himself. But that was wishful thinking. He wondered about the possibility of his mother someday losing her wits about *her*. But, when he looked into her eyes, he was convinced that she would probably out-live him. In any case, he needed a living-trust to secure her future for the rest of her life. He would look into taking out an insurance policy on himself, to ensure her security when he was dead.

For the rest of the day, Vincent and his Iris did exactly what she wanted to do, which was to show him off to her friends. He hadn't seen so many curious, old women in his life. They all wanted to know if he was married, why wasn't he married, did he have children, why didn't he have children, was he going to move back to Baton Rouge, why wasn't he going to move back to Baton Rouge and everything else about him.

He went to the church that he used to attend as a young boy, to watch his mother in choir rehearsal. While inside, he was afraid that God was going to strike him down for daring to enter his holy house. Vincent was convinced that he was a sinner beyond saving and that God was sending him to eternal damnation. But, he didn't let his mother see his true feelings; instead he clapped and sang along with the people in the choir, all while his mother smiled at him from the second row of the pews.

The memories of attending church as a child took him back to a time in his life when everything seemed right. His parents had insisted that he and his brothers know that God is watching. The thought that, God was watching, used to scare he and his brothers as a kids because they were all afraid of being stuck down, when they were jacking off under the covers and being bad in general. He wondered now, if it was all catching up to him because his parents had warned him that he would become corrupt if he moved to "the big city." Was this the "crows coming home to roost" for real?

After rehearsal, they were invited to dinner at Mr. and Mrs. Le Beau's home. Vincent sat on the living room sofa next to his mother, answering the same questions that the older people seemed to ask him. They sipped lemonade out of the most beautiful antique glasses he had ever seen.

"Mrs. Le Beau, you have a beautiful home and what unique glasses these are. May I ask where you got them?" Vincent asked as he lifted his in the air and examined the intricate detailing on them. The room suddenly got very quiet.

His mother looked like she had just seen a ghost and Mrs. Le Beau was speechless. When Vincent realized that he had just asked a question that was, for some reason, making everyone uncomfortable he immediately changed the subject. "Not just the glasses, but your furniture and paintings are lovely as well. I've always admired the turn of the century look."

"Thank you child," Mrs. Le Beau said.

"Dinner is served," Mr. Le Beau said, as he poked his head out of the kitchen. Everyone rose to enter the dining room. "Could you point me to your facilities?" Vincent asked Mr. Le Beau.

"Around this corner son," he said pointing. Vincent followed his finger, entered and closed the bathroom door.

He felt alongside the wall for the light switch, but couldn't find it. When he was about to re-open the bathroom door, in order to use the hallway light to see inside, he heard a voice. At first he thought it was Mrs. Le Beau, instructing him where to find the light switch. But then he realized that it wasn't her voice, it was... "It ain't so, boy. It ain't so. If ya wanna know da truth ya betta com sees me. Don be afraid. Even these people know 'bout my ina eye. I see everyting, an it ain't so."

Standing in the dark, Vincent froze, his heart pounding. He had to pee really badly, but he wasn't about to pull out "junior" while he was hearing voices in the dark. He reached for the doorknob and turned but it wouldn't budge. He panicked and tried again, this time realizing that he had locked the door. Nervously, he unlocked the door and walked out of the bathroom. He stood in the hall for a few minutes in order to regain his composure before entering the dining room.

"What in the hell is going on?" he whispered to himself. "This is not a dream. This lady is real and she wants something from me, but what? And why me?"

He closed his eyes and started to pray: *"Dear Heavenly Father above, below, to my left, to my right, and within me...I know I have sinned and am being made to pay for it. But, I pray for your forgiveness, and especially for the protection of my family. If I am being haunted or punished, may your will, please protect my family and friends from harms-way, separate from my own shame. Amen."*

He opened his eyes, expecting to meet the grim reaper but saw only an empty and well-lit hallway. He made his way back into the dining room and sat down to eat the meal prepared by Mr. Le Beau. Understandably, the dinner conversation went unnoticed by him.

For the next couple of weeks he received visions of the Truth-Seeker, saying the same thing over and over again. And, even though he was having a much-needed vacation and a great time with his mother, he decided that he couldn't take it anymore and had probably put his mother in harm's way. So he decided to tell her everything going on with him inside his body and his mind.

Iris was usually on the porch swing, playing with the cats during this time of the evening but when he went downstairs he noticed that she was not there. He crept back upstairs to see if she had gone to bed early and was relieved to see that she had. Because of this, he could hold off telling her his eerie story for now.

Suddenly, he was overtaken with the urge to confront his fear of this Truth-Seeker. So without thinking, he walked out of the front door and headed in the direction of the Genevieve La Rue Plantation. In the darkness he walked for what seemed like hours, though it had actually been only minutes. Not knowing exactly where he was going made him walk all the faster.

Finally, when he decided that he had probably been walking in circles, he walked across the street to ask for directions at a gas station. He hadn't asked earlier because he didn't want anyone to know where he was going and he especially didn't want the word to get back to his mother that he went to the Genevieve La Rue Plantation.

While in the middle of the street, he suddenly saw two headlights heading straight for him. He began to trot, to get onto the sidewalk faster, but the headlights turned in his direction. A panicky feeling struck, as though he were the target of some assassination plot. His life flashed before his eyes just as he thought that he was going to be struck down. The truck came to a screeching halt, with the headlights having stopped only inches in front of him. He stood there trembling, stupefied and unable to move or speak.

"Ya gon stand in da middle of da street boy, or ya gon git in?"

"Oh my God! That's that crazy Truth-Seeker," he thought to himself.

"Well, come on. Ya probly wasn't gon find it in da darkness anyways so I came to give ya a lift."

Without thinking as though in a trance, Vincent walked around the side of the truck and got in. The Truth-Seeker sped off like a raving maniac. She, nor Vincent, said one word while they rode in the darkness. Finally, she turned off onto a dirt road and went through a heavily bushy area until they got to a clearing. There, Vincent saw one little wooden house with a lantern on the porch and a fire burning from inside an old, metal trashcan.

"Git out," she said to him. Like a little boy, Vincent obeyed her. She walked over to the trashcan and put her hand into the flames. Vincent winced, as though he could feel the pain she should be feeling, but she showed no signs of feeling pain. Instead she pulled out what looked to him like bones. Chicken bones!

"Sit down on dat ol' tree stump and watch and learn." Vincent obeyed again. He walked across the yard and sat on the log, as his mouth hung open, part in fear and part in awe.

While watching her in the firelight, he wondered if she was one of Hattie Mae's relatives. He looked for any signs of that good looking trait that his mother spoke of, but found none...except for her slammin' ass body!

The whore in him couldn't help but think to himself, "If I put a paper bag over her face and just concentrated on her body, then I might be able to..."

"Git yo mind out da gutta boy," she said snapping him back into reality. "Dat's what got ya in da trouble ya in now. Now look at da bones I got here." But Vincent didn't want to look at her chicken bones; he wanted to know how she had just read his mind.

"Yeah, so. Chicken bones, is what I see. What do you see, Truth-Seeker?" he asked her.

She threw the bones at his feet in disgust. "What I see? "What I see is ya."

Vincent looked at her with a lack of understanding. She saw that he was confused as she began walking towards him. Vincent could see straight through that dress she wore and was glad to see that she still did not wear anything underneath it. As she approached him, she got on her knees and picked up the bones again. She looked into his eyes. "Ya sick, huh?" Vincent turned away from her. "Ya know why ya ain't talked to nobody 'bout ya sickness, boy? 'Cause it ain't so!"

Vincent turned to face her again. "What do you mean?" he asked very softly. His heart was softly breaking in shame, as the realization of his secret illness was becoming clear to her.

"I mean," she said as though talking to a child, "Ya ain't sick!"

Confused, Vincent stood up and started walking around in circles. "You mean to tell me that you've been using that damn witchcraft to come into my dreams and into my head just to fuck with my intelligence? Who and what are you? And by what authority do you have the right to prey on me, like I'm a fucking animal!?"

She was very calm. "Them be ya words, not mine."

"Well what *are* your words, Ms. Truth-Seeker?"

"That ya ain't sick, boy!"

Vincent put his hand to his forehead as if he had a headache. "You're crazy, you know that?"

"Nah I ain't. I just know dat ya ain't sick," she insisted.

"And how do you know that I am, or am not, sick?"

"'Cause ya tol me," she stood facing him.

"I didn't tell you shit," he said angrily.

"Ya spirit tol me."

"And how can you hear my spirit?"

"'Cause ya let me in to hear."

"When did I do that?"

"On da train."

Exhausted with the whole ridiculous scene, Vincent sat down on the log in defeat, putting both his hands to his head. The Truth-Seeker watched him for a while and then she sat down next to him. Vincent was surprised how good she smelled...like wild flowers...like his mother!

"When my mama was heavy wit me, she came outside dis here house screamin' in pain fo somebody ta help her birf me. Nobody was round, sept fo two young girls pickin' wild flowers in da field, 'bout a quarta mile away. Da one girl, ya know her as Mrs. Le Beau, did what she could to help me be born, 'cause I was breech. Da other girl, ya mama, stayed back 'cause she had been tol dat we was witches, or somethin'.

When I finally was born in dat field ova dere, my mama tol da one girl to go to da house an take da box of old antiques sittin' on da porch, as her appreciation. When she came back, carryin' da box, my mama ate my umbilical cord in front of da girls, to prove dat she was tellin' da truth, 'bout us not bein' witches; dat if she ate it, she was tellin' da truth. Da girl dropped da box and broke everyting in it, sept fo some drinkin' glasses.

Well, da girls ran off an neva tol nobody what happened. After dat, my mama tol me dat it was my duty to seek da truth 'bout people who done helped us. An I grew up havin' a ina knowing 'bout people dat my mama knew.

On ya mama's marriage day, my mama lef a bottle of homemade smellin' water, on da church steps. She made it from da wild flowers in dat field ova dere. She did some tings fo Mrs. Le Beau too. When ya was on da train comin' here, I heard yo worries. An 'cause yo ya mama's son, I had to tell ya da truth; dat you ain't sick, like some lady don fooled ya into tinkin'. An dat ya heart would be betta off wit dat girl you can't stop tinkin' bout. Ya got some choices to make, boy. Ya betta git to 'em."

Vincent sat there on the stump listening to the most incredible story that he had ever heard. He couldn't believe that he was trippin' off some backwoods, crazy shit anyway. The fact that one of his many women friends, could make up something like this, made complete sense to him because he was a D.O.G., and probably deserved it. But who? Who would do such a thing? Better still... who the fuck was this lady and how did she get all mixed up in his life? He went inward to find the answer.

Karma. What goes around...comes around. And some way, somehow, his belief, love and fear of God Almighty had knocked his ass to his knees for the scandalous life that he led. And maybe because God felt Vincent had genuine remorse, He sent the Truth-Seeker to save his sorry ass.

"   Could that be it?" Vincent wondered. "I had to be relive my upbringing in the church, through my mother, to be reminded that God is watching…that everything is connected…that what we put out will come back to us, one way or the other."

Somehow, though he kept fighting the urge to believe it, his body kept trying to tell him that he didn't have HIV, but his mind wouldn't let him listen. But the Truth-Seeker seemed to have all of the answers. He would be a fool to believe one word of it, but too many things added up; like Mrs. Le Beau's beautiful drinking glasses that he had seen with his own eyes; the fact that his mother always smelled like wild flowers, even when he was a child and so many other things that he was having a hard time rationalizing.

But, there was one lingering question that he had to confront the Truth-Seeker with. The answer would either plunge Vincent's reality into a pit of death and fire, or re-awaken his knowledge of God and all his glory. "Are you a witch?" he asked with an uneasy feeling.

"Nope. Nah was ma mama, new nobody else in da family."
She had answered his question so believably so that he wanted to believe her. "Then why do people, even to this day, think you are?"

"Pure 'n simple ignance, boy."

"But you do have a gift?"

"Gift from God, I spect. Ain't neva used it fo no evil."

"Well you sure scared the hell out of me, on more than one occasion."

"Dat's 'cause ya was too thick fo me to git in ya head. I had to make ya believe me first. My family owe yo family da truf. It worked didn't it?" She smiled that weird smile.

"Yeah," he paused for a few seconds, "it worked." Vincent sighed, then he relaxed, then he smiled, then he cried.

(10) – Joseph – Cold Feet

"Where have you been Joseph? I've been waiting here forever," Veronica asked from her sitting position outside of her fiancé's front door.

"What are you doing here? I said I would be by your place later on today," he said looking down on her…literally and annoyed. He was hoping that she wouldn't start an argument with him because he already knew he was wrong. If she had had the inclination to come check up on him, it was because he had given her plenty of reason, due to his recent behavior.

Their wedding was fast approaching and he was being less and less attentive towards her. He knew he was wrong, but he just couldn't help himself. "I'm sorry baby. I just don't like it when you check up on me. If I said I'm going to be there, then I'm going to be there," he said as he helped her to her feet.

She stood to face him. "I wasn't checking up on you Joseph. Should I be?" she asked, looking at him closely.

"We're getting married in two weeks, so I don't think you have a reason to." That seemed to ease her mind, so he opened the front door and led her into his apartment. He was relieved that he had decided to spend the night with Jacqueline in a motel rather than to bring her back to his place last night. He just hoped that he wasn't smelling like pussy right about now.

"Where have you been anyway?" Veronica asked.

"Shit!" he thought. "She is checking up on me. Think fast, think fast, think fast," until he finally said, "I was helping

George with his car. Homeboy called me early this morning begging for my help. Then he had the nerve to throw that, 'Well I am your Best Man' shit in my face. So I helped him out." When she didn't say anything else, he figured she bought it.

He wasn't exactly sure how stupid his excuse sounded just now but he would bounce it off of George later to see what he thought. "Let me take a shower right quick. I'll be right out," he yelled from the bathroom.

He was nervous as hell that Jacqueline might call, even though she had never done so before, but he had to bathe before Veronica got a whiff of him close up. She was probably already mad at him for not giving her a hello kiss. Why he got himself into these predicaments was beyond him.

All he knew is that he was minding his own business, trying to be faithful to Ronnie and then this sexy ass woman comes along in the middle of the night and starts to give him action. He would be a punk if he didn't take the pussy. Wouldn't he?

By the time he got out of the shower he was feeling a lot better. Now all he had to do was to spend some quality time with Ronnie, fuck her good and send her on her merry way. Then he would have to call Jacqueline before it got too late, because she was a hard one to catch up with. He knew that he was playing his cards too close to the vest, by playing two women at the same time, but for now he had to have both of them. If either of them found out about the other, then…well he would deal with that when and if the time comes. In the meantime, he was just about the happiest man on earth.

"Hello in there. Are you out of the shower yet?" Ronnie was yelling from the other side of the door.

He opened the door and exposed his wet naked body to her. These days, even a strong wind made that girl horny. Must be hormones from recently having a baby. "What were you doing in there, jerking off?" she asked with a smile.

Approaching her, he said, "I don't have to. That's what I have you for." He took her into the bedroom and lay on top of her. As tired as he was from his strenuous night and morning with Jacqueline, he tried to summon up every inch of strength to give Ronnie what she wanted.

They began kissing one another with the passion of familiarity. Joseph touched her face while looking into her trusting eyes, while hoping that he would be able to pull this thing off. He kissed her lips, her forehead, her cheeks and neck with such gentleness and care. She trembled at the mere touch of him and began to writhe wildly underneath him.

But he needed more time because as he wasn't able to get an immediate erection like he usually did. So he continued to touch and fondle every inch of her in order to give her some kind of satisfaction.

He nibbled on her ears, licking the inside of them, soaking them with his saliva. Next he sucked at her neck and then unbuttoned her blouse to expose her erect breasts. He played with one nipple, pinching and twisting it out of proportion as he sucked anxiously on the other. She moaned in ecstasy while enjoying wonderful pleasures. Still, Joseph was embarrassed with himself because not only was he not able to enjoy the event, he was still unable to get a hard-on with Veronica.

Time was beginning to become his enemy because even though he was skillful at sexually pleasing a woman, he was not used to having his own body betray him with a willing subject…especially his fiancé. So he continued his foreplay activities with her, in the hopes of reaping the awaiting benefits.

Joseph unzipped her jeans and slowly slid them, along with her panties, down past her round hips. She helped him by anxiously pulling them down past her thighs. Then he assumed the position as he raised both her legs in the air and laid in-between the "V" of her love.

Playfully he began to stroke the inside of her thighs with his tongue. He plunged in and out of her pussy in a relentless effort to give her pleasure. Through it all, she used her hands and feet to stroke him in every area she could reach, to get him ready for the big plunge. She must not have noticed the look of panic on his face and on his dick, because he was as limp as last month's celery stalk.

The thought of prolonging this pre-empt to pleasure by climbing on top of her face in typical 69 fashion crossed his mind, but that would be the end of his masquerade in hiding the fact that he just couldn't get it up.

Jacqueline had sure done a number on him in the last 12 hours. Their first union of sex, a week ago, had proved how well they suited each other in the bedroom. Last night was just one of their many erotic evenings together when they fucked each other's brains out.

Veronica, on the other hand, was one of those women who receive all of the pleasure without putting much effort into it. Well, today she was in for a surprise. Because not only would she not be fucked, but she would also be left with the nagging question of, "Why?"

"What's wrong baby?" she asked with disappointment. Joseph stood and walked toward his bedroom balcony window and stared into space without answering her. He was trying to hide his limpness from her, though he doubted she would have noticed. That's what was wrong with Ronnie; she was not an experienced lover and 100 years of teaching her probably would not do any good.

He tried to convince himself that he wanted his future wife...the mother of his children, to be Bambi in the bedroom, but he was lying to himself. He liked...no he was driven toward an unusually high level of eroticism with the women he made love to. He simply could not get a hard on with Ronnie because he had found in Jacqueline what he thought he needed...animal attraction. And although this episode of limpness was only temporary, he wondered how it would affect his relationship with Ronnie in the future.

"Ronnie," he said, "let's go get the baby and head over to the zoo."

"Just like that?" she responded with hesitance.

"What do you mean just like that? Oh, you mean because we were right in the middle of something." He turned to look at her and smiled. "Well, there's plenty of time for that. Besides, I gave you what you wanted, didn't I?"

"Gave me what I wanted! Gave me what I wanted! No Joseph! You didn't give me what I wanted. I wanted to make love with you. All you did was give me head and make me want you even more. Now what's wrong with you? Is it me? Am I a turn off?" she demanded while putting her clothes back on in a huff.

"No you are not a turn off. How can you ask a stupid thing like that?" he said approaching her.

She pointed to his penis. "Well just look at it. It's just hanging there like it's sleep or something." Veronica placed her hands over her face and began to cry.

Joseph was torn between going to her and comforting her and just walking away so she would leave him. His first thought won him over. He put his arms around her. "What are these tears for, huh? Now you know you are too pretty to be crying. Come here?"

She turned to him and buried her face in his chest. "Joseph," she said through her tears. "I know you're scared of getting married, believe it or not, I'm scared too. But I love you. I love you so much it hurts. And I know that you love me too, I'm just not sure if you're in love with me." She held on to him in an effort to receive the satisfaction that she needed. He held her and tried to soothe her with comforting words that would make her believe that everything would be ok, even though he didn't believe it himself.

They cuddled up on the bed watching television for the entire morning. He was cautious when glancing at the clock on the nightstand as to not arouse her attention. As much as he tried to deny himself, he could not wait to rendezvous with Jacqueline again tonight.

There he lay in limbo, holding on to the woman that would soon be his wife and looking forward to being with the woman who rocked his world. Just the thought of the other woman brought him an erection. He thought for a moment that he would take Ronnie now and pretend that she was Jacqueline. That way, he tried to rationalize; he could satisfy Ronnie and be with Jacqueline at the same time.

That just might be the answer to his problem. Maybe he could get through this dilemma by marrying Ronnie as planned and always keeping Jacqueline as the focal point of his dick. Genius!

Soon Ronnie was asleep in his arms. After watching Gilligan's Island, American Gladiator's, and Soul Train, Joseph felt like taking a nap himself. He dosed off soon after hearing Don Cornelius' "Love, peace and soul…"

Next he found himself walking down a deserted street. He could hear church bells ringing in the distance and although he didn't recognize the neighborhood, he knew where to go. He was walking in the middle of the street while a fierce wind tried to push him back. It was as though he were in a battle with nature; his will was driving him onward while the strength of the wind was trying to defeat him. When he approached the steps of the church with the ringing bells, the doors swung open invitingly. He slowly ascended the steps to the accompaniment of music…the wedding march. Inside the church there were rows of people on both sides. Everyone seemed to be dressed in white. At the front of the church there waited a bride in white, with a thick veil over her face. He began what seemed like an eternal walk down the center aisle, as the crowd of spectators stood. Their faces were all unknown to him, which made him think that he was at the wrong church, until the awaiting bride extended her hand to him in anticipation. No sooner than he grabbed for her hand and held on to it, did the church turn icy cold. He looked around for George, who was to be his Best Man, but couldn't find him. The minister, who stood before them, was unknown to him, nor could he hear what he was saying, even though the old man's lips were moving. Suddenly, he was able to hear the minister say, "…speak now or forever hold your peace." Joseph turned around as he heard a woman's voice yell, "Stop!" The woman was dressed in a black dress with a veiled hat. He was not able to determine who she was, as her face was hidden from view. Suddenly, without warning, the audience began to throw stones at him from every direction. He could see that their faces were contorted with anger as they screamed and shouted at him. He still was unable to recognize any of them and so he turned to his bride for comfort. He found his bride standing next to the woman in black, while holding one another for comfort. He tried to speak, but no words would come out. He grabbed for his throat in desperation for an understanding, but the faceless mob soon jumped him and placed a noose around his neck. They dragged him outside and took him to a wooden platform. Through the crowd, he could see the two women crying together. He extended his hands to them in a plea for help, but his hands were grabbed and tied behind his back. The noose was then swung over the platform and a cloth sack was placed over his head. At that exact moment he knew that he was about to die. Before the bottom of the platform dropped from underneath his feet, the faces of several women flashed before his eyes; the faces of the women whom he had loved and left in various ports around the world. The faces of Veronica and Jacqueline stood formidably amongst them. A moment later, he felt like he was being choked to death. He tried to grab hold of his throat but could not raise his hands. He felt dizzy and was soon tired of the struggle, so he decided to rest. He closed his eyes and took a deep breath. His lips mouthed the words, "I'm sorry…I'm sorry…I'm sorry," over and over again until he could hear his voice again. His voice got louder and louder and louder…

"Joseph, wake up! Joseph wake up, baby! What's wrong?" Ronnie was saying while stroking his back, trying to nudge him awake.

Waking up from a deep sleep and covered in perspiration, a very groggy Joseph said, "I'm sorry!" He sat up in the bed and looked all around him. He saw Ronnie sitting next to him with a weird expression on her face. He took his hands and felt his throat. "What's wrong?"

"I was about to ask you the same thing. Are you alright? I think you were having a dream or a nightmare or something."

Again, panic struck over him. "What did I say? Did I say anything?" he asked her anxiously, hoping to God that he hadn't said anything incriminating, if anything at all.

"You kept saying, 'I'm sorry', over and over again. Damn, you must have really done something wrong in that dream for you to talk in your sleep, baby. I've never heard you talk in your sleep before. You wanna tell me what you dreamed about?" she asked with concern as she wiped the perspiration from his forehead.

Joseph found himself getting off the bed and walking away from Ronnie. He put on his jeans and turned to face her. "I don't remember exactly," he lied. "I think it had something to do with the fight that broke out on the Cruxia." Joseph was hoping that this fictitious story would be enough to keep Ronnie at bay, until he could figure out what in the hell that dream did mean. When she didn't press him for any further information, she got up from the bed and straightened her clothes.

They left his apartment and headed for her mother's house to pick up Sayla. It was around 2:00 in the afternoon and they decided that it was too late to go to the zoo. Instead they took Sayla to the park and let her attempt to throw popcorn to the ducks. She preferred to try slobber all over the popcorn rather than throw it.

After their cozy little family gathering, Joseph couldn't drive fast enough to drop her and his daughter off. Ronnie asked him if they could spend the evening together, but he insisted on going home alone. He told her that he was going over to his mother's house after he caught up with George and work on his car some more. He promised her that he would call her later and kissed her and his daughter sweetly before he turned to leave.

When he got home, he called Jacqueline only to find her answering machine on. He left her a message telling her that he would call again and to not make any plans for tonight. And although he knew that he was acting like a schoolboy with a hard-on, he couldn't seem to help himself. She was sexy, intelligent, exciting and even more than that, she was confident.

He had never met a woman with so much confidence before...in and out of the bedroom. Just thinking about her made him feel like a man...like he was the only one who could tame her. Idiot.

When he turned the radio on and jumped into the shower, he bathed himself to the sound of Sade singing, "This Is No Ordinary Love." He couldn't help but think out loud, "You got that right." Getting out of the shower, he laid on his bed naked and wet. He listened to the music on the radio, thinking about what to wear that evening and about the day's events. Things were getting too close for comfort with this Veronica and Jacqueline thing. So he began to analyze the bizarre dream he had earlier in the day.

He assumed that the bride standing at the alter was Ronnie and the lady in black was Jacqueline. But then, he remembered the faces of all the women he had been with overseas.

The woman in black could have been anyone of them. The veils could have represented his inability to see what's in front of him; the white attire could have meant the purity of love and marriage. Oh hell! He could have racked his brain all night and still not know what the dream was about. But one thing he did know; he was fucking up, and it was just a matter of time before it caught up to him.

In the meantime, he made sure that his answering service was turned on, with the volume turned up and the ringer turned off. The last thing he needed was to be disturbed by Ronnie. He was hoping that Jacqueline would call and he would answer the phone only if he heard her voice. But he was sure that she wouldn't because she barely phoned him since they had met. Maybe she was playing hard to get or something. Whatever it was she was doing, it was working.

By six o'clock that night he was fully dressed and sipping on brandy out on his balcony. He had called Jacqueline at least three times over the last hour. Her answering machine was still turned on and so he hung up after each unsuccessful phone call. The radio was playing Baby Face's, "When can I see you again?" It's funny; every time he turned his attention to the music on the radio the song seemed to capture his very thoughts.

"Where in the hell is Jacqueline," he thought. Hadn't he made it clear to her that he wanted to spend the entire weekend with her? He listened to song after song tell of his very thoughts; Janet Jackson's, "Anytime, Anyplace," R. Kelly's, "Bump N' Grind" and Queen Latifah's, "Weekend Love." Apparently the radio station was in some kind of love mood and it was beginning to get on Joseph's nerves.

He had put on a pair of his good slacks, a nice shirt, tons of aftershave and had bought an extra box of condoms. The only thing missing was a woman. When finally he had decided to give up on trying to get in contact with Jacqueline, he phoned George and planned an evening out with him instead.

"What's up man?" George asked as he climbed into Joseph's car.

"Nothing," he said pathetically.

"Well damn! Don't sound so happy to see me. What's wrong with you?"

"You know me. Same o, same o," Joseph said trying to avoid the subject and a pending lecture.

"Yeah, I know you're ass, which means a woman has got something to do about your attitude," George replied. "Could it be that sexy thing you met over my ma's house?"

Joseph was backing out of the driveway and hearing George's question made him abruptly hit the brakes. "What about Jacqueline? Have you seen her?" he asked impatiently.

George looked at Joseph with curiosity. "No I haven't, but you obviously have. Man, what are you doing now? You're about to get married in two weeks. Haven't you soaked your oats enough?" He was a tiny bit jealous.

"Man," Joseph said, "she's different." He put the car in park. "She's tough enough to make me fuck up everything I have with Ronnie."

"Does she know about Ronnie?

"Not exactly," he answered slyly.

"Well, either she does, or she doesn't, so I take it she doesn't," George insisted.

"No. She doesn't," he said weakly.

"And you'd like to keep it that way until your wedding day, right?"

"Right."

"Ok by me." George fastened his seat belt and assumed a nonchalant position. "Where do you want to go tonight?"

"Let's go to Newton's," Joseph said as he put the car in reverse and backed out of the driveway.

Joseph had intended to talk to George about Jacqueline and his dream. But he was feeling so guilty lately he didn't want to bring up any uncomfortable conversations. Even though, George was the one who knew most everything about him, the timing just wasn't right.

When they pulled up in front of Newton's, there were cars everywhere looking for somewhere to park. "Looks like the party is in here tonight," George said.

"Good," Joseph replied. "I need a distraction."

They found a parking place and went inside of the club. Some jazz band was playing on the main floor and some people were dancing on either side of them. The air was thick with cigarette smoke and glasses were being lifted in toasts all around. For a minute, it looked like they had stumbled onto someone's private party. But when they found a table and sat down and weren't questioned, they decided that it was alright for them to be there.

"I should've known that you and Jacqueline would get together," George finally yelled over the sound of blaring music.

"What makes you say that," Joseph yelled just as loud.

"When you two met over my ma's refrigerator, I saw how you were looking at each other."

Joseph couldn't help but smile; obviously busted in his attempt to appear nonchalant. "And how were we looking at each other?"

"Well, put it this way," he said. "I could've sworn that you guys were fucking without even touching."

The waitress approached them and asked them for their order. George ordered two cognacs. When the waitress walked away, George turned to Joseph. "Joe? I'm going to ask you one question, and then I'm going to drop the subject altogether."

"Shoot."

"Do you know what you're doing?"

Joseph was a little put off by the question. He figured that George would ask a more typical question like, "Why did you get involved with this girl when you're about to get married?" or something like that.

He took a moment to think about the question. "That's a good question man," he finally said. "The fact is I don't know what I'm doing. I know that I love Ronnie. I know that I love Sayla. And I know that life is not supposed to be perfect. So I guess that I'm supposed to do the right thing by marrying her, but in the meantime I'm trying not to think about the upcoming events, while kickin' it with someone else." He knew he sounded stupid, but he didn't have a better answer.

"Well what are you going to do when you finally say, 'I do?'"

"That's two questions." Joseph laughed nervously.

"Come on man," George pressed. "You don't mean to tell me that you're going to try and play both of them, even after you're married?"

"I would be a fool to try," Joseph responded. "No, George. I'm just having a little fun, that's all. I'm sure I'm not the only man in Jacqueline's life 'cause she's too fine for that. I'm just getting all I can before I become an old married man."

"Well, if that's the case, can I get with Jacqueline when you're finished with her?"

This question pissed Joseph off. He grabbed George by the collar. "If you try, I'll fuck you up!"

George slapped Joseph's hand away with force. "Punk! You're pussy whipped. You're acting like she's the one you're marrying. You better get your punk ass together, boy! And if you ever grab me like that again…it's on!"

The both of them sat there silently listening to the band play on. The waitress returned with their drinks and George reached for his wallet. Joseph held up his hand. "This round is on me."

After they began to relax and forget about their little episode, they began talking again and commenting on different women as they walked by. George got up from his seat and began his rounds of flirting, as usual. He would wave to Joseph across the room while he pursued different women, while Joseph would wave him on with either thumbs up or thumbs down.

That was the difference between him and George. It wasn't like he purposely pursued women or anything like that; they just seemed to be lured to him for some reason. The fact that he had been involved with several women during his sailing adventures was purely what all of the men did. So he didn't know why he always seemed to feel guilty about it. He wasn't a playboy or a womanizer he just liked women…what's the harm in that?

George, on the other hand, actively pursued women like they were going into extinction. His approach was not the most flattering either, which is why Joseph thought that most of them were put off by him. But, he still got his share of the women. Some women enjoyed being treated like a piece of meat...so he obliged them.

They both were enjoying their evening venturing from table to table flirting with different women all night long. The jazz band was playing a tune by Take 6, by mixing their different instruments into a sweet sounding blast of harmony.

Everything was going alright for them. Joseph had even forgotten about the disappointment of not being able to get in touch with Jacqueline, even though he was pissed off at her for standing him up. If he saw that bitch again, he had every intention of kicking her ass to the curb. Although, he knew that he was just bullshitting himself into thinking that he could have his cake and eat it too. Besides, it was just a matter of time before he would have to break things off with her anyway. Right?

But for now, he and George grabbed hold of two fine women and started dancing on the floor. Joseph noticed how the woman he was dancing with kept grinding her body closer to his. She was definitely giving him the green light for getting to know her better. He, being typical of his nature, probably would have taken her up on the offer. Until, through the loud music and the rustling of voices, he heard a woman laughing in the distance.

There was nothing unusual about the laugh, except that it sounded like someone he knew. He danced his partner around in a half circle until he could see in the direction of the laughing. And that's when he saw Jacqueline.

She was hanging-out in front of a table with about five other people, laughing so hard that she was holding her side. For a moment, Joseph imagined that they were laughing because she was telling them that she had stood him up. He didn't know why but that made him feel stupid for a lot of reasons. If she didn't give a shit, why should he? But then, he didn't give a shit about how he was feeling. All he knew is that she was in the same place as she was, and that was good enough for him.

Before the song had even ended, he politely excused himself from the woman he was dancing with and walked away. George was too busy putting the grind on the woman he was dancing with to notice.

As Joseph approached the table where Jacqueline stood, he wondered how he would approach her, seeing that he wasn't sure if one of the men at the table was with her. "Fuck it," he said to himself as he took a deep breath and started in her direction. He pushed crowds of people politely out of his way as he made his way towards her. She was still laughing and joking around when he finally walked slowly up behind her.

He tried to play if off for a minute, as though he were just a part of the crowd. But then, George walked up to him and said, "Hey Joseph man, why'd you leave? I thought we were going to get busy with those two lovelies over there."

George had spoken before Joseph was able to tell him to lower his voice. It was too late for him to run for cover because Jacqueline had already turned around after hearing his name. She was looking good as usual, though she only wore a pair of jeans, a clinging black bolero jacket and a pair of black pumps. Her cleavage was shown off easily through the opening of her jacket, and her hair was piled up high on her head. It looked something like a soft serve ice cream cone. It was sexy.

"Joseph?" she said after seeing him.

Joseph decided to play along. "Jacqueline? Hey, what a coincidence."

She turned to George. "Hi. George isn't it? Do you remember me? We met at your mother's. How is she by the way?"

"Of course, Jacqueline. I could never forget anyone as lovely as you. My mother is great, thanks for asking," George replied, turning to Joseph with a puzzled look on his face.

"Have you been here long?" Joseph asked Jacqueline.

"No, not long."

She was making things very difficult for him by only giving simple replies. Maybe she was with one of those guys sitting at the table or, maybe not. None of them seemed to be paying her any particular attention now. He went for it. "So how are you feeling, lovely lady?" Joseph asked her, looking for something to say.

"Well I feel fine Joseph. Don't I look fine?" she said smiling.

His smile broke a little of the anxiety he was feeling about talking to her. George felt like a third wheel, so he simply melted into the wood works and vanished. "You know you look better to me than that." He pulled her closer to him. "Did we cross signals this morning, or weren't we supposed to get together tonight?"

"We must have crossed signals," she said. "From what George said a moment ago, I thought you were looking for anyone to get with tonight."

Damn! She did hear what George said to him. "That wasn't my idea it was his. I'd rather spend my time with you," he said, sounding like a complete wimp.

"Is that right?"

"Yes. That's right."

"So what did you have in mind?" She sounded as though she was coming around, like she was just as turned on as he was.

"Me and you, alone," he whispered.

"Well, I did hitch a ride tonight. But right now?"

"Yeah, why not? My car is right outside. I'll take you anywhere you want to go, as long as I can go."

Staring at his beautiful body as she spoke, she was hoping that he wasn't too good to be true. "What about George? Are you going to leave your buddy hanging?"

"No. I'll take him home first. You don't mind riding along, do you?"

"You better check with your friend first," she said. "I wouldn't want to interfere with any plans you two might have." She was teasing him, of course. And though her youth and her fantasy-filled life allowed her to play games, if provoked, there was no reason to play games with Joseph. So far, he was the real thing.

"The only plans I want to have tonight are with you."

"And what about next month?" she said as she rubbed up against him and kissed him lightly on the lips.

"Next month and the month after that," he said before thinking.

He walked off looking for George to tell his friend that the evening was over. It was up to George if he wanted to hang around and find his own ride home. The fact that he caught up with Jacqueline, in Newton's of all places, was great. He had been coming to this place for years, and could not recollect ever seeing her in here before. And cussing her out for standing him up was least on his mind. He was just grateful that he would be able to spend another night with her.

Disappointed as he was, George agreed to call it a night. Jacqueline waved good-bye to her friends and left with the two men. As Joseph drove towards George's house, they all engaged in small talk.

Jacqueline seemed to be pretty interested in the lives of sailors. George was more than happy to talk about their adventures. Whenever he got too close to the subject of all the women they had access to, Joseph would interrupt him. But, he was able to talk around that subject and still keep Jacqueline's attention.

In turn, he asked her about her work and what she did for fun. She told him about the research work she did and explained to him that she liked doing almost anything that involved spontaneity. Of course, George thought this to mean that she was a freak. But he kept that to himself.

When Joseph dropped George off at home, he was relieved that he finally had Jacqueline to himself. "Where would you like to go?" he asked her as he began driving down the street.

"Let's go to your place," she said. It was time she checked Joseph out a little closer.

He hadn't figured on her saying that because they had always gone to a motel whenever they were going to have sex. But tonight, he figured that it was no big deal since it was so late, Ronnie had already done her checking up on him for the night. He would simply take Jacqueline home very early in the morning just in case Ronnie decided to pull one of her early morning visits again.

He drove to his building and led her upstairs to his apartment. As he led her into the front door, his mind began to visualize inside, to recall if there were any signs of Veronica. He recounted his morning with Ronnie, and was not able to determine if she had left anything behind.

Jacqueline already knew about Sayla, so he didn't have to worry about hiding any of his daughter's belongings. Jacqueline had never asked him how old his daughter was, so he never volunteered. Though he figured if she knew that his daughter was still a baby, she would have asked about the baby mama.

After she sat down on the sofa, Joseph offered her a drink. She didn't want one so he turned on the radio and joined her on the sofa. "I'm glad you're here," he softly said to her.

"How glad?" she said in response.

"This glad." He leaned toward her and started kissing her on the neck. He moved his hand onto one of her breasts.
She suddenly tore away from him, stood and walked a few feet away from the sofa. "This is a nice place you have here."

Joseph sat there with the look of confusion on his face. He figured that she was just playing hard-to-get...again. "Thanks," he said quickly. Then he stood up and followed in her direction.

When he stood right in front of her, he realized just how small she really was even with her heels on. She was a petite woman compared to Ronnie. She looked so feminine…so sexy…so edible. "Is there something that I can do to make you more comfortable?" he asked her.

"No. I'm very comfortable thank you," she said. "Why? Is there a problem with me just standing here and not ripping off my clothes so you can fuck me?"

He was put back by her question and it showed all over his face. "No, of course not." He lied.

"Joseph, look," she said, "the circumstances under which we met were funny and mysterious and fanciful. And yes, we were very attracted to one another. But I must make it perfectly clear to you that I am not your sex kitten. I enjoy a good sex-session just like any other red blooded American girl but by the same token, I say when, where and how."

Joseph stood there a little dumbfounded. It was a trip how this woman could say any little thing and make him stand to attention. Of course he didn't have to take it, so when he did take it he was confused even more. She obviously didn't give a fuck about him or their little love affair, or did she?

After stunning him into submission, Jacqueline changed her colors again. She stood on her tippy toes, bending his neck down with her hands, and licked across his lips. When he stuck out his tongue to greet hers, she pulled away. She then walked around to his back and put her arms around his waist. She pulled his ass closely into her body. He couldn't see her face but she could hardly keep herself from cracking up out loud.

Next, she began to fondle his penis through his pants. She could feel that he was already rock-hard. Joseph just stood there like he was the woman and he let her have her way with him. That's what he liked about Jacqueline; she was a take-charge kind of woman.

At a remarkably slow pace, she began to undress him. She took her time on purpose just to see how cool he would try to be. To her amazement, he was going along with the game. After she had removed every article of his clothing, she said, "Dance for me."

Joseph was standing there butt-naked, rock-hard and looking stupid. "What?" He couldn't have heard her right.

"Dance for me, baby. That really turns me on."

It just so happened that "In Between The Sheets" by the Isley Brothers was playing on the radio. Joseph didn't know quite what to make out of her request, but because he was hornier than a dog in heat, he started wiggling his ass, just knowing that his efforts would pay off in the best sex with Jacqueline to date.

So he danced for her, doing every move he could think of without embarrassing himself too much. Jacqueline sat down on the sofa and opened her purse. She opened her wallet and began to throw dollar bills at his feet.

He watched the money fall to the ground. "You know, possession is nine tenths of the law," he said without missing a beat.

Jacqueline just smiled and continued to throw money at him. Eventually she began to undress herself. He approached her and tried to help undress her but she slapped his hand away. She undressed herself just as slowly as she had undressed him and she could tell that this was driving him wild. When she was also naked, except for her pumps, she called to him with her finger. He was only too happy to come to her.

They made love on the living room sofa, with Jacqueline being the aggressor, as usual. Joseph didn't mind one bit. He liked the fact that he could receive so much pleasure with so little effort for a change. Jacqueline rode him like a cowgirl from the old west, all the while whispering sweet nothings in his ear for extra effect.

The heat that they created was enough to keep them warm for the remainder of the night, so they slept in the same position they had finally collapsed in. Jacqueline had succeeded in teaching Joseph a lesson in love; that the girl is not always the one who is getting fucked.

Joseph was still asleep with a smile on his face, clinging on to Jacqueline's butt when the sun started rising. Jacqueline slipped away from his grip and into the bathroom for a long soak in his bathtub. She was careful not to wake him up until it was actually time for him to take her home. She didn't want to make love to him this morning, figuring he had had enough to last him for a minute. She didn't want to give away too much, too soon, as her mother would say.

While in the tub, she couldn't help but think about Vincent. "Where in the fuck is he?" she kept whispering to herself. Ever since she caught him red-handed, she had been doing everything to keep herself away from him. But when she finally broke down and called him, only his answering machine picked up. That wasn't unusual because Vincent was the type to be bothered with only those he felt like being bothered with. Still, she couldn't help but wonder because he hadn't been himself lately.

She was truly concerned. She knew that deep down inside Vincent was a confused and lost little boy. But it was totally up to him to ask for help from somebody. It might as well be her, since she loved him just because. However, she decided she would not pursue a dead end. If Vincent wants to be a love-less whore for the rest of his life, then so-be-it; she had better fish to fry. The skillet was already hot, and the hot sauce was on the kitchen table.

After she finished her bath, she was quiet to tip toe to the living room and pick up her clothes. Joseph was still sleeping on the sofa with that stupid look on his face. Jacqueline looked at him and thought, "He's really cute. I hope he's as nice a guy as I think he is." She took her clothes into his bedroom to get dressed. Afterwards, she walked over to his balcony window and looked outside. The sky was a deep purple and pink color. She always did like this time of morning...coming home from the club.

After her nostalgic gaze out of the window, she decided to wake Joseph up so he could take her home. As soon as she turned and headed towards the door, his phone made a noise. It startled her a little, because it didn't ring, it just clicked. She figured that the caller had hung up before it could ring. But before she could get out of his bedroom, she heard a woman's voice coming from his answering machine. She didn't make anything out of a single man receiving phone calls from women. He probably had several women lined up. But what she heard next stopped her dead in her tracks.

"Joseph, what is your machine doing on this early in the morning? Are you there? Anyway, I just wanted to catch you early and tell you that the minister wants to meet with us this morning after service for some last minute pre-marriage counseling."

Jacqueline found herself turning slowly to look at the machine with a bewildered look on her face. Her first thought was to go and pick up the phone, but she changed her mind after realizing that it would be her dumb ass looking like a whore. She heard the other woman's voice say, "Call me when you're on your way to pick us up. We love you."

"We love you? That must be his daughter's mother," she thought. "The son of a bitch is going to marry his baby's mother!? And from what the chick said, 'last minute pre-marriage counseling,' the wedding is coming up really soon."

Were all of the men she knew dogs? After this new revelation, she was convinced that they were. Damn!

Jacqueline walked quietly into the living room and saw that Joseph apparently had not heard anything and was still sleeping. She decided not to raise any hell about what she had just heard from the voice on the answering machine. She would play it cool and play him even cooler. She leaned over him and whispered, "Wake up, baby. Wake up."

Joseph moaned a little until he finally opened his eyes. "Good morning, sexy," he whispered back.

"It's time for you to take me home, sleepy head." She was biting her tongue the whole time, as she held back the urge to cuss him out. She kissed him on the lips. He grabbed hold to her waist and pulled her down on top of him. She began to stroke his penis, as it quickly grew in the palm of her hand.
"Later, baby. I've got something to do this morning, but I promise I'm going to do something to you that you'll never forget."

Joseph smiled at her.

She smiled back.

(11) – Gregory – Meet, Greg

The weeks that followed Gregory's confrontation with Sara, showed him that he had to finally face the truth; that he was being reckless with his life because he wasn't able to handle the pressure. But surprisingly, his mother had taken such a firm grip on the situation she wasn't going to let him fall even if he wanted to.

You see, the first thing each morning, she would call to make sure he didn't over sleep. At the first sign of Gregory becoming agitated in any way, she would miraculously walk through the door and tell him what he needed to hear. And whenever he thought that he might crack in front of the board of directors, she would show up and give him that famous Thomas Childs line: "Of course you can pull it off. You're a Childs, aren't you?"

Sara was slowly but surely filling the shoes of her children's father. They were all becoming more dependent on her for all kinds of support. None of this went unnoticed by Louise. She had nearly blistered every inch of her lips by trying to keep herself from interfering with the kids and their mother.

Although Louise was not a selfish woman, she couldn't help but wonder about any other motives that Sara might have in regards to the kids, now that Thomas was not around to protect them from her. But every opportunity she got, Sara would march her way up to the Childs front door.

Theresa was usually the first to open it and greet her mother with wide-eyed joy. Louise would stay away from the family during these times, retreating to pool house or the surrounding gardens. The situation was awkward enough with having an estranged mother trying her damnedest to reconcile in her house. So Louise said nothing, she just kept her ear close to the grind.

The family, except for Sara, didn't know the extent of what Gregory had been going through; from his weird sexual behavior to his prescription drug usage. So he did his best to shield them from his drama while trying to kick his bad habits and become normal again.

Whether he wanted to admit it or not, his mother had come around just in time before he completely self-destructed. Who else could he have talked to regarding something as intimidate as what he was going through, but an estranged mother?

Anybody else would have had him committed or something, but, not Sara. She would do anything to get back in the good graces of her children. And when she was gathered together with all of her children in the study, she and Gregory would always have a strange communication going on between them that the others were not a part of.

One Friday evening after Gregory, Jeremy and Theresa made it home; Louise had a big surprise waiting for them in the back yard. She had spent the entire day instructing the staff on how to prepare the perfect barbeque on the open grill. They were all used to Thomas, donning his chef's hat and apron and firing up the grill on rare occasions. So the fact the Louise would even attempt such a gathering was a special treat.

The estate was large enough to host a celebrity golf tournament but no one ever took advantage of all that it had to offer, but her and the grandchildren, who were on their way with Lisa. Everything was set for a fun filled early evening with the children she loved as her own. "Louise? What is this?" Gregory said smiling as he approached her in the garden.

"You surprised?" Louise asked hesitantly.

"More like astonished," Jeremy said, as he brushed past Gregory and headed for the table overflowing with food.

"Why didn't you tell us you were going all out tonight? You know we could have come home early to help you with all of this?" Gregory asked.

"Then it wouldn't be a surprise," she said with a slight laugh.

"I don't know why you didn't tell us," Theresa said as she threw her book bag down on the sofa. "Didn't you know that our mother is taking us out to dinner tonight?" she added with a distasteful tone.

Gregory turned to her with an angry look. Sara stood there with her mouth gaping wide open and Jeremy was too busy tasting everything with his fingers to hear anything. "Theresa, you are tactless, you know that? There's no need for such a distasteful attitude," he said to her, sounding more like his father than he would like to.

Theresa quickly tried to turn on the little girl charm. "I didn't mean it like that Gregory. I just meant that mother will be disappointed if we don't go out with her like we planned." She turned to Louise. "I didn't mean anything by it Louise...really. But you do understand that we're going with our real mother tonight." Again, she plunged her hurtful little knife further into Louise's heart.

Before Gregory could try and smooth over what his little sister had said, Louise dashed past the both of them and ran upstairs as fast as she could. "What's wrong with you, girl?!" Gregory asked her furiously.

"Nothing is wrong with me. What's wrong with you? You act like she's our mother or something, and she's not, Sara is. Why do we have to pretend like everything is hunky-dory around here anyway? Pops is not around here anymore, so why is she?"

Gregory had to hold back his urge to slap her. But she was young and silly and for reasons unknown, probably didn't know any better. "Because whether you like it or not she is part of this family. She was Pops wife for cryin' out loud! She took care of your spoiled, little ass when Sara was not around; this house is partly hers, and because I said so."

Lisa and her four children had come in through the back yard just in time to hear Gregory yelling at Theresa. She led them into the family room and put the sleeping baby in his bassinet. Then she joined her brother and sister in their heated discussion. Jeremy finally took interest in what was going on and followed behind Lisa, with a rib bone stuck between his teeth.

"Hey...hey...hey, what's going on you guys?" Lisa asked, taking a stand in between the two of them.

"Ask your little sister. I'm going up stairs to try and undo what this brat just did to Louise." Gregory gave Theresa another hard look before walking away. He could hear Theresa whimpering out her pathetic little story to Lisa and Jeremy as he climbed the staircase. He approached Louise's room very quietly and then he placed his ear to the door to listen for any noise. When he didn't hear anything, he knocked.

"Come on in Gregory," she said.

Gregory slowly opened up the door and walked in, closing it behind him. "How did you know it was me?" he asked carefully.

"I recognized your ear against the door," she said with a failed smile. She was sitting in her lounge chair with her knees cupped up to her chin. He knew that she had been crying even though she tried to hide it

"Pops spoiled that girl rotten," he said trying to break the ice. He took a seat at the end of the bed and faced her.

"That girl is a grown woman, even if she doesn't act like it all of the time. But, still...she knew what she was saying. She has every right to her own opinion."

"Yeah, but she doesn't have to have everything her way. That girl has got to learn that sometimes other people's feelings have the right of way sometimes. And if anybody's feelings deserve special treatment right now, that would be yours." He took a deep breath.

"Louise, you don't think I know how difficult this transition has been for you? You lose the man you love...you get stuck with four kids who you didn't give birth to...and a woman who you probably despise has come back to claim what's hers. You're pissed off, and you have every reason to be."

Louise looked up at Gregory with tears in her eyes. "What am I still doing here Gregory? I don't belong anymore. Maybe it would be best for me to leave."

"Over my dead body! Gregory insisted. "You're not going anywhere...nobody is going anywhere. We're family Louise. Too many years have gone by for us not to be considered a family."

"But what about your mother Gregory? She wants you all back. There isn't room for the both of us."

"Says who? You're giving up too easy. This isn't the woman I remember making me eat my vegetables before I could eat dessert. Or, who made Jeremy fight back in school. Or, who taught Lisa and the brat how to handle boys on a first date. No! The woman I remember is a fighter...a fighter for her man and his family. So the bottom line is, you're stuck with us, whether you like it or not. And as far as Sara is concerned, Theresa is the only one who really missed having her around. The rest of us are pretty much just going with the flow."

Gregory was trying as best he could to drive home his point across to Louise. He respected his father's wishes that Louise belonged in the house with everyone else. Hell, chances were if she were to see an attorney of her own, she could probably kick everybody out of the house and claim it as her own. They were legally married through common-law...anything is possible.

"I'm glad you feel so strongly about having me around Gregory," she was saying as he drifted back from his own thoughts.

"Huh?"

"I said...I love you too!"

After his talk with Louise, Gregory headed back downstairs to see what the rest of his family was up to. His nieces and nephews were all busying themselves in front of the television. Lisa, Theresa and Jeremy had not moved. Jeremy spoke first. "Is she alright, man?"

"No, she's not alright. Would you be alright if someone you raised, and love, told you that your services were no longer required?"

Lisa said, "Look you guys, we're all adults here and we are all going to have to make this sticky situation with Sara and Louise less sticky. Now it's not going to be easy, but Resa realizes that she made a mistake. Don't you?"

"Yeah. I didn't mean it the way it came out. I just don't want Louise to try and keep me from being with my mother." Gregory was about to speak out, but Theresa threw up her hands in protest. "But I'm sorry that it all came out wrong like that." She looked at Gregory. "Is she really mad at me?"

"No, Theresa. Her feelings are just hurt, that's all."

"Well, I'm going up to tell her that I'm sorry, OK."

"Yeah, do that. And why you're at it, why don't you tell her that you love her too. She would probably like to hear that from you...from all of us."

They all agreed that Louise should be made to feel like a part of the family...still. The entire situation had evolved because Theresa had neglected to tell the rest of the family that Sara had invited them all out. She just assumed that everyone else had no other plans and would be as willing and eager to go out with Sara just like that. So it was up to her to call Sara and cancel the plans for the evening. They were all going to spend the evening with Louise...their mom.

"Did you call her and cancel, Resa," Lisa asked as Theresa approached the picnic table.

"I called her, but there was no answer. She must be on her way over here already."

Gregory looked to Louise to get her reaction, but she was hiding it pretty good by busying herself with the twins. "When she gets here, I'll talk to her," he said. Everyone nodded their approval.

Just then Gregory got an idea. "Hey?" Everyone looked up at him in surprise. "What if we invite her to stay here and eat with us?" Louise gave a look of disappointment. "I mean, what if we invite Sara to dine with our family so we can all get to know her better. Louise, me, you, you, you..." he was pointing around the table. "...all of us. If she wants to be a part of our lives, then she should do it out in the open, in front of Louise. This has been our family for years and years and no one here should be made to feel out of place in their own home."

He looked around the table in defense of his statement. No one argued, not even Theresa. Louise looked up at him and smiled a sincere smile. "Good," he said. Now, at least Louise doesn't have to feel like the odd wheel. And Sara...well, Sara would just have to deal with it!

"Pass the potato salad please," is all Jeremy had to say. Where did he put all of the food he ate?

When the doorbell rang, Gregory rose to answer it. But before he could stand upright, Louise stood and said, "I'll get it." Gregory froze, afraid to speak and afraid of the monster he might have created. But he sat back down and looked around at his brother and sisters. None of them seemed to have a problem with her answering the door. He was the only paranoid one...as usual. Oh how he would love to be a fly on the wall when Louise opened the door for his mother. He wasn't looking for a cat-fight; he just wanted Louise to get what she deserved in her own house...respect.

Several minutes passed by before Louise emerged with Sara. "Kids, your mother has accepted our invitation to dine with us this evening." Louise gave a quick wink to Gregory, which he quickly returned. She returned to her seat at the table and then asked Sara to have a seat.

"Mother, I tried to call you to explain about the mix-up, but it was too late and Louise had already made us this big dinner and nobody wanted to upset her, not that anybody wanted to upset you but we couldn't let all of this good food go to waste and now you can eat with us and we all still get to be together anyway." Theresa was talking so fast that no one could put a word in edge wise.

"Theresa slow down. You're running all of your sentences together," Sara said with a slight laugh. "Besides, Louise was kind enough to explain the mix-up and I still get to eat with my beautiful children."

"Hello Sara," Lisa said, followed by Jeremy.

"Well hello there yourselves. And look at my little sprouts over there," she said pointing to Lisa's kids, who ignored her and continued to pester Louise. "Louise, the food looks wonderful. It looks like you cooked enough for an army." Everyone grew silent and looked to Louise for her come back.

"No, not an army, just Jeremy." Everyone started to laugh so hard that food started falling out of their mouths. No one noticed that Sara wasn't laughing.

When the chit chat from Louise's funny comment died down, Sara said, "I don't get it. You mean to tell me that my skinny boy over there has a large appetite?" Again, they all started to laugh. No one even bothered to answer her. Mother or not, she sure did not know her kids as well as she would like to believe she did.

Dinner flew by. It was all working out to everybody's satisfaction...except maybe for Sara's. Without even realizing what they were doing, they were all confirming to her that they were a family, and had been for a long time. But Sara pretended not to be affected by the whole thing. Even her precious little Theresa betrayed her by continuously asking Louise her opinion about one boy or another.

After dinner, Gregory lit the outdoor fire place and they all gathered around on the lounge chairs and blankets. The kids were playing in their playhouse that their grand pop had built for them a few years ago. Louise was lying on a blanket with Lisa and the baby. Jeremy and Theresa were trying to get a dance step, called the Electric Slide, together.

"So," Sara said walking up behind Gregory. "I can see that you've all been taken care of very well."

Gregory turned around to face his mother. "What made you realize that?"

"By the way you all act together."

"You mean, like a family?"

"Yes. Like a family. I can see that Louise really loves all of you very much. And you all love her too...don't you?"

"Without a doubt. She'd go through hell and back for each and every one of us. She's a good woman. Pops was lucky to find her after..." He let his final comments disappear into silence.

"I'd better get going now," she said. I can tell that you're feeling much better these days. That's all I ever wanted."

"You can stay and enjoy the family for a little longer. You're amongst a friendly people here. We won't bite."

"I know sweetheart, but I don't want to wear out my welcome," she said.

"Now how could that be Mother, you'd have to be around longer to do that." Right after he said it, he realized how mean it must have sounded. "No pun intended," he said, as a weak attempt to apologize to her, but he knew that it still stung her a little.

She smiled. "None taken."

Sara joined Jeremy and Theresa in their dance step. She was still a very youthful and beautiful woman. Gregory guessed that she had danced the night away in many nightclubs all over the world.

Tonight, he needed to dance...to feel his youth again. He left the backyard picnic without disturbing anyone, because he didn't want to break up the party. It was a picture perfect moment. If only his father could have been around to see Louise and Sara in the same place, breathing the same air. Even he would have gotten a kick out of that.

Gregory drove down the street heading nowhere in particular, as long as he could unwind. He found himself driving north on Pacific Coast Highway in Malibu approaching Gladstones. He pulled into the always crowded parking lot and entered the restaurant.

At the bar, he was tempted to ask for a glass of his favorite brandy. It would be easy to get swept away into a state of oblivion and not have to think about all the things that had gone wrong in his life. But instead he settled for a bottle of beer.

The restaurant was filled with its usual crowd of yuppie type people. Most of them were over paid and under skilled. He wondered if he fit the bill, too. Music was blaring in the bar section, as men drooled over skimpily clad women. Some of the women were flirting to any and every one, while displaying their all too obvious silicon breasts. Yes, the crowd was a lively one alright. This was just the place to set his progress back a hundred years.

Tired with the busy scene of Gladstones, Gregory downed the last corner of his beer, paid his tab and walked into the cool ocean breeze. He could see that a full moon was shimmering over the ocean. It was as though it were beckoning him to come closer. So he did.

He walked down the flight of stairs leading to the beach. It might have looked a little funny for anyone who might have noticed, to see him with a suit and tie on. He stopped at a bench and took off his expensive shoes and socks, stuck them in his jacket pockets and walked towards the calm shore. There, he looked into the sky and saw the moon smiling at him. It was a peaceful night and he was just glad that he could walk the shore alone and undisturbed.

As he started a slow stroll down the beach, thoughts of his father, once again, entered into his mind. He would have felt foolish talking out loud to the old man, so he let his inner thoughts communicate for him.

"Pops, are you there? Can you see me? It's me Gregory. You should have been at the house tonight, Pops. It was something to see. Sara showed up as proud as a tiger, but Louise held her ground. I think in time the two of them are going to come to some sort of understanding about their positions in the Childs family. Theresa almost made a mess of things, but I think we got that all straightened out. She's spoiled Pops. How did you let that happen? Well, I think I know. She was your baby, right? You just did what any other over protective and doting father would do, right?

By the way, how am I doing as CEO? Are there any pointers you have for me? I know that I still have a lot to learn, but I think that I'm finally getting the hang of it. It's going to take me longer than I expected to be able to handle the pressure and the wealth, but I'll try.

Pops, when did you get so rich? I mean, I knew we were rich, but I never knew about all of the assets you had stashed around the world. I wish I were better prepared for all of it. And as you know, I've already done some stupid things with the money. Hanging around that tramp Venus, sure took me for a loop. She was just in it for the money. And she did anything for me to get it. Some women are a trip, huh Pops? But I guess you knew that. That's why you got with a woman like Louise after mother. She didn't want you for your money, did she Pops? She wanted you for you. You two were good for each other. You were lucky. I hope that one day I'm lucky enough to find a woman who wants me for me and not for my money.

Well, Pops, I hope you're flying high up there in Heaven. You're probably making major business deals with the Angels up there, huh? Don't double cross them. We wouldn't want anything to keep you from getting your wings, big guy. Anyway...I hope you can hear me...and I hope you can see me. I miss you Pops. I'll talk to you again...soon."

After his silent prayer, Gregory continued his slow paced walk along the beach. His pant legs were getting wet from walking too close to the water. Not only did he not notice, he didn't care. A ruined suit was the least of his worries.

He was set for life, if he was as smart as his father. Peace of mind was all that consumed his thoughts at this moment, and someone to love. He never thought that he would think a relationship could help him to cope better. But after talking to his father, he assumed that a healthy relationship could take a man a lot further than if he were by himself.

But where does a rich man go to find a woman who will love him for him?...certainly not in a place like Gladstones. Rich people frequented that place more than the average earning folk, even though most of them tried to dress themselves down with holey jeans and T-shirts. No. He would have to find a woman in a less conspicuous place. And aside from that, he would have to let fate play its role in things.

A good thing is hard to find...so it's probably better not to look. Let it find you instead. That's easier said than done though. Most people can't help but try and find love. Especially when you think you need it in order to survive. That's how he got in trouble with Venus. He wasn't about to let that happen again.

After a while, he got tired of walking so he just sat there on the sand. There were several people, here and there, who were walking around, kissing, or just enjoying fires that they had built. Gregory tried to ignore them all. He didn't want to think anymore, but to instead just sit. The moon was moving in its direction. It was slowly trying to hide itself behind a small patch of clouds. "I wonder what you're running from," Gregory said quietly to himself.

His eyes followed everywhere the moon went, until he could see it no more. Without the moon to keep him company, he suddenly felt cold and very alone. But he continued to sit and try to seek out the dimly lit stars in the sky.

The bright lights of the city, mixed with the constant smog, was always making it nearly impossible to see the light show the sky has to offer. Sometimes, like when he was a little boy, he wished that he could just float away into the sky and talk to the constellations face to face. To get lost in the black hole would be a trip, if not frightening. Well, those were the things that little boys thought about. He was no longer a little boy, but a grown man. And what is it that grown men think about? Money and women, which brought him back to his original thoughts.

So he decided to create an alter ego of himself that was not as extravagant as he actually was. That way, when he met people he would automatically present himself as one of those average earning people - like the ones in that restaurant.

"Yeah," he said to himself. "The next time I talk to a woman, or a man for that matter, I'll just pass myself off as an average Joe. I could be a clerk or a foreman, or something like that. And instead of earning six figures a year, I could earn in the low five figures. That way, I'm sure to deal with other average people like me. And I won't have to keep my guard up all of the time." That was that. The next time he introduced himself to someone, he would be plain old Greg.

He would have to keep a pair of Jeans in his car. Better yet, he would have to stop driving the Jag everywhere and get a jeep or something. And he would have to remember not to give out his business cards. Instead, he could scribble his number on a piece of gum wrapper paper with a pencil instead of a Mont Blanc Pen. That's it! An alter ego is all he needed to make himself feel normal...isn't it?

He was so excited with his idea that he immediately got up from the sand and started trotting to his car. It was still early enough to find some clothing store open. Why put off tomorrow what you can do today, was his thinking. He was eager to start his double life. And first things first, were to take off his expensive suit and shoes and trade them in for some jeans, T-shirt and some athletic shoes.

And as he neared his car, he wondered where he could go to find his spare clothing. Well he was at the beach, in the summer time. He was sure that one of the beaches would have a clothing store still open for business. So he drove off in search of one, and luckily for him he found just a store.

After changing into his new outfit, he felt like a new man. He was proud with his decision to go out into the world and be somebody else for a change, even if it was for after hours and weekends. Besides, he had no desire to hurt anyone or even deceive them. He just wanted to be Greg. And he found out soon after changing his clothes that people began to look at him differently...like he was going to rob them or something.

"How funny," he thought. "Just a minute ago they were all looking at me like I was going to start throwing money at them, and now there looking at me like I'm going to start demanding it. I guess clothes do make the person."

The next step was to lose the Jag, so he pulled in to a used car lot. There he found just what he was looking for, a 1987 grey Cherokee Jeep. He whipped out his American Express Gold card and purchased it outright. The salesman thought he had just died and gone to Heaven. When asked what he was going to do with his Jaguar he said, "I'll have it towed home."

He wrote a note for Louise explaining that he had bought another car and sealed it in an envelope to be given to her, upon the arrival of the tow truck. He waited for the tow truck to arrive and hook up the Jag and he took off into the night in his new used, jeep.

He was beside himself. There he was, driving around in a car he had just purchased with a credit card, wearing ordinary clothes he had just purchased, pretending to be someone other than himself. If Sara could see him now, she would probably disown him.

She was so into high fashion and society that she would surely think that he had completely lost his mind. But be damned of that. He was going to be normal, if it killed him. Oddly enough, in his jeep he was still receiving inviting stares from women in passing cars, probably because he looked macho driving around with the top off and a T-shirt on.

"Maybe I should get an earring," he thought. But soon shrugged that thought off his mind. He didn't want to change that much. By transforming himself into this new guy, it had almost certainly transformed him into a bigger target for bigoted policemen too. He would surely die of embarrassment if one ever stopped him to ask him if he were affiliated with a gang...simply die.

But for now, he wanted to test out his new identity, but where? He couldn't go to a dance club dressed like this. And no one would be able to see him in a movie theater. So where was an average guy to go on a Friday night?

When the answer didn't come, he began to feel foolish about the entire plan. Who did he think he was, anyway? Someone who could buy things, just like that, and change who they really were? Hell! He was still the same person who thought just the same way as before. And the truth to the matter was...he was just a simple kind of guy, who didn't know where to go or what to do. The only thing he was good at was mixing in with the wrong kind of people for the wrong reasons. And God knows he didn't want to go through that shit again.

Depressed by his shock back into reality, he decided to go home. He would go home and maybe play a game of chess with Jeremy, if he was home, which probably wasn't the case, because if anybody had adjusted to the life of being rich and normal at the same time, it was Jeremy. Maybe he could get a few pointers from his kid brother? But that would be embarrassing for him. Asking his brother, "How do you cope with being rich and normal, Jeremy?" Oh, what the hell. Computer chess is just as challenging.

But before he turned off of PCH, he approached the Santa Monica Pier. He could see that the lights were still burning bright, which meant that the amusement park was probably open. So he turned into the parking lot and began another stroll on yet another beach.

The atmosphere at this beach was much more different from the one in Malibu. People were burning fires and kissing, but their level of energy was much more noticeable. Some people were splashing and playing in the water, just as though the sun were out instead of the moon.

Several large crowds of people were having what seemed to be a birthday party. That was a great idea - to have a birthday party as a night time beach party. He walked past lots of activities on the beach, and for the first time, he felt completely normal. He hung around for a while watching the activities around him.

He sat on the sand, just as he had done in Malibu, and looked into the sky. Here the moon seemed to shine even more brightly than before. Though he wondered how that could be since there were more lights in this area. Just the same, he took in his surroundings and was glad that he had decided to spend his Friday night at the beach.

When he got up to go the pier, the closer he got the louder the voices of people got. When he climbed the stairs to the pier, he knew why. Hundreds upon hundreds of people had apparently flocked here tonight to take advantage of the warm summer night. He could have sworn that he was at Disneyland...with the vagrants, of course.

Every time he saw a homeless man or woman, he was compelled to take out his wallet and give them the contents. But he couldn't tonight. Gregory would do that, not Greg. He walked past them with eyes unseeing and kept his hands in his jean pockets. He went into the arcade and cashed a $50 dollar bill to get quarters to play with. He had so many quarters that he could hardly stuff them all into his pockets, so he gave hands full of them to different children who were watching and not playing.

When he ran out of quarters, only after about 20 minutes, he cashed another $50. By the time he ran out of those quarters, he was pretty good at Donkey Kong and some other games. The children loved him. They knew a good thing when they saw one, especially one who had so many quarters.

Outside he could hear the bumper cars going at it. So he bought five tickets and jumped in one of the beat up cars. The cars jerked to a start, and he was off, bumping into and against the other beat up cars. Each ride seemed shorter and shorter, but he was having fun. After his fifth ticket, he was used up and he became a spectator instead. Watching the children play was just as amusing as watching the other adults go at it.

Crowds were cheering their friends and family on, as though they were driving in the Indy 500. Little heads were being snapped back and forth. You would expect them to start crying or something, but everybody was getting off on this. Most of the people there were Hispanic, so when they yelled out to their friends and family all Greg could do was smile as to say, "Yeah, you look like you're having fun." Soon after, though, the bumper cars were becoming boring. So he turned his attention elsewhere.

The far end of the pier looked to be interesting. He could see that rows of people were fishing from it. As he walked toward them, he watched as they cut up various kinds of fish they used for bait: Mackerel, Anchovies and Mussels from what he could tell.

Most of them skillfully cut and stuck the bait on the ends of their hooks and flung their lines into the dark ocean below. Others were not as experienced. They looked as squeamish in trying to put on the bait as the bait itself. But all in all, they fished as if to save their lives.

One Hispanic man pulled out a large fish and started flinging it around in victory. He presented it around and held it up to Greg as he approached him. He said something that Greg didn't understand. Greg just shook his head and smiled. "No habla espanol, partner," he finally managed to say as he walked past the lucky fisherman.

The full moon must have been a lucky time to fish, because everybody seemed to be doing well. Although, he couldn't always tell which fish was the bait and which was the catch.

At the far end of the pier, he was able to find an empty railing to rest upon. He was tempted to take out his handkerchief and wipe it off first, but thought this would be something Gregory would do, not Greg. So he leaned on it and looked down into the dark ocean. It was easy to see his reflection in the water, with the moon towering above it. Every now and again little bubbles would surface and burst...probably little fish.

This was great, he thought. Looking out into a void of space and time was just what he needed to lift his mind of the pressures he faced. Changing his persona didn't hurt either. All it meant was that he had the opportunity to drop some of his defenses and be a simple person from time to time. Pretty much like the people that were on this pier. Maybe he'd buy a fishing pole himself? It seemed easy enough. God knows he needed an outlet.

Well, why he thought about that, time must have passed him by, because when he looked up, at least two-thirds of the people who had once been on the beach and the pier had vanished. Nearly alone, at least on the far end of the pier, Greg sat down on a bench, spread his arms to either side of the bench and closed his eyes.

When he concentrated really hard he could hear many different sounds; the crash of the waves, the murmur of faint voices, the ringing of a bell, the roar of plane engines, and footsteps approaching him from behind. He quickly opened his eyes and turned around to see if he was about to be jacked. All he saw was a figure of a woman dressed in dark clothes walking to a section of the railing. She didn't even seem to notice him.

Greg watched as she went through some of the same motions as he had when he approached the railing. He wondered if their thoughts were the same too. After a moment, he closed his eyes once again and tried to find those sounds again, but he couldn't.

"I wonder if my car made it home OK?" he said to himself. At the same time he had to restrain himself for reaching for his cell phone to call home and check. Besides, he left the phone in the trunk of the Jag with his clothes. This business of trying to be a simple kind of guy was going to take a little more practice than he thought.

He couldn't help but laugh out loud at the idea of it. When he laughed, the woman leaning on the railing looked up to see who was there. Apparently he startled her. As he looked in her direction he tried to see her features by moonlight. "I'm sorry, I didn't mean to scare you," he said to her.

"It's OK," she said. "I should have looked around to see what my surroundings were before drifting off." Then she turned her attentions back to the black sea.

Greg didn't want to bother her, but she seemed upset. He could tell by her body posture that she had some troubles of her own. But he didn't say anything else to her, he just stared.

He could tell that she was medium brown in complexion with her hair in a hanging ponytail. It looked like she had on some black jeans and a dark shirt with maybe a black leather jacket. The only thing he knew for sure is that she had a sweet sounding voice.

As he watched her, his eyes began to adjust to the darkness, and though he only had a profile view of her, he was sure that she was beautiful. He thought to himself about what an average guy would say to an average girl on a pier, on a Friday night. He didn't have a clue. Luckily for him, she gave him an idea as she looked up into the sky at the moon.

"Have you ever seen it so big and bright before?" he asked out loud.

Without turning to face his, she answered. "It's just like a light bulb turning on in your mind."

Greg was confused by her answer. She sounded almost philosophical. He thought he was the only one feeling nostalgic tonight. "I wish I were there tonight," he said.

"I'll race you."

"Actually, I'd like to get swept into the black hole out there."

She placed her hand underneath her chin and thought for a minute before responding. "I'd rather just see the view of the earth from inside it and maybe throw meteors at selected individuals." She laughed.

"Damn. I wouldn't want to be on your shit list," Greg said to her, trying to sound like any other brotha.

"I didn't mean it like that," she said. "I'd just like to see who can jump their way out of situations, and who can't."

"And if someone can't move out of the way in time?"

"Hey. We've all gotta go sometime." The both of them started laughing at her comment.

"Let the water soak up all of your anxieties. That's what it's here for, you know?" Greg said to her.

"Yeah, I know. Good thing for me there's lots of it. And you? Oh yeah, you want to live in outer space somewhere, right?"

"No. Just visit the constellations and the black hole and be back in time for dinner."

"If you had a choice of transportation, would it be by rocket or by astro-traveling?"

"Slow down. I haven't gotten that far in my thinking yet. Oh, you're just trying to get rid of me so you can have this whole pier for yourself, huh?" he said with amusement.

She was amused too, and said, "No. I'm just trying to help you get where you wanna be." Again they laughed.

Their non-topic conversation went on for another 20 minutes or so. Neither of them moved to get closer to the other. It would be like invading the others obviously needed space. Their sarcastic view of the world and the people in it was almost identical. They laughed easily at each other's jokes without pretense. Neither of them flirted with the other, nor did they care what the other thought of them.

Greg was receiving the best opportunity he had had all night to be just an average guy. She seemed to be really smart, tough and fragile all rolled up into one tight package. Greg thought it too bad that someone had put her in a defensive mood. She probably was a lot of fun when she was in a good mood. Anyway, he didn't want to get into her business by asking any personal questions, so he kept all of his questions as vague as possible. "Are the bumper cars still at it up there?" he asked.

She hesitated before answering. "By the time we came up, they were just shutting them down," she answered.

"We?" he thought to himself. "She's here with someone else?" But he kept these questions to himself. Maybe the person she's with is over on the other side fishing. After answering him, her body posture seemed to tell him that she was upset with whoever she was here with. After a while, she placed her hands on her hips and started walking down the other side of the railing. From what Greg could tell, nobody was over there, but she walked towards the other end anyway.

Every few yards or so, she would stop and look over the railing into the water. After several minutes of doing this, she returned to her original spot near Greg. He didn't want to disturb her. The conversation he had had with her was so nice he didn't want to bring up anything unpleasant. So he waited for her to speak first. Unfortunately for him she didn't speak first, so he had to say something to break the ice all over again. "Did you find a spot where no one would find the body?" Again, he was fortunate to get her to laugh.

"You must really think I'm mean, huh?" she said through laughter.

"No, no. Actually you seem to have a plan in mind. And from the way you've been talking, your plans probably work."

"Well, you're right about me having a plan, but it has nothing to do about getting rid of someone - more like keeping them around."

Greg was convinced that she had it in for someone. And it didn't sound to him like she was trying to hold on to a guy either. It sounded more like she was going to punish somebody and make them like it. "She's good," he thought.

"We need more people like that on our administrative team." Both of them looked up after hearing faint footsteps heading toward them on the pier. "Oh well, I guess our secret hiding place is old news now," Greg said. As he looked at her he figured that she knew the man walking their way.

"It was just a matter of time. What's a girl to do?"

Before Greg knew what came over him he said, "She could call a guy."

She turned from the man approaching them and looked at Greg. "That's nice."

"What's nice? The fact I asked you to call me?"

"No. The fact that you didn't come on to me, and then ask to call me, is nice."

Greg suddenly felt embarrassed and out of place. Why had he just asked this stranger to call him when he hadn't even seen her face? Well, believe it or not, I'm one of the good guys. And besides, I liked our conversation about nothing in particular, didn't you?"

"Sure. It was a load off of my heavy mind."

"Mine too." He took out a stick of Dentine gum and a pencil from his pocket. He put the gum in his mouth, and wrote down his phone number on the tiny gum wrapper. "Here," he said as he stuck the paper into a groove of the wooden bench beside him. He stood and began walking away from her and back towards the beach. "Call me if you need to talk. Better yet, just call me."

He walked off into the night. After he was a good distance away, he turned to see if he could make her out in the darkness. A smile covered his face as he thought he saw her bending to pick up something from the bench. The smile faded as the man who had been approaching them on the pier put his arms around her.

Greg returned to his jeep and headed for home. He had no idea he had just met his crossroad.

(12) – Jax – The Cosmos Must Be Crazy

I can't believe I've been up half the night thinking about all of this "men" shit going on! After I refused to fuck Joseph without an explanation again last night, I told him to take me home. For all he knows I have, yet, another headache. But I've just been trying to decide how to deal with his up-coming wedding that he still hasn't told me about.

I've been going over to his place every night since I found out, trying to get his fiancé to catch us together. But he must think he's got this thing wrapped up; wanting his cake and eating it too. And her ass ain't showed up at his place while I've been there. She has a right to know what she's getting herself into and I have a right to get his ass back! Surely he has no idea that I'm the wrong girl to play games with...but he will.

Even though I enjoy being around his fine ass, he's not getting anything more from me except for what I think of to do to him. And Vincent has been using up every inch of my answering machine tape trying to get a hold of me. These fucking men deserve whatever they get in life. Shit!

I can't even think of the perfect plan to get back at either one of those ass holes. Ordinarily, I'd be fantasizing about finding the perfect man I imagine my pen-pal, Frances to be...or fucking a complete stranger in public...whatever. It's all lived out in my mind, waiting for the day I start writing my play. But now all I do is obsess over controlling this shit I done got myself in. And I'm cussin' to damn much too! "I gotta get my ass back in church."

Time and time again, I continue to open myself up and start to care for "dogs" and look what happens? Now that nice guy, Greg, I met on the pier seemed to be a little different. I could tell right away that he was real. He didn't have anything to hide which is what I would want in a guy, if I were looking, but at the moment I happen to have my hands full. Besides, I don't even know if I still have that small ass piece of paper with his phone number on it. Oh well, I guess I'll look for it later 'cause right now, I'm plotting.

I left my answering machine on low all night and already it had three messages waiting for me to check. Who in the fuck was blowing up my machine like this? Who else? Why was Vincent so eager to talk to me all of a sudden?

The last time we spoke, I told him where to stick it. Even though I knew he would call again, just like I know Joseph will call again and again and again. Do these guys get attached to any particular brand of pussy or is it just unleaded? I swear for the life of me, I will never understand men and the control their dicks have over them.

All of this thinking was making me hungry so on my way to the kitchen I walked down the hall to my mother's room. Her door was ajar and so I peeked in and I could immediately tell that her bed hadn't been slept in again last night. "She's probably hanging out with Mr. Nichol's," I thought. "I sure hope she doesn't marry him before I get a chance to move out."

So I went downstairs into the kitchen and was scavenging the refrigerator for food when I heard the doorbell ring. I walked to the living room and saw my reflection in a mirror. Oh my God, I look like shit! There is no way I'm answering the door looking like this.

Instead of taking a chance on seeing someone that I should look presentable to, I ran upstairs to get a better look out of my mother's bedroom window. Of course I couldn't see anyone because her window is above the front door. But I did see a car parked on the street in front of the house, and it was Vincent's.

"What in the hell was he doing here at this time of morning without an invitation?" I asked myself. He must be full of himself today. Or maybe he's desperately sick and wants to tell me he's dying or something. No. If something was wrong he would have told me a long time ago, right? But he had been acting funny lately and never really told me what was going on. Maybe he's ready to tell me now.

Well, whatever the case may be, I do not like surprise visits. Those are the rules and Vincent knows that. So he'll just have to make an appointment like everybody else. I'm tired of treating him with preferential treatment. From now on, I'm going to treat him just like the rest of the whores.

Yeah, well, all that big talk is easier said than done. The fact is I had to keep myself from quickly gargling with some Listerine, wiping the eye crust away and opening the door. But somehow I was able to keep myself from doing it. I hadn't forgotten what he put me through and I wasn't ready to let him off the hook.

Vincent had some explaining to do and *I* would set the scene for when and where. In the meantime, he would have to continue his effortless attempts to try and get in contact with me. I'm screening all my calls from now on out, 'cause I don't wanna be bothered by no man until I have something to say.

This should convince everybody exactly how I feel and where I stand. I mean...men and women all play games in relationships - whatever that relationship may be; whether you're just cuddling, snuggling, fucking or sucking. But whatever kind of relationship it is, it's got to be an honest one.

Everybody needs to be able to decide if they're down with it, or not. Let me make my own fucking choices, 'cause otherwise you trying to control me and that shit ain't happening.

Mom is always saying, "Jacqueline Marie Winters, you are the youngest person with the oldest soul I have ever met. You're in the body of a young person but you act like you've been around since the beginning of time; always thinking somebody is out to get you. Girl, you better stop thinking so hard and start looking for a husband."

How can I find a husband if every man is a liar? If you act like you're interested in them, then they reveal some kind of game that they're playing. So all I do is make sure that I am outplaying them, that's all. It's not like I want it to be this way, but it is what it is. I either deal with it, or I don't. But, in the case of Vincent and more recently Joseph, I definitely intend to deal with it.

As I sat on my mother's bed and watched Vincent slowly retreat to his car, I expected him to pull off at any second. But to my surprise he sat in the car staring at the house. I couldn't believe what I was seeing. Vincent Cruthers is sitting outside of my house waiting for me to appear. It was the funniest thing I had ever seen. Mr. fine, proud and mighty lover man was trippin' off of a tenderoni like me. Damn I'm good!

I was somewhat flattered but more confused and even more curious as to why he wanted to get in touch with me so bad. I expected him to pull off at any second, but he didn't. He just sat in his car as though he were trying to "will" me to open the door. Well, as long as I kept myself looking as tacky as I was looking, there was no way that I was going to open that door. I didn't wash my face, I didn't brush my teeth, I didn't comb my hair, I didn't put on any deodorant, I didn't do anything. And as long as I was looking like this, nobody was seeing me.

The longer he sat there, the creepier it got. I started thinking about news headlines of women being stalked by crazy men. But that's foolish, because Vincent never showed any traits of being crazy. But damn, when you think about it, those are the ones who usually snap; the ones who act normal. Frightening thought, but I didn't buy it. He was just missing me, that's all. And as long as he was missing me, I was in the driver's seat. Perfect; it gave me something to think about, as far as getting back at him. One down and one to go. Joseph is number two on my list.

I was getting bored with watching that idiot out of my mother's window when my phone rang. Even though I had no intentions of answering it, I did want to listen to whoever's voice it turned out to be. So I made a mad dash for my bedroom in time to hear the voice begin to speak on the machine.

"Where in the hell are you? And better still, where have you been? It's me, are you alive?" It was Sabastian's voice.

I picked up the phone. "Hey girl."

"Hey girl your damn self. Where have you been? Are you alright?" she asked with concern.

"Of course I'm alright. I've just been out of touch, that's all."

"Well that's not hard to figure out. I know that much, but what have you been doing?"

"You mean aside from busting my ass at work?"

"Yeah," she said. "Welcome to the world of making a living."

I took a deep breath before explaining. "Remember when we all went to Newton's?" I asked her.

"Yeah, I remember. And you left with two guys. I hope you knew them. I had a weird vibe when you walked off with them. Is everything alright?"

"Yeah, everything is fine. And you have a weird vibe every time the second hand on a clock changes. Anyway, I've been pretty involved with one of them."

"I bet I know which one," she said.

"Right. The taller of the two."

"Yeah and..."

I was hesitant in telling her the rest of the story because all of a sudden I knew she was going to lecture me on the ways of men and how I should have known from the very beginning that trying to get back at Vincent was going to back-fire on me. But I needed to talk to her now, so I took my chances. "Girl, you aren't going to believe this."

"What, what? Don't keep me hanging," she said anxiously.

"Well...he's engaged."

"Engaged in what?" she asked.

I couldn't believe she just asked me that. "Engaged to be married!" Silence swept over the phone line. Either she dropped the phone, or she was reaching for one of her magic crystals to perform a cleansing spell over me. "Sabastian, did you hear me? I said he's engaged to be married."

"I heard you, I heard you. Damn, girl, what have you been doing with a soon to be married man? I thought I knew you better than that."

In defense of trying to save my reputation I quickly replied, "You do know me better than that. That bastard lied to me!" I took a deep breath. "I found out by accident that he going to marry his baby mama."

"How did you find out, girl?"

I began the long and tedious details of how I found out that Joseph was engaged to be married. Sabastian listened and commented on various sections of the story. She was surprisingly sympathetic to my dilemma and hadn't once called me a home wrecker...yet.

If I dared to tell her what I intended to do with the S.O.B. since finding out that he was a liar, she would surely put up her hands, stomp her feet and try to stop me. So I conveniently left out the part about how I was going to teach him a lesson.

After I was finished telling her all of the details that I wanted her to know, I said, "And that's why I've been so hard to get in contact with lately."

"What a story," she was finally able to say. "I knew when I saw him at the club his vibe wasn't right," she said again.

"Well, that's not the half of it," I said to her.

"You mean there's more?"

"Yep. Guess who's stationed himself outside of my front door right now?"

"Joseph?"

"Nope. Vincent!"

"Vincent? Girl you must be running a circus over there, huh?"

"Yeah, it seems that way doesn't it? Well, you know they say that the chickens always come home to roost."

"What? Oh, so you think that Vincent is tired with his slutty way of life and has decided to change his evil ways to be with you solely and completely?" she asked with sarcasm.

"Let's not get carried away. I just meant that he misses the pussy, that's all."

"My queen sista has the pussy of gold. You go girl," she said with a giggle.

"Well, why else would he be blowing up my answering machine every other minute and then park his ass outside of my house?"

"Maybe he has something important to tell you, Jacqueline."

It's just like Sabastian to turn things around into some kind of moral issue of humanity when talking about men and women, or else anything for that matter. Didn't she know that the third leg of a man is always the reason for anything they do? Well, I wasn't about to get into it with her and try, once again, to explain the behavior of the birds and the bees. She would simply have to find out for herself how these things work.

Besides, it was obvious that Vincent had something to tell me, but whether it was important or not was up to me to decide. But the bottom line was that he wanted to get back into the panties, after all this time. I wonder who slapped him back into reality?

"You know, I've always thought that I was a good judge of character," I finally said to her. "And I still haven't changed my mind but...it simply amazes me what people will do for their own gain. The direct approach always pays off the most dividends, don't you think so?"

"Yeah, but most people don't think like you. Most people feel that they might as well get over on you before someone can get over on them, even if no one is trying to get over on them. But that's life, sweetheart. Once you acquire certain stripes, it's hard to rearrange them."

Now that was the most impressive thing I think I have ever heard her say, until she kept talking.

"Besides, Venus is in rising right now, and the cosmos are all mixed up."

"Sabastian, we aren't talking about the galaxy, we're talking about men and women." As soon as I said that, I remembered the guy I met the other night and how we too were talking about the moon and stars and shit.

While half listening to what Sabastian was saying I began searching around my room and under my bed trying to find that piece of paper with Greg's phone number on. I didn't know what I was going to do with it when I found it; I just found the whole thing coincidental. When I did find it, I decided not to tell Sabastian about it. She would have just insisted that there is no such thing as coincidence and that I should find this guy and marry him right away. No, I'll keep this one to myself.

"...so what next?" she was saying.

"What?" I was busted.

"What's next with Vincent?"

"Oh. He can sit his ass outside all damn day if he wants to. I have nothing to say to him." As soon as I said that, I heard my mother's car pulling up in the driveway. Damn! That means he is going to follow her into the house. "Sabastian?" I said in alarm. "You at home?"

"Yeah. Where else would I be?"

"I'm on my way over right now!" I hung up the phone before she could even respond. I had to get out of the house through the backdoor, fast. I ran to my dresser and grabbed some panties, a bra, some shorts and a tank top. I slipped on my sneakers, picked up my purse and ran into my bathroom to grab my tooth brush. Then I ran down the hall, down the back stairs and headed for the backdoor. As soon as I heard my mother's voice ring out from the living room telling me I had a visitor, I dashed for my car, skidded out of the driveway and made my great escape!

I looked like hell driving down La Brea Ave. My hair was all over my head, my robe was covered with moth holes and I didn't have on a drop of make-up. If I were to have an accident and die, my mother sure would be disappointed when she identified me in the morgue. So I ignored the other motorists the entire time. There was no way that I was going to have eye contact with anyone looking like this.

Thank God I got to Sabastian's house in no time flat. I waited until the coast was clear and no one was entering or leaving her building and ran full speed with loaded hands to her front door. When I got there she opened the door before I could knock.

"What took you so long?" she asked with a smile.

I laughed, giving her a big hug around her skinny neck. "Hey girl. Thanks."

After I showered and changed into my clothes, I went into the living room where Sabastian was sitting on the floor, dressed in a long flowered dress with her legs crossed in a very uncomfortable looking position. She had her eyes closed and was taking in very large breaths of air. I thought maybe she was choking on that weird smelling incense she had burning in every corner of the room, but then I remembered that she was doing her daily meditation.

So as to not disturb her, for a few more minutes anyway, I went into her bedroom and started looking for a belt for my shorts. When I found them in the closet, arranged like a mural on the walls, I shook my head in disbelief. "This girl is a trip," I said under my breath. But the arrangement looked so pretty that I didn't want to disturb anything. So I decided that I would go without a belt. Then I looked on her dresser to choose which perfume I would wear. I smelled one called Orbit and decided that this had to be the one.

I waited a few more minutes before checking in on her again. When I did, I found her in the kitchen this time making breakfast. "What you making?"

"French toast," she said. "Now that you're finished snooping, you wanna tell me why you ran over here looking like Nurse Hatchet?"

I walked over to the kitchen table and sat down. "Girl you would not believe the shit I'm having to deal with right now. I didn't want a confrontation with Vincent this morning, so when my mother conveniently invited Vincent into the house, I ran."

"So where you runnin' to?"

"I'm running to you baby. You know I need your ever-knowing knowledge to get me through." She looked at me with a weird expression and we both started cracking up. "No, seriously, I'm not running, really."

"Then what would you call it?" she asked.

"Delaying the inevitable."

She handed me a plate of French toast and a glass of milk and sat down with me at the table. "And what about Joseph?"

I stuffed a fork full of toast in my mouth. "You know," I said after I swallowed, "I don't really blame him. Let me explain before you think I'm stupid. But, I just realize that men are people too. And I'd rather think that he just got himself mixed up in a situation that he couldn't get out of. Not that he had to go about the thing the way that he did, but like you said, some people can't change their stripes."

"So are you going to let him go?"

"It's not up to me to let him go, Sabastian. It's up to him to do the right thing whether it's marrying his fiancé, or whatever. I really have nothing to do with the whole thing. For all I know, he's just marrying her because he doesn't know how to be alone. But that's ok, because he can do anything he wants to with his life. I, on the other hand, am going to do what's best for me and my life."

Sabastian looked at me with a snicker. "What in the hell does that mean? Are you going to get back at that bastard or aren't you?"

Wow! That took me by surprise. I guess there's hope for Sabastian after all. "Let me put it this way, he's going to regret having fucked with me!"

The two of us ate our remaining breakfast in silence. It was cool the way she was letting me take some time out of my personal life and hang out in her eclectic apartment. She made sure that I had access to everything I needed to make myself look like I had dressed at home and then she went into her bedroom and left me in the kitchen. I went ahead and washed dishes and straightened up her place. When I got to her incense, I just left it alone; I didn't want to get hexed by it.

I needed to meditate myself, in dealing with both Vincent and Joseph. So I sat down in Sabastian's rocking chair and turned on the radio to a jazz station. Listening to the classic sounds of Ella Fitzgerald, Billie Holiday and Miles Davis, just to name a few, brought me closer to feeling like I could do anything that I set my mind to. Something about the blues made my blues go away.

After about an hour had passed by, I was suddenly filled with burst of energy. It was nearly ten o'clock in the morning and I didn't have any plans for the day. Seeing Joseph was not an option at this point. And my option to see Vincent was killed when I ran out the backdoor from him. So my only other alternatives were to either, kick it with Sabastian all day and become influenced in the ways of the modern guru or to do something productive. The latter was the choice I made.

So I thanked Sabastian for her hospitality and told her that I would call her later. "You better," she yelled after me.

I headed straight for the office. I could kill two birds with one stone there: clear my desk for Monday by getting some work done and continue my thoughts on how to stick it to Vincent and Joseph. I didn't want to become obsessed with plotting and scheming on them so this would serve as a good outlet.

When I got there the place was empty. Of course I didn't expect anyone to be there but it wouldn't have been unusual for my step-father to be busily working away. I sat at my desk and began doing the tedious tasks of my job that really required a secretary to do. I would have to ask Harry about getting me an assistant someday. Yeah right, like I really expected him to comply.

Anyway, I got so involved with my work that I had forgotten all about revenge. When I got up from my desk to file away some papers, the file got stuck on the corner of my desk and splattered all over the floor. Damn! That meant that I would have to pick up each piece of paper and arrange them back in order within the folder.

I got on my hands and knees and started picking up every large and small piece of paper on the ground. Lucky for me, the file belonged to TCI. It wouldn't be too difficult in putting everything back in place because I was personally familiar with that account. As a matter of fact, it was the first account that I had been given when I started with the company.

It was just a matter of time before I was done placing this form on top of that one and that one behind another one. The familiar signature of Gregory Childs showed up on most of the forms, while Thomas Childs' showed up on others. I remember Harry telling me a while back that Gregory had taken over the company when his father died, which explained the two signatures to me.

I had done such a good job clearing my desk, that come Monday I might not have anything to do. But knowing Harry and his pursuit to make every major and minor company in this town a client, I doubted it.

I walked to the ladies room to check myself in the mirror. It was hard to tell, by the way I looked, that I hadn't gotten dressed at home. Usually when a woman gets dressed anywhere except from her own dressing room, she tends to look or at least feel out of sync. That wasn't the case with me today. Had I not known it, I would have sworn that today had started out like any other.

Out of habit, I blotted my lipstick with a piece of tissue and threw it in the waste can. Then I remembered that I had another piece of paper in my purse; that guys phone number. I took it out of my purse and read the name on it. It read, Greg, along with a phone number.

I considered calling him but I couldn't justify a reason right away until it hit me; He was my sarcastic counter-part the other night. He just might be the one to give me some insight on men and how to get back at them. Even though I had a pretty good idea on how to do it, I thought that it might be interesting to get his point of view on the whole thing.

I called him from my desk. When I heard the voice on the other end of the line answer, I immediately thought that I had dialed the wrong number. The voice sounded very familiar to me. "Hello. May I speak with Greg please?"

The voice on the phone briefly hesitated before answering. "This...uh...this is Greg. May I ask whose calling?"

"This is your dark, shadowy friend from the other night," I tried to say with a bit of humor though I know it must have sounded really stupid.

"Excuse me?" he replied.

I knew I sounded stupid. "This is Jacqueline, Jackie, Jax...from the other night. We met on the pier. Well, actually we didn't meet, we just sort of talked. Do you remember?"

"Oh. Of course I remember. I was just thinking about you."

"Right," I thought. "Oh, really. Well, isn't this perfect timing then?"

"I'd have to agree with you, Jackie. May I call you Jackie, like the classy Jackie Kennedy?"

"Uh, sure." Another nick-name might help me keep track of all these damn men, she thought. "I hope that I haven't called at an inopportune time?"

"Not at all. I just returned from playing tennis in the back...uh...I just got back from playing in the park."

"Great. Hey listen," I said, wanting to get straight to the point and forget about all of the small talk, "do you have any plans for this morning?"

"Wow! You really are reading my mind. And no, I don't have any plans, yet."

"Good. I was hoping that I could see you today. I know that this must sound very presumptuous of me and not to mention straight forward, but I really enjoyed talking to you and I was hoping that we could sort of continue where we left off." There, I said it.

"That would be very nice...uh...cool, real cool. Where can I come and pick you up at?"

"I'm at my office right now."

"Oh, where do you work? I'll pick you up from there if you like."

"Well, that would be fine but I just finished up here, so tell you what, why don't we meet at...say...Griffith Park. I love the Observatory and we were talking about the galaxy and stuff. Don't you think that would be appropriate?"

"That's cool. And very appropriate. What time would you like to meet there?"

"Say...one o'clock?"

"Perfect. I'll meet you at the Griffith Park Observatory at one o'clock. But how will we find each other? We don't know what the other looks like."

"I'm dressed in white. I'll be the one in the white shorts, sitting on the front steps of the observatory, gazing into the sky."

"Cool. I'll see you then."

"Bye." I hung up the phone and put his number in my desk. He sure likes to use the word cool a lot. I locked up the office and headed for the Griffith Park Observatory. I wanted to get there well before one o'clock to decide on how I was going to approach Greg. Dating him was the furthest thing from my mind. I simply wanted to pick his brain on a few subjects. Since we hit it off last night, I'm sure we'll hit if off again today.

When I arrived nearly an hour before I was to meet Greg, I took advantage of the beautiful day and walked around outside. Flowers were in bloom everywhere and kids were playing all over the place. Apparently I wasn't doing too bad my damn self. Men of every color and race were giving me second and third glances even though I didn't think I looked my best. Looking into the faces of those different men gave me the opportunity to try and figure them out. What makes them tick? And how does one blow up the ticker?

I was consumed with all sorts of feelings about the subject but it would have been a lot easier if I didn't care about either one of them. But that wasn't the case. I cared very much for both of them in entirely different ways and for entirely different reasons.

Friendship's with them was possible if I could figure out the basis for it. Round and round I went on with my obsession until I realized that it must have been close to one o'clock. I didn't have on my watch, so I asked a woman passing by me. She confirmed that it was five to one, before she looked me up and down and rolled her eyes at me. Again, I took that as a confirmation that I was looking good.

Quickly I began to walk to the front entrance of the observatory. I wanted to be in position before Greg got there. When I arrived at the steps I didn't see anyone in particular that could be him. So I found an empty spot on the least occupied stretch of steps and plopped down. Unfortunately, I left my sun glasses in the car. It would have been nice to conceal my face for a little while longer when I met him. But, that wasn't to be. Besides, I had to keep telling myself that I was not here for him but for myself.

When about 10 to 15 minutes passed me by I started getting worried. Maybe I was going to be stood up? Maybe I got here too late and he decided to leave? Or maybe I was sitting at the wrong steps? I looked all around me checking out everyone who went up or down the stairs. I didn't see anyone who reminded me of Greg. While my head was half looking to the right of me, I heard a voice to my left.

"Jackie?"

It was his voice. Shyness over took me for some reason and I was hesitant to turn and face him. Slowly, I turned around. "Greg?"

"Yes. Sorry I'm late but I couldn't find a parking space. This place is crowded today," he said to me.

"Yes it is." He was cute. Actually he reminded me of a little boy, sort of neat and proper. But his clothes seemed to be all out of character for him. Well, who am I to judge? Maybe all he can afford is jeans and a T-shirt. Anyway, he seems harmless enough. I think my decision to call him was a good one. And meeting him in this public place was a good idea too. I extended my hand to greet him. "Greg, it's nice to meet you."

He took my hand and shook it. "The pleasure is all mine. And thank you for calling. I think your idea to meet here was perfect."

"Well, thank you. Would you like to sit here with me for a while or would you like to go inside?" I asked him.

"I'd like to sit out here a while, if you don't mind?"

"Not at all. Take your choice of seats." I gestured with my hands to all of the many steps that he could sit on. He sat only inches away from me.

"This is a pleasant surprise, I must say."

"And what is that?"

"The fact that you are intelligent and beautiful."

I blushed. "Oh well, that's very sweet of you but I didn't ask to see you to flirt with you but to continue our conversation from the other night, ok?"

His expression changed to that of a business face. And with a very business-like tone, he said, "Ok. Where would you like to start?" We both laughed.

"It's very easy to talk to you," I said through laughter. "I was hoping that our cosmic energy would still be intact today." Oh Lord! I'm starting to sound like Sabastian.

"Yeah," he said, "I think that we clicked right away too. So, what did you want to talk about?"

"Well, nothing in particular." I lied. "I just wanted to pick your brain on various views of the world. You know; politics, current events, relationships..."

"Ah ha! Relationships; you're having boyfriend problems, aren't you?" he asked with a grin.

"Of course not. I don't have a boyfriend."

"I see." He was confused.

"I just want to shoot the breeze. You know, like we did before."

"Well you would have to sneak up on me like you did before."

"Well, would you like me to leave and then come back when you least suspect it?"

"Oh no, don't do that. I don't want to take the chance of losing you...in this crowd, I mean." Again we both laughed. Hmm. This was going to be interesting. "So, tell me, do you believe in the relevance of astrology?"

"Jackie, are you asking me what my sign is?" he said with a smile.

"No, I swear I'm not going to use an old '70's pick up line on you. I swear," I said as I tried to hold back yet another smile.

"I'm just kidding," he said. "But to answer your question honestly, sometimes yes sometimes no."

"Oh yeah, why?" I asked.

"Well, he started, "I think that the stars might be able to chart atmospheres and moods. But on the other hand, I think that we as people chart our own decisions and lives."

I couldn't help telling him about Sabastian and her view about this whole topic. "That's a very interesting answer. But I must tell you that my girlfriend thinks that the entire universe is scripted by the stars. She even went so far as to tell me..." I hesitated. I didn't want to tell him that she said that I should marry him, so I said something else instead. "...she even went so far as to tell me that Venus is in rising." I started laughing at my own words. But he wasn't laughing back. As a matter of fact, he looked down right pale. "Did I say something wrong?" I asked.

"No, no. It just so happened that I once knew someone named Venus. It just took me by surprise, that's all," he explained.

"Oh I'm sorry. I didn't mean to bring up any undesirable subjects."

"Honey, you don't know the half of it," he said mysteriously.

Anyway, we got passed that and got more into the business of talking about nothing in particular, once again. We got along so great. He was a smart guy, and seemed to want to hide the fact that he was intelligent. I on the other hand was just being myself, as usual.

We talked about everything from Adam Ant to the Zulu Warriors. It was like talking to a girlfriend but with a twist: You have to be more careful of what you say and you have to make sure that your lips stay moist looking. It was obvious that this new found friendship could easily turn into something more.

You can tell by the way a man looks and talks to you that he likes you. Well, Greg really liked me. I found it quite impossible not to like him either. But I was in a pretty weird period in my life right now. With having two men to fuck over, I just didn't see how I was going to be able to fit this nice guy into my busy schedule.

As time went on, we got up from our seats on the steps and started walking around the grounds. It was his suggestion. I suppose he wanted to see how tall I was standing next to him. Whatever his motivation for it, we made a perfect fit, literally speaking that is. He was tall and not too slim, just like I like them. But more importantly, he had a perfect ass. I tried my best not to walk too close to him while on our little nature walk. I didn't want him to get the wrong idea.

Anyway, he was proving to be invaluable to my cause. He answered every question about whatever I asked him. But more importantly, he told me how to get back at a man without even knowing it.

We approached a man with a hot dog cart and ended up eating them underneath a tree. He offered to take off his T-shirt for me to sit on. He said that he didn't want me to ruin my pretty white shorts. I thanked him for his valiant efforts but declined. The last thing I needed was to see him even partially naked. That would mess up everything.

The hot dogs weren't that bad. I just hoped that they wouldn't have a side-effect on my stomach and make me scramble for a bathroom. But luckily, the food stayed put without a fight. "So," I said after I finished my hot dog and finished re-touching my lips with lipstick. "You never did tell me what you were doing at the pier."

He was wiping away crumbs from his lips. Those lips... "I was just kickin' it," he said. "You know, just trying to unwind from a hectic day. And you? What were you doing there?"

I liked the way he mixed slang with proper English like me. "Oh me? I was there with a friend, just hanging out."

"I didn't see you with anybody." He lied.

He must think I'm stupid. Not only did he see me with someone, he just wants me to admit that it was a man. "Oh, don't you remember the gentleman who was approaching us towards the end of our conversation?"

"Oh, him." Busted.

"Yes. Surely you remember giving me your phone number on the sly?"

He smiled. "Ok, you got me. I didn't want you to have any unnecessary problems with him by having him think that I was trying to talk to you. So, yes, I stuck the piece of paper to the bench so you could pick it up when I was out of the way. I think I saw that in a movie somewhere."

"See there, that wasn't too hard. You could've told the truth in the beginning."

"I'm sorry. I was just trying to be a gentleman by not getting into your personal business."

He looked so cute I couldn't stay mad at him for long. "Ok. You're off the hook this time." We both laughed and continued to have a great time.

When I asked him what time it was he informed me that it was nearly four o'clock. I hope that you don't have to leave."

"No not at all." I wanted to know because a lot of the people were starting to clear out of the area and I didn't want to suddenly get stuck in the dark with him. But the sun was far from setting and there was no chance of a total eclipse today. Just the same, I suggested that we return to the observatory.

I wanted to take advantage of the air conditioning and see if there was anything to see on their powerful telescopes. When I suggested it to him he was agreeable. So we made the short walk back to the building and went inside. Lucky for us, a gigantic group of kids were making their way out as we made our way in. "Perfect timing, huh?"

"Absolutely."

Once inside, we walked around and commented on the various things we saw. It had been so many years since I had been there that mostly everything was new to me. He said that it had been just as long since he had last visited too.

We took turns looking out of different scopes and then we sat in the auditorium, with eyes to the ceiling, trying to figure out the stars. He found a few of the zodiac signs, which I never would have found. But I found the big dipper or was it the small dipper? Anyway, I found one of those dippers.

While sitting side by side in the auditorium chairs, with our bare arms brushing up against one another, I thought I would die. For one thing, I already know that I'm over dramatic when it comes to men and another thing, the last thing I need in my life is another man. I've got too many of them that don't even belong to me. But damn he felt good. We both tried to play off our reactions to the touch. But I could see that he was holding back because I wanted him too.

"I won't bite you know," he finally said.

"What do you mean?" I asked knowing damn well what he meant.

"I mean, I won't bite you. I'm feelin' you, alright? I think you're a beautiful and funny and intelligent woman who is obviously fed up with a certain kind of guy. I just hope that whoever he is, he hasn't messed it up for guys like me."

He caught me off guard. I never expected him to make a play for me...right away anyway. "Greg, things are a little complicated for me right now and...," he cut me off before I could finish.

"Things are just as complicated for me Jackie. Boy are they complicated. But so what. It seems to me that the two of us can probably help each other out. Our flow of communication is good, our attitudes on most everything we've discussed so far is good, and we're both nice people who would like to have other nice people in our corner. What's wrong with that?"

"Nothing is wrong with that Greg. But if that is to be the case..." I hesitated trying my best not to get in over my head. "...then I should at least know a little more about you. You know, like what you do and who you are."

He smiled sort of nervously, but finally said, "I'm just a clerk in a pretty nice sized company. I'm working my way up but I make a pretty good living for myself. But the real story is that I'm an all-around good guy. I've just put through the ringer a little lately and I'm trying to get back on the right track. You seem like a lady who has got it going on. I like that in a person. I like having people around me who have it going on, like you."

"Well that's sweet. I'm glad you think that I have it going on. You're not so shabby your damn self."

I told him about recently graduating from college and starting work for my step-father earlier this summer. He seemed to be very impressed. He told me enough about himself for me to know that I was dealing with a hard-working man and an all-around good guy. "Well, now that I've gone through my check list, I guess I can stop giving you a hard time now," I said.

"Thank you, dear lady. You won't be sorry," he said, sounding so sincere I had to believe him.

"So Greg, where are your people from?"

"Ohio."

"Really? "I like to know where a man's people are from to make sure that we couldn't possibly be related."

"That's a great policy."

"Yeah. It's my mother's greatest fear that I'll either end up an old maid or that I'll marry a long lost relative."

"Your mother sounds like a lot of fun," he said with a smile.

"Yeah. A real riot."

"Well, I'll tell you about my family sometime. It makes the Adam's Family seem normal."

"I can hardly wait," I said with a smile. "In the meantime what's your last name, so I can pencil you in my rolodex?"

"Pencil? I guarantee you'll want to pen me in, right away," he said with a new confidence.

"Oh, so you think you have that much potential, huh?" We were both playing around with the words and having a good time.

"Uh huh."

"Well ok. Mr..."

"Childs. Greg Childs. Pleased to meet you."

He extended his hand to me and without realizing the name I had just heard, I took hold of his hand and said, "Jacqueline Winters, better known as Jackie to you. The pleasure is all mine, I'm sure." We shook hands very ceremoniously and he kissed the top of my hand while looking into my eyes.

At that very moment, I realized what he said his name was; Greg Childs. Could it have been a coincidence that I had just spent most of the morning with a company file with Gregory Childs' name all over it? Sabastian said that there are no such things as coincidences. I couldn't be sure at the moment, but at the same time I had to keep a straight face so he wouldn't ask me if anything was wrong. "Greg Childs. Well that has a nice ring to it," I said with a smile.

"Well thank you madam. Your name is very fitting as well."

"I take it your full name is Gregory, or no?"

He hesitated. "Uh...yes and no. But please call me Greg."

I smiled. "Ok. Greg." I tried to think of another question that would clarify my suspicions about who I thought he was. It would be tacky of me to ask if his father recently died so I tried another approach. "So what's the name of the lucky company who has such a dedicated clerk?"

"A company named TCI. You've probably never heard of it though," he said.

I had to use my hand to keep my jaw from dropping into my lap. I couldn't believe what I had just heard: Greg Childs who works for TCI, but he said he's a clerk? He's lying! He's no damn clerk! I should know because I've seen enough of his signatures lately. He's the fucking CEO of that company! His father was filthy rich! That makes him filthy rich! That fucking liar!

I ought to give him a piece of my mind that he'll never forget, or better yet I should stick it to his ass like I'm planning for the other two. But maybe he has a reason for lying to me. Maybe he's just being cautious. Hmm.

I can't decide on what to do with this information right now. So I'll just keep it, and him, in my pocket until I figure out how to kill three birds with one stone. "TCI?" I finally said with as straight a face as I could manage. "Hmm. So, when can I see you again?"

(13) – Vincent – Starting Over

ow he remembered the reason for not making an appointment with a doctor when he heard that he was infected with HIV; he hated them. But Vincent sat firmly in his seat waiting for his exam just the same.

Though the Truth-Seeker had given him a clean bill of health, he wanted to check it out for himself. However, based on a deep feeling he had about that strange woman, he knew that he could believe everything she told him.

His first reason for being in the doctor's office was to make sure that his "hot water" episode didn't do any permanent damage to his back. He thought about calling a dermatologist first, but then decided to just go for the whole physical thing.

Oddly enough, Vincent had begun to lose interest in continuing his exercise routine when he thought he was dying. The opposite should have been the case since doctors have always said staying fit was one way to slow down the process. He couldn't help but wonder if he stopped on purpose so he could die sooner, or if deep down inside he knew he wasn't really sick, therefore a slack-up on exercising wouldn't hurt him. Whatever the reason, he was feeling supercharged now.

He thumbed his way through at least a dozen magazines while waiting in the reception area, though he wasn't really looking at anything at all. Jax was the main thing on his mind. He couldn't blame her for not wanting to see him based on the way he had treated her lately. But the truth was he missed his best friend. He needed desperately to talk to her and to explain things.

The Truth-Seeker had made him promise that he would do it right away, but Jax wasn't having any part of it. He couldn't believe that the girl had actually snuck out of the back door and drove away when he went to see her Saturday.

It kind of made him smile to himself. "She's a rare one, that girl," he thought to himself when he thought about the whole thing. But she could run all she wanted to. She couldn't hide from him forever, which is why he intended on confronting her at her job today. It would be impossible for her to make a scene there...wouldn't it?

Vincent sat patiently in the waiting room while different faces came and went. The receptionist on the other side of the glass kept giving him these seductive stares. He thought she should either look somewhere else, or visit a plastic surgeon before looking his way. At this point in his life, flirting was not his main agenda. That was a different part of his life altogether...wasn't it? I mean, the fact that he had been put through such a terrible ordeal in the first place was because he was promiscuous. "So she can look all she wants," he mumbled to himself. "I'm not in the market anymore."

Well, saying it didn't necessarily make him believe it like he should have. Too many years of living the life he had led was going to be hard to let go. But he promised himself that he would try...hard! Just the thought of a real lady...a lady like Jacqueline Winters should be enough to keep him in line. But would Jax go for it, was the question?

In the time that it would take for her to cool herself down from her anger, Vincent would be done with his medical examination and have all of his former worries tucked away. Soon he could be looked at as a different person, altogether.

Though he thought, because of his encounter with the Truth-Seeker, that he was a better person now, he knew that he would have to take it several steps further. The one thing that he dreaded most was getting a job! "A job?" he blurted to himself. "The only thing I know how to do really good is..." He let his thoughts drift off as a smile spread widely across his face. But before he could let his imagination run wild, he was interrupted by a voice calling out his name.

"Vincent Cruther?"

"That's Cruthers. C.R.U.T.H.E.R.S. Got it?" he said to the receptionist as he approached her.

She looked at him and smiled. "Yes Sir. I have it."

A cold chill ran down his spine after hearing her words. His guess was that she was referring to more than just the spelling of his last name.

The routine of his physical examination had taken more out of him than he had expected. And so, by the time he left, he had spent most of the day in the medical building. At first he was going to go home and take a quick nap before trying to catch up with Jax at her job. But he quickly decided there wasn't enough time for that. If he gave her the opportunity to get home, she would play dodge with him again and he would be stuck waiting to see her until tomorrow. No, Jax was going to see him today whether she liked it or not.

He had a good feeling about himself as he drove down the highway. The tests results that he was able to receive today were all favorable. One of the medical assistants had even commented on the fact that he was in such excellent physical condition. He smiled just thinking about it.

He'd known all along that his body was his key to success in this town, but now he would probably have to use some of the office skills he had picked up through the years.
Studying up on different office tasks had mainly been a way of getting closer to women in libraries and other pick-up locations. And although that had been his way of thinking in the past, he figured that now it could qualify him for a job.

He knew that he could call up a variety of successful business women who could hook him up. He also knew that these women would want to be compensated in a way that only he could provide, too. Damn! Would there ever be a way out of this way of living?

The closer he got to Jax's place of business, the more he began to sweat. For the life of him he didn't understand how this one woman could possess so much power over him. It wasn't like she was the richest or most beautiful woman in the world, but more like she was the one who had the most sense.

Jax was very well rounded and independent of everyone. Maybe he needed someone who was able to match him mentally? Or maybe it was the way she played hard to get, even when she wasn't playing. He knew that all women were a trip, but this one...she yanked the hell out of his chain.

A while ago, he had already decided that he wasn't going to present himself like he wanted her to be his woman, or anything like that. He simply wanted to re-establish his relationship with her, and to add on some new benefits if she insisted. The main thing for him was to just get her back into his life. Things seemed to be a whole lot better for him when she was.

The moment he parked his car, he tried to overcome his fears by quickly getting out of the car and rushing to the front of the building. The quicker he "ate cheese" with her, the better, at least, that's what he was hoping for. And he also hoped that her office would be filled with people up the ass, so that she couldn't raise her voice or run away.

So when the elevator doors opened and he was standing in the hallway of Research Limited, his heart nearly leapt out of his chest when he only counted three people in the entire building. "Is today a holiday, or something?" he asked himself under his breath.

"May I help you?" one woman asked him.

"Yes. I'm looking for Jacqueline Winters, please."

"Do you have an appointment with Ms. Winters?"

Vincent looked at this square faced little woman coldly and thought to himself. "Do I have an appointment? Do I have an appointment? I'll show your ass an appointment in the nearest hospital if you don't get your fat ass out of my face!" But instead of saying that, he opted for, "Why no. I'm sorry, is it very necessary?"

The woman answered him with an annoyed look on her face. "Yes Sir. Ms. Winters has issued instructions that any walk-ins must have an appointment."

Vincent just stood there at a loss for words. He had no idea that Jax would go to any means to keep him from seeing her. Of course this "screening" of walk-ins was designed for him, who else would it be for? He was beginning to get the feeling that she didn't want to see him...ever.

"Sir?" the woman was saying. "Sir, is there something else that I can help you with, otherwise you'll have to leave."

Vincent thought that was very rude of her. For all she knew he could have been an important client who just flew in from out of town to see Jacqueline. He decided the intimidation approach. "May I have your name and the name of your supervisor, please?" he asked her as he pulled out a Mont Blanc pen and a piece of paper from his jacket pocket.

The woman looked at him with bug eyes. He thought for sure that they were going to blow any second. "Well...why?" she asked with uncertainty.

Vincent took an even tougher approach. "Young lady, if I am to be treated by you in this manner, then I want to know who you and your superiors are, so I can report the both of you to Harry personally!" Now, that should do it. Throwing out Harry's name like that was sure to put the hot irons to her ass.

"Oh," she said as she threw her hands to her cheeks. "I'm sorry. I had no idea that you know Mr. Townsend. Well right this way, Sir. Ms. Winters is away from her office at the moment, but she will be returning any minute. Right this way, please." The girl was so frightened that he actually felt sorry for her. She walked him to Jacqueline's cubicle and offered him a seat. Before she left him, she turned to him and said,

"Sir, I'm really sorry for the confusion. Please don't tell on me."

She sounded pathetic. He decided to put the final touches on his charade. "Just make sure that this never happens again. By the way, what is your name?"

"Pam Watson, Sir. And again, I'm very, very sorry." She walked away with her head down.

Vincent had to keep himself from laughing aloud. "So that's Pam. I bet Jax will thank me for that," he mouthed softly.

Well, that was the first step; getting into the office without giving out his name, or being seen by her. The next step, in getting her to talk to him, was not going to be as easy.

In the meantime, he positioned his chair so that she would not be able to see his face when she entered her cubicle. He needed as much as a head start that he could get. Even before he could really begin to collect his thoughts on what to say, he heard footsteps approaching. "This is it," he whispered to himself.

Jax's voice rang out before she even entered her cubicle. "I'm sorry for the delay, Mr..." Her words cut off as she stepped into the cubicle and looked at the back of a stranger. She was about to say something else, but then she must of realized whose back it was. "Vincent? Is that you?"

He took his sweet time slowly swiveling around in his chair. When he completed his turn and faced her, she did not look amused. "How dare you pretend to be a client," she said in a hushed voice.

"How else was I going to get to see you?" he pleaded.

"You weren't," she said as she walked behind her desk and sat down.

"Oh, so you were just going to leave me hanging forever?"

"I didn't leave you hanging, Mr. Cruthers, you left me hanging."

He smiled his charming smile. "I did some stupid shit, huh?"

"Stupid?" she asked. "No. I wouldn't call them stupid, Vincent, I would call them typical," she said with sarcasm.

"Well, I'd call them stupid, Jax, which is why I'm here. Baby, I need to talk to you like you would not believe. I have so many things that I have to...no...that I need to explain to you, girl. You would not believe the things that I have done or seen."

"I bet I have a pretty good idea. Believe me; you don't have to draw me a picture."

"No, no, no, it's not what you think, Jax really," he insisted.

"Look, Vincent! Maybe you haven't noticed that we are at a place of business, at my business. So I suggest you take your business somewhere else. I don't have time, nor do I want any of your shit! Understood?" She had to control her voice and her temper while expressing this to him. But he looked so good sitting there.

Vincent looked helplessly at her. "Have I fucked up that bad, Jax?" he was finally able to ask her.

She hesitated before answering him. "You fucked up that bad, Vincent."

His heart dropped. She was being so mean and so hateful. And he was so sure that she would at least give him the opportunity to explain things to her. He guessed that she had just taken as much as she could and couldn't take any more. He rose from his seat to leave. When he looked at her, she pretended to be writing something down on a piece of paper, but he could tell that she was doodling. He stopped just inches from the door. "You can't get rid of me that easily," he said with a last effort and a smile.

She tried to hold back her smile, and then threw her pen at him. "Damn you, Vincent Cruthers. This shit better be good." He rushed over to kiss her, but she held up her hands in protest. "Don't touch me."

He was slightly confused about her reaction. Hadn't she just given in to him? Oh, who knows what her motivation is? But he was pretty sure that he was going to have to pay a high price to make it right with her again.

Vincent took his instructions from her and stopped dead in his tracks. Instead he decided to sit on the edge of her desk so that she would have a close up look of what she had been missing. He casually opened his suit jacket to expose his chest and stomach through his shirt and placed his hand on his thigh. He watched her eyes as they examined his physique. "I knew this would get to her," he cockily thought to himself.

Her eyes eventually made their way up to meet his, and in a nonchalant tone said, "Get your ass off of my desk and stop the bullshit, Vincent. I would appreciate it if you would take a seat, like a big boy, and proceed before I change my mind."

Damn, that girl can be vicious. But he did what he was told...for now. And though he can only take so much of her fucked up attitude, he figured he deserved at least a little of it.

After taking his seat across from her once again, he began to talk to her very slowly at first. He wanted to make sure that she heard everything that he was going to tell her, from beginning to end. And he especially needed her undivided attention when he got to the part about the Truth-Seeker. She was probably going to think that he had lost his mind. If he were in her shoes, he would. But, that was a chance that he was going to have to take. If he was going to get his life back on track, Jax just had to be there to help him. Who else cared enough to do that for him?

Slowly and clearly he told Jax everything. He explained from beginning to end about the incident which started their fall out; the unknown caller's bad news. Jacqueline seemed to be listening and looking with amused eyes, as he continued to speak. He wasn't going to lose this opportunity to speak with her. It was somewhat difficult for him to tell her about his HIV scare, but she had to know. However, he was very quick to explain to her how, deep down inside, he always knew that he was healthy; and how he would never expose her to anything dangerous or life threatening. Which is the reason, he explained, that he began to withdraw from her sexually. And, though he still wanted and needed to be near her, he simply could not perform the rituals that they had both become so accustomed to.

Jax looked surprised when Vincent mentioned that he had been out of town. Apparently, she thought that he had been ignoring her, but he readily explained that he had had a longing to see his mother and father. And when he spoke about his feelings of loneliness and despair on his train ride to Louisiana, it seemed to bring about a look of caring in her eyes.

The whole story sounded like some delusional fairytale with an eerie twist, which is exactly how he wanted it to sound to her. It was very important for him to get her sympathy before he could get anything else from her again. And still she listened.

He was grateful to her for letting him explain the smallest of details at her place of business. But he knew that she was the boss' daughter, and had a lot of pull around the place. But the short version of the story was not an option, which is why he took his time. She listened, and from time to time she would show different expressions on her face, or simply readjust her sitting position. Vincent assumed that he was striking a positive cord with her, and so he played on it.

When, in his story, he got to the part about meeting the Truth-Seeker in the park, she made a snicker; such as that of a jealous girlfriend. But by the time he finished telling her about the strange lady, her eyes squinted a bit. Perhaps she was trying to visually see the story as he told it. But, all in all, he was sure that she believed that he could not make up such a fantastic story.

He was sure not to skip a thing in this part of his story; from the voices he heard in the night, to the chicken bones the strange woman threw at his feet. He went on and on and on, until finally there was nothing else to tell her. That was the end of the story and he hoped the beginning of their alliance. He was grateful to her that she was patient and even quiet, as he told his bizarre tale. And when it was all over, he looked at her as only he could and asked, "Do you believe me?"

She raised a pen to her lips and leaned back in her chair. Then she closed her eyes, patting the pen to her lips. When she opened her eyes again and looked into his, she answered him. "The problem is not whether or not I believe you, Vincent, but rather, are you capable of being this honest with me all of the time?"

A huge weight seemed to lift off of his shoulders. Finally, he had come clean with Jax and it was apparently going to pay off for him. Until this very moment, he hadn't realized how stressful all of his secrets were to him. But he was confident, especially now, that Jax was the remedy. She was his best friend after all. Now all he had to do was to say something clever to get her back in the sack. His dick was getting hard just looking at her.

"Yes, Jax," he said. "I am capable of being this honest with you all of the time." He was sure that this was what she wanted to hear. All women like to hear that honesty stuff...didn't they?

After hearing his last comment, she let loose with laughter. "Vincent? Just who in the fuck do you think you're dealing with, huh? You didn't write the book on being a dog all by yourself, I contributed to it, remember? And yes, sweetie, I believe your story and your anguish, and I am very sorry to hear that you chose to go through all of that alone. But I once heard that animals cannot change their stripes. So don't sit over there and promise me something that is just not in your nature to do."

Vincent had to keep himself from losing his temper. "Didn't you just hear everything I had to say? I poured my heart out to you and your acting so damn smug sitting over there! Damn, girl! Who made you so damn bitter?"

"You did!"

"Nah, I couldn't have possibly done this shit by myself. Something else is going on with you. We had something Jax…something worth making a big deal out of, and you're sitting over there trying to make an ass out of me. How long do you think I'm going to stand for this shit anyway?" he demanded. She didn't say anything. "Good," he thought to himself "I'm sure she'll come to her senses now."

But without speaking one word to Vincent, Jacqueline rose from her chair and walked around her desk to face him. She was wearing a beige linen dress, which fell about three inches above her knees. The sleeves were short and the dress fit snugly around her breasts, waist and hips.

Slowly, she sat on top of her desk and crossed her legs. Her dress rose a few inches as she settled into position. Vincent could easily see that she was wearing stockings, being held up by a black garter belt. She leaned back on the desk with one hand, while the other rested softly on one knee. If she was trying to make him all hot and bothered, it was working. Vincent couldn't take his eyes off of her. After all, it had been a while since he had been with a woman…long for him that is.

Finally, after a few moments of saying nothing, she looked at him until his eyes met hers. "It's on you, baby." With having said that, she slid off of the desk and stood, hovering nearly on top of him. "Now, if you'll excuse me, I have a lot of work to do."

Vincent looked at her with cold eyes. He could easily hate her for the way she was treating him. He stood up slowly and carefully, as she was taking up most of his space. On his way up to a complete standing position, his face brushed against her body. He immediately recognized that she was wearing a perfume that he had bought for her.

As he rose to a complete stand, he towered over her and had access to the best view he had had of her cleavage in a long time. Obviously she had no intentions of moving out of his way, so he had to inch his way around her to get clear.

Who in the hell did she think so was, anyway? Did she think for one minute that he was going to stand for this shit and bang on her door forever? Not. But before disappearing behind her cubicle wall, he turned to her and said with a monotone voice. "Later, Jack."

Without turning to face him, she childishly replied. "Goodbye, Joseph. I mean Greg. I mean Vince."

Vincent fumed out of the building. He couldn't believe that she had just acted that way...that bitch! Who did she think she was dealing with, some punk? If that's how she wants to play it, fine! It was OK by him if she didn't get over it, and get on with it.

He jumped in his car and slammed the door. As he fumbled around for the ignition, he stopped dead in his tracks. "What? Goodbye, who? Did you say what I think you said, Jax?" He was talking to himself, but he wished he had had sense enough to react when he was in her office. "I've never mentioned another woman's name in your face, and you have the nerve to pull some shit like this?"

He was fit to be tied. That was it...end of it...over...finished...through. "Fuck her! If she's going to act like that, then I'm glad to be rid of her." He started up his car and began to drive dangerously down the street. There had to be somewhere he could go to release the rage that he was feeling. But he was stumped. He couldn't think of anywhere to go, or anything to do. He headed in the direction of his home. The first thing he would do when he got there was deprogram his phone of her phone number. Then he remembered, he only wrote it down in his mind.

By the time he got home, he had cooled down a bit. He took off his tie and jacket and threw them on the sofa. Then he went into the bathroom to splash his face with cold water.

He thought back on the order of events which had just taken place with Jax. That girl sure knew how to push his buttons. He decided to look at things from her point of view...just for a second: If he had caught her with another man, innocent as it was, and lied about the entire situation; and if she had denied him sex with her, without an explanation; and if she had disappeared for weeks without telling him, he would be through with her too. He guessed the question was; did she have a right to be pissed? As much as he hated to admit it, he knew she had every right.

When he let himself think about the fact that she had accidentally called him by the name of two others, (though he almost certainly knew that it was no accident), he was enraged. But why? And why was he so possessive of her; that just the mere thought of her being with someone else upset him? Hadn't he done nearly the same thing to her since the beginning of their relationship?

Of course, he knew the answers before he asked the questions. But it's different between men and women. A man doesn't like the idea of "his" woman being with someone else...anyone else. That shit is just not done! But, he was dealing with Jacqueline; the girl who broke the rules on occasion; the girl with enough spunk to dare to make him care. "Oh, Jacqueline," he said out loud. "What am I going to do with you?"

Right then and there, Vincent decided that he was not going to go out like that. If Jax really wanted him out, then she would have to just say it. He was confident enough to know that she was trying her best to teach him a lesson, and that she wasn't really through with him. But he didn't know how much his massive ego could take either. He had wanted to come clean with the whole unpleasantness of the entire situation and ditch all of the other women he knew. But now, he wasn't exactly sure if he would soon require something, or someone, to fall back on.

He went into his bedroom and found his treasured, "little black book," (some might call it an encyclopedia), and began to thumb through it. So many names so many memories. A man would be a fool to throw away such a treasure. He definitely was no fool! He put his book back where he could easily reach it in case of an emergency. "Nothing is that serious," he said to himself, with a smile.

As he lay in his bed, looking at the ceiling, he tried to visualize Jax with someone else; in their arms... kissing them... fucking them. "I can't take this anymore," he said to himself. "I'm starting to act like I'm in love or something." Oh shit! The "L" word. He had been keeping himself from saying that word for years. How could he be in love with her? He didn't even know what the word meant.

She had been purposely trying to get back at him ever since he got back into town, and he was allowing her to do it. If she thought that this was the last of it, she was out of her mind. The Truth-Seeker had healed him from all of his anxieties and Jax was supposed to be the icing on the cake. But nobody told him that it was not going to be smooth sailing in trying to put everything back together. He wished someone had.

The first thing in the morning, Vincent went out to get a Los Angeles Times. He had an appointment with the classifieds section. Though he had enough money to get him through the next several months, he didn't want any excuses to call up any of his "friends" in order to make ends meet. And though, he needed to get his rocks off...really bad, he was going to try his best to hold off and let Jax be the recipient of the pleasure. He had also started his daily exercise regime again. Top physical condition was going to come in handy when he chose the woman he was going to pump, and pump good.

He did his sit-ups, his weight lifts and his pushups. It felt good to get the juices flowing again. A clear mind, body and spirit is the road to the successes that Vincent intended on achieving. Jacqueline was merely a consolation prize. He intended to show her that he had what it took to conquer all. Surely even she could appreciate that.

Yet, he hadn't forgotten about the fact that she was probably fucking someone else. "It couldn't be as good as what I can give her?" he thought. "She's probably just doing it because I wasn't around." Whatever the case was he had driven her to it.

If he hadn't been so arrogant as to not see the "goods" standing right in front of his face when he had them, he wouldn't be in this position right now. But she was human just like he was. Her feelings counted for something too. So, one way to prove to her and to himself that he could "cut it," was to make some serious changes in his life. It was a matter of life and death, as far as he was concerned. Because if some woman could randomly call him up and tell him that he had given them Aids, then something was terribly wrong with his current lifestyle.

And though he believed in his heart, that it was just a matter of time before she forgave him and started acting normal towards him again, he knew that some things in his life would have to change...forever.

Page after page of the classifieds proved to be a dead-end for him. He had never really held a decent job in his life. He never had to. And the qualifications needed for some of the ads he read proved to be a bit much. If he had his pick of the ideal job, it would have read something along the lines of: *Wanted; a tall, dark, and handsome fellow with a perfect body and a taste for sophisticated women. You must be educated, refined and readily available for all sorts of physical tasks. Short hand optional. The job pays 125K, and has excellent benefits."*

Now that would have been the perfect advertisement for him to respond to. Unfortunately, this was the real world, and Vincent would have to use his mental skills rather than his physical ones to get him where he wanted to go.

After a while, he became pretty depressed with the whole thing. Mediocre jobs lined the pages of the paper and he thought it a waste of his time. He decided to wait until Sunday to get the big picture of the jobs being offered in the newspaper. Until then, he would simply have to make do. So he went into the bathroom and turned on the shower. After taking off his clothes, he stood naked in the mirror observing himself.

He turned to the side to try and get a better look of the blisters which had scarred his back. The doctor had told him that they weren't too bad, and he agreed. The ointment that the doctor provided would quickly heal and remove the scarring from his back. It was a good thing for him that no permanent damage was done to his skin tissue.

Once in the shower, Vincent grabbed his soap on a rope and worked up a good lather all over his body. He took his time letting the soap and water do it's magic on his tight body. And although, he knew full well that Jax was the one who had supplied him with a year supply of this brand of soap on a rope, he tried not to think of her.

The shower had proved to be a very good idea. He was suddenly revived and full of energy. With this kind of energy, he could easily go for several hours for some pure unadulterated sex, but he opted for something else. He would go to a job agency to continue in his serious pursuit of a job, even if it killed him. Once he was on his feet, he intended to help out his mother, by sending her a portion from his paycheck every month. Not like she was in dire straits or anything. Actually, from the look of things when he visited her, she was doing just as good as he was, if not better.

"Hmm," he thought. "I wish Jax could have met my mother. If she had, I know she would be panty-less, on her way to see me after work." He shook his head, hard. "I have to stop thinking about this shit! It's going to drive me crazy," he demanded of himself. "But what am I supposed to do? Shit, it's been too long for me to go without. I can't take it anymore." With having thought that to himself, Vincent grabbed hold of his penis and began to stroke. He was going to get his rocks off today one way or another.

His climax proved to be a "little dud" but at least he was able to get rid of some of the tension that had built up inside of him.

After getting out of the shower, he toweled off and headed to his bedroom closet. The idea was to wear something business like, not tycoon like. If he looked like he already had a lot of money, the agency probably would not take him seriously. He wanted to impress them, not make them standoffish. But what to wear?

He didn't own a whole lot of average looking clothes. The women he knew had treated him right, providing him a collection of designer and custom-made suits. The only thing for him to do was to mix and match a jacket and pants, get a white shirt, and a simple tie. That should do it. He wasn't going to break any hearts looking like this but he was sure he'd be filing some lucky lady's boss' papers tomorrow.

Before leaving, he changed the message on his answering machine. He didn't want to receive any call backs from the agencies he was going to visit, hear him saying, "I'll pick up the phone after I hear your voice." Oh, no. That would send out the wrong message for sure. He would say something simple like, "Please leave your name and number." That would probably sound more professional, so that's what he did. Then he tore away a few pages from the paper containing the addresses of several agencies, and headed out of the door. Today was a good day.

His first stop was a bit of a disappointment. When he walked through the door, all eyes turned to him. There were several white women standing around, looking like they were sent by the unemployment office. They all looked desperate and despicable. It looked to him that they resented the fact that he had even showed his face in this place.

There wasn't another black face in the joint, and suddenly he felt like he was going to be the victim of a hanging. But he didn't know where this feeling of panic was coming from because he had "dated" women of all races and colors. The "color thing" was never a problem for him. He called it, "Equal Opportunity Advancement," meaning; he'd fuck them and fuck over them if they wanted him to. But these women, ugh!

"Yeah," one woman sitting behind a desk said. "You lookin' for somebody?"

"Oh that was good," he thought. "No, I'm here to fill out an application for employment."

"You don't look like you need a job," she said.

"Do you go on appearances only?" he asked.

Everyone in the office was listening to their conversation. He was feeling very uncomfortable. He knew when he wasn't wanted, but he wasn't about to give up yet.

"What can you do?" she asked.

Vincent didn't like the way the conversation was going - standing in the middle of the office with no seat being offered and no hospitality whatsoever. "Excuse me, but is this the proper format for our discussion?"

"Format? What do you mean, format?" she asked curiously. Obviously she didn't have a clue about professionalism.

"Never mind, lady." Vincent turned on his heels and walked out. One down and four to go. Today was an average day.

When he arrived at the second agency on his list, he was greeted with a sign that read, "We have moved two doors down." So he walked two doors down and pulled on the door. Locked. He moved one door to his left and pulled. Locked. All of the doors looked the same to him.

The entire outside of the building was made of mirrors, so how was he to know which of the doors was the right one? So he decided to walk over three doors to his right and pull. Locked. "What in the hell is going on around here? Can't anyone see me out here?" he thought.

People were walking past the building, as he stood there looking like an idiot. He was beginning to feel like today was a conspiracy. The address on the building was no help either. There were many doors and only one address. He didn't know how these people expected to get any clients if it was impossible to find them. Oh well. Off to agency number three on his list.

The third agency on his list was easy to find. When he entered, he found an organized looking bunch of men and women taking care of business. He was immediately acknowledged and asked to sit down at a desk. The woman who acknowledged him proceeded to ask him a series of questions as to his reason for being there, the kind of job he was looking for, and if he was looking for permanent or temporary work. Vincent answered her questions and was handed an application to fill out. "Do you have a resume?" she asked.

Damn. He knew he had forgotten something. "No, I'm sorry I don't."

"Well, that's OK. We'll prepare one for you."

"That would be great, thank you." She instructed him to a nearby desk to fill out his application. The first section was easy to fill out: name; address; phone number; social security number. The second part was not so easy: name of last three employers; positions held; salary earned. The only positions Vincent had had in the last several years were X-rated. Surely they didn't want that information from him. Obviously, he hadn't thought this whole job thing all the way through. What could he possibly write down: Paper route at age 10; Stock boy at age 15?

"Hi," the lady said as she approached his desk 10 minutes later. "How's it going?" She looked at his empty piece of paper and crossed her arms. "I see we're having a little trouble filling this thing out, huh?" Her tone was timid and reassuring. "Let's see," she said, pulling a chair up next to his. She took his application and looked at him. "What would you like to say that you've done before?" she asked discreetly.

Vincent was surprised, and the look on his face showed it. "Excuse me?"

"You do want a job, don't you?"

"Yeah, I want a job. But as you can see, I don't really have any references...at least not the kind you're looking for."

She began to get impatient with him. "Not a problem. Do you have a problem with bending the truth a bit?"

"But how will it be verified to the employer that wants me?"

"Don't worry about that. We'll take care of it."

He didn't like her attitude. This place was obviously crooked, and it was just like his luck that he was being set up for a big future fall. "Isn't there a way that we can do this thing on the up and up?" he finally asked her.

She looked at his application and then back at him. She had a sort of smirk on her face. "I don't see how that will be possible, Mr. Cruthers." She put his application on the desk and stood up. "When you make up your mind, let me know." With that, she walked away and greeted a woman who had just entered the office door.

Life's a bitch! You can't do good without first doing something bad. Vincent felt that he had already done enough bad in his life. He was searching for a way to do the right thing from now on. But how could he? He had no job, no work experience and no job references. The ones owning the companies who employed everybody else had probably lied and screwed their way to the top. Why should it be any different for someone just trying to make an honest living? Everybody did it, didn't they? How in the hell would he know. He's never had to do it before.

Finally Vincent stood up to leave. On his way out of the office, the lady looked in his direction from behind her desk. When he passed by her, he tore up his application and threw it in the waste basket. "Thank you for your time," he said to her as he walked out of the door. Today is a shitty day!

He didn't have the energy or the courage to venture out to agencies number four and five on his list, besides, it was time to grab some food. He was in the mood for Mexican so he went to Casa Maria's. Sitting in his booth with a bowl of greasy tortilla chips and runny salsa, Vincent barely glanced at his menu.

Today's events were a heavy toll on his mind. And he was wondering if he should just go back to agency number three to get a job, honestly or not. But deep down inside, he had a slight worry that if he did anything wrong, the Truth-Seeker would come back into his dreams. Silly as the thought was, he didn't want that crazy lady following him around for the rest of his life. "No. I'll just go to another agency...and another...and another, until somebody can help me get a job the right way."

He didn't see the waitress standing beside him when he was blurting this out to himself. "Senor?" she asked curiously.

He looked up to see her looking at him. "I'll have the #4 lunch special."

She wrote something down on her pad and nodded her head at him. "Si Senor."

He guessed that she understood him. Anyway, Vincent tossed his menu to the side and mechanically began to dunk a tortilla chip into the salsa. Both of them were so bland that he couldn't taste either one of them. But he continued to eat them anyway. It was his first accomplishment of the day.

When his food came, he picked at it. It was as bland as the chips and dip. He thought it a little strange, because the last time he was there with Jax, the food was delicious. As a matter of fact, that was the last time he had been out with her. Their date to the movies would have been the last, but he didn't want to think about how that night ended up.

After he finished his disgusting meal, he contemplated whether or not he should continue his pursuit of a job today.

His ego was already a little shaky from the earlier events which had taken place, which was a new and strange feeling for him.

Vincent was always in control. This take on his new life was proving to be more difficult than he had expected it to be. There had to be another way of going about straightening out his life. He didn't want to find rejection at every turn. Maybe he just needed to re-think his priorities. "Yeah. Re-think my priorities," he thought.

He picked up his check and paid his bill at the register. He was not about to lose his confidence now, instead he was headed home to seriously figure out how he wanted to live the rest of his life.

His day was about to start over.

(14) – Joseph – Who's Doin' Who?

J oseph was going to marry Veronica in less than one week and nothing was going to change that. The invitations had been mailed out, the church, minister and reception hall was scheduled, and his tuxedo had already been fitted and altered.

This was going to be the beginning of a life with the woman who bore him a child. It was the right thing to do...he was sure of it. No longer was he afraid of the decisions which had plagued him for such a long time. His father would want his son to do the right thing and marry the girl that he got in trouble.

"If it's good enough for my father, then it's good enough for me." He no longer felt it necessary to try and make up excuses and to decipher dreams about the whole thing. It was just a matter of biting the bullet. And Veronica could not have been more pleased about the approaching nuptials. So he figured that if she and the baby were going to be happy, then it was good enough for him.

This past weekend, he served his time working in the Reserves for the Navy. Since he was getting married he wouldn't have to report for at least another month. He was also going to receive a permanent station at the Long Beach Naval Yard. Married men didn't have to be stationed around the world, if they could get the right signatures to get them out of it. Yes, everything was just going to be hunky-dory from now on.

But there was still some unfinished business that he was going to have to deal with; to sow his royal oats. And he didn't mean with Jacqueline either. No, he decided that she was too dangerous to be involved with, especially so close to the wedding. He had acquired feelings for her that were sure to bring him nothing but trouble. So, since she was already pissed at him, though he didn't know why, he figured he'd leave it there. If he were to go near her now he'd just fuck everything up and probably get caught by Ronnie in the process.

So instead, Joseph intended to call every woman he had ever known, before, during and since he got involved with Veronica, except for Jacqueline. He intended to fuck his way down the wedding aisle. If it was good enough for his father, and his father before that, then it was good enough for him.

He wasn't quite as nervous as he had expected he would be. Being on the Cruxia, around his buddies in the Reserves had probably put his mind at ease at bit. It must have been the roar of the sea, or the allure of adventure. Whatever it was, he always had a hell of a time when they all got together.

His best buddies from the ship were all going to be in the wedding. George, of course, was going to be his Best Man, and Green, Carrera and Paul were going to be the escorts. And while at the shipyard Joseph handed out a few wedding invitations to more of his friends.

Captain Grey was one of the invited guests. It would have been a big deal for Grey to show up to his wedding. Most of the guys always thought that the Captain was partial to Joseph anyway. Having him attend the wedding would confirm that. Joseph knew what he was doing. Now that he was about to take that final plunge, he wanted to ensure some real security within the Navy. And Captain Grey was the ticket.

Over the weekend, Joseph was also able to catch up on everything everyone else had been up to this past summer. On Sunday night, before everyone headed for home, two dozen of them snuck out a military vehicle and went hanging out on the north side of the harbor. The chances of them of getting busted, was slim to none. All of the big wigs had already left, and the guys responsible for the trucks, were among the two dozen.

Most of the men were still talking about the fun they had had in Fiji. But that was somewhat of a sour note with Joseph. He had a deep guilt over the way he had left the woman whose name he tried to forget. He had long since thrown away everything, including the sketches that reminded him of her, as well as the others he had met along the way. The names of these women were no longer important, only the memories of their faces.

While hanging out at a bar, a sailor named David recalled the morning that the big brawl occurred in the kitchen on the Cruxia. "Man," he said to the group, "I was socking anybody who got in front of me."

"I think I popped your ass a couple of times," another sailor said.

"Couldn't have been me, I'm too quick," David responded.

Joseph was listening to them with little interest. He couldn't forget the embarrassment of having broken his hand on that particular day. And now, he found himself subconsciously massaging it.

"Hey Joseph," a sailor named Luke asked, "Are you sure you injured your hand during the fight in the kitchen, or was it in the infirmary?"

It was a sarcastic question and Joseph didn't like it. Had Luke just asked him what he thought he had just asked him? If that was the case, then the word had gotten out about the two faggots who were in the bed next to him. He was pissed. "What did you just ask me, Luke?"

"You heard me man. I said are you sure about how you broke your hand?" His tone was more demeaning than before.

Joseph had to save face...and fast. "I told George that if he was going to let that crazy story out, to tell it right. And for your information, Luke, I was about to kick some serious ass when I found two faggots doing the humpty dumpty in the same room with me!" His tone was filled with testosterone. "There's no way the guys could think that he had something to do with that shit," he thought.

One of the other guys said, "I heard that they drugged you and made you suck their dicks."

Joseph said, "The only man who's going to suck my dick, is your mama!"

The guy jumped to his feet ready to fight, but three others jumped up and held him back. Joseph was ready for him. He stood up, brushed off his clothes and took a few steps towards them. "Let the mutha fucka go, 'cause I'm down for mine! And I'm not about to let some fucked up story mess with my reputation. Now, since the shit is out, I'll tell you everything I remember. So get out your paper and pencils, 'cause I'm only gonna say this shit once."

They all looked around at each other before sitting back down. Joseph faced the crowd. "I'm gonna kill George," he said to himself. He readied himself to speak. "The morning after I kicked ass in the kitchen, you all know that I broke my hand on somebody's face. When I was taken to the infirmary, some stupid ass gave me enough pain killers to stop a whale in its tracks. I can deal with that, because it did hurt like shit and it got me out of working for a while." Everyone laughed.

"When I was lying on the cot, all drugged up and with a big ass cast on my hand; I started having this really weird dream. And before y'all start trippin, let me explain." Joseph started smiling to himself. "I was dreaming about a fine ass freak, who had somehow snuck on the Cruxia and was fucking everybody she could get her hands on." The men all started laughing and commenting out loud.

"Yeah, I fucked her first," one man shouted.

"How could she fuck you first when she was with me?" another yelled out.

All of the men got into the discussion of what this "dream woman" did to them and in which positions. The group got totally side tracked and it became a battle for control over her.

Sneaking a woman on board a Navy Ship has always been a fantasy for sailors. They all fantasized about it on one occasion or another. So the fact that Joseph had dreamt about it happening, struck a chord with them...a common bond, so to speak. When each and every man had had his chance to say what he had done, or what he would do to a female stow-away, Joseph was able to continue his story.

"Now you guys know how I felt. I mean, here I am dreaming about this fine woman and what she was going to do to me. It was cool, and very real. Anyway, the dream was getting louder and louder and louder, when finally, I thought I was going to reach out and find the bitch in my bed. But when I opened my eyes, and realized that I wasn't dreaming anymore, I still heard her voice...only it wasn't her voice anymore; it was a man's voice."

Once again the men all started to laugh and comment on how Joseph had been dreaming about a man dressed in drag. Joseph couldn't keep himself from laughing and commenting about it too.

"Anyway, because of the drugs and shit, I still thought I was dreaming. But then, I knew I wasn't, because I could hear the ships engine. So I jumped up and turned on the light and yelled out, "What in the fuck is going on around here?" Naturally, the two "queens" didn't want to tell me what they were doing or who they were, but the *what* they were doing part, was easy to figure out. One of them said, 'I thought we could be alone in here?' or something like that. I wasn't trying to hear what they were saying; I was too ready to kick their asses."

One man asked, "Who were they?"

Everybody asked the same question out loud. "Yeah, who were they, Joe?"

I don't know," Joseph said confused. "I really wish I did. And you know what else?"

"What?" they all answered in unison.

"I recognized one of the voices. And the way he was acting was like..." Joseph was about to tell them that the man's voice that he recognized, was acting as though he knew that someone was in the room all along. But Joseph wisely decided to leave that part out. The men would surely get a good laugh on how somebody on the crew was setting him up for a booty call. So instead he continued by saying, "...he better not let anybody see him."

"Well, what's so strange about that," David asked. "Anybody would have acted the same way. I mean, nobody would want to be found out, right?"

The crowd all agreed.

"Yeah, I know," Joseph said. "But it was something else, too. It was like...it was like he would be ruined in a big way, you know what I mean?...like he would lose some really big stripes." Again, the voices of the men rang out at once. They were still discussing the possibilities of who could lose the most if they were found out when they left the bar and returned to the yard.

They were totally engulfed in darkness as their debate continued. Interesting suggestions arose, as well as, some weird experiences others had run into on the Cruxia. Joseph was happy to know, that his brush with the unknown was not an isolated one. He listened to this new information with an open mind and a steady ear. It really would be nice if he could figure out who those two men were. That way, he would know exactly whose ass it was he would kick, and where he could find them now.

He couldn't help but take a look at the faces of the men around him at that moment. For all he knew, it could have been one of them. No one was safe from the speculation, at this point. His reputation was closer to being ruined by the guys, than it had ever been before. Not including the fact that most of them were envious of his relationship with the Captain.

One by one, they all spoke up and told of the unusual things that they had too, seen and heard. The more they talked about it, the more they were possessed with finding out who had been responsible. Joseph realized that some of them were probably making their stories up so they wouldn't feel left out of the group. But, on the other hand, too many of the stories sounded like it had relevance. But, no one had experienced anything as interesting, and so close, as had Joseph.

Time and time again, one man or another would insist that Joseph, "Think harder," in order to reveal the culprits. But all Joseph could tell everybody is that they were both white.

"I told you, all I saw was two white dudes running out of the door from behind. They both had their asses hanging out, and their uniforms were wrapped around their ankles as they fumbled down the passage way."

"What colors were their uniforms?" a voice rang out.

Joseph froze. "What colors were their uniforms?" he asked himself. Joseph contorted his face in thought. The various debates continued around him as he wandered slightly away from the rest of the men. That was a very interesting question: What colors were the uniforms? If he just thought hard enough, he might be able to concentrate and figure that one out.

He went over the events in his mind again and again and again. But everything specific seemed to be a big blur. He knew that it had been the sedative which was making his thoughts blurry, but still...blurry or not, a color is a color. And he knew that by knowing which color the uniform was, and then he would be able to at least narrow the ranks down.

Close to midnight, most of the fella's were anxiously moving about the docks. They had all exhausted their stay and were ready to head for home. Most of them didn't mind hanging out like this because they only had to report once a month for the Reserves. But that would soon change for some others.

Some of them were going to receive permanent postings in other states, cities and countries. Others of them were headed back out to sea soon, to create more adventure stories. So in reality, this was the last chance Joseph would get to spend time with the original bunch of the Cruxia clan.

"Too bad George wasn't here," someone said.

Someone else replied, "Why? All he would do is get drunk and cuss everybody out. Then he would get his ass thrown off into that nasty ass water." They all laughed together for the last time. Joseph knew that they were just joking...even though it was probably true.

When Joseph pulled up into his parking space in his apartment building, he was exhausted. He hadn't realized how tired he actually was until he finished driving. So he dragged himself into his apartment and instinctively headed to his answering machine. He suspected that Veronica would have left at least a million messages by now, seeing that he didn't come home right after work. He was almost relieved to find that he didn't have one message from her, or from anyone else for that matter.

He went into the bathroom to run himself a hot bath. When he knelt to turn on the water, he saw one of Sayla's rubber ducks sitting in the bottom of the tub. He raised it to his nose and smelled it. The softest, sweetest scent was all over the little toy. He sure loved his daughter. He was glad that she was going to be living with him all of the time.

After he bathed he turned on the television in the living room. He couldn't sleep for some reason, even though he was dead tired. The butterflies in his stomach probably had something to do with it. He was getting married this Saturday.

"Too bad I didn't make any arrangements to have a freak here tonight," he murmured to himself. "That would have been the ticket." Yes, it was count down time for him. And he was serious about getting with a few more women before Saturday.

He could have easily called someone over without fear of Veronica showing up in the morning. But, most every woman he knew had to go to work in the morning, just like Ronnie. He and his sailor buddies were the only other men he knew that lived like bums half of the time, by sometimes having to report for work, and sometimes not.

As he curled up on his sofa, he quickly found comfort and relief. Soon, he was once again, thinking about who the two men in the infirmary could have been that night. Without the others being there, he could easily make any assessments that he wanted to. He could speculate about anybody and point the finger at anyone. That's not something that he would want to do in front of a big crowd...in front of nobody really, except maybe for George. But George had the biggest mouth this side of Compton.

Joseph was the kind of person that didn't like to let his right hand know what his left hand was doing...especially since it had healed up nicely. He felt that he could remain in charge that way. Knowing something that someone else didn't know seemed to be the best way of life for him.

But lately, too often, he was beginning to slip. George knew that the talk of those particular events could have ruined his reputation. And if he was going to blabber like that, he should have at least had the decency to tell him about it. But that was George; impulsive, stubborn, and a pain in the ass. His Best Man. "I'll get that punk later."

But how was he going to find out who was doin' who on the ship? If he was going to do some investigating into the matter, he was going to have to hurry up. The people involved could easily be two of the people leaving for new stations soon. So Joseph began to try and think about the "color of the uniform" theory, once again. He had not thought of that before or maybe he just didn't want to think about any of it before because that might be the answer.

Then he began to think about the voices that he heard. And then the voices he heard with the color of their uniforms. He was sure he was getting closer to the truth, now. His heart began to beat faster and faster. The sound of the ships engine was again ringing in his ears. He could taste the salty air on his lips. The chill of the open sea filled the room. His body began to sway back and forth, as though on open water. The blurriness was beginning to fade. He could see a color now. It was...it was... Damn! It disappeared.

It was on the tip of his tongue, but he had lost it. "Forget it," he said as he turned off the TV and headed for his bedroom. He crawled between the sheets and grabbed hold of his pillow. "I wish this pillow was a woman right now," he said softly.

A perfectly gorgeous Sunday night passed by him as he lay alone in his bed. And though he would have preferred a pretty lady to be by his side, he was anticipating conquering several women before his wedding; right down to the wire. He promised himself that as soon as he was a married man, he would never again be unfaithful to Veronica.

The remainder of the week was going to be a busy one. He needed to take care of the final wedding details, since Ronnie had to continue to go to work for the entire week. When he woke up on Monday morning, the very first thing he thought was to line some chick up for the evening. So he rammed his brain trying to figure out which of the many women he knew, would accommodate him.

Mostly everybody knew that he was getting married, so it would be almost impossible to try and convince a woman that will be more than just sex. His mother had remained friendly with most of the women he'd known through the years, and she had made it a point to tell as many of them as she saw what the plans were for her son. So his only approach would have to be the honest approach. If he brought up the subject in the wrong way, he might end up beating off on himself rather than beating in-between some woman's legs.

He called Leslie, and luckily for him she was still at home. Leslie was always ready to get with Joseph. Actually, she might have been one of his steadies, if she wasn't so possessive of him. When their conversation began, she was the first to bring up his up and coming nuptials. "I thought you were getting married."

"I am," Joseph said pensively.

"Oh. So what is this phone call about? Don't tell me that you're trying to get some last minute hanky-panky going on?" she asked curiously.

Joseph had to answer this question delicately. He didn't want to beat around the bush, but he did want to get her in his bed. "No, Les," he said gently, "I'm just calling the very best of all the friends I've made through the years...men and women. Now that I'm getting married, I didn't want these friendships to become strained by the change in me." He waited for a response from her. He hoped that he didn't sound too much like a nerd, but hey, whatever works.

Leslie took a few seconds before responding. When she spoke, Joseph was convinced that this would be his approach line for every other woman that he called in the days to come. "That's really sweet, Joseph. And I'm sorry that I couldn't be the lucky lady to get a ring, so I guess I should see you again as a single man, as opposed to a married one. Ronnie might not want us to be friends after the wedding," she said.

"Oh no," Joseph insisted, "I'm going to keep all of my friends whether she likes it or not!" He lied. "But...I'd really like to see you before the big event Les. We really had a special kind-of-thing back in the day." He figured that was enough buttering up. "So can I see you tonight...alone?"

"What time?"

After lining up his plans for the night, Joseph got started with his morning. He wanted to take care of everything before any unexpected interruptions could get in the way of his evening with Leslie. He got out of bed and busied himself around the house, cleaning up this and that. The kitchen was the cleanest room in the house since he never did much eating in it. And he was lucky enough to find a couple of bottles of wine in the cabinet. He took them and put them in the refrigerator so they would be chilled for later. A bottle or two of wine, and him, was all he needed to get Leslie in the right mood.

While in the refrigerator, he grabbed four slices of bread, and buttered them. He threw them in the oven to brown and then got out the peach jam and a carton of milk. While the toast was cooking, he went into the bathroom to run a bath. He noticed his dirty uniform on the bathroom floor. He picked it up and hung it in his bedroom closet. He would have it dry cleaned whenever he got around to it.

Veronica had asked him on several occasions, if he was going to wear the tuxedo for the wedding, or his official uniform. He had insisted that he was going to wear the tux, but now he wasn't sure. Anyway, after getting his bath going, he went back into the kitchen to make his jam toast and down the rest of the milk in the carton. After eating in record time, he gave out a big belch, returned to the bathroom and climbed into the tub for a good soaking. "Life is good," he thought.

He had a woman who was understanding, he had a military life that suited him perfectly, and he was still able to be his own man. If his father were around to see him, he was sure that he would have been proud of him. Everything that he did was for or about his father. His father would have wanted him to make the choices that he was making...wouldn't he? Well, he was pretty sure of that answer.

On his way out of the front door, he grabbed the checklist of "things to do" that Ronnie had prepared for him. His first stop was to head over to the travel agency. Those tickets for the honeymoon in Mexico should be ready for pick up.

He thought he should've been thinking about flying off with Ronnie, but his thoughts were mostly focused on the next few nights he would share with other women. "Some things are going to have to improve in Ronnie's methods," he thought. "If I'm going to be married to her for the rest of my life, she's going to have to be a little more creative in the bedroom." Mexico was as good as any a place to teach her. And just like he planned, the agency was opening up for the day just as he drove up. But unfortunately, the tickets were not ready for pick up.

The lady explained that there had been some kind of computer mess up, and his tickets hadn't been printed yet. She assured him that his name was the first on the list for printing, and that he didn't have any reason to worry. Though he doubted what the lady was saying, he didn't have the time or the patience to listen to her for long. So he reiterated the importance of his having those tickets in his hand no later than Thursday. The lady was agreeable to that, and Joseph turned to leave. His next stop was the limousine company.

Unfortunately, dealing with the limo company wasn't any better an experience. Nobody could find any record of their request for two limos on that day, and they were all booked up for the next two weeks. "But I need a limo this weekend, not in two weeks," Joseph fumed.

Some weird looking lady with a cigarette hanging out of her lips, and orange hair looked at Joseph nonchalantly. "Just hold on a minute," she said through clenched lips. "If your fiancé made arrangements, then I'm sure we'll find the record.

Joseph stood standing next to the counter. He was amazed how tacky the whole place looked. Ronnie had, no-doubt, ran her fingers through the yellow pages to find this place. There was no way that anybody in their right mind would drop in from off of the street. Joseph was convinced that their advertisements must be the sole reason for their business. "Do you know how long this is going to take?" he asked. "I've got a lot of things to do today."

The woman was bending over a stack of unarranged papers. She didn't even bother to raise her head when she answered him. "You can stay or come back later, it's up to you."

Joseph took that as meaning, "Fuck you, pal," so he turned and bolted out of the door. He didn't have time for this shit. He had a schedule to keep to.

His next stop, at the flower shop, was to see if they had the order together. The florist explained to him that the arrangements would not be made until the night before, and the morning of the wedding. They did, however, show him samples of what the arrangements would look like. "Everything is on schedule, Mr. Pride," the man behind the counter said to him. "We've done hundreds of weddings, and have never had a dissatisfied customer."

Joseph nodded and left the flower shop. "At least somebody knows what they're doing," he told himself as he jumped into his car. Now if only he could take care of the limo, he would be all done with his list for the day. Then he would have the rest of the day to think about all of the things he was going to do to Leslie. So instead of driving back over to the limo company, he jumped back out of his car and went to the pay phone.

A yellow pages phone book was dangling from the end of a chain, so he opened it up to find the phone number. When he saw the advertisement, he knew why anyone would use their company. In brilliant color print it said, "Limo Luxury. Experience the ride of your life. All of the amenities anyone would require. Professional. Courteous. Discreet. Let us take you where you want to go...in style." It was a pretty good add, Joseph thought. "Now let's just see if they can live up to it."

He called them up, and he assumed the same lady in the office was the lady on the phone. When he asked about the request for his limo, the lady said that she was looking at it right now. Joseph didn't want to take her word on it. He wanted to make sure that she wasn't tripping, or something. So he bit the bullet, and drove back across town.

When he arrived, sure enough, the dingy lady had his request in her hands. Joseph was a little leery, but he put up an advance for it and got a receipt. He figured that they knew what they were doing if they had been in business for eight years. "Everybody in the place couldn't be as disorganized as her," he reassured himself.

Finally, he needed to check with the caterers to make sure that they were on track. Ronnie had insisted that he visit these places instead of making the confirmations on the phone. "They feel more threatened when you do it in person," she had told him. Well, the travel agency and the limo company didn't seem to care about his presence, why in the hell should the caterer? If anybody got an attitude with them, they could just piss in all of your food. So Joseph decided to approach them with kindness, even though he had gotten himself a little worked up about the other fuck-ups of the day.

When he got there, he was pleased to find out that their menu was accounted for and ready for preparation the day of the wedding. With having completed his check list for the day, sort of, Joseph headed for home. Leslie would be getting off work in a couple of hours, and he wanted to speak to Ronnie first, to get her out of the way for the night.

As soon as he walked in the front door, he heard his phone ringing. He ran to answer it before his answering machine could pick it up. It was Ronnie. "Good," he thought, "Time to get her out of my hair for the evening." "Hi, baby," he said to her.

"Hi back. How did your day go?" she asked lovingly.

"It went right as planned," he said to her. He was in no mood to get into the details of the day. The conversation could easily lead into a long discussion if he were to bring up the negative stuff. So he told her that he had completed his check list for the day and was about to settle in for the night. When she tried to persuade him into coming over for dinner, he was quick to remind her of her own idea of not seeing each other again, until their wedding day.

"I know I said that Joseph, but how's a girl to get through the week without seeing the man she loves?"

"I know, I know," he said. "I'm just as anxious to see you too, but, we have to wait it out Ronnie. It'll be more exciting that way."

"You always know what's best, don't you?" she finally said in defeat.

"I try to do what my heart tells me," he said.

After their long exchange of terms of endearment, Joseph hung up the phone. He thought about one of the things he had told her; that he tried to do what his heart told him to do. He wondered if that was entirely true, since his heart seemed to ache at the very idea of getting married. Was it marriage with anyone, or just marriage with Ronnie? There was no time to think about that now; his date was going to be arriving soon.

With the arrival of Leslie, came an evening of ecstasy. She was as willing, ready and able as ever. There was no doubt that she knew what the evening was all about, because she came over straight from work with a purse full of goodies.

There was some whipped cream, some candy sprinkles, two party hats and two small paper horns. She told him that if she was going to watch him get married to someone else, they were going to party first. And party, they did.

The entire night was filled with delightful and experimental sex. It was as though Leslie was going to change Joseph's mind about getting married, or have a lot of fun trying. Together, they must have reached half a dozen orgasm's; signaling each one with a toot on their party horns. Yeah, the evening had turned out just the way Joseph had hoped. And with the close of that night, he had only four more to go before he would be off limits.

After that, the week seemed to speed by. On Tuesday, his mission was to pick up his mother and drive her all around town to make sure that she had everything she needed for the wedding. They got started at about 9am, and they didn't finish until 6pm. For the life of him, he couldn't understand why women needed to take up every ounce of sunlight to accomplish things.

His mother, however, was very meticulous in wanting everything done ahead of time so she wouldn't have to rush the last day before the wedding. Joseph was able to line up both Brice and Toni for the night. They were into that kinky shit, so he could be with the both of them at the same time. If he had thought better of it, he should have gotten with them for the whole week. But it had proven just as well, because he would have been burnt out for his own wedding night.

On Wednesday, he had to catch up with the men in his wedding party, one by one. He had to make sure that they all remembered he was getting married, and that they had their tuxes together. And, of course, each stop he made was an invitation to a celebration drink, or a "sorry" toast. Either way, by the time he had left the last man's house for the night, he was drunk.

He had nearly forgotten that Brenda was going to meet him at his place at 10pm that night. But when she arrived, he was ready for her. It was a miracle that he was able to drive himself home after being with the guys, let alone answer the door when she knocked. However, the mere sight of her, and the knowledge that his days were numbered, seemed to be enough to snap himself back into reality. Two more days to go before Joseph Pride would submit himself totally unto his wife. In the meantime, it was on!

When Joseph awakened on Thursday, he was a little surprised to find Brenda gone. He hadn't even realized when she could have slipped out of the bed. But better for him, he thought. There was no need to prolong the inevitable goodbye with one another.

Each woman that he was with knew what their evening with him was going to be about. And he guessed, by their agreement to get with him, that women were just as horny as men were, otherwise he wouldn't have been able to line up so many women, so close to his wedding day. Whatever the reason, he was truly grateful.

So as he scrambled out of bed and picked up his list, he saw that the only thing remaining was the honeymoon tickets to Mexico. This meant that he could relax for the day and not have to rush to do anything. He decided to make the phone call to check on the tickets instead of just showing up. When he did, he was pleased to find that the tickets were there for pick up. "Cool," he thought. "I can take my time today."

Joseph walked around the house stretching as he moved. His week had been one of those incredible stories that men talk about all of the time. He was just glad that he was able to pull it off like he did. And from the look of his bed, he had a good time last night too, though his memory was a little blurry. But slowly, the memory of Brenda began to re-visit him, and he suddenly found himself blushing at the very thought. "Damn!" he said out loud. "That girl is wild!"

Soon after, he realized that he should put some fresh sheets on the bed. He and the others had fucked around the house, but he and Brenda did most of their fucking in the bed. Joseph realized that it probably wouldn't be a good idea to have Samantha come over and fall into a creamy bed, though he didn't mind it at all. So he pulled off the sheets and put them in a pile on the floor. He decided that he would do his laundry while he had the time.

Joseph opened the closet to grab together clothes that needed to be washed. Most of his dirty clothes still hung on hangers. Hanging up his clothes, dirty or clean, was a habit for him. There, he noticed one of his uniforms sitting on a hanger. It should have been dry cleaned days ago, but of course, Joseph's attention had been elsewhere. When he reached to grab it, he suddenly felt a sense of urgency. The feeling was telling him that he should wear his ceremony uniform to his wedding, rather than that stupid tux.

"Yeah, that's what I'll do. I am a sailor," he thought. But there was one problem; his good uniform was back at the base. He would have to pick it up now to make sure that it was ready to wear. So, to make sure that his day would not be rushed, Joseph got dressed to go take care of the final things on his list right away. That included starting a few loads of clothing in the buildings wash room, taking his uniform to the dry cleaners, and finally picking up the honey moon tickets to Mexico.

The last thing he would do would be to drive up to the base to pick up his other uniform, and then go home to wait for Samantha. He could change his mind about what to wear if he wanted to. He was to pick up his tux on Friday and then he could make his final decision at that time.

Anyway, he did what he had to do, and set out for the base. When he got there, he saw that it was nearly deserted. Most of the activity had usually been on the weekends. But he knew that things was going to change soon, because most of the men's new orders had been given, which meant permanency at the base for a lot of men, including him.

He checked in at the front gate, and drove his car straight to his destination. When he got out of the car, he was approached by an on-coming military vehicle. It was Captain Grey. "Sir!" Joseph threw his hands in attention and knocked his foot heels together, as the Captain drove up beside Joseph.

"At ease," the Captain said, as he saluted back. "What in the hell are you doing here, Joe. Aren't you supposed to be getting married this Saturday?" the Captain asked.

"Yes Sir," he said ceremoniously. "I came to pick up my uniform, Sir."

"Your uniform?" the Captain asked. "You sure waited long enough before you had to get it, didn't you sailor?"

"Yes, Sir!"

"Hey, by the way, how's your hand?"

"Fine, Sir!"

"You still drawing, sailor?"

"Not exactly, Sir!"

"Not exactly?" the Captain asked. "What does that mean?"

"Not really enough time for that now, Sir!"

"Carry on, then." The Captain saluted Joseph again and began to drive off. Joseph was about to enter the barracks when the car stopped again. Captain Grey stuck his head out of the window and yelled one last command to Joseph. "When you finish here sailor, head over to my office...clear?"

"Yes, Sir?" "I wonder what that's all about?" he asked himself. "Oh, he probably wants to turn down my wedding invitation," Joseph told himself, as he headed into the barracks to get his uniform.

When he retrieved it, Joseph carefully carried it out to his car, hung it up on a hook in the back seat, and locked up the car. He was going to walk the short distance over to the Captain's office and didn't want any jokesters to mess up his uniform or find and take his honeymoon tickets, which he had placed in the glove compartment.

Joseph walked up to the Captain's office door and knocked. "Enter."

Joseph entered the office. "Reporting, Sir!"

"At ease, sailor." Captain Grey was sitting in his big chair behind his desk. His desk and chair were so big that it looked overwhelming to Joseph. It looked like it was consuming all of his body. Anyway, Joseph stood standing with a rigid posture, waiting to hear the Captain's commands. He barely noticed what his superior was doing on the other side of the desk. "Pride," the Captain said, "you've been of a great service to the Navy. I'm sure that your father and your grandfather would be proud of you."

"Thank you, Sir!" Joseph gleamed.

"How much do you love the Navy, boy?"

Joseph was a little confused about this question. He figured that the Captain was trying to get an idea of his loyalty since he was about to get married. "The Navy is my life, Sir!"

Captain Grey smiled. "And what would you do for the Navy, boy?"

"Anything it asked of me, Sir!"

"And have I been good to you, boy?"

"No question about it, Sir!"

"Good." With that, the Captain swiveled around in his chair, turning his back to Joseph. Only the top of his head was barely peaking over the chair. He seemed to be slightly rocking himself from side to side. "There's something that I want from you sailor," the Captain said. "And if you are as smart as I think you are, you'll do it. Otherwise, you will have some major set-backs for the rest of your career. Do you understand me, boy?"

Joseph had no clue as to what this man was trying to say, but, he was careful to listen, because Grey was a very powerful man. And Joseph knew that anything this man said about you could make or break you. He had been very lucky up to this point because the Captain was always very kind and accepting of Joseph. His hope all along had been that the Captain would take notice of his loyalty and see to it that his Navy career blossomed. But the Captain's last question stumped Joseph, and so, he had to verify it before he could answer it. "Sir?"

"I said, what will you do for the Navy?" His voice was much more authoritative than before.

"Oh...I mean anything, Sir?"

The swaying from left to right stopped. "Give me your oath, on your life as a military man and on the lives and reputations of your father and his father before him, that what happens in this room today, will stay in this room."

Joseph was more confused than ever, but he wanted the whole thing over with. He figured that the Captain was just pulling a power trip on the closest peon around. He needed to get home in a hurry. So without much thought to the whole thing, Joseph answered, "Yes, Sir!"

The Captain motioned for Joseph to come to him. Joseph did as instructed. When he was standing next to the Captain in the over-sized chair, his eyes could not believe what they were seeing! Captain Grey had his pants wrapped around his ankles, and was holding his puny pink dick in his hand!

Joseph's chin nearly hit the ground. "Suck it, boy!" the Captain commanded. "Then you will bend over...understood!" His voice thundered throughout his office.

Joseph was enraged! His first thought was to kill the son of a bitch! And his next thought was to do a Lorena Bobbit on his ass! The truth of the matter was he didn't know what to say or do. But sucking somebody's dick, even if it would mean the end of his Navy career, was not an option!

All within a flash, Joseph knew who at least one of the men in the infirmary was on the night he was there with a broken hand. "It was you!" Joseph roared, forgetting who he was talking to and what the consequences would be. "You and somebody else were butt fucking that night on the Cruxia!"

The Captain seemed unaffected by Joseph's anger. "That's right boy," he said. "You know you wanted to get in on it. And if the drugs that I you shot up with hadn't worn off, you would be so addicted to my dick right now that I'd have to beat you off with a broom!"

Suddenly Joseph felt nauseous. He had to get out of there, right away, before he did something that would lock him up for the rest of his life. He turned to leave the Captain's office.

"Where are you going? I haven't dismissed you, boy!" the Captain demanded.

Joseph kept on walking. He wasn't about to give that "fruit" the time of day. As he slammed the door to the Captain's office, and probably to his Navy career, he could hear him yelling out orders and commands for Joseph not to do anything stupid.

Joseph knew that meant if he told anybody, his career would be over. But at this point, he really didn't give a shit! A man had just come on to him...and aside from that, it was the man that he admired most, next to his deceased father.

Joseph ran to his car, started it up and skidded out of the base gates. He was as angry...as pissed...as disgusted, as he had ever been in his entire life! He gritted his teeth so hard that he thought they would all break within his mouth! The rage was overbearing. He wanted to kill that man...to wrap his hands around his faggot neck and strangle the fuck out of him!

Joseph was a dangerous man at this moment. He was out of control and he knew it. He had to get off of the streets before he killed someone and himself. Tears of anger began to stream down his face. He didn't remember the last time that he cried...maybe his father's funeral? He wasn't sure. But he knew that he had to let the tears fall now, as an outlet for his anger.

He drove around, not knowing where he was, or where he was going. The pain of betrayal was more than he could bear. His second home, the Navy, was what made him a man! It made his father and grandfather men too, didn't it? But now, it seemed to be all a lie. But how? How could Captain Grey portray himself so masculine, and then behave so bizarre? It was beyond Joseph. But he knew that he was sick to his stomach behind all of the lies.

His own betrayal towards everyone in his life, and the betrayal of Captain Grey towards him, brought everything to a head. So without even knowing how he had got there, he found himself pulling into Jacqueline's driveway. She was an understanding, intelligent and rational person, and perhaps the only one he could share this secret with.

He barely noticed the car pulling out right next to him. But as he scrambled to the front door and found Jacqueline standing there, he turned into a nervous wreck, clinging to her as if for dear life. His tears of anger and disgust were falling even more now. He was a pathetic, broken man holding onto this woman...the woman his heart truly wanted for himself.

And as he and Jacqueline fell to a clump on the front porch, she held him as if he were her child. Joseph spilled out his guts to her about Veronica, about Captain Grey, and about everything else in his entire life.

She wiped away his tears and whispered soothing words in his ear. "Shhh," she said.

Joseph was stripped of his dignity and stripped of his manhood. He felt he had nothing to lose by telling the truth. So he told Jacqueline that he was going to marry Veronica for the sake of their child, but that he wasn't in love with her. He looked Jacqueline in the eyes and told her that he loved her...that it was she that he wanted to be with.

"You give me the word Jacqueline, and the wedding this Saturday, is off!" he said. "Maybe she'll give me some sympathy pussy," he thought.

She looked into his tear streaked face. "Shhh," she continued to whisper. "We'll talk about it tomorrow when you can think straight. On Friday night we'll chill at the beach and get everything out in the open. I got you now baby," she said as she continued to embrace him. "I'll get you," she whispered in her thoughts.

(15) – Gregory – Life Savers

The drive home from the observatory was as pleasant a drive as he had ever known. Gregory took the long way home so that he could retrace every moment that he had just spent with Jackie.

It was clear to him that he had stumbled onto something that could change his life. And he was positive that she was impressed with him too. Thanks to his new and improved simplistic style. Greg was on top of the world and he owed it all to Jackie. *He* had already become fascinated by her - now it was just a matter of time before he could introduce Gregory to her.

She seemed to be as fed up with the opposite sex as he was. And there was a bonus to it; she wasn't looking for anything other than happiness. He could be the one to give it to her. Greg was sure that she would accept his alter ego Gregory, the money, and all the rest of it.

She was the new bright spot in his life, and it showed. Meeting her had been totally accidental, so that meant fate or the stars must have had something to do with it. Right?

When he finally made it home and pulled into the long winding driveway, he looked at his Jaguar parked at the far end. To think that it would take an old used Jeep to find the woman of his dreams was incredible. "Jackie...Jackie...Jackie," he found himself uttering over and over as if she had just saved his life. She would be a sophisticated addition to his family once they were married.

He had purposely been avoiding everyone at home ever since his new personality emerged. The idea of trying to explain his new look and his Jaguar being replaced by a used Jeep wasn't something he was looking forward to. Jeremy, however, had seen Gregory many times since; had even played a few games of tennis with him earlier and he didn't seem to notice a thing. He should be so lucky if the ladies in his family didn't notice either. "Just as well," he thought. "I might as well explain this new look to everybody at the same time."

To his surprise, when he walked into the house he seemed to go unnoticed. Everyone spoke to him as they usually did, but no one commented on the fact that he had his car towed home, had replaced it with a used one, or that he was wearing jeans. "But I never wear jeans," he said to himself.

He took a seat on the family room sofa and surveyed his surroundings. Jeremy was on the phone, obviously talking to a woman Theresa was watching television while painting her toe nails and Louise was walking around watering the plants. Something had to be wrong. "What's wrong?" he finally asked out loud. Everyone looked up at him as though he had just yelled, "Fire!"

"What are you talking about?" Theresa was the first to say.

"I mean, what's wrong? Everybody is hanging around here like we're the Brady Bunch or something. There has to be something wrong," he said.

Jeremy was hanging up the phone. "Man, there's nothing wrong with us. What's wrong with you?"

"I knew it," Gregory said. "I was wondering when somebody was going to mention my new Jeep and my new jeans."

"What new Jeep?" Theresa asked.

"The one he bought the other night," Louise said.

"Yeah," Jeremy commented. "If you were going to buy a new car, shouldn't it have been new?"

Theresa was looking up from over her wet toe nails. "You bought a car?" she asked.

"Yes, Theresa. And the reason I bought a used car is because I wanted to save some money."

This brought Jeremy and Theresa to tears and laughter. Louise just looked on and continued to water the plants. "Save who money...you?" Again he and Theresa started laughing. Gregory wanted to laugh too, but he kept it in somehow.

"Leave your brother alone," Louise said mildly. "If he wants to buy a car and save some money then what's the matter with that?"

"Thank you, Louise," Gregory said.

"But I can't help but wonder," she said. "What's with the jeans?"

All eyes turned to Gregory and the jeans he was wearing. It was as if he were just diagnosed with a contagious disease. "Hey," he said defensively, "what's wrong with them? I think they look kind of good."

Theresa returned her attention back to her toe nails and the TV. "If you say so."

"Yeah, man," Jeremy said as he stood to leave the room, "If you say so."

"Where are you going?" Gregory asked him.

"Who me?" he said jokingly. "I've got a date, big brother. You do remember what a date is, don't you?"

Gregory smiled to himself as he watched his brother leave the room. "Yeah, I remember," he smiled to himself.

Well, it looked to Gregory that he would be able to live out his alter-ego as Greg, without too much interference from his family. Apparently they were into their own lives. This was the best scenario he could have imagined, because if he was going to turn himself into an average Joe, he was going to need a little space in order to pull it off.

The thought of moving out of the house, at 28 years old, and getting his own place had crossed his mind but he thought that to be a little drastic. Besides, this was his home and if he couldn't be comfortable where he lived, then something was definitely wrong.

Relieved he didn't have any explaining to do, he focused his attention on Louise. "Louise, how are you doing today?"

Louise put the water jug down and sat down beside him. "I'm fine, child. Why do you ask?" she said curiously.

Gregory could see that Theresa was looking at them from the corner of her eye. "I just wanted to make sure that I didn't leave too soon the other night," he said.

Theresa seemed bored and returned her eyes to the TV. "Oh that," Louise said. "That night was a revelation, child. We carried on for a while after you left. I think your mother had a nice time too."

"Really," Gregory said. "Well, that's great though I'm sure you two won't become the best of friends."

"Well, that's a silly thing to say," Louise said annoyed. "Don't you know anything about women, Gregory? They can get along when they need to, but they won't tolerate each other when they don't have to." She and Theresa glanced at each other and winked

"Did they know something that he didn't?" he thought. Gregory decided to leave the subject alone. If they were OK with it, then he was OK with it. Besides, he was taking Jackie to dinner later and he didn't really care about anything else. He was happily surprised when Jackie had asked to see him again so soon; he could barely contain himself.

He let his mind wander up into his bedroom closet while trying to decide what to wear that evening. The thought had never occurred to him to go buy some new clothes for his alter-ego, rather than jeans and a T-shirt. That meant that he had to wear something expensive which is all he owned. Finally, his mind decided on what he would wear, right down to the suit, shirt, tie, socks and shoes. But when he began to think about which restaurant he would take her to, he had to be careful.

He had acquired quite a reputation in the restaurant circuit lately, with all of the carrying on with Venus. And he was sure that somebody at one of them would be sure to recognize him. He didn't need that kind of attention. The less Jackie knew about the old him, the better. If she found out that he had been a reckless maniac it might scare her away.

When finally he decided upon Spago in Beverly Hills he had to immediately re-think his choice. Spago was an expensive restaurant and might cause Jackie to become suspicious. "Would a man working as a clerk take a woman to Spago on their first date?" he had to ask himself. "Yes, if he paid with cash and not with an American Express Gold Card," he replied to himself. But he didn't have any cash on him. That meant he would have to go to the bank to get some. "Are banks open on Saturday?" he asked out loud for Theresa or Louise to hear.

"What, are you going to buy another car," Theresa said without turning around.

"No smart ass. I just need to go to the bank."

Louise responded. "I don't know Gregory, why don't you call."

"Oh, yeah." Gregory jumped up and grabbed the phone. He dialed 411 for information and called his bank. Unfortunately, his bank was closed. That meant that he would have to go and find an ATM, somewhere. "Where is the nearest ATM?" he again asked out loud.

Theresa looked at him with annoyance. "I don't know, why don't you try the nearest 7 Eleven."

"That girl really needs to get laid," he thought.

"Gregory, why don't you use the ATM at the bank? Where is your mind anyway, child?"

"Oh yeah. Banks do have ATM's, don't they?" Without having to explain himself any further he jumped up and headed out of the door. It was dark and he wanted to get some money in his pocket before picking up Jackie on the other side of town. Only God knew what kind of neighborhood she lived in.

He decided to drive to the company bank in the Wilshire district, taking a nice long ride in his Jeep to think about his plans with Jackie. He wanted everything to run smoothly, without any hitches. Hopefully there would be celebrities at the restaurant, so he could watch Jackie light up with excitement while living in his world. Yes. Gregory was on top of the world. Nothing could possibly go wrong tonight.

As he parked and approached the ATM outside of the bank, he was startled to hear police sirens directly behind him. When he looked up, he felt a sense of relief. "Thank God," he thought. "Now can I withdraw my money with some peace of mind." He turned back around to continue his transaction. The next thing he heard was the first time he had ever heard it.

"Raise your hands slowly and step away from the ATM," one of the officers said.

"What?" he said in disbelief, as he quickly turned around.

"Hold it right there buddy!" the other officer raised his voice and drew his revolver.

Gregory was livid, with raised arms. "Are you gentlemen talking to me? Is there a problem, and if so, would somebody please be kind enough to tell me!"

The two officers looked at one another in amusement. "Just keep your hands where we can see them and walk slowly towards us," one of them spoke.

Gregory was sure that they were making the biggest mistake of their lives. What had he done that would have precipitated them into acting this way toward him? Who did they think he was? And why were they treating him like he was a criminal? He was rigid as he slowly adhered to their commands.

"Right there," one of them said when he was close enough. "Place both hands on the hood of the car."

Gregory did what he was told, but his tone was enraged. "Look officers, I deserve to know why you think you have to treat me like this!"

The white police officers avoided his questions as one of them eyed the jeep, and reported his finding into his walkie talkie. The other stared at Gregory without saying a word. "Hello...hello, do you speak English? I said, what's going on?"

"Shut up and wait!" the officer demanded. When his partner was done with his conversation into the walkie talkie, they gave each other a certain look, and then turned to face Gregory. "Sorry for the inconvenience. You can go." They started getting back into their police car.

"Wait a minute," Gregory said as he turned to face them "I demand some sort of explanation for your behavior, right now!" He began approaching the police car.

"Whoa...hold it. We don't have to explain anything to you. We were just doing our job, that's all." He placed his revolver back into his holster.

Gregory stopped just short of their car. "You call that, doing your job? What was the reason for the hassle? Do I have a reason to fear for my life, from you?" Gregory was trying his best to hold his temper. He was alone out here with two white police officers, and didn't want to wind up on the local news.

"You just looked kind of suspicious, pal. Usually only big-wigs and business types use this bank. You just looked out of place. Is that OK with you?" one of the officers said.

"Would it be alright with you?" Gregory snorted.

One of the officers turned beet red, and started walking in Gregory's direction. "You wanna make something out of it, boy?"

"Murphy! Hold it got dammit!" the other yelled. "He hasn't done anything wrong, so leave 'em alone."

"You trying to defend this piece of scum? Billy, look at him. He's probably one of those Bloods or Crips. He ain't got no business being on this side of town. Let him go to his own bank in South Central somewhere!"

"Boy!?" Gregory realized what the whole thing was about; the fact that he was uptown dressed in jeans, a T-shirt, driving an old Jeep and he was black. He was being profiled! He would make a mental note of everything being said and done. He wasn't going to let them get away with this shit!

"You think I'm a gang member?" Gregory asked with scorn. "Just because I'm dressed casually and happen to bank in the Wilshire District?"

Officer Murphy answered him. "Not anymore. We know that you just purchased this Jeep recently. But you're lucky - the papers were just filed with the DMV. You could have been explaining yourself downtown."

"Explaining what, that I was minding my own business trying to use the ATM when Starsky and Hutch decided to respond to code B.L.A.C.K. M.A.N!"

"Hey, these things happen. And like I said, we were just doing our job."

Gregory decided to give them a taste of their own medicine. "Hey Murphy. Hey Billy. You're out of the Mid Division, aren't you? Yeah, you guys are sponsored yearly by my company at the Policemen's Ball. I wonder how your Chief, or better yet, the Mayor, would like to know how the CEO of your largest contributor is treated?"

They looked at each other in bewilderment. "What's this clown talking about, Billy?" the younger cop asked.

"I don't know, but if he knows what's good for him, he'll shut up or be brought up on charges."

Gregory decided that he should shut up. They could easily do anything they wanted to him, with nobody around to see it or hear it. He would deal with them on an upper level. They obviously fucked with the wrong black man, today! "Never mind. Good day, gentlemen."

The policemen mumbled as they retreated to their car. They watched as Gregory returned to the ATM and began his transaction all over again. When they finally pulled off, Gregory turned to face their direction, shaking his head in disgust. "All it takes is a pair of jeans and a black face."

He felt sorry for them, and the others out there like them. And though he had never gone through anything like that in his life, he was ashamed that it had taken him so long to. If he had, he would probably already be the kind of man that he wished he was...normal like Greg.

When he collected his money, he jumped into his Jeep to head for home. He was still furious from the humiliation that he had just been put through. And as he drove, he wished that the evening could still be spared...that he could go out with Jackie tonight and not become agitated about the incident. He had just learned, firsthand how the brotha's on the other side of the tracks must feel all the time. He sympathized with them...and now he shared in their views.

By the time he arrived at home, the pressure of the incident had built up in him like a stick of dynamite. The whole drive home, his mouth was salivating for a pill or two to calm his nerves. He walked through the front door, slamming it hard enough to rattle the chandelier in the entry way.

Louise came running into the front room. "What's the matter, Gregory?" she asked out of breath.

Gregory walked past her in a fury. He threw his car keys down on the piano in the living room, scratching the shiny black surface. Louise followed him. "Those sons of bitches!"

"Who? Who's a S.O.B?" Louise begged.

"The damn police, Louise! I was out minding my own business, when these two cops, came at me like I was a common criminal!"

Louise grabbed for her chest. "Oh my goodness! Are you alright, child?" she asked.

"Yeah, I'm alright," he fumed. "Lucky for me that they didn't drag me downtown."

"Well, what did you do to provoke them?" she asked concerned.

Gregory turned around slowly to face her. He could see the innocence in her eyes. She had the same look in her eyes, as he had had before this. "I was using the ATM, Louise! I was standing in front of the damn machine, retrieving money out of my account."

"Well that just doesn't make sense."

"No, it doesn't. But look at me. Look at what I'm wearing, Louise?" he asked.

"You look very nice, Gregory. Comfortable and clean - so what?"

"So what is that I was wearing this, plus driving a common vehicle around in the Wilshire District," he explained.

"And?"

"And that's it! I was harassed by two white idiot policemen...dangerous men with guns who told me to raise my hands in the air." Gregory went to the liquor cabinet and poured himself a brandy instead of calling his dealer. "It was the most embarrassing thing I've ever gone through in my life!" He gulped down his drink and poured another. Just then the doorbell rang.

"I'll get it," Louise said and hurried off to the front door. Before she returned, Gregory could hear voices in the front of the house. The voices were getting closer and closer to the living room.

"Darling, are you alright?" his mother was asking as she rushed toward him.

Gregory looked at her viciously. "What in the hell are you doing here Sara?" He had had just about enough of her hovering and scaring off his different drug connections.

"I was in the neighborhood...never mind about that. Louise was telling me about your brush with the police."

"It wasn't a brush Mother, it was more like a hot comb!" he growled.

Sara Childs was a black woman who passed for white earlier in her youth. Though she had never used a hot comb on her own hair, nor her children's, her son's choice of words reminded her that they were still black...regardless of the money. "I'm sorry you had to go through that Greg."

"Don't call me Greg" he yelled. "You know how much I hate it when you call me that!"

"I'm sorry, dear. But please, let me help. Maybe I should call the chief of police and have those two men reprimanded," she said, trying to soothe her son. Louise just stood at the doorway and listened in dismay.

"No! That's all I need - to have my mother tell on the bad men for me! I'll handle it myself."

"Whatever you say, Gregory," Sara said. She was a little confused as to why he didn't want to be called Greg, when her sources told her that was what he preferred these days. But she didn't want to upset him any further.

Gregory turned his attentions toward Louise. "Louise? Would you do me a big favor?"

"Of course."

"Would you find Pops' file on the Mid-Wilshire Police Department? It should be in his filing cabinet."

"Sure, but don't you think that the file would be in the office?" Louise asked.

"Yeah, but I've learned that Pops always kept two records of everything - one for the office and one for home." Gregory gave his mother a hard stare when he said this.

Louise rushed out of the room, leaving Gregory and Sara alone. Gregory gulped down his second drink and was about to pour himself another. "Greg...I mean, Gregory, haven't you had enough to drink?"

Gregory stopped and looked at his mother. He gave her a wicked smile and then continued to pour. "What's it to you?"

Sara rushed to his side and put her hand on his arm. "Because I know what it can do to you...and so do you. OK, so the police pissed you off tonight, so what. Deal with it in the way that your father would have. And that doesn't mean drinking yourself into a stupor, either."

Gregory ignored her. Sara took on a tougher tone. "Are you going to let yourself revert back to where you were heading to before? Look at yourself, Gregory! You're a Childs…start acting like one!"

Before Gregory could respond to his mother, Theresa ran into the living room with some man on her arm. "Guess what? We're getting married!" She ran around the room holding out her left hand, displaying a tiny ring with an even tinier diamond.

Gregory grabbed for his head in disbelief. Sara gasped out loud with the look of sheer terror. Louise walked in on the news and dropped the file to the floor. Theresa was smiling from ear to ear. And her fiancé, stood with his hands in his overall pockets.

"Has this family gone insane?" Gregory was finally able to say.

"Theresa, baby?" Sara began. "What is this non-sense you're talking about?"

Theresa walked next to her intended, and slipped her arm through his. "It's not non-sense, Mother, we love each other."

Louise was next. "Since when? I've never seen him before. Have you, Gregory?"

Gregory was leering at the young fella. "No! But we're about to have a little talk, right now."

Gregory walked towards the young man and pulled his arm in his direction. "Wait!" Theresa yelled after them. "What are you doing, Gregory?" she pleaded.

"I'm looking out for your best interest, you silly little girl!" he yelled back to her.

When Theresa tried to run after them, Sara grabbed hold to her waist. "Wait a minute, Theresa!"

Theresa struggled with her mother trying to run after her fiancé and her brother. "Mother let me go! I have to stop Gregory from destroying my life!"

Sara continued her grip. "What do you know about this man, Theresa?"

"I know that he loves me for me and he doesn't treat me like I'm a baby!"

Louise kept her distance. "Who treats you like a baby, Theresa?"

"Everybody Louise, including you!"

"Do I treat you like a baby?" Sara asked.

"How in the hell would I know?" Theresa blurted. "You're damn near a stranger to this family!"

The shock of the words hit Sara as her grip turned to jelly. Theresa finally tore from her mother's arms and made a mad dash for the door. Louise grabbed her this time. "What a horrible thing for a young lady to say to her mother!" Louise roared. "How dare you talk to your mother like that!"

Theresa, being held by Louise's tight grip, looked up in disbelief. "You're defending her?"

Sara looked at Louise with a look of knowing. Louise looked into Sara's eyes as she spoke. "I know what I know," Louise answered. "Sara is your mother, and how dare you talk to her like that."

Finally Theresa stopped her struggle. She turned to face her mother, who had now faced away and was leaning against the piano. "Well, I guess I didn't mean it the way it came out," she said in defense.

"You have a habit of saying that, don't you?" Louise said.

Theresa looked at Louise again. "You are a hard one to figure out." She walked to the sofa and sat down. She began to stare at the tiny ring on her finger. "I just miss Pops, that's all. I figured that Alan could be the one to make up for that - you know, to treat me like I was the only thing that mattered."

"Well, you aren't the only one that matters," Louise said defiantly. "Now apologize to your mother."

Sara looked up. "Thank you Louise, but that isn't necessary. I know how everyone must feel about me, having shown up after all these years. Who did I think I was fooling anyway?" She looked at Louise. "Certainly not you. In all trueness of the word, Louise...you are their mother now."

"Sara, there is no reason or excuse for the way this girl has just spoken to you. The fact of the matter is she's spoiled rotten. She always has been. Thomas lavished everything on this girl that a girl could want. And how does she go and repay him - by leaping head first into something that she knows is not right.

Now don't get me wrong, child," she turned to Theresa. "I'm not saying that this Alan is not the one for you. But what I am saying is that no one in the family has even had the opportunity to meet him, or even see him before. What's the rush girl, are you pregnant?"

Louise's question got the attention of both Theresa and Sara, who dropped their jaws to the carpet. "Of course not, how could you ask me that?"

"Well, what do you expect us to think? And why do you think that your brother is in the other room talking to your young Alan right now, huh? Do you think he's asking him what movies the two of you have seen together? No. He's making sure that the young man has acted like a young man with you."

Theresa jumped up from the sofa and ran out of the living room crying. Louise and Sara could hear her stomping her way up the stairs. "Are you going to go after her?" Sara asked.

"No, and you shouldn't either," Louise said. "She should be alone to think about what's going on in her head. That girl needs to grow up, Sara. It can't be healthy the way she carries on sometimes."

Sara sat down on the piano chair. "And how is that?"

Louise sat across from her on the sofa. "She doesn't act like a young lady her age. It seems to me that she prefers the attention that a child gets, rather than that of an adult."

"What makes you an authority on human behavior?" Sara asked with the instincts of a defensive mother.

Louise looked at her with squinted eyes. "Oh, I suppose 20 some odd years of watching her behave, that's all."

This must have really hit Sara where she lived. Tears began to streak down her face. Louise watched her without compassion. Finally, when she regained her composure Sara spoke.

"I'm sorry. But it's hard you know - looking at your children from the outside looking in. I do love them, Louise, I'm sure you know that. But I want to be much more than just a formality to them." She held up her hands. "And yes, I know that the perfect come back line for that is, that I should have never left them in the first place, but things were different then. It was a different time for men, and women, and relationships, and the whole world seemed so different then. And unfortunately, I wasn't able to handle much of anything back then. I guess I was weak. And it breaks my heart to see that my children might be ending up the same way." She tried to regain her composure by wiping away her tears and clearing her voice. "I wonder what's keeping Gregory with Alan."

Before Louise could answer her, they arrived through the doorway. "Did I hear somebody mention my name?" Gregory said. Alan looked as pale as a ghost.

"What did you do to the boy?" Louise asked.

"Nothing. We just had a little talk." Gregory was patting Alan on the back.

"Uh...yes ma'am...we just had a little talk. Is Theresa around?"

"She went upstairs, dear," Louise said.

"Good," Gregory said. "I hope she's getting her act together up there. Besides, she can wait until tomorrow to hear what Alan has to tell her."

Sara stood. "Oh, Gregory, what have you done? You haven't done something that she'll hate you for, have you?"

Gregory ignored his mother. Instead, he grabbed Alan by the arm and walked him down the hallway towards the front door. "Later Alan," they could hear Gregory say.

Gregory reappeared into the living room. He turned to the two women. "Alan and I have come to an understanding that he and Theresa will have to see a lot more of each other to establish their relationship. I simply told him that they were moving a bit too fast and that we would not stand by and do nothing about the whole thing. And I take it, from his reaction, that he would much rather be the friend of a rich girl, rather than married to a poor one."

Louise looked at him with pride. "Your father would be really proud of you, child."

"Thank you, Louise." He walked toward the window. "I don't know what's happening to us. First me and the police and now, Resa and her little fantasy. What's next? Is Lisa going to leave Michael? Is Jeremy going to get some young lady in trouble?" He walked around the room with his head down. "These are some strange times in which we live."

Gregory saw the file that Louise brought to him earlier, and picked it up. Out of the blue he asked, "Where's the gun?"

Both women looked at him. "What?" Louise asked.

"The gun? Where's Pops gun?"

Sara ran to him and stood directly in front of him. "Why Gregory? You aren't going to do anything drastic to that boy, are you?"

Gregory pushed her gently to the side. "Hell no, woman. I just want to know where it is." He raised his eyebrows in thought and then snapped his fingers. "I think I know exactly where it is." He rushed out of the room leaving the two women alone again.

"What is this insanity?" Sara asked Louise.

"I haven't the slightest idea."

Gregory returned no sooner than he had left the room. The file and the gun were nowhere to be seen. "Tonight I learned a little more about the world ladies, and I plan to be prepared for what goes on in it. But not to worry, I have a feeling that everything is going to work out just fine. You'll see what I'm talking about soon. Talk to Resa when she feels better and tell her what went on with Alan down here, OK? Now, if you'll excuse me, I have to prepare for my date." He walked out of the room, again.

"We'll see that *what* is going to work out just fine?" Louise asked while nervously settling down in a leather recliner.

"A woman. He's talking about a woman, Louise," Sara said with concern as she paced the room.

"Well, how do you know that?" Louise asked confused.

"I've seen him try to put all of his eggs in one basket before. And I'd bet my last dollar that he thinks *she* can make his world sane." Sara was worried.

"And what about the gun?" Louise asked nervously.

"I can't figure that one out yet."

Meanwhile, upstairs Gregory was getting ready for his date with Jackie. And when he bathed, dressed and slapped on a little Cartier Aftershave, he dashed out of the house with the directions to her house gripped tightly in his hand.

She gave exact directions and he found it without any problems. When she opened the door, she was drop dead gorgeous. She was wearing a sleeveless, ankle length, rose colored dress with a split up the front. Her hair fell to her shoulders in soft loose curls, and Gregory noticed that her shoes and handbag had sparkles in them, like diamonds. At that moment, he realized tonight she deserved to be driven around in the Jaguar and not the average looking Jeep. But, he also knew that Greg didn't own a Jaguar...Gregory did.

"You look absolutely beautiful," he said to her as she allowed him to enter the house.

"Thank you. You don't look so bad yourself," Jackie replied.

Greg looked around the house. "This is great. You said you and your mother live here?"

"That's right."

"Well there's definitely enough space in here, huh?"

"Sure. This house is big enough for us. I just hate the way rich people try and show off their money with a house big enough to house the U.S. Congress, don't you?" She was looking for a reaction.

Greg ignored her question and thought to himself, "You ain't seen big, yet." Instead, he responded, "You ready to go?"

"Yes." She smiled.

They left for their night out on the town. Greg had the time of his life showing off this beautiful woman on his arm. He watched every move she made, every gesture, every remark. He wanted to make sure that she was as perfect for him as he had suspected she was. They dined and danced the night away.

Much to his surprise, she had an enormous appetite for such a petite woman. She ordered the most expensive items on the menu, without even knowing what the prices were. When asked if she wanted a cocktail, she insisted on champagne. And she did all of this without appearing greedy, or shallow. Instead, she asked for, and received everything with a sense of style...with class. It was as though she herself lived among the wealthy.

None of the glitz and glamour fazed her at all; if anything, it bored her to death. She grabbed the attention of men everywhere she went...like she was catnip or something. Jackie was full of surprises and more than ever, Greg was convinced that she would take his news in stride. Moreover, he was sure that she was the answer to his prayers.

The time he spent with her came and went entirely too fast for Greg. He asked if he could see her again, and she agreed right away. They enjoyed the next few evenings doing whatever Jackie wanted, and they were definitely consistent - dining in the finest restaurants, drinking the most expensive champagne, and living it up to the extreme. It was hard for Greg to hold back his good news; that he could easily afford their evenings together. But he wanted her to think that he was worthy – that he would stretch his finances to the limit just for her.

Either way, she didn't seem to care about the money. She simply required the best of the best. Greg suspected that she was the kind of woman who could just as easily open up her pocket book and pay for their nights out as well. He, of course, would never allow such a thing.

Greg was falling in love with Jackie, and he was going with it, full force. He figured there was no need to fight the obvious; that he and she belonged together.

At work his days seemed to breeze by, due of the enormous amount of energy he found himself with lately. Board meetings were a breeze and the business had never been running better. Timothy Callahan had even assured Gregory that Stanley Bunch would no longer pose a threat to the company. He had been indicted on two counts of tax fraud, and would probably be spending the next 10 years in prison. Gregory just smiled at the news and thought of Jackie once again.

He imagined she would be waiting for Greg to come home after a long day at the office. She would be dressed as immaculately as the night he had first taken her to Spago. They would do everything together, like couples in-love do. It could be the perfect marriage; it could be his last chance at a perfect life.

He also imagined that the reason she had not yet given herself to him, was because she was a virgin, or required long courtships. In other words, he knew Jackie was waiting to be swept off of her feet and not sleeping with men for kicks. After being with a tramp like Venus, it was good to finally run across a woman with some real class.

And Gregory was convinced that he had met Jackie because of his transformation into Greg. He often wondered if he had been Gregory out there on that pier, if she would have given him the time of day. But the more he thought about it, the more he didn't think so. He was positive that he had done the right thing, and for the right reasons.

Justifying his deceit was the only thing he could do. If he began to feel guilty about what he had done...was doing...then he probably wouldn't be able to live with himself. No, Jackie was the reason for his actions. And he would only need to hold off for a little while longer before he was able to explain the truth and introduce Gregory to her. He was sure that she would understand.

As the days came and went, Gregory became a better man at work and at home. Theresa had adjusted to being Alan's girlfriend instead of his fiancé. Lisa, Michael, and the kids were doing well and Jeremy was as unaffected by anything as usual.

But the most incredible transformation of all was Louise and Sara were getting along. Not like sisters or anything like that, but like alliances. It was as though they joined alliances for the sake of the family. Nobody could figure out why those two constantly had their heads together, like they were up to something. It was shocking to believe at first, but eventually everybody got used to it.

For the first time since his father's death, Gregory was on top of the world. Everything was going right, and nothing could possibly go wrong. He owed it all to Jackie. His siblings were constantly commenting on the transformation that he had gone through. They also suspected that his run-in with the police, and a rumored new woman in his life was the reason for it.

They were all very curious as to why he hadn't brought her around yet. But he couldn't tell them that the reason for the secrecy was because of alter-ego named, Greg. They would just have to wait to meet the, soon to be, addition to the family.

Curiously, Louise and Sara didn't say much to him about the changes he had undergone, but they sure were eyeballing him all of a sudden.

On Wednesday night, while in the study, Jeremy and Gregory were having a friendly discussion about women. Gregory decided that he couldn't keep Jackie a secret any longer. "I've got something to tell you," Gregory said.

"Hot damn, I knew it! You're in love, aren't you?" Jeremy said with a smile.

Gregory couldn't help but blurt out his happiness. "Yeah man. I'm in love, and it feels...it feels like Heaven!"

Jeremy slid to the edge of his chair and began rubbing his hands together. "Well, who is she...where is she?"

"She's Jackie Winters. She's fine. She's smart. She's classy. And she's all mine."

Jeremy looked impressed. "Does she have a sister?"

Gregory started laughing. "No, she's an only child."

"Did you just hear the irony of what you just said?" Jeremy asked his brother.

"No. What are you talking about?"

"She's an only child. She's to be the new addition to the Childs' isn't she?"

Gregory couldn't hold back. "That's what I'm hoping for, little brother."

Jeremy stood up and walked over to his brother. Gregory stood up to meet him and they embraced. "I'm really happy for you, man. I wish you a lot of luck and happiness."

"Thanks, man." They both returned to their seats.

"Have you asked her to marry you yet?" Jeremy asked his brother.

Gregory bit his lip. "Well...there's one problem."

"What?"

Gregory didn't know where to begin. "Well...umm...."

"Spit it out man," his brother said.

"She doesn't know I'm rich," he was finally able to say.

Jeremy looked relieved. "Oh, is that all. Good, most of the women I date don't know I'm rich either."

"But she doesn't know I'm Gregory Childs."

That stumped Jeremy. "What do you mean she doesn't know that you're Gregory Childs?"

"She thinks my name is Greg Childs and that I'm a clerk for TCI."

"What! That's a good one, Greg. So how, but better yet, when do you plan on telling her the truth?"

"Tomorrow," he said pensively. "I'm going to tell her the truth and ask her to marry me, tomorrow."

"How long have you known this woman?"

"Long enough to know that I'm in love with her."

"OK. Do you have the ring?" Jeremy asked.

"No, that would be a problem. If I buy her a ring...say a five carat diamond, before I tell her the truth, then she's going to think that I robbed Tiffany's or something."

"You've got a point there."

"So, I'll tell her the truth first, and then I'll propose, and after she accepts we'll go and pick out her ring together."

"You sure it's going to work out?" Jeremy asked.

Gregory thought about it for a minute. "It's just got too."

The next day, Gregory rushed over to Jackie's house after work. He took a deep breath and rang her doorbell. She was looking as beautiful as ever, as he kissed her on the cheek and walked past her into the house. He took his time settling on the sofa and making small talk before making his big confession.

His palms were sweating and his heart was pounding. That, he figured, was expected since he was still fighting urges to pop those damn pills. But when finally, he couldn't hold back the truth any longer, he told her.

He started from the beginning and told her everything about himself; that he was actually Gregory Childs, CEO of TCI. He spilled out his reasons for pretending to be Greg; for his own sanity; for a real shot at happiness. And then he explained why he kept the truth from her, that he had fallen in love with her, and wanting her to marry him.

Jackie listened without budging or flinching...like she had already read his mind. And much to Greg's or Gregory's, surprise she didn't make a big fuss or throw anything at him. But unfortunately for him, she didn't leap into his arms and say, "I will," either. In fact, Jackie just sat there with an iron knowing look about her.

Finally, she rose from the sofa and said, "I'll think about it, Gregory. I will honestly give everything a great deal of consideration, and I'll tell you tomorrow."

"Tomorrow? So soon?" Gregory asked stupefied.

"Yes, tomorrow," Jackie said as cool as a cucumber.

Gregory stood to face her and kissed her on the cheek, again. "I'm sorry that I was trippin' when I met you, and had to be someone else for a while. But now I'm OK...thanks to you."

Jackie just smiled and told him the time and the numbered lifeguard station he was to meet her at Dockweiler Beach. She then told him not to be late. "I'll give you my answer then...at the beach...where we met"

"I'll be there. So, I'll see you tomorrow then?" Greg was ecstatic.

"Yes."

"I can't wait to see you again, Jackie."

"I can't wait for Friday night either Gregory."

He left the house with a good feeling. He knew she had a lot of thinking to do tonight in deciding to become his wife, and he would give her the space she needed, for now. As he jumped into his car and backed out of the driveway, he was on such a high cloud that he barely took notice of the car pulling into the driveway right beside him.

(16) – Vincent – Life's a Bitch

V incent couldn't remember the last time he had worked so hard in all of his life. The time he'd spent in libraries was paying off for him.

He was able to find books to teach him how to do his resume and give them just the right look. He'd use old jobs that he had over the years and embellish some stuff; his length of employment, his dates of his employment and his salary.

Good for him the places where he used to work had all changed ownership or had been closed down for years and there would be no way for anybody to check up on his facts. He was determined to do things on the up and up, as much as possible.

He decided not to go to the library where he met Jax, since that would have distracted him too much. No, she was not his primary focus at the moment. First, he would make some changes in his life and then impress the hell out of her. If this didn't do it, he didn't know what would.

He became distracted as the hairs on the back of his neck suddenly stood up. Something was happening around him - women...and lots of them were stampeding into the library. He obviously chose a library that was near some college, because swarms of attractive looking young women were settling down all over the place.

When he thought about it, another semester of college had just started. "Damn, time flies," he heard himself say out loud. It wasn't so long ago when he met Jax doing research for her final exam, or thesis, or something. She was so...so easy to talk to back then. Now, she wouldn't even give him the time of day. She had to be fucking somebody else.

Vincent constantly found himself refocusing his thoughts to the work ahead of him. When he finished jotting down information out of some reference books, he went into one of the private rooms to use a typewriter.

It wasn't going to take him much longer before he completed his resume. Aside from being a lover among the best of the best, he was a pretty good typist too. And by the time he had finished with his resume, he read back to himself what his accomplishments had been in the work force for the last 15 years. It all sounded pretty good to him. But he knew that it wasn't going to be enough.

Most of the people competing for the top notch jobs in reputable corporations, generally sought after college graduates, still green behind the ears. They preferred to get their hands on them first so that they could do the type of "molding" that would be fitting to their company.

Vincent, on the other hand, would be labeled a seasoned veteran, which could play out either as an asset, or just as easily as a liability. The more he looked at his situation, the more he realized how pathetic he must look to someone who did not understand his way of life. It had suited him well, but now he was convinced that it was time to change. And though his natural instincts constantly tugged at his pant legs, he kept the faith.

The Truth-Seeker had reminded him what his parents taught him about faith and prayer. She taught him things that he didn't know he needed to learn. Because of her, he knew that he had a second chance at life.

When he was all done at the library, he was too full of energy to just let it die down at home. So he decided to visit an old friend who could possibly give him some pointers on how to assert himself when seeking employment. He was sure that she would have a pretty good idea of how he should present himself.

She was an A&R person for one of those top record labels. And often, she had told him how she made instantaneous decisions on whether a singer "had it," or not. Well, tonight he was hoping she could guide him on if he "had it," or how he could get it.

He knew he would be taking a chance on driving up to her house without calling, but he figured what the hell. By the time he drives through that 405 freeway traffic to get to Sherman Oaks, everybody should be home. And if she had another car in her driveway when he got there, he would simply turn around and head back for the city. It was that simple. Luckily, when he arrived he saw that her Lexus was sitting alone in the driveway.

He knocked at the front door and a Mexican lady opened the door instead of Alexandra. "Si?"

"Is Ms. Dupree here?" Vincent asked curiously.

"Who are you?" the lady asked with a thick accent.

"My name is Vincent Cruthers."

"One momento." She allowed Vincent to have a seat in the main entrance and then she left to find Alex.

He took his seat and looked around. "Wow! Things must be looking up for her. The last time I was here, the place was nearly empty. Now she has some tough shit up in here, with a housekeeper to boot!" Vincent spoke under his breath as he looked around in awe.

Moments later, Alex was briskly walking toward him with a black leather pant suit on. "Vincent," she said with surprise. "My, my, where have you been keeping yourself?" She embarked on him as he stood and kissed her full on the lips.

"I've been here and there, Alex. But look at you. You look great. And your place has come along quite nice."

"Thank you. Please, please come in." She grabbed him by the hand and led him into her family room. "Can I get you something to drink?"

"No." Vincent took a seat on a bar stool and looked at her. "You sure look good, girl."

She sat across from him on the other side of the bar and poured herself a glass of wine. "You always had something nice to say to me," she said before she took a sip. "But what on earth are you doing here? You couldn't have just been in the neighborhood."

"No, I drove up here specifically to see you. I'd like to tug at your ear if you have the time."

"Sure, anything for you."

"Well," he began, "I've taken somewhat of a new direction in my life Alex, and I need some advice."

She looked puzzled. "A new direction? What exactly does that mean, Vincent? You want to become a performing artist?"

"No."

"Good, because as far as I'm concerned...you already are." She gave him a wicked smile.

That was exactly what he had been trying to avoid all along. But unfortunately, the only women that he had ever really dealt with - he'd also slept with them. Now, he was bound to be tied to sexual connotations for the rest of his life. But he could deal with that...as a matter of fact it was great. However, he was trying to do something different now, and this was not the time for sex talk. "Alex, I'm serious."

"So am I."

He leaned forward in his seat. "I'm talking about a career." He stopped her with his hand before she could speak. "A business career within a company. A respectable position within a respectable company. And my question to you is do you think that I have what it takes?"

She looked at him with serious eyes. "You're looking for a job, Vincent?"

"Yes, Alex. I'm looking for a job."

Alex tapped her chin with the wine glass in her hand, and rolled back her eyes in thought. "Vincent, you are an incredible man. You have been doing just fine...better than fine, for a long time. But, if you're serious about getting a job, I don't think that you're going to have any problems."

Vincent was glad to hear it. If anybody knew, she did. "Really? I mean, what about the age thing? Aren't company's looking for the spring chickens right out of college?"

"Sure, in some cases. But look at you. You've got the look, baby. And if you have the skill, you're in. But sometimes you can be in, even if you don't have the skill."

"Thanks, Alex. I really needed to hear that." Vincent said with a smile.

"It's all true, Vincent. But why do you suddenly need affirmation from me? You are the most confident brotha I know."

"Yeah well, you're the expert Alex. You're in the kind of business where as you have to make snap decisions, and I want your opinion. He meant it, but hopefully it would flatter the hell out of her, as too.

"My, my, my," she said. "You really have changed, haven't you?" She stood up and walked around the bar and stood directly in front of him. "But I'm curious to know what the change is for. Could it be love, Vincent?"

Vincent resisted the urge to pull her into his arms, which is exactly what she probably wanted him to do. "Yeah, love of self."

"Is that all you love?"

"Of course not. I love everything and everybody."

"Oh, have you turned into a nature lover, since last we were lovers?"

"I guess you could call it that." Vincent was getting a little uneasy as she continued to stand directly in front of him. When she finally walked away he exhaled.

"So, tell me, what kind of work will you be seeking?" She moved cat-like across the room.

Vincent thought for a minute before speaking. "I really don't know. But whatever it is, it'll have to be something that

I enjoy. I'm not the kind of person that can put up with something that I have no real interest in."

Alex moved to open the sliding glass door, leading out onto a terrace. "Come join me out here," she said as she went outside. "I was thinking about getting into the Jacuzzi tonight."

Vincent stood to follow her outside. He would have liked to watch her put on a bikini, though he had no intentions of getting into the Jacuzzi with her. He found her leaning on the terrace railing. He joined her outside. "It's as nice out here as I remember."

"Yes it is, isn't it? It's one of my favorite places in this whole house."

"So why are you still living out here by yourself. A woman as beautiful as you should have a man to take care of you."

"Are you volunteering, Vincent?"

Her question caught him off guard. He was already trying his best not to come on to her tonight. "Uh...that's not what I mean. You know, what I'm asking you - when are you going to get married?"

"Married? Hell, I don't think that I've ever thought about that before," she said.

"Oh no. Hmmm...I could have sworn that you used to tell me how you longed to share your life with someone."

"Yeah, but that didn't have anything to do with marriage. I'm having too much fun on my own right now." She looked at him in a familiar way. "We used to have a lot of fun, Vincent. I guess somebody else got to you before I could, huh?"

Vincent didn't want to hurt her feeling by telling her about Jax, or about anybody else for that matter. "You couldn't want to be with a guy like me." He didn't know what else to say.

She touched his arm as she began to walk back into the house. "I knew you'd cop out on me." He turned to watch her vanish through the door. When he walked into the house to follow her, he noticed her disappearing down the hallway leading to her bedroom. His heart leapt with excitement. It had been a while since he had been with a woman, and he was feeling as though he could settle for anyone right about now.

And when she returned, just as he thought, she was dressed in something more comfortable; a sleek black see-through nightie with lace. Her back was bare, and the split went straight up the middle to her navel! She topped the outfit off with black stiletto boots. He couldn't help but think how much she looked like Elvira.

As she walked towards him, she held the split of her nightie open, to expose herself to him. She had that look in her eye...the look that told him that she was his for the taking. It seemed like an eternity before she finally ascended upon him and plunged her nearly bare breasts against his chest. Vincent tried to contain himself from throwing her down on the floor. Then she moved her red lips up to meet his right ear. He was anticipating the warmth of her tongue on his lobe. He closed his eyes, as to ready himself for his surrender.

"You have to go. I'm expecting company," she purred.

It took about three seconds before for the reality of what she said sunk in. When it hit him, he opened his eyes. He was cock-hard as a pipe, but he wasn't about to give her the satisfaction of seeing him suffer.

"You're right. I do have plans for the evening." Vincent leaned down and kissed her on the cheek. He turned and walked out of the family room, down the hall, and through the front door. When he was outside he looked down at the bulge in his pants. "Damn. I must be losing it." He got into his car and sat for a moment. It felt strange to him, not having any real plans with a woman for the night.

He got back on the 405 and headed south. His buddy Tony should be home right about now. At least his dick wouldn't get hard around him, though he was bound to talk about nothing but women.

The urge to pump Tony for information on getting in at his company, didn't last long. If he were to mention that he was even thinking about getting a real job, it would fuck up his reputation forever, in the eyes of the guys who thought he led the perfect life. No, he would just let them find out gradually when he was already employed somewhere.

Tony was one of those guys who thought about nothing except pussy and his pension. He'd been working for the same company since he first got out of high school, and had no other desires in life except to receive a retirement check.

Up until now, Vincent thought his was a boring life. But now he was gaining a new respect for those who found a place in the working world. And he was even a little surprised that the urge had not gotten to him sooner, since just about everyone he knew was successful in their careers. Even he, to a degree, had been successful in his kind of work. But the kind of work he was in to could kill a fella.

Vincent knew Tony was at home the moment he pulled into the driveway. He could hear laughter echoing out of the window. That meant Tony was trying his best to woo some young lady over to his house and into his bed. That had been his mission in life ever since his woman finally had the sense to leave him.

When Vincent closed his car door, Tony's head popped out of the window to see who was coming up his front walk. He recognized his friend and hailed him to the door. By the time Vincent got to the front door, Tony was kissing his phone date off the line. "Yeah baby, let's do that...and soon. I'll be thinking of you - and only you. Yeah, later baby."

Vincent had to keep from laughing at his friend. He always gave it his best shot. "Did I interrupt a love connection, man?" Vincent asked as he shook friends with Tony and walked through his front door.

"Of course not. She's crazy about me, man. She'll be back, as Arnold would say." He laughed and patted his friend on the back. "Come on in, man. Come on in. Now talk to me and tell me what in the hell's been going on with you." The two men walked into the spare bedroom that Tony called his den.

Vincent sat across from Tony on a bamboo chair. "Ain't nothin' man. I just got back from seeing Alexandra. You know Alex, the one that works with singers?"

Tony rubbed his hands together. "Yeah, I remember that sweet thang. Umm! You sure get the hot one's man."

Vincent didn't want to get into any discussions about Alex, especially since she had just blown him off. He wasn't mad at her but he knew that it was going to be somewhat impossible to retain his relationships with women if he wasn't going to give them a stiff one, every now and again.

Alex was no exception, nor were any of his many, many female friends; maybe except for…Jax. And it was now that he realized he was going to have to make some choices. He didn't want to lose his acquaintances, but he didn't want to exploit himself anymore either…unless he felt like it, that is. No, Vincent was insistent upon gaining a new kind of respect from his peers, even though he didn't have the slightest clue as to where to start.

Would he have to lie to his friends, like Tony, and keep them believing that he was still banging the women of his choice? Should he ignore the talk about women with his friends, and then have them think that he was losing his touch? The questions were ones that needed to be answered, and quick. Because Tony wasn't going to let up on his interrogation on Alex, until he heard all of the juicy details.

"Not tonight, man. She was plugged up," Vincent said, opting to get off of the subject with some dignity intact.

"So what," Tony said. "That never stopped you before."

"Yeah, well the difference between me and you, my friend, is that I give the lady the option."

"Always a gentleman, huh?"

"I try." That was close. He already felt like Tony was looking at him funny. But he couldn't tell if that was good or bad. He didn't even know why he was there anymore. What in the hell was Tony going to do for his motivation?

No way was he going to be open to his friend's new goals in life. No, that's not the way it works with men. Once you've acquired a great reputation, especially among the ladies, then you are expected to carry on until you die. Those who change in mid-stream are usually seen as failures to the entire gender. So as it turned out, Vincent was stuck between a rock and a hard place. The only way out of this mess was to lie, and let the rest of the shit fall into place later. "But the night wasn't a total failure. There's nothing wrong with her mouth, you know."

Tony seemed elated at the news. "That's my man!" he said, clapping his hands twice.

Though Vincent saw his visit with Tony as a total waste of time, he decided to prod him on his feelings about work. He wanted to get some kind of idea as to the satisfaction that working people have. But he did it in a roundabout way; making it seem more like he was interested in the women that worked there. Tony was more than happy to talk about his job and the pension he was going to receive in another 20 years. The thought of all of that work made Vincent sick to his stomach.

He didn't have the head-start that Tony had, which meant that he had some serious catching up to do. And the way Tony told it, you had to do what you're told without talking back, show up early to get the brownie points and compliment your ugly female manager's when necessary. In actuality, a job was that same as having a woman at home: Agree with what she says, take her out occasionally and fuck her well. This job business wasn't as foreign to him as he thought.

The night slowly passed as they talked about work and women, and the work you have to do to keep your women pleased. When it was all over, Vincent was glad that he stopped over his friends place. Tony did have some important things to say after all. So he left, telling Tony that he should call up a freak or two before it got too late. "They'll wait for my call, man," he said.

Vincent just laughed as he walked out of the front door. "Yeah, I'm sure they will." He got into his car once again, and headed for home. As he drove, he realized how strange the current events in his life were. And though he hadn't shared his experience with the Truth-Seeker to anyone else except Jax, he felt as though the whole world was laughing at him.

Jax wouldn't laugh, he was sure of that. She was probably the only one who could take him as he was...whatever that may be. And now all of that might be un-repairable. He had alienated the only person who cared for him regardless of himself. It was not going to be easy to get back into her good graces, but he felt he had to keep trying.

Everyone else saw him as just some piece of meat, or some stud. But a man can't go through his whole life living up to someone else's expectations, can they? And although those titles he received from friends never bothered him before, now he felt as though he had entered a cross-roads in his life.

Once in his apartment, he instinctively checked the messages on his answering machine. To his content, he found that he was just as popular with the ladies as ever. But this time, instead of just listening to each message to decide who to call back first, try to get them to come over, and then fuck them, he wrote down each of their names and their occupations.

One of them was bound to be able to help him get his foot in at one of their places of employment. Still, he knew that all of them would want sexual favors for it, but he would have to work his way around that later.

Joan was the first to leave a message. She was a nurse for the county hospital and probably didn't make a whole lot of money. Besides, he had no desire to work in a hospital or to be exposed to only God knows what kind of diseases.

The second to leave a message was Unique. It had been quite a while since last he heard from her. She had been on the road traveling with some band, and had probably recently returned and wanted to renew her intimacy with him. She wasn't a hopeful either.

Thirdly, a message from Lorna brought Vincent hope. She was the V.P. of Personnel for a major corporation. If anyone could find him a job, it would be her. The only problem with Lorna was that she was 50-something, lonely, and boring as hell. He knew without a doubt that she would accept no less than a hard stiff one for a long time to come.

To Vincent's surprise even Alex had called and left a message. She wasn't offering him a job though. Instead, she was telling him of her disappointment that he didn't take her when he had the chance.

"That girl is sick," Vincent said to himself. "If the bitch needs it so often she ought to get herself a vibrator like the rest of 'em." He thought to himself for a minute. "She's just the type to leave a fucked up message like...like..." He found it hard to believe that Alex might have been motivated enough to cause him so much distress. But she *was* trippin' so he wasn't going to put it past her.

His fourth call was from his mother. As soon as he heard the woman's sweet voice, he looked at the clock and saw right away, that it was too late to call her back. He listened very closely to her message and her voice, and was assured that nothing was wrong at home. "I'll call her first thing in the morning," he thought.

After being uplifted from his mother's message, he was beginning to believe that maybe even Jax had found the nerve to give him a call. But as he began writing down the name of the next caller, he knew he was mistaken.

Gala was a sweet and unexpected surprise. She had been avoiding calling him ever since her husband found out that she was cheating on him. Gala didn't work, but was filthy rich. Actually it was her husband who was rich, but that didn't stop her. She wanted the cake, the diamonds, the house, the cars, the furs, the maids, her husband, the icing and Vincent, all wrapped up in a nice Chanel silk scarf. Vincent was sure that her husband would not give him a job within his winery empire.

His final message was a big let-down. He was still hoping that Jax would have called, but instead he received a message from Penny. She was a nice girl, but didn't have the sense to call home with. She held several part time jobs, from waitress to aerobics instructor. No. Penny couldn't help him with his desire to work...except on his push-ups.

"This is a damn shame. All of these messages from all of these women, and not one of them, with the exception of Lorna, can help me get a job."

He was frustrated with the thought and started tearing off his clothes in frustration. He threw on a pair of sweat pants and a T-shirt and decided to do some more thinking while taking a brisk run through the park down the street. When he was outside, he did a few warm up exercises on the sidewalk and then darted off for the park.

The lights were fully lit up and the sky was as clear as glass, allowing him to see the rarely visible sky of Los Angeles. Other runners were taking advantage of the clear night as well. Most of them were more agile than he was, but he ignored them and kept to his own pace.

After about 4 1/2 laps around the field, he bent over on his knees to pause for a rest. In the darkness, he heard whining coming from underneath the bleachers. The crying was no doubt a puppy and he was sure that the mother dog would soon go scampering underneath the bleachers to comfort it.

He took this as an excuse to rest, and so he walked over to the bleachers and sat down. He had nearly forgotten about the puppy, as he was lost in his own thoughts. But as soon as the other runners on the field zipped past him, he snapped out of it. He could still hear the whining, and there was no sign of the mother.

Before he knew it, he was starting to get a little worried. And it wasn't that he was an animal lover or anything like that, it probably had something to do with the relationships he used to have with the farm animals in Louisiana. And so, before long, Vincent found himself crawling underneath the bleachers, looking for a stray dog.

When he finally was able to locate the little thing, his heart nearly fell out of his chest. The dog was so puny and little, Vincent was sure that it would not survive the night. He didn't think that the mother would abandon the puppy, unless she was hit by a car or something. But one thing was for certain, if he left the little thing alone, it would surely die. So he held the little brown ball of fur and bones in his hands and took it home.

Once there, he placed the puppy in a card board box filled with balls of newspaper, and set it next to the stove. Next, he felt the urge to warm some milk. And because he didn't have any dog food, he threw on some rice. "A good mixture of rice and milk should taste good little fella," he found himself saying to the dog. The little animal just whined and squirmed with as little energy as Vincent had ever seen.

Once the rice and milk cooled off a bit, with the assistance of ice cubes, Vincent placed a plastic bowl in the box with the dog. He could see that the animal smelled the food and wanted to crawl towards it, but just did not have the energy. So Vincent pushed the food directly underneath its mouth and the puppy tried without success to sap it up.

Vincent finally realized that the puppy was too young to feed itself. It couldn't be more than a week or two old, and so he would have to bottle feed it if it was going to survive the night. "How do you bottle feed a dog without a bottle?" he asked himself. He didn't have the slightest clue, so he ran to call somebody...anybody on the phone to tell him. But as soon as he picked it up, he stopped. "If people already think that I've been acting strange lately, this'll really do it." So instead he decided to figure this one out on his own.

After a few minutes of thinking and watching the little puppy suffer, Vincent got an idea. He would put the food in a blender and squish it up together, then put it in a plastic bag. With a small corner of the plastic bag cut open, he was sure that the little fella would be able to swallow the food. And sure enough, after he tied close the top of the bag, picked up the puppy and stuck the open end in its mouth, it sucked at the food like crazy.

The puppy was swallowing the food so quick that Vincent had to slow him down so he wouldn't choke on it. Soon it was all gone, and so he made another big batch. When the puppy's stomach was protruding past its legs, Vincent stopped the feeding. He was so taken by this little brown and helpless puppy with floppy ears. He only hoped that he wasn't premature in taking the animal from the bleachers, in the event his mother returned. So he decided to keep an eye out on the park in case the mother returned for her baby.

Before he got ready for bed himself, he took some extra sensitive steps for the dog. First he gave it a good bath. Next, he got out a hot water bottle from underneath the bathroom sink (the one usually reserved for Jax when she was PMS'n) and filled it with warm water. Then he replaced the newspaper in the box with an old piece of cloth and put the water bottle underneath it.

The puppy could stay warm all night that way, and Vincent wouldn't have to keep the oven on overnight. "Pretty damn ingenious, if I do say so myself," he said as he turned off the kitchen light and left the puppy to its dreams. If the mother dog didn't return first thing in the morning, Vincent would take the animal to the S.P.C.A. At least that way, he knew that somebody would take care of her.

After he took his shower and then watched out of his bedroom window, for what seemed like hours looking for the puppy's mother, he went to sleep. And when he woke up the next morning he watched out for her as well. She was nowhere to be seen, but the puppy was soon to be heard.

The whining coming out from the kitchen was a big sign that the little puppy made it through the night. And boy was she hungry. So Vincent got up to see for himself. Sure enough the puppy was moving all around trying to get out of the box. It looked like she was going to be OK. He called his mother while at the same time preparing the puppy's breakfast. "What's that sound, son?" his mother asked on the other end of the phone.

"A puppy," Vincent answered her.

"What you doing with a dog? I didn't think you could have animals in your apartment."

"We can't. I found it last night without its mother. The poor thing was starving to death, so I brought her home to feed him last night before taking him to the animal place."

Vincent poured a new batch of food into a new plastic bag and picked up the puppy. The whining got louder and louder before the puppy's mouth finally found the entrance.

"That sounds like a little bitty dog, Vincent," his mother said.

Vincent smiled to himself. "It is. It's a little bitty brown puppy with big floppy ears, whose eyes have just opened."

"Ah," she said. "I bet it's the sweetest looking thing."

For some reason, his mother's doting on the dog was starting to get to him. He himself didn't want to get too attached to it because he knew that he couldn't keep it with him. But the more he talked with his mother, the stronger the bond became. He had to get off the phone with her before he started crying over the damn thing.

When he hung up, he looked at the fat little puppy that was gnawing at his thumb. It was too late...he was attached... time to name her!

Before running out of the house to drop off his resume to several companies that he found in the paper, Vincent put his laundry basket over the puppy's box. It was bad enough that he had already pooped in his box. There was no need to have him poop all over the apartment too.

He would care for the poor thing up for a couple of weeks before giving her to a friend - someone who liked animals. "Jax," he said out loud. "Jax loves animals. She loves animals more than anybody I know."

He smiled triumphantly to the caged puppy. "You're gonna be alright. If anybody will take care of you, it's her." Vincent strolled out of his front door a pleased man. Somehow, that puppy was going to put him back in Jax good graces.

He hustled all morning, making unannounced visits to every major company that he could think of. His list of prospective employers proved to be entirely too small for the amount of energy he found himself with. The odds would eventually be in his favor if he just kept on with it and persisted.

Nothing good in life ever came for free, and Vincent knew that all too well. Had he really charged women for his services, he could have easily been a rich man by now. But this way was going to pay off for him one way or another. Whenever he put his mind to something, there was usually no way to stop him. But he also realized that he was not in the driver's seat this time. When "The Man" decides to hire you, he makes sure that he can get more out of you than what he'll pay.

Sometime during the afternoon, Vincent thought about the puppy. "I bet she's hungry again. I better go home and feed her." That was becoming a little weird for him. Not only was he thinking about something other than his own problems, he was becoming paternal towards the dog, as well. "I'll give it to Jax tonight," he told himself, as he instinctively returned home to give the puppy another feeding. And much to his surprise when he walked in the front door, the puppy was sitting in the middle of the living room gnawing on one of his house shoes.

"How in the hell..." He walked into the kitchen and found the laundry basket flipped over on its side and dog poop all over his floor. "This must be wonder puppy," he thought as he returned to look at the dog in the living room. Sure enough, it looked like the same puppy...only bigger.

Apparently the puppy was older than it looked last night. In fact, all that the puppy probably needed was a little nutrition and a little love to bounce back.

Though he wanted to call her at work to tell her about her present, he resisted. He knew that somehow God had given him an excuse to approach her again. But he wanted to be somebody's new employee before he asked her forgiveness. However, there was no telling how long that would actually take. So he would use the puppy, as it was probably intended to be used.

But he would have to stop thinking of the dog as simply, puppy. Surely he could call it something else before giving it to Jax...something like Madison. "Nah, not a woman's name," he said. "Maybe, Lady? Nah, that's too not good either." Vincent snapped his fingers in excitement. "I got it...Bleacher, your name is Bleacher from now on, or until Jax decides to change it."

With having picked out a name for the puppy, Vincent scooped the little thing in his hands and headed for the bathroom. "But first, you stink. I think you can handle another bath right about now." Bleacher lapped happily at his fingers.

All while he bathed the shivering Bleacher, he thought about how he was going to approach Jax with her. Should he say that he bought her? Should he say that he rescued her from the dog pound? But then asked himself, why would he lie about it in the first place? He would simply knock at her front door, apologize again for any hurt he may have caused her, present Bleacher as a piece offering, and then tell her he loved her? "What!" He snapped out of his thoughts.

"Why is it, every time I think of her, the "L" word sneaks up on me?" he asked himself. He didn't know why he denied it so often, because the fact was that he did love Jax. He was sure that she loved him too. He just wasn't sure if she'd take him back.

With Bleacher in tow, Vincent knocked at Jax's front door. He felt stupid after a while when she didn't open the door because he knew she was home because her car was in the driveway and her bedroom light was on. She obviously had no intentions of speaking to him, but would rather see how long he would wait outside.

Eventually, however, she did open the door and looked at him with an annoyed face. "Yes," she said with the tone of an ice princess.

"How are you?" he asked, trying to be pleasant.

"I've been better," she said with one hand on her hip.

"May I come in?" he asked.

"Vincent, you know that I don't like company without a phone call first."

"I know, but had I called first, would you have received me?" he said as innocently as he could.

She seemed to think about it for a minute. "What's behind your back?"

He had nearly forgotten that Bleacher was sound asleep in his hand behind his back. That poor dog must have been through some hard times to be able to sleep anywhere. "Something for you."

"I'm not accepting any bribes."

Damn! This was not going to be easy. "It's not a bribe, it's a symbol," he said. Slowly he held out his hand, presenting the sleeping Bleacher to Jax.

"Ah," she said, sounding just like his mother. "It's a dog!" she said with excitement as she gently took the present from Vincent's hand. "It is a symbol." She looked him square in the eyes as her smile turned to stone. "It could only be a dog!"

Vincent smiled. He set himself up for that one. "Jax, may I please talk to you?"

"I'm very busy Vincent, what do you want?" She was nuzzling Bleacher.

"You know what I want," he said extending his hand to touch her face.

She pulled back from him. "Don't touch my face with doggie all over it."

He looked at her softly and tried a different approach. "There are some things that we need to work out."

"What? Did you find out that you do have Aids?"

That one stuck to his ribs. This girl was pissed the fuck off at him, and wasn't going to let him forget it.

"No!" Vincent raised his voice. "I told you how some stupid bitch played a game on me, Jax; probably some jealous, tired tramp who got tired of being second to you!"

Jax's expression changed into one of surprise. "That's right, Jax...you. You are my best friend - I never made any secret of that. The fact is, before you, I was much more of a dog than I am now. But I was never that way with you, Jax. I told you everything...well at least I meant to."

"What does that have to do with now, Vincent? What about now? Did you think that we could go on being lovers like that forever? Did you think you would be able to keep me in your little black book like the others, forever?"

"No, I never thought of you like that, Jax. You were the one I could come home to - you know what I mean?"

"No!"

"You, Jax, were...are my best friend. Not Tony or anybody else...just you. I was afraid this would happen the moment I got to know you."

"Afraid what would happen?"

Vincent told himself, "Time to bite the bullet, buddy." "I was afraid that I would fall in love with you, Jacqueline."

Jax looked up from looking down at the puppy. "Love? Vincent?"

"Yes love, Jax. Did you think that I was incapable of it?"

She looked back down at the puppy. "No."

"Well, do you believe me?"

"Of course I believe that you love me, Vincent. I just don't think that you're in love with me."

Vincent turned his back on her and started to count. 1-2-3. Why do women always think they know what's going on in a brotha's head? He slowly turned back around to face her. "And why is that, Jax?"

To his surprise, even she had to think about one of her quick come back answers. "Because we never had the kind of relationship where we could fall in love with each other."

He grabbed her free hand and brought it up to his chest. "Then what is this I feel in here?"

With a very sweet and concerned voice she said, "You feel that I've been fucking someone else, Vincent. No man likes to think about the woman he cares for sleeping with someone else."

He turned red hot. "And are you?!"

She took back her hand from his chest with a forceful tug. "Let's not play tit for tat Vincent. I don't like that game."

Vincent leaned against the doorway. "What are we going to do, Jax? Our relationship has changed in so many ways. I don't want to lose you and I've got so many things to tell you and to explain to you."

"Not now, Vincent, I can't think straight."

"Then when?"

"I don't know...this weekend, maybe...I don't know."

Vincent saw a spark of hope and went for it. "OK, no pressure. I'll be looking for a job all day tomorrow, so I won't bother you." Jax's eyes bugged wide open at this news.

"You'll have plenty of time to think tomorrow and Friday. So let me pick you up Friday night and we'll go and talk somewhere in private."

"No, that's no good. What if you get on my nerves and I want to leave? No, I'll meet you instead."

"Great. Where?"

"You tell me?"

Vincent thought long and hard. He wanted their meeting place to hold some good memories for them - a place she loved - somewhere private. "The beach," he finally said. "We can meet at that life guard tower...you know the one, closest to the entrance, so you don't have a long way to walk."

"Fine. What time?" He mentioned a time to her. "Alright." She moved back to close the door as he began walking away. "Vincent?"

He turned around. "Yes?"

"What's..." she turned the puppy over to see its genitals. "...her name?"

Vincent smiled. "Bleacher. I found her in the park crying underneath the bleachers.

She suspiciously smiled as she closed the door.

Vincent felt good as he climbed into his car and drove off. Come Friday night, he was going to woo Jax back into his life...his bed. And before Friday night was over, he was sure that she was going to change his life, forever.

(17) – Jax – Pimpin' Ain't Easy

When I woke up on Friday morning I was nervous as hell. My knees were wobbly and my head was spinning like I was on LSD. In other words, I was fucked! I stumbled out of bed thinking about all those close calls in my driveway last night, and all the shit I had gotten myself into for tonight.

Realizing I had just setup three different men, on the same night, at the same place, should've been just a fantasy in my head, but my dumb ass had to go and turn it into a reality. But my reality right now is to get to work. Yeah, I was about to make one of the biggest decisions of my brief life, but I still had a job to do.

After showering and throwing on my regular Friday jeans gear, I relived my dilemma in my mind. How in the hell could this have happened to me anyway? I was a good girl who played by the rules, most of the time. I wasn't a liar, they were…all of them! Vincent, Joseph and Gregory were the ones who put me in a position to come out swinging.

It's so like my mother to attract lots of men all of a sudden, and then have droughts when not even one man looks in her direction. It got her three different husbands, and neither of them has worked out for her so far. I could be taking after my mother in the men department too. Damn!

I dragged myself downstairs, first checking on Bleacher and refilling her kitty litter box. I then fed and petted her, all the while wishing for once, that my mother was home to give me some advice. But wouldn't you know it, she herself was too busy to butt her way into my business these days. That new man of hers, whoever he is, has her sprung. I don't think she knows if she's coming or going, and today, neither do I.

Thank God for Fridays and the way they seem to inch by very slowly. I've never been more grateful to have a day take so long to get started. And by the time I got to my office it was a relief to see that my work load was close to nothing and I could think all day long. Perfect.

Now, up until this point I'd tried to let myself think that all of this attention was a present from the universe. But now I don't know. I'd have to be a pimp to hold down all three of those fools, wouldn't I? But if I got it like that then why not? I'm not true player material, but I hate when I'm being played. But what if the universe is testing me?

"Oh hell!" I screamed in my mind. I really had to decide what to do, and there was no way around hurting someone either. Hell, I could get hurt my damn self. If either of them finds out what I'm up to it's gonna start some shit. But Do I care if they all hate me and I walk away from this whole crazy situation without a man?

The bottom line is nobody told them to piss me off like this and then unknowingly put me in the driver's seat, knowing damn well that I drive like a bat out of hell! So determined to weigh the pros and cons of my situation, I picked up a pen. The first of them to scrutinize was Gregory.

After I discovered who he really was, I took it upon myself to do some digging up on him. Fortunately for me, he still doesn't know who I am and that I work for a company who does work for his. Unfortunately for me, during my digging I found out that no management company employee's or affiliates are allowed to become romantically involved with one another.

Thomas Childs added this rule into his company bylaw's years ago when he apparently got involved with an affiliate employee. After realizing he didn't want to jeopardize the integrity of his company, he made the rule irreversible and obtained cooperation and signatures from all of his inner company and affiliate company heads.

Harry's signature was among them, having signed it after he received the contract with TCI. I guess in a way it makes good business sense. But in another eerie kind of way, Thomas Childs remains in charge of his company. And I have no way of knowing if Gregory knows about this rule.

Should I be so presumptive to think that Gregory would be willing to give up his position as CEO to be with me? I don't see why not. If he's crazy enough to ask me to marry him after a few dates and he already has lots of money, then I guess he can do anything else he wants to do. He was even a stock broker in New York, so I'm sure he could do that again. But would he want to?

If he asked me to marry him only after knowing me a short time, he'd probably do anything I asked of him. My mother would be so proud. But if I had to resign from my job what kind of work would I do? Not to mention that it would break Harry's heart if I left his company.

But if Gregory set me up in my own business, Harry would understand that it was a great opportunity for me to move on up, right? I could be CEO of my own company. Hmm, this could be interesting.

All of this bullshit could have been avoided if he had just told me the truth…and who uses an alter ego anyway, except maybe in their padded room? Maybe there's something else about Gregory that I don't know.

Well, whatever he knows, he put me in a fucked up position, jeopardizing Harry's company and my job. If my step-dad ever finds out what he's been up to, I feel sorry for him. Harry's one protective ass black man you don't want to fuck with! Like step-father, like step-daughter.

GREGORY:

PROS   CONS

Filthy rich	Liar
CEO of TCI	Not if he dates or marries me
Gentleman	Shy
Handsome	Sexually compatible???
Refined	Weird
Wants to marry me	Wants to marry me so soon

Gregory's pros and cons should speak for themselves, but without having had sex with him I'm stuck on whether or not I should take a chance on a man who could have a small dick.

Next on my list was Joseph. I knew he was a man's man the first time I laid eyes on him. More than that, I should have known that a woman would already have him on lock. And I know that he said that he wasn't in love with, what's her name, but so what. How do I know that if I were to get with him that he wouldn't get with some chick behind my back? Besides that, he has a kid and I don't even particularly like them, especially when there's a mother attached to them.

That's what I hate about some men; they feel that they have to lie about everything...like the truth is going to kill them. The fact that he has a baby with this woman, not to mention that their wedding day is tomorrow, is a trip. If he calls it off because of me, he and I both might end up on a hit list.

Do I want to watch my back for the next several years behind breaking up that girls wedding? Is it even moral for me to get in the way like that? Ah man, I don't know, but he sure picked a fucked up time to discover what he wants out of life. How can I be responsible for my feelings when they were born because of a lie?

My heart really did feel for him when he cried in my arms last night. The fact that his horny captain made a pass for him has him twisted big time. Who knows if he'll even have a Navy future ahead of him? Could he and the captain both carry out their jobs at the same base? It's crazy just thinking about it.

Why do I get involved with the weirdest of men and their fucked up predicaments? One thing I know almost for certain; a woman scorned is a dangerous thing. And only God knows if this woman will even let him see his child again if he leaves her. Joseph is in a real pickle of a position, and the punk has placed me right in the middle of it. I wonder if he's worth the trouble.

JOSEPH:

PROS	CONS
Fine as hell	Liar
Hell of a body	Has a fiancé
Loves children	Has a child
Great career	Court martial???
Sexually compatible	
Well-traveled	
Loves the sea	
My age	

Joseph's list is tempting but... drama!

Vincent is last, but definitely not least. I should've known when I met this one to run the other way. But then our relationship grew and I couldn't help but love him anyway.

It's sort of sad that a grown ass man can know so many people but still be alone. And Vincent doesn't make it easy on himself. He thinks that he has to live up to some kind of unwritten standards. If I decided to bite the bullet and try to form a real relationship with him, how would he be able to handle that?

How could I be sure if he really threw out the "Little Black Book?" And what would stop the hundreds, maybe thousands of women from knocking at his door? But am I being fair to him? I knew exactly what kind of man he was when I first met him - I'm no fool, but still he's proven to be a liar when he didn't even have to lie…like he couldn't help himself.

All of their traits are either a wonderful dream, or a cosmic joke gone wrong. But Vincent is the one who started the whole thing. He is the one who schooled me on what to look for in a dog in the first place. And now he says that he's changed. Right! Like I just stepped off of a turnip truck.

I'm sure that weird lady in Louisiana he told me about scared him, and I'm even surer that his little HIV episode shook him. But I'm not so sure that Vincent Cruthers can go out into the world, find a job, be faithful to one woman, and live happily ever after. But knowing that he loves me makes it very hard to resist him.

VINCENT:

PROS	CONS
Gorgeous	Liar
Mature	Egomaniac
Sexually inventive	Flirt
Sexually compatible	Knows too many women
Well-groomed	Fucked too many women
Confident	Might fuck too many women
Resourceful	Job???
Classy	
Hell of a body	
My best friend	

Vincent's list is my worst nightmare. Ah man, I should just start running now!

It was plain to see, as I looked down at my list of men, that their pros were more than any woman could ask for, individually or combined. And their cons were typical of most of the men that I've known before. It was all nothing new.

That's what gets me; if I was a man dealing with three women, nobody would even trip off it. How's that for a double standard? See that's why I gotta represent my sista's. I'm not good at reading somebody that really has something to hide, but I'm horrible at turning the other cheek!

I was temporarily interrupted, when the phone rang. I answered it and who was on the other line but Sabastian. All she wanted to talk about was Bart this and Bart that.

Apparently the little tike she met was still hanging tough with her. I was glad, but obviously had too much on my mind to deal with her cosmic ass today. So I got her off the phone without even telling her about my dilemma. If I had, she probably would have given me some sensible advice. But I was in too deep to hear anything sensible right now.

Reading their lists over and over again was only adding to my stress level so I leaned back in my chair and closed my eyes to relax for a minute. In the darkness of my mind all I could see was one big mess.

Each of them were reaching for me...pulling me in different directions. None of them could see the other man standing in the night with me. And there I was, the maiden in despair, not knowing which way to turn. The walls were closing in on me. Their faces were popping in and out of my mind. I started to sing a little tune; Money, Navy, Hoe...oh oh. Money, Navy, Hoe...oh oh.

Then I realized that I was singing the Butt Song. I swear I need psychiatric help for these damn day dreams of mine. It doesn't matter when or where, but my mind does wander from time to time.

I found myself banging my head against the back of my chair. First of all I couldn't believe how dumb I was by considering hooking up with one of them. It should have been all about payback, but I couldn't help myself. When the universe offers you champagne, you drink it, you don't pour it out. If I were to kick all of them to the curb, then what would that leave me with? I'd be the winner of a game with no one to celebrate with.

So finally, at 3 o'clock in the afternoon I knew what I was going to do. I had solved part of my problem and I knew who I wanted to be with. I guess it was right there in front of me from the very start. Now all I had to do was cleverly meet with them and summon up the courage to tell the other two that we could only be friends.

Nobody likes to be second best, but what's a girl to do? It wasn't like I could really try and pimp all three of them at the same time, was it? Hmm...no. I just want one man who wants me back. So I'm going to march my ass to that beach and do what I have to do.

I barely made it home from work and had to be at the beach in a little over an hour. That left me very little time to hurry up and freshen up, before I show up and show out. So I turned on the radio to keep me company in the shower.

I was hoping for some soothing music that would help to relax me, but instead I got Snoop Doggy Dog talking about doing a "1-8-7" on somebody. Shit, for all I know that could be me tonight. "Why didn't I turn to the jazz station?" I asked myself as hot water fell over my body. Snoop kept on rapping so I kept on bathing.

After I toweled off, I began to unsteadily rub myself down with lotion. My hands were trembling so much, the lotion was flying all over the place. By the time I was done I couldn't tell you which part of my body was lubricated or ashy. But I didn't give a damn 'cause I still had to brush my teeth and comb my hair. My teeth got clean, I guess, but my hair was doomed from the start. Shit, why didn't I put the damn shower cap on? I was trippin'.

I was as nervous as the night Lewis Riley took my virginity from me...a long time ago. My hair turned into an afro, like that girl who sings "Afro Puffs." I looked like

Whoopi Goldberg on steroids. I swear I'm going to scare them away before I get a chance to fuck with them.

Finally it was time to find the right thing to wear. So I asked myself, "Do I wear something casual that I can fight in, or something I can run for my life in? Or do I wear something sexy so at least two of them will remember what they'll be missing?" I decided on something in-between. I wanted to at least look sexy while I was running for my life.

I put on some black leggings with a long, clingy, V-Neck sweater and some Converse. I decided to pin my hair up, since it was going to get even frizzier at the beach. My makeup was short and sweet...lipstick. I didn't have time to deal with the rest of my make-up drawer. My final touch was perfume; searching my vanity for the right scent, I finally settled on was Escape.

When I was fully dressed, I lay across the top of my bed and watched the clock. I had wanted to get ready a little early so I could concentrate on the upcoming events. There was no turning back, as I took in deep breaths to clear my mind and ward off stress. I had a long night ahead of me and I didn't have any heart pills to prepare me for this shit.

So now that I had a little free time for myself before heading down to the beach, I thought it appropriate to reminisce about the two men that I would not be seeing with romantic intentions, anymore.

Each of them had characteristics that I admire in one way or another. They both were kind and good men, I'm sure. But they were not the ones for me. I only hoped that someway...somehow, we would be able to part as friends. Fate dealt me this hand of cards and it's time to play them!

I had stalled long enough, and as I watched my new clock blink to the new time reading of 6:35, I knew it was time for me to make my way over to my first tryst of the evening.

For just an instant, I thought about leaving a note for my mom to let her know where I would be, and about bringing a kitchen knife with me just in case one of them tried to man handle me. "No, what am I thinking? Didn't I tell myself that they were all gentlemen?" I said out loud. I was paranoid at first but then I deep breathed that thought away too. So instead I picked up my keys and walked out of my room.

I made one quick stop in the pantry to check on Bleacher and she was fine. I refilled her puppy food and whole milk mixture. The little pooch was fast asleep on the pile of old pillows I laid out for her. I wanted to pick her up for a good luck hug but I didn't want the scent of a dog on me just yet...that was coming soon enough.

It really was one of the sweetest things that Vincent had done for me; another plus for him. He knows that I love animals a lot, but I had hesitated in getting one because I was afraid that I would neglect it. But after holding Bleacher in my arms, the little girl has a home for life. She's so innocent, trusting and loyal and she loved me from the start. That's all any girl wants. I took one more look at her and closed the door before I woke her.

In my car, heading down Imperial Highway, I imagined how things would turn out if I were to carry out my original plan of revenge. Finding out about all of them, at the same time no doubt, had done something to me. I had actually fantasized about lining up all three of those ass holes and doing horrible things to them. But that would have been a disaster. Who did I think I was Cleopatra Jones?

When a man is cornered he's likely to go off to save face. And that was the last thing I needed - to have three big men go off on little me. No, I think I made the right decision in choosing to meet all three of them separately. Besides, my feelings for them had changed. I no longer wanted to see any of them hurt. I cared for them, in spite of themselves and was hoping for a peaceful resolution. So now I just prayed that I could find the words to salvage the friendships of two men and be with the one of my choice.

When I arrived at the beach I was happy to see that there were a few people scattered about. The sun was setting directly over the ocean in a display of boldness like it was waiting center stage for the drama about to unfold. I looked at my watch and noted that I had arrived a little early. Good. I didn't want to work up a sweat trying to run in the thick sand to keep my 7 o'clock appointment. This way, I could take my time and gracefully make my entrance to my first stop. Plus, I knew that if bachelor number 1 was watching me, he wouldn't be able to read my body language.

No, I want to be able to hear him out before telling him how I feel. There was no way that I was just going to blurt out what I had to say and then trot down the beach to my next appointment. I had to handle this with a style and grace all my own. 'Cause who else could have gotten themselves in a no win situation like this except for me? So I began to pray for courage and strength, ending my prayer with, "Amen" and then I took a deep breath.

I got out of my car, carefully tiptoed down a small hill and headed for lifeguard station #48. I didn't see him anywhere, so I figured that I was the first one to arrive. The ocean air was soothing to my mind and spirit, allowing me to relax while I strolled. But once I got there the wait was agony. Where was he? Already five minutes late meant that I only had about 45 minutes left to deal with him. And then, I saw him walking towards me.

He had this big smile on his face, indicating that he had no idea of what was to become of us. I smiled back as I leaned on the railing of the platform. When he approached me, he kissed me on the cheek and handed me a single red rose. Then he took my hand and led me up the ramp of the lifeguard station. I had to hold onto him tight so I wouldn't lose my balance...my nerve...my mind. He was looking really good, dressed in all black.

After we made it to the top, I ignored the sand that had built up in my shoes. I had a more important agenda at hand. "I'm not that late am I?" he asked.

"Oh, no. I've just been here for five minutes or so," I said nervously.

He checked me out, looking me up and down. "You look good as ever." Then he took on a serious look about him. "I want to tell you everything…about the lies and everything. I never meant to hurt you that way."

I just looked at him as he began this long story about why he did what he did and why he was sorry he did what he did. I listened without interrupting him because he deserved to get these things off of his chest. I couldn't look him square in the eyes without feeling guilty. He seemed so genuine, so sweet. I thought I would just break down and cry while hearing this man pledge his devotion to me. But I was sure not to let it all go to my head. He was a man and capable of anything to get what he wanted. But it was nice to hear anyway.

When he was done with his sermon, I casually glanced at my watch and looked at him. I had exactly 15 minutes to say what I needed to say and get over to my next appointment. I didn't know exactly what I was going to say so I winged it. "Thank you for telling me everything. It's nice to know that a girl can have a friend like you."

Uh oh. He didn't like hearing the "F" word. "Friend?" he said suspiciously.

I got tough. "Yes. You are a friend that I will cherish forever, didn't you know that?" I got softer. "In the time that we've known each other I find that my life has been touched by something special. I don't want to lose that. I want to keep you forever in my heart. And being your friend is the best way for me to do that." Whew!

He grimaced. "You're turning me down, aren't you?"

"No," I said sternly. "I guess I'm being both practical and selfish because I don't want to lose you. 'Cause if we were to get together like you're talking about, we'd start off with dishonesty and are probably doomed from the start. Wouldn't that be a disaster?" I searched for his eyes in the fading light.

He hesitated before answering me. I could see that he was upset, so I decided not to say anything else. A few minutes ticked by and he saw me looking at my watch. "Oh, am I keeping you from something?" he asked rather rudely.

I just looked at him sideways. "Just think about what I said. I've thought about it and I think it's best...for me at least." After that, I turned my back on him. I wasn't trying to be hurtful I just wanted him to get the message, agree with it and be my friend. Besides, a tear was starting to stream down my face and I didn't want him to see it.

Finally I heard him stir behind me. "And there is nothing that I can say to change your mind?" he eventually asked.

I didn't answer him, but gently shook my head "No." I heard his footstep fade from the platform. After a minute or so passed I turned to see him walking in the distance. I looked at my watch again, and saw that I only had three minutes to make it to the next lifeguard station.

As I began stumbling down the platform, I looked at the red rose in my hand. I didn't know what to do with it. Do I take it with me or leave it here? It would be mean to just throw it away. So I decided to leave it for now and come back for it at the end of my mission.

When I approached lifeguard station #49, I could see that someone was already standing at the top of it. The sun was nearly gone and it was getting more difficult to see. But as I approached with caution, I noted that it was bachelor #2. "There you are," he said to me as I ascended to the top. "I thought I was going to have to come looking for you."

That would have been a disaster. "No, no, I'm fine. How are you?" I asked him trying to change the subject and catch my breath.

"I'm better now," he said with a great big smile.

What is it with these damn smiles? I cut through the shit. "You have some explaining you wanted to do?"

His smile faded. "Right. Look, I didn't mean to put you in the position that I put you in. I lied to you and expected you to understand and forgive me. I realize now that couldn't possibly be the case without a real explanation."

I listened to him give me the big speech about how he thought that I was the one and how he wanted me to trust him. Again, I decided not to look into his eyes either. Looking into the eyes of a handsome man is not a good thing when you're about to give them the boot. So I just listened attentively, with my eyes looking more at his Adams apple than at his eyes.

He sounded so sweet. I must be crazy for not choosing to be with this man, or the other one. Who knew that I wouldn't be the bitch to just let them beg and plead, and then turn to them and say, "Fuck off!" No, I couldn't do that now if I tried. This was a man with potential standing in front of me. But fate hadn't dealt me any decent cards to work with. If *she* had, I would have met these three desirable men at totally different times in my life. But no...I had to meet all of them during the same fucking summer!

When he was done with his reasoning and such, he grabbed my hand and kissed it. He had this look in his eye like I was just going to jump in his arms or something. And God knows I wanted to, but I couldn't. He was not the one. For whatever reasons I had in my head, this gorgeous man standing in front of me was not the one. I think he eventually saw it in my eyes...what I was thinking. "Did I say something wrong?" he asked.

"No. You said everything right, sweetie. A woman would have to have a good reason for not being able to be with a man like you. I just happen to have a good reason." His mouth dropped a foot. I held my hands up to stop him from talking. "It's not you...it's me. And I know that sounds like an old cliché but it's the truth." I walked closer to him for reassurance. "This is not a brush off either. We can be friends for life, if you want to. You are one of the kindest, sweetest, gentlest men that I know, and I don't want to lose that."

He looked at me like I was crazy. "You want to be friends?"

"Yes, more than anything."

"Just like that?"

"That's all I can give at this point in my life. I change every time I encounter something or someone new. You had something to do with that change in me too, you know."

He turned his back on me. "So I'm a fool?"

"Not in my book."

He turned back to face me. "Then what am I?"

"You're my friend."

I gave him a hug and kissed him on the lips. "I'll talk to you soon," I said before leaving to walk towards lifeguard station #50. I made sure to walk slowly and to look over my shoulder often, to make sure he wasn't following me. The sun had disappeared leaving a blazing trail of colorful hues, but I think he left. Anyway, nobody was walking behind me.

When I climbed the top of my last platform for the night, I looked around and saw nothing. I had finally arrived to the place where I should be, but where was bachelor #3? From below, I heard something move so I looked over the railing. It was him, holding onto the sides of the platform as he walked through the sand. "Is anybody home?" he asked as he walked to the top.

I was standing directly in front of him when I answered. "What does it look like?"

"I think it looks like there's somebody home," he said. We smiled at each other. It was as if we had some unspoken connection which told us that we should be together. But I wasn't going to let him have me that easily. No. He was going to have to dig himself out of the dog house too. So when he tried to touch me I pushed his hand away.

"I'm sorry," he said.

"For what? For lying to me?"

He stuck his hands in his pockets. "For a lot of things, and especially for lying to you."

"Go on," I insisted.

"Can we sit?" He took my hand and helped me sit down. Our feet were dangling from over the side of the platform. He looked at me and began talking. "When I first met you, I knew you were trouble and I knew there was no way that I was going to be able to run for long. So I had to lie to keep you. And I know that sounds like a bullshit way out of things, but I'm not looking for a way out, I'm looking for a way in. For some reason, you seem to be the one who can save me from myself."

Listening to him talk was like being in a pool of warm hot fudge. The way the words slid off of his tongue could make anybody forgive him. I tried my best to look at him as though unaffected by his words. "And what about the next woman to come along?"

"I've had my fill to last me for a long, long time. But I think...no, I know you're the one to keep me in check - not to mention that I can't resist you." He looked into my eyes looking for an answer. When he was sure he found it, he kissed me.

I was consumed with his tongue inside of my mouth. The warmness of his hands clinging to my face gave me the reassurance I needed in knowing that I had made the right choice. It was difficult to pull myself away from him to ask a stupid question. "Are you sure?"

He looked into my eyes, hesitating only for a moment. Then he kissed me on my nose...my eyelids...my forehead...my cheek...my ear, and finally, again on my lips. Then he took both of my hands up to his mouth and began to suck each of my fingers, one by one. I was getting the impression that he was pretty sure. "It's you girl," he said as he sucked on one of my fingers.

When he completed tasting all 10 of them, he stood up and pulled me to my feet as well. Then he pulled me close and began kissing me on the neck. The chills that ran down my body were unexplainable. It felt so right, even though it was sure to hurt so many. His kisses fell lower and lower until his nose was nudging away at the center of my chest. I let my hands begin to explore his body - inviting his face to venture into the privacy of my blouse.

His mouth found one of my nipples, and he began to titillate the swollen mass with his tongue. One of his hands found my other breast and he slowly massaged it. I was in a haze full of desires with this man. He looked so good...smelled so good; it was as if my wildest fantasy had actually come to life.

I could feel the hardness of him coming to life against me. His large frame was pushing me up against the side of the lifeguard station, locking me into position. I would be lying if I said that I didn't want him. The truth of the matter is I wanted him then and there, but something wasn't right.

The sun was gone and we were safe from being seen, but I had a weird sensation - like we were being watched. However, I was too indulgent in the moment to stop him. I felt so good I didn't care if the whole world was watching. When I couldn't help myself any longer, I started to slide my blouse down below my breasts. He began helping me with one hand while tugging at my pants with the other.

We were consumed with each other, trying to unleash the clothing that was keeping us apart. I could feel the chill of the night touching my body. I stopped him from pulling down my pants because I heard a noise and I knew we weren't alone.

"Look at you? Just look at you, you fucking slut?" a voice rang out from behind us.

He and I were both stunned back into reality after hearing the angry man standing at the entrance of the platform. When we both looked up, we could clearly see that he was holding a gun. I grabbed hold to the arm of my man, to stop him from rushing the other. My heart was pounding over the surf of the ocean, but I found the strength to speak. "What are you doing? Did you follow me?"

The gun he held uneasily in his hand was all the reply I needed. He was crazy. I didn't know what to say, but my man found the words. "Who in the fuck are you calling a slut, mutha fucka?"

"She's a slut!" he yelled. "She must have been seeing you the same time she was seeing me!"

The man I was holding on to for dear life looked at me. "Is that true? Were you seeing both of us at the same time?"

I was speechless. Never in my wildest dreams did I think *I* would be put on the spot. I could give a shit that the jig was up but I didn't like the look of that gun pointing at me. "I never promised anybody anything!" I was finally able to shout at the both of them.

"You told me you loved me!" the crazy man insisted.

"I did not! You're delusional! I said that we could be friends, and now you go and pull a gun on me!?"

"It's all your fault! You women are all the same!" He was waving the gun in the air as he taunted us.

"Let's talk about this for a minute," my man was saying as he slowly began to push me behind him.

I couldn't let him do that...put himself in the line of fire. "No, don't."

The crazy man must have thought that he was hurting me. "Don't you touch her you son of a bitch!

Before anybody knew what was going on, the gun went off. It was a ripping loud surge of noise that flew right past my face. I could see the smoke and smell the gun powder lingering in the air. That pissed my man off, so he began to charge at the mad gunman. I heard myself screaming "No!"

Suddenly, like a flash of lightening, I saw another man leaping at the gunman knocking him off the platform, onto the sand. My man tore himself away from me to join in the fight. They were all struggling over the gun. I ran closer to see the three men tussling on the sand. I could see that the gun was waving left to right. Finally when I saw a finger inching its way over the trigger of the gun, I feared that one of us was going to die.

I wanted to run and snatch the gun out of his hand, but before I could blink I heard a woman's voice scream. "Gregory, No!"

Another loud shot fired into the night. This time I couldn't see the direction the bullet took. I felt numb...then cold. I watched, in slow motion as two men savagely beat the third. What appeared to be an older white woman threw herself into the fight trying to break them apart, but she got knocked down and shoved to the side.

I started to sweat profusely, so I used my sweater to blot my face. The sticky fluid dripped from my face, to my sweater and then down my body. Two men finally stood up, leaving the third man moaning on the sand. Then I clearly saw Vincent and Joseph kick Greg in the head and body before running to my side. I'd never felt so wanted in my life.

I tried to tell them how I felt but my words were slurred. My eyes began to flutter as I struggled to keep them open. There was so much to say to them, but I didn't have time because a bright light appeared in the sky and distracted me. All I could think of was getting to that light! I tried to do just that, but I slumped to the ground before I could reach it. I heard someone say, "Oh my God, she's been shot!

I looked at the lady crawling on the sand towards Greg. I assumed she was the one who had been shot because Vincent held me up on the right and Joseph held me on the left, and both of them seemed fine. They looked soooo good. I looked at them both and smiled as a warm and loving feeling swept all over me. I started to get very sleepy. I knew I was about to fantasize about something heavenly.

I'm such a lucky girl.

Epilogue

My first instinct was to selfishly pull her out of that fool's arms, into mine, but I be damned if Jacqueline didn't know him too; just by the way she had looked at him. He wasn't just somebody walking by deciding to join a fight, with two other brotha's and a gun. This was personal to him.

So instead, I anxiously stood up, picked up the gun and started to run down the beach at full speed, only briefly yelling to homeboy sitting next to her, "Keep her safe, man! And keep pressure on the wound...I'm going for help!"

He was saying to her, "Hold on baby...hold on!

"Baby? Who the fuck is he? I'll deal with his ass later!" I was torn between running after and killing the man who shot her and the woman who helped him get away. But they took off running in the opposite direction. I had to make an instant split decision on what to do. So, I decided to get help for her first, find and kill that crazy mutha fucka later!

While I ran I snapped pictures in my mind so I would never forget. I was gonna remember this; the who, the what, the when, the where...all this shit!

My own life flashed before my eyes; the life I intended to have with her; our wedding; our children; our future. If only I hadn't wasted so much time playing games with her, just trying to get mine, none of this would've happened.

My heart was pounding as I zipped past lifeguard station after station, all lined up along the beach...as though they would go on forever, until finally the phones came into view.

"I gotta get one of those fucking cellular phones," I was

saying to myself; huffing and puffing as I picked up the sticky receiver. Silence!

"Fuck!" I was so pissed off I slung it against the wall and watched pieces of it crumble to the ground. I picked up another one and thankfully heard a dial tone. I nervously pressed the buttons.

"911, what is your emergency?" the man on the other end of the line asked lazily.

"My girlfriend's been shot! Please send help to Playa Del Rey Beach, please!" I shouted into the mouth piece.

"Sir, please lower your voice and speak calmly and clearly," the operator responded.

I collected myself and lowered my voice. "Please, please send help right away. She's been shot in the head!"

"Alright Sir calm down. Now, who's been shot?"

"Jacqueline Winters!"

"OK. And who shot her?"

"I don't know, some man!"

"So a man you don't know shot your girlfriend?"

I was about to lose it. "Yes…no, she knew him. I think she was dating him."

"So you're her boyfriend but she was dating someone else, huh?"

This mutha fucka is gonna let her die! "What the fuck difference does that make!?"

"Do not swear at me Sir. Now where is she and the man who shot her?"

"I don't know where he is - he ran off — but she's at Playa Del Rey Beach at life guard stand #50!"

"Sir, Playa Del Rey is a city not a beach. Do you mean Dockweiler State Beach in the city of Playa Del Rey?" These stupid people.

I'm adding this fool to my hit list. "Yeah, that's it! Hurry, she's dying!"

He sighed. "Sir, before I can send help the responding police officers will need to know who and where the perpetrator is."

"I said I don't know – some man shot her, dropped the gun and ran off with some old white lady!"

"So the perpetrator is a white man?"

"No he's not white he's black; the old lady he was with is white!"

"OK. And where's the gun?"

I looked at the huge 9mm in my sweating hand while I spoke. "I have the gun! I took it from him when I kicked his ass!"

The operator cleared his voice. "Oh, Sir you're going to have to surrender yourself and the gun before the LASD can approach the crime scene."

"OK, no problem – you're wasting time man! *Now* she's gonna need a helicopter or something! If she dies it's on you! What's your name?"

The operator ignored him. "Sir a medevac and the LASD are on their way. That's the Los Angeles Sherriff's Department," he said to make sure the caller understood him.

"I know what LASD means! What, you think I'm stupid?"

Silence.

"Hello? Hello?"

As soon as I realized that bastard hung up on me, I could hear the chopper approaching over my head; heading towards my woman and…

"Homeboy is down there with her alone," I was talking to myself making a mad dash back to the woman I loved. But before I could get all the way there I was suddenly stopped by flashing lights surrounding me from every direction.

They were serious. "Freeze! Throw down the gun and get on the ground – now!" At least 6 police cars had appeared out of nowhere, with guns drawn and itchy fingers on the triggers – blinding lights shining in my face.

I threw the gun in their direction, got on my knees and put my hands behind my head. I could see the helicopter landing down the beach…finally! "I didn't do it! I'm the one who called you guys! The shooter ran the other way! He's gonna get away!" I was yelling at them.

"Lay down flat on the ground with your arms spread wide!"

I quickly did what I was told. They were inching towards me…like cowards. One of the cops picked up the gun I had just thrown in their direction and tucked it away in his waistband behind his back. Another cop ran up on top of me, kicking me in the ribs before stabbing his knee into my back. Next he slapped handcuffs on me, whispering, "Nigga," in my ear before they all swarmed me.

I was sweating like a hoe in church, but I *was* able to peep his badge number. "It wasn't me – I'm the one who called you guys!" I was hoping they wouldn't lynch me before their supervisor arrived on the scene.

One big ass, red looking cop said, "Then where did you get this gun – from one of your homeys?" He helped the other cop snatch me up from the ground.

"I was with her when she was shot! I tried to defend her and was able to get the gun away from him – me and the other dude down there with her!" I was trying to look down the beach, into the darkness to see what was happening with Jacqueline. I could see the flashing lights and hear the swirling blades of the helicopter over the crashing sound of the ocean as it lifted off into the night sky.

"Please officers, I'll cooperate. Please tell me how she is? Is she OK? Is she alive?" I was pleading with them but they ignored my questions and instead started asking me a bunch of questions including my name, my relationship to the victim and my version of the events that had occurred.

A cop cruiser arrived on the scene and I think it was their supervisor who finally said, "Put him in with the other one."

As I was roughly thrown into the back of the cruiser I was relieved to see the fool who had been with my woman already inside...handcuffed just like me...blood all over him. "How is she man? Tell me she's alive."

The other brotha's first angry words were, "What did you do man? How could you set her up like this? Did you follow us here or something, and got your little feelings hurt seeing us together?"

"Fuck you! She was with me when this shit went down! You saw that crazy mutha fucka with the gun – who the fuck was he?" I turned toward him to get a better look. "And who in the fuck are you?" It was a good thing I was restrained 'cause I wanted to fuck him up bad!

He finally said in a softer voice, "She's alive...barely. At least she was before they flew her off to the hospital."

I sighed and was a little relieved at hearing she wasn't dead but I knew she wasn't out of the woods. I don't know if the bullet did any real damage or if it was just a flesh wound. I just knew I needed to get out of here and get to the hospital to be with her. "Did she say anything to you? – before they took her away?"

"Yeah," he looked down and paused, "she told me she loved me."

"No...no," I said to myself. "I don't believe it; she's confused. She must've thought *he* was me. I should've been there...it should've been me with her!"

My thoughts were interrupted with the hustle and bustle of the cops investigating up and down the beach talking to witnesses. I was sitting closest to them so I leaned out of the window to listen to what they were saying.

"...yeah and they're rushing her into surgery at Poly Catholic Hospital," one cop was saying to another. They don't know if they can save her...or her baby."

My heart sank!

"You can release those two; their stories hold up. But we don't have any leads on the shooter and his accomplice. So get on it, now!"

"Yes Sir," the cop replied and released us.

I began to stumble down the beach, reliving what just happened; Jacqueline was shot and pregnant with my baby. I wasn't about to tell that fool; I guess he'd find out sooner than later.

Yellow tape and investigators kept me from going back to the scene of the shooting so I made my way over to the nearest lifeguard stand to think...to plan...to make them pay for what they had done to us.

When I got to the top I found a red rose lying on the railing. It reminded me of the floral arrangements Ronnie had picked out for tomorrows wedding which would never take place. No, now my priorities had changed forever: Figure out what Jacqueline had been up to tonight; then find the psycho and the bitch who shot my woman; and oh yes, deal with Captain Grey's faggot ass.

I sketched everything in my mind before heading to the hospital to be with the woman I loved and the baby we were expecting together. But when I surveyed the beach one last time, I saw homeboy walking in the distance. I decided to follow him.

As he drove off in a black Mercedes 560SL, I kept my distance. First he's gonna lead me to his house so I can get some answers from him, and then I'm going to lead him straight into hell!

The End.

To Be Continued with Joseph's Story...

www.ingramcontent.com/pod-product-compliance
Lightning Source LLC
Chambersburg PA
CBHW050901250626
47155CB00001B/49